A History in Blood

Chris DeFazio

A History in Blood

Blood Trilogy, #1

Copyright © 2013 Chris DeFazio

All rights reserved.

ISBN-10: 1495924939
ISBN-13: 978-1495924934

Published by TouchPoint Press
www.touchpointpress.com

Editor: Tamara Trudeau
Cover Artist: Colbie Myles, colbiemyles.com

This is a work of fiction. Names, places, characters, and events are fictitious. Any similarities to actual events and persons, living or dead, are purely coincidental. Any trademarks, service marks, product names, or named features are assumed to be the property of their respective owners and are used only for reference. If any of these terms are used, no endorsement is implied. Except for review purposes, the reproduction of this book, in whole or part, electronically or mechanically, constitutes a copyright violation. Address permissions and review inquiries to media@touchpointpress.com.

DEDICATION

This book is dedicated to the memory of my aunts, Katie and Mary DeFazio. Although not quite 6000 years old, they were ninety-five, and ninety-seven, respectively, when they died in 2012, only three months apart. They lived together, and independently for their entire lives, cooking magnificent, Sunday afternoon, Italian feasts for my children and me. Right to the end they were razor sharp, completely supportive, and wonderfully quirky. I miss them a lot.

PROLOGUE

The Roman soldier Titus Acilius wandered through the narrow streets of Alexandria, lost in thought. Old by the day's standards at forty-five, he'd served for nearly thirty years and had risen to the rank of Primus Pilus, or first spear, the most senior centurion in his entire legion. Equivalent to a captain, or perhaps a major in modern times, Acilius was a gifted, loyal soldier, and the trusted advisor to the legion's commanding general. In a few more years, he could have retired, and perhaps ended his days as a farmer. Or, if he chose, he could have re-enlisted and become a "lifer" in the army. All was in jeopardy now.

The battle of Actium had just ended Rome's latest civil war; Octavian had defeated Antony. Acilius had been in one of Antony's most loyal legions, the Twelfth. It was the very last one to go over to Octavian when it was clear that he would be the victor. They'd escaped the endgame with their lives, but because of the tardiness of their defection, Octavian would surely punish them. When all was settled, Acilius was sure his legion would be sent to a horrible backwater assignment—or more than likely, it would be disbanded altogether.

He'd walked away from the ongoing victory celebration,

hopefully unnoticed, to ponder his predicament—and also because he'd always despised and distrusted Octavian, and respected Antony. He'd served with Antony for years and had developed a brotherly love for the man. He didn't feel it was right to celebrate his old commander's demise.

His walk began at dusk, and before he realized it, it was full night. He was lost in a slum area dominated by mud buildings and narrow streets. Although the city still suffered from sporadic violence, Acilius wasn't concerned, as he was a well-trained Roman soldier. He was, however, annoyed with himself for getting lost.

As he turned about, trying to get his bearings, he heard a low growling noise coming from his right. He turned to face it, expecting to see an animal, but he was surprised to find only a small boy not twenty feet away. The filthy, unkempt child was dressed in a rag sack and down on all fours. The stench emanating from him was overpowering, and his eyes savagely reflected the moonlight with a harsh, unearthly silver glint. The guttural growling continued, getting louder, now punctuated by odd, high-pitched barks.

Acilius' long military experience would not allow the boy's small size to influence him. Over the years, he'd seen many of his comrades killed by assailants they'd misjudged as nonthreatening. Titus Acilius was never one to make such a mistake. This child-animal was clearly mad and radiated menace. Acilius' feet naturally took a ready, defensive posture, and his hand dropped to the hilt of his sword. He said in fair Egyptian Arabic, "Stop that noise, child. Go now and find your mother."

The response was a hackle-raising howl.

CHAPTER 1

"Julian, I want a divorce."

The statement was clear enough—five words, simple content. It should have been easy to grasp. But even though I heard it quite clearly, I didn't understand.

Suddenly, my surroundings felt surreal, alien even, as if I'd been whisked to a dark, nasty parallel universe in the span of one sentence. My wife had said something that was completely incongruous with my life as I knew it. On autopilot, my mind clicked through the day's events.

Slept in…check. Read the paper with too many extra cups of coffee…check. Did some work on the computer and set the ER schedule for next month…check. Boring swing shift in the ER, home before midnight…check, check. Glass of wine, read a bit, and off to bed…While this was my normal routine, I knew I would not be checking off those last few things tonight.

I looked around my home, feeling dazed, and tried to ground myself in reality and return to my side of the looking glass.

The kitchen looked the same as it always did: large, marble-topped island right smack in the middle of it, kitchen table off to the side, surrounded by stainless steel. I looked out into our living room: comfortable, oversized chairs, leather sofa, and the flat screen, which was now muted and silently blabbing away the late news.

Finally, I looked at Lisa. She looked the same: dark hair pulled back, high eyebrows, intense brown eyes, and a slim, fit body that marked her more-than-successful battle with the ravages of age. Everything looked the same—so why did I feel like I'd been hit in the head with a mallet? The best I could do was ask, "Could you repeat that, please?"

She did.

Her words started to penetrate my thick skull, but I guess my mind wasn't quite ready. It took off on yet another tangent. My life could be looked at as one continual misbehavior, punctuated by brief periods of civility that, in one way or another, were usually forced upon me. Given the fact that I had gotten away with an awful lot of crap through the years, I reminded myself of all those time-honored words of wisdom, like "Fair is fair," "You have to take the bad with the good," and "Take it in stride." But that's a lot of baloney. No matter what type of life you may have led, when the shit hits the fan and splashes directly onto you, it sucks—plain and simple. It was beginning to dawn on me that I was indeed in the midst of such a fan-propelled shit shower.

I may not have had my arms fully around the problem, but even in my shocked state, I knew this was an instance that required careful reflection and an even more careful response. I tried—really tried—to do just that. But my mouth has always been my enemy, and careful reflection and response have never been my strengths, especially after I've been mallet-whacked.

Despite this inborn disadvantage, I strove on diligently to come up with a well-thought-out reply. What I mean by "strove" is that I took about as much time as it takes an Olympic-level Asian table tennis player to wallop back a lightning-fast serve. You know, the kind of player who holds the paddle upside-down and backward. After super-deep consideration of the problem at hand, a nearly Shakespearian phrase flew from my lips: "You're fucking kidding me, right?"

I thought it had a certain dignity about it, a certain panache, but evidently, Lisa didn't agree. She stood there, her arms folded over her chest, silently staring at me like I was someone she didn't know, someone she didn't care about. I studied her face, looked into her eyes for some hint of warmth, some hint of affection—hell, some hint of *anything*. All I found was a closed book, nothing I'd come to know and love for the last fifteen years.

Maybe this is a joke, I thought. Lisa could pull off a good one every now and again; she did have a bit of a mean streak in her. But my hopes were quickly dashed.

"No, I'm not kidding," she replied all too calmly.

I felt weak and sat down at the kitchen table. After a moment, she did, too.

When I thought I'd gathered myself, I took a deep breath and blurted out, "Well, since we've established that you're not kidding, what the fuck? As far as I know, we're great together. You never gave me one hint that you were unhappy, let alone a single discussion. We've been married for fifteen years, for Christ's sake! You're going to piss it all away? I feel like I'm in one of those crappy romance movies you like to watch."

She sat there silently, not moving, looking out our kitchen window. It was infuriating. It took some effort, but I managed to get myself partially under control.

"I'm sorry I raised my voice, Lisa," I said, "but I think you owe me more than 'I want a divorce,' followed by the silent treatment."

She turned toward me. Her face was blank and emotionless, like nothing I'd ever seen before. For a moment, I didn't even recognize her, and it scared me.

"It's not you, it's me," she intoned blandly.

"Okay, that's something, I guess. But can you maybe tell me a bit more?"

Even more blandly, she answered, "There's someone else."

I felt like I had been kicked in the gut. Women can be so fucking mean. A mallet to the head would have been kind, compared to this. "Well, that's just great," I answered. My voice sounded distant. I stood on shaky legs, but at the same time, I could feel my temper rising and turning red-hot. My temper was an ugly thing, and I worked hard at keeping it in check. I knew that if I lost it, there was no telling what I'd do. I headed for the door.

"We need to talk," she said. "Where are you going?"

I rounded on her with my fists and teeth clenched. I think even my balls were clenched. "Out!" I spat. "And maybe *you* need to talk, but it's about the last fucking thing in the world I need to do right now."

I slammed the door with a dramatic flourish, *thank you very much*, and flopped into my car. I felt like shit. I sat there for a while, trying—and failing—to come to grips with this catastrophe. In retrospect, what I was actually doing was stalling, in hopes that Lisa would come out and stop me from driving off. It wouldn't have taken much—a kind word, a smile, a touch. But she never came.

I drove mindlessly around town. Considering my state, I was lucky not to crash my car. But at midnight, in a sleepy suburb like Needham, Massachusetts, there really wasn't much around to crash into. That famous single, "How Could This Happen to Me?" kept playing over and over in my head. I got an occasional break from the song's sonic repetition by singing along with its equally famous B-side, "What the Fuck?"

I pulled into the town's deserted, starkly lit commuter rail parking lot to stew. The cold, steady drizzle did little to improve my mood. Lisa had blindsided me; she'd pole-axed me without a hint. After fifteen years, the fireworks were pretty much gone, but things were still pretty good, and I'd been a good husband to her.

Hasn't it been said that when someone has an affair, it's because the involved party was driven to it by something bad in the home life or the relationship? I'm sure I read that somewhere, or at least saw it on *Oprah*. I mean, how could Lisa do this if everything was hunky-dory? And I truly thought it was. It didn't add up. I'd been around the block a zillion times, and I couldn't believe I hadn't seen this coming. I'd done nothing but treat her well, and now this?

I must be the biggest dope on the planet, I thought, *or she's the biggest bitch.* And frankly, I was beginning to lean toward the bitch thing.

I'd gotten myself good and pissed while sitting alone in my car with all this shit flying around in my head. But as time passed, all the crap and guilt and "what-ifs" and "how-could-shes" and "what-happeneds" distilled further and further down, like a fine port reduction. When the sauce was finally finished, it evaporated to three little words: *There's someone else.*

That summed it up. She'd said those three horrible words in the same flat tone she might have used to say, "The mail's here," or "Fold your laundry," or a lot of other banal three-word phrases that I was too flustered to think of.

I'd thought I was pissed before, but that was just an artificial Sweet'n Low pissed, because at that moment, I was doing a red-hot slow burn, fueled by 100 percent pure cane sugar. The pulse in my temples steadily marched up and down my skull, getting stronger with each and every beat.

There's someone else.

It was like tossing gasoline on a fire. My breath was coming fast, and my skin flushed as I began to lose control. I came to the brink of full-on rage, but with a final shred of effort, I reeled the anger in. My breathing slowed, and I felt myself calming. The pulses in my temples lightened. I took a deep, cleansing breath and said to myself, "I'm going to find this 'There's someone else' and kill him."

Oh shit.

CHAPTER 2

My head snapped up off the headrest. The sky was brightening at that in-between time right before daybreak. I'd fallen asleep and had spent the entire night in my car. *Great*. I felt uncomfortable and jittery. I stepped out into the lovely April morning, which was cold, damp, and drizzly — pretty much status quo for Boston.

I had an old friend in Montreal who sent me a pack of mini-Cubans every now and again. I thought a smoke might be the ticket to settle my jangly nerves. The first drag hit me as it always did: smooth, but thick and oily at the same time. The smoke had so much substance, it felt like I could almost drink it. Just standing in that lonely parking lot and smoking my cigar made me feel a little better. For a moment, my mind wandered as if I were meditating. But then, out of nowhere, Lisa flew back into my head with all the subtlety of a shotgun blast.

My calming nerves re-jangled, and I sacrilegiously tossed away my half-smoked Cuban and got back into my car. There was only one thing that would settle me down. I rummaged around in my briefcase and pulled out two small test tubes of discarded blood that I'd scored in the ER. I popped the lids, drank them down, and instantly felt better.

I'm not a weirdo or a psycho or a fetish freak. Nothing like that. I'm a vampire. Drinking blood is kind of our thing.

You see, for the past hundred years or so, I'd been depressed and had an identity crisis. I'd begun to feel as if I had lost my last shred of humanity. Did it matter? Probably not, but that didn't mean it didn't bother me.

My vampire friends assured me that I had retained some of my human nature, but what did they know? They were vampires. You would think the "newbies" would be able to give me some perspective, but they were so enthralled and/or screwed up from being recently turned that they were of virtually no help.

To make a long story short, the entire thing had come to a head when my dog died. I loved him to death, and I completely lost it over a freaking dog. Can you believe it? Well, one thing led to another, and I decided to bury as much of my vampire self as I could. I got an extremely humanistic job as a doctor and married a human, while hiding my true nature from her. I tried to behave as humanly as possible. Pretty stupid, huh? Needless to say, most of my kind thought I had gone insane, and I was never that far from crazy to start with. And now, here I was.

It had been many years since I had killed for the hell of it; I had restricted myself to doing so only in self-defense. It had been even longer since I'd drained a "donor" to death, unless it was by accident. Since I was over two thousand years old, I was well past the days when I required large amounts of blood to survive. But even my vampire friends who thought I'd still had some human left in me, didn't see this behavior as humanistic, but rather as a sign that I was a wimp. All in all, most thought it a sad state of affairs.

My latest profession, a physician, was not chosen randomly. I'd done it, or similar jobs, a few times before.

This time, I'd made my choice mostly because I genuinely wanted to help people. But also influencing my decision was the technology of the era. Modern scientific advancement gave me a chance to research the physiology of my not-so-delicate condition. There were many legitimate vampire researchers out there who were much better at it than I could ever be—but I've always liked doing things firsthand.

However, there was a more self-centered reason to work in the medical field: blood. No, I didn't go prowling around the blood bank late at night, working out complex schemes and heists. I love the term "blood bank," though. It sort of rolls off the tongue, doesn't it? It makes me feel good all over.

Anyway, since I worked in the ER, getting blood was simple. When patients with serious complaints came in, the nurses drew blood in what was known as a "rainbow": six or seven tubes topped with different-colored stoppers to indicate which chemicals were inside and what kind of tests they would be used for. The colors ranged from blue to purple to red to green.

I know it sounds like a massive amount of blood, but considering each tube held only ten to fifteen milliliters, the usual rainbow had about three ounces of blood total. As you might imagine, not every tube was used on every patient. Sometimes, none were used at all. The discarded tubes were thrown into a disposal container for contaminated goods, in the "dirty utility room" in the ER which, as you might imagine, was the room where we dealt with contaminated specimens, urine and the like.

That room wasn't high on the list of places to hang out for obvious reasons, and also because it usually stank. It should have been named the "stinky utility room." Anyway, the room's lack of popularity gave me ample opportunity to score bunches of those discarded tubes on a day-to-day basis. So when I worked, I got to sneak down several of these little blood shooters. It was my version of an energy drink, and much better for me, too, since it didn't have all that caffeine.

Fresh blood directly from a victim was by far the best, but the rainbow stuff wasn't so bad, once you got used to the aftertaste from the chemicals. This scavenging behavior may have appeared to be beneath me, and many vampires would have agreed with that assessment. But what was I supposed to do, ignore all that blood? It was there, easy to get, and I'm a vampire. It helped quench my essential thirst and reduced the number of necks I needed to sink my teeth into.

I couldn't say my career was a bad choice—I was a good doc. In addition to being able to perform vampire research, I got the perk of easy-to-obtain extra blood. The marriage, on the other hand, wasn't my best idea. I hid who I really was from Lisa, and she must not have suspected. Otherwise, she'd never have sprung this surprise divorce on me, out of fear for her life.

I admit keeping things hidden from your wife, even if it's something like being a vampire, isn't the basis for a good relationship or a healthy marriage. But other than that, I truly was a good "human" husband. And look where that had gotten me: cheated on, with an impending court date for divorce. I'd have to keep my temper in check while dealing with this. After all, killing was in my nature. I would have hated to make Lisa my first homicide victim in twenty years...wouldn't I? Well, in any case, killing her would have been unseemly.

Given this potential danger to Lisa, I decided, for her own protection, to avoid going home—or perhaps I was being a chickenshit. She was a VP at a real estate agency in town and was out of the house by eight thirty every morning. My plan was to stall around town until after nine o'clock, then slink home. After that, I pretty much had no plan.

I started at Dunkin' Donuts and continued on to nearly every coffee shop in town, carefully avoiding the ones Lisa frequented. Fifty-two cups of coffee and a few hours later, I started the short drive home. Although my bladder felt ready to burst, I was happy that my great avoidance caper had gone so easily—until I saw her car in the driveway. She'd been waiting for me.

Fuck it, I thought. I took a deep breath and went in.

She was where I had left her last night, in the kitchen.

Being a grandmaster of the obvious, I asked, "You still here?"

"Where have you been?" she responded, sounding annoyed. "I've been waiting for you. We really need to talk."

Now *I* was annoyed, too, since she'd been only waiting, not worrying. More importantly, she'd totally fucked up my plan for ducking her.

"No, 'we' implies both of us," I said, "and frankly, I'm not feeling the need. What I *do* need is to get out of here and spend a few days at the Vineyard."

We'd bought a beach house on Martha's Vineyard about eight years ago, and I loved it. The thought of heading down there on a cold, rainy April day would normally never have occurred to me, but given the circumstances, it seemed like a good idea. And besides, it would allow me to execute another Lisa-ducking maneuver. Maybe this time it wouldn't get all fucked up.

She said disdainfully, "If you have to, go ahead. But we're going to have to discuss this sometime."

"*Have* to? What's there to discuss? You seem to have

already made a whopper of a decision. I'm sure there's nothing of importance I could possibly add."

She glared at me. "Fine. Be a child. It'll only delay things."

Even though I was angry, I couldn't help but notice how good she looked. Her long, dark hair was casually pulled back, and she had on just the right amount of makeup to bring out her cheekbones and eyes. She wore a knee-length black dress that showed off her nice legs and exposed a little cleavage, but not too much. A smart jacket and half-height fuck-me pumps completed the ensemble.

Now wait a damn minute! The way she was put together started to sink in. She looked too good for a workday. I didn't get a look half this good even on our "date nights." She obviously was all dressed up for "there's someone else," and unless this guy was a chronic house hunter, it had to be someone at work. A nice piece of deductive reasoning, but I didn't need to be Sherlock Holmes to figure that out. *Of course it's someone from work. Duh.*

I choked down my anger for the moment. My first thought was, *Screw her. She cheated on me, and I'm going to blow this thing up and move on.* But for some reason, I softened. I hadn't even heard her side of it. Didn't I at least owe her that? Of all the human and vampire women out there, I'd chosen her to be with, to help me heal, to help me find myself again.

Granted, my plan was ill-conceived and hadn't worked at all. Frankly, it sucked. But that didn't change the fact that I had married her. I'd loved her when I did, and maybe I still did. Even though she'd made it clear that we were done, I owed it to her and to myself to swallow my anger and pride and try to salvage things one last time. I guess I wanted to play human to the bitter end.

I took a deep breath and said, "Lisa, before we move things too far along, I want to know that I still love you, and I want us to stay together. Is there anything that we…that *I* can do to give it a try?"

She looked surprised for a moment and then let out a short laugh. I had put myself out there, and the bitch laughed at me. This was too much.

She said, "Now *you're* the one who's kidding, right?"

I was too dumfounded to speak—a rare thing.

She went on. "Jules, you've basically ignored me for the last three years."

I opened my mouth to retort, but she halted my response with a hand. I shut up and let her have the floor.

"Oh sure, we've done a lot of things together," she continued, "but the things *you* wanted to do, like dragging me to all those hospital functions. And all the trips…but we always went where *you* wanted to go. I could barely get your attention, because you were usually prowling around some old ruins with your nose stuck in some history book. And by the way, how do you know all those weirdos we meet all over the place? Everywhere we go, some cretin crawls out of the woodwork and gloms onto us."

Those vampire friends of mine would have been quite insulted to be called "weirdos" and "cretins."

"I'm a popular guy, what can I say?" I replied before I could stop myself.

She wasn't impressed. "Very funny, Jules. You wonder why I'm leaving. Can I go on?"

I nodded.

"When I ask you to go out with some of my friends from the office, you make me feel like you're being put out. I can't think of the last time we visited my family."

"Mumble, mumble," I said quietly, barely catching

myself in time.

"What did you say?"

"Nothing." Actually, what I had meant to say was something like, "That's because they're all assholes." I avoided her gaze by suddenly finding the floor remarkably interesting.

Finally, she went on and got rolling. "We have dinner and do the 'how was your day' routine. Did you notice that neither of us is listening anymore? At home, you do some paperwork or read, and if I should dare speak to you, you honor me with a grunt. Then I'm stuck with the TV for company."

"You work at home, too."

"But not all the time!" she yelled. "You used to be so romantic. What happened to that? Never mind sex. You hardly touch me anymore. You used to touch me all the time. I loved that. And now you take me for granted."

I was starting to feel guilty. A lot of what she was saying was true. It wasn't like I had done any of it on purpose; well, except for not visiting her family—they really *were* assholes. And I did grumble when we had to go out with her friends, but that was just me being me. I thought she knew that. Assuming your partner knows what you're thinking was such a rookie mistake, and especially embarrassing at my age.

For a moment, she looked like she was going to cry—but unfortunately, she didn't. "Jules, do you know the last time we made love?"

I almost said, "Do you mean, 'fuck'?" Personally, I think the term "make love" is plumb dumb. Thankfully, this time, my mouth stayed closed. But the sad truth was I didn't know how long it had been. I could only shake my head.

She said unhappily, "Three months, Jules. *Three months.*

And before that, two months, and before that, about a month...but you fell asleep halfway through it, so I'm not sure it even counts. Do you want me to go on?"

I shook my head again. I felt like crap. Vampires are sexual creatures, and in many circles, I was known as a man-whore. I must have been seriously depressed. I had taken my human middle-aged man pretense too far, even into the bedroom.

She looked into my eyes. "Jules, how is that okay with you?"

I had no answer, but managed to croak out, "Why didn't you tell me?"

She sighed. It was one of the saddest sounds I'd ever heard, and I'd heard a lot of sad sounds. "At first, there was nothing to tell. We'd been good together, and I figured it was only a phase, but it went on and on. I tried to tell you so many times, tried to get your attention. The lingerie, the suggestions for romantic trips and date nights, but none of it worked. Then I started to get angry. Why were you doing this? Why should I have to tell you? You should have known, Jules. We'd been together so long, you should have known. How could you treat me like this?"

She paused, not to be dramatic, but to ready herself to say the next part. "When the affair started, I felt guilty...guilty. Again, I thought it was just a phase, and in the end, we'd be okay, you know? I thought I'd stop a dozen times, but I couldn't. It went on and on, and you know what? I started to feel alive again, good again. I thought this happened to us, Jules, because it could—and that we weren't meant to be. I thought of coming to you and talking about counseling, and then I remembered what you'd always said about that."

I intoned weakly, "Save the money...just get on with the

divorce." I really hate it when my own axioms rear up and bite me in the ass.

For the first time in the conversation, she actually smiled. "Just get on with the divorce," she echoed. "After that, it was simply a matter of finding the courage to tell you."

What could I say? I decided to go with the classic lame response in these situations. "I see."

"Jules, I'm forty-one, and hopefully I have a lot of good years left. But I don't want to fritter away time trying to salvage the unsalvageable. I don't want to hurt you; I want to be happy again. And I'd like it if you were happy, too." She smiled again. "Why don't you let one of those nurses who chase you around the hospital finally catch you?"

It was my turn to smile. How civilized this was all turning out. "Not likely." I wasn't sure if I was talking about the nurse part or the happy part. I still felt like shit, but I was starting to think that maybe this was going to be livable. Then I asked the question that made everything spiral out of control. Was it a macho thing or curiosity? Maybe it was a "women can be so fucking mean, but men can be so fucking stupid" kind of thing.

I could have said my civilized goodbye and promised her we'd start working on the civilized specifics. I could have gone over to the Vineyard and spent time in our civilized beach house. I could have meditated, contemplated, taken several deep breaths, smelled the salt air, the coffee, that sort of thing. I could have come back and had my amicable lawyer work with her amicable lawyer and arrange all of the amicable details of an extremely amicable divorce. It would have been the most civilized, amicable event in the history of the world.

But instead, I asked a question that I wasn't ready to hear the answer to. I fooled myself into thinking that feeling a tiny bit better than dog crap meant that I was ready.

I wasn't.

Maybe I never would have been truly ready, but if I had waited, I think I would have been more ready. No matter, because my big mouth asked the question, all by itself. "So who's the boyfriend?"

She stiffened, and her cheeks flushed. She said rigidly, "Jules, I don't think it's such a good idea to talk about that right now."

Now I was convinced that I was actually feeling oh-so-sweet, so I said oh-so-sweetly, "Oh, come on. You've already done the hard part. What difference does it make at this point? You might as well get it all out there." Somehow, by the time I had finished that sentence, I had dropped two full levels on the sweetness scale, precipitous by any standard. And she looked a bit nervous. Was I enjoying that?

"I don't want to go into this now," she replied. "Let's take it a step at a time."

Then our eyes met, and I got it in a flash of intuition, like a direct transfer of information from her head to mine. Vampires do have a rudimentary telepathy. Lisa was resistant to vampire telepathy, like many other humans, and this kind of specific information transfer was unpredictable, and usually only possible with direct physical contact. Well, things change, and we vampires are like fine wine; we keep getting better with age. I certainly had quite a bit of age under my belt.

I couldn't tell if it was telepathy, intuition, or something else. But it didn't matter, because in that instant, I knew exactly who the man was. The thought of it made me want to puke. "Donald Leland?" I blurted out. "You're bipping that old buzzard, Donald Leland?"

Lisa went pale, but she couldn't deny it. There was no

point. I knew I was right.

This couldn't have gotten much worse. Donald Leland was the self-proclaimed "king" of Needham real estate, who happened to own Lisa's company. *What a coincidence.* He was a faux-charming windbag, a know-it-all, aging lothario who'd recently gone from a Trump-like comb-over to a heinous-looking toupee or weave. He was highly involved in town politics, as long as it put more money into his pockets. Everyone in Needham loved him to his face, but hated him behind his back.

He had to be sixty, and had been married probably four times. Lisa herself had told me he'd slept with every woman in the office. Up to now, my wife had been the exception that proved the rule. Boy, was that tired and misquoted saying kicking me in the nuts at that moment. This was truly a fucking nightmare. If you can imagine having your significant other cheating on you with someone right at the top of your *People You Absolutely Would Not Want Your Significant Other to Cheat on You With* list, that's where I was.

Now I was starting to wonder how exactly Lisa had made VP at her office. *Hmmm.*

"You told me yourself he was a chronic womanizer and a cheat," I said. "How could you fall for someone like him? He's slept with almost every woman in this town, and what is he, like, seventy? And there you are, lining up this great catch so you can be Wife Number Five."

The color in her face came roaring back, and she glared at me. My god, how I hated her at that moment. *So much for amicable*, I thought. "Civilized" was heading for the nearest exit.

"He's fifty-seven, and he actually pays attention to me, something you forgot how to do a long time ago!" she shouted. "He's committed to me, and when our divorce finalizes, I've already agreed to be Wife Number Three, not Five, you asshole!"

That took the wind out of my sails. This was way down the road. I'd been living in my own little world and missed the whole damn enchilada. I paused for a moment, gathered myself, and sighed. In a believably sincere, slightly sad, and maybe even contrite voice, I said, "Lisa, I'm sorry. Can I ask you one thing?"

Her look softened a little and she bit, the dumb bitch. "Okay…what is it?"

"When you're fucking that geezer, how do you get past that old-guy, saggy-ass thing? You must have to keep the lights off, right?"

"Get out…Get the fuck out!" she screamed.

"I'm going, and when I get back, we'll get this show on the road!"

"Run away, Jules. It's what you do best. Run down to that shitty little island. And while you're gone, I'll be fucking Don left and right in our bed. And his dick is way bigger than yours!"

Ouch.

The two of them fucking in our bed was bad enough, but a bigger dick? *No way*, I thought, at least I hoped not. Comments like those were a surefire way to hurt a man, but it didn't stop me. I was on a roll. Recalling Donald's dopey only son who worked at Lisa's office, I retorted, "And watch out for that retarded son of his. He'll probably try to fuck you, too. You know what they say—like father, like son."

She was about to say something else, but checked herself. I thought I saw a hint of a smile on her lips, which bothered me.

"You're not going to drag me down to your level, no matter what," she said. "I've got houses to show." She turned to leave.

"Run away," I said mockingly. "Run away, Lisa." I admit it wasn't my best retort.

She kept walking and came back with the extremely original phrase: "Get yourself a good lawyer, Jules."

Serve and volley. "Get yourself a consult at Hair Club for Men," I chided. "That boyfriend of yours looks like someone crazy-glued road kill onto his bald head." *That was better.*

The slamming of the front door was music to my ears. I made myself some coffee and sat down to read the paper. I thought I'd feel awful at some point, but I didn't. I actually felt fine. Was that a good thing or a bad thing?

CHAPTER 3

On a small farm in the middle of Iowa, Bill Harrison leaned against the office door, watching his wife, Helen. He was yet unobserved, as she remained focused on her computer screen. Bill, as usual, was as silent as death. Helen's face was lit harshly by the computer's glow, in contrast to the room, which was barely illuminated by the feeble early morning light.

Although the unforgiving fluorescent light showed every line and contour of her face, Helen looked robust—the picture of health. Bill thought nobody would even guess she was sick, let alone terminal. Her dark hair was streaked with gray, and her angled features sharply contrasted against her well-worn bathrobe. She looked like the typical grandmother, one who might be up early to prepare the Thanksgiving turkey, or perhaps start a batch of cookies.

It was her eyes that gave her away. They told a different story—a story as different from that of a typical sixty-one-year-old Iowan farm wife as anyone could imagine. Her eyes were deeply intense and the darkest black, so black that sometimes it appeared that she didn't have pupils at all. People meeting her for the first time frequently did a double-take, trying to find those camouflaged pupils. Those eyes gave her an otherworldly appearance.

Being the poor sleeper that she was, Helen often did her research in the early morning or in the dead of night. As she stared at the screen, she drank in the information with such absolute concentration, it seemed as though she could draw data from the mainframe by sheer force of will. She wasn't looking at a recipe for how to make a better apple pie, but rather following through on an idea on how to better kill vampires. She was known as "the Genealogist," the most-feared vampire hunter of the modern era.

The sky had lightened a bit and started to illuminate her comfortably furnished office. It was cluttered with the usual mixture of well-used furniture and bookshelves stuffed with a wide variety of literature. The one oddity was a large easy chair and ottoman positioned behind her desk, to the right of her desk chair. It made no sense there, given the flow of her office, or any office, for that matter.

Taking a break, she leaned back in her desk chair, lifted her glasses, and rubbed her eyes. Bill winced as she reached for her death—a pack of cigarettes—and lit one up. She tilted her head back, absently blowing smoke toward the ceiling.

Bill finally broke the silence. "You really ought to quit those damn things, Helen."

She smiled and turned toward him. "A little too late to quit, sweetie. You ought to stop sneaking up on me like that. You're too darn quiet. And it's too early. Why don't you go back to bed?"

Bill Harrison slowly ambled into the office. He sat in the misplaced easy chair, put his big feet up on the ottoman, and completed the room. Helen spun her desk chair to face him.

"Naw, the bed gets too cold when you leave," he said.

"That's what you get for marrying an insomniac."

"I wish I'd known that before we got hitched," he said.

They'd married young, while still in college, forty years ago. Even though Bill had never been a man prone to sentimentality, he couldn't stop thinking about the fact that they wouldn't make it to their fiftieth anniversary. The thought sometimes brought him to the verge of tears. He hoped he'd hidden it from Helen, but through the years, he hadn't been able to hide much from her.

She winked at him. "Back then, we didn't do a whole lot of sleeping."

"No, we sure didn't," he replied with a laugh. But his mood quickly sobered as he thought about what he needed to say. "Helen, I know you don't want to hear this, but I think you should reconsider going through the treatment at the Mayo Clinic."

She leaned away from him and took a long, defiant drag of her cigarette. "We've been through this. Those saw-bones don't know what they're talking about. I looked it up, and so did you. With this kind of lung cancer, there's no hope. They'd carve me up and give me their poisons, but I'd still be dead in a year. Their way, I'd be in a hospital most of that time, feeling like crud. My way, I've got maybe six or eight months of doing okay, so I can go on with my work."

He grumbled, "You and your damned work."

"What's that got to do with anything?" she said harshly. "It's simple. I'm dead within the year, no matter what. Get used to it."

It wasn't the first time she had tongue-lashed him. But the way she referred to her impending death with such nonchalance surprised him. *She knows it will crush me, so why does she talk like that?* She might as well have slapped him in the face.

"So sue me for wanting to take every chance to keep you

around longer," he shot back. He felt his throat begin to tighten, but he got it under control and stood up. "I'd better go put on the coffee."

She stood quickly, catching him by the arm before he could leave the room. He was six foot two, nearly a foot taller than she was. Although they were mismatched in height, they were remarkably well matched in nearly every other way.

"Wait, I'm sorry," she said. "I can be such an ass sometimes. I shouldn't have said that. I don't know how you've put up with me all these years."

They hugged.

"Oh, it wasn't so hard," Bill said. "I wouldn't mind having a bunch more years, that's all."

She looked up at him and reached her hand behind his head. "Come down here."

He bent down, and they kissed long and deep. It was a kiss that younger people wouldn't be able to fathom, or maybe they'd even find it grotesque. But the Harrisons' contemporaries would have understood it just fine.

When they broke the kiss, he said, "Damn it, girl, you always take my breath away. Now I'd better go get that coffee going, or I might drag you back in the bedroom. And I know how you hate to be interrupted when you're working."

She smiled at Bill and returned to her computer. As he made coffee in the kitchen, he thought about how they'd come to this point, and how'd they'd started their long careers in killing vampires. Helen's family had gotten her into it, and she'd brought him along in turn. He recalled the story that she'd told dozens of times over the years.

Helen was only seventeen, and her maternal grandmother, affectionately known as Nonny, was dying.

Lung cancer...again. How the wheel of life turns. Nonny's husband, Gus, had been a farmer who dabbled in bootlegging. Years before, Chicago mobsters had killed him during a deal gone bad, and Nonny was left alone with two young children.

Before Gus died, she'd been strong and vibrant. But afterward, she'd spiraled into alcoholism and depression and had never recovered. Through the years, she and her children moved from family member to family member, living on their goodwill. Thankfully, goodwill was something that Iowans possessed in abundance.

On her deathbed, even though they weren't particularly close, Nonny told Helen what had really happened to her husband. Bill had never met Nonny, but even so, he sometimes cursed the memory of her for telling Helen the tale. The mobster story had been essentially correct, but it had lacked one crucial detail.

One of the Chicago mobsters had been a vampire.

In the aftermath of the shootout, the vampire had attacked Gus, draining him. Gus accidentally turned, and for some reason went home to make a meal of his family. Although Nonny had been bitten and was in shock, she was a mother defending her children. She managed to kill Gus by lighting him on fire with a kerosene lamp, along with the rest of their farmhouse.

Helen initially thought the tale was a bunch of baloney, but didn't say so out of respect. She asked her grandmother why she'd been chosen to hear the story.

Nonny replied, "Well, child, you don't expect me to carry this to my grave, do you? Besides, you've got a cold streak in you from your father's side. You'll probably do fine with it. Now run along, girl. It's time for me to die."

Three hours later, Nonny was dead. The thought of that

dying statement chilled Bill's blood, even after all these years.

For months, the story had bothered Helen because it possessed such great detail and had the ring of truth to it. But it wasn't as if she could do anything about it. She thought the tale would simply fade, but it never did. Instead, it stuck with her like a loyal companion.

Two years later, at the University of Iowa, the nightmares about vampires started to come. Helen decided she had to put this to rest once and for all. While she was working for the school newspaper, she learned skills that she used to research what had happened to her grandfather. Bill, already being quite enamored with her, offered his help, even though he thought the story was crazy.

Strangely enough, they found that a few days after Gus had been declared dead, three different people had seen him—very much alive. Granted, it was nighttime when he'd been spotted, but two of the witnesses knew him, and the third described him accurately. This first bit of investigation had jump-started the Harrisons' unbelievable careers.

Now, four decades later, this seemingly harmless little lady commanded a network of over six hundred agents, all dedicated to the eradication of vampires. At first, she'd gone into it purely for revenge, as payback for the ruined life of her
kin—but now she saw it as her life's work. Helen was brilliant at devising strategies for ferreting out vampires and their human helpers. She'd developed an interest in genealogy over the years, and those skills had greatly enhanced her vampire-hunting abilities, earning Helen her nickname.

Vampires, being so long-lived, had become adept at falsifying papers and electronic documents in order to avoid drawing attention to themselves. They became so experienced in this that most of these bogus documents easily passed inspection, unless they were discovered accidentally. But creating a detailed "family history" to fool an educated eye was another matter. Genealogists have those eyes, and Helen was the best of them. She'd become, in essence, the vampire boogeyman.

Bill was the perfect merciless counterpoint to her brilliance. He relished his role in wreaking havoc upon the monsters and their human helpers. At first, all the killing had unnerved him. But it had quickly become a matter of routine. *Maybe not so surprising,* he thought. He realized he was a harsh man by nature, and he'd soon earned his nickname in this unusual venture: "Bloody Bill." He had earned it in part for his substantial skill at killing vampires. But it also came from his exquisitely cruel treatment of their human helpers. He considered them lower than the animals and took great satisfaction in torturing them in the most viciously imaginative ways.

Bill had become a true innovator when it came to torture. He did it ostensibly to obtain vital information, although this wasn't quite true. The real reason he did it was that he enjoyed it. Everyone in their network knew that, and although they respected Helen, they feared Bill.

In the last forty years, they'd killed 120 vampires and countless numbers of their human followers. One hundred twenty might not seem like much to the average person, but considering the vampires' scarcity and enhanced physical attributes, it was akin to DiMaggio's 56-game hitting streak.

Bill went back to the office with a pot of strong coffee. Helen looked like she was dragging, and the coffee would be just the pick-me-up she needed. He brought her a cup.

"You really need to get some new pajamas," she said.

"I'm sick of those ugly gray sweats."

"I like them. They're comfortable."

"They're too big for you. You're skinny as a rail as it is. Those damn things make it look like somebody stole your butt."

Bill recognized the tone. Helen got cranky when she was overtired. He didn't respond right away, and they sat for a bit, sipping their coffee.

He said, "So what are you working on?"

She shook her head. "Not much. I thought I had something up in Canada. A few names kept popping up—O'Sullivan, Callaghan, Flaherty, and a few more down south. But they all turned into a big, fat nothing. I'm pretty sure about that other one I've been tracking in Shreveport. I'm nearly zeroed in."

"Well, at least there's that. But we probably ought to be slow and careful, anyway. We don't want another debacle like New York."

She snapped. "Well, it isn't like I've got all the time in the world, is it?"

"Now, Helen—"

"Don't 'now, Helen' me! What are you trying to say, Bill? Are you saying I rushed the job and got our whole team killed? Because if that's what you think, come out with it."

In truth, that was exactly what Bill thought. Helen's having less than a year left had affected her judgment, and they both knew it. The job was rushed; it had clearly needed more research and surveillance. He thought those things, but he would never say them. "I don't think that at all. Maybe—"

"Maybe it was because *you* didn't prepare them well enough!"

Now his anger flared. "Now you hold on a damn minute.

The team was totally prepared. Do you think I'd send out my own nephew if it wasn't?"

"I don't know what I think, Bill. But you ought to remember who's running this network."

He was a prideful man, and he hated it when she took this attitude, especially since he never bucked her or questioned her authority. Lately, since the diagnosis, she'd taken to reminding him who was in charge, and he'd had enough of it. "You might come up with the plans, but you don't run things, I do!"

She slapped both hands down on the desk and glared at him. "And I run you!"

That took Bill aback. They didn't fight often, but when they did, it could quickly reach monumental proportions. He didn't like where this was going, so he decided to stave it off. "That's not fair, Helen. I've never questioned your decisions. I've always supported you, and you know it."

She leaned back and ran her hand through her hair. It was something she did when she was agitated.

Helen was already beginning to feel badly about what she'd just said to Bill. She'd always been an even keeled person in the past, but ever since she was diagnosed as terminal, mood swings seemed to be running roughshod over her. "I'm sorry. You didn't deserve that. It's this damned cancer. My time is so limited that I want to do something big and important before the end, that's all. I think I did send that team out too early. I'm so darn guilty over it."

Even though it was Bill's blood nephew who'd been killed, he'd felt no sorrow over it. He'd never cared for the boy. "Doesn't matter if you did or you didn't. You're the boss, and we're in a dangerous business. People get killed. I just like keeping our tally ahead of theirs, that's all."

She smiled at that. "Me, too, but if I keep going like this, I'll get the whole lot of us wiped out."

"I doubt that. And you know I'm always one hundred percent behind you. As long as you promise not to screech 'I run you' at me anymore."

She laughed. "I promise."

"Say, you've got an awful lot of open tabs on your screen. What else you up to?"

She lit another cigarette. "I had this silly idea that if we could search for people with no health insurance and cross them with some of our other research parameters, we might find a few vampires in the mix. But the group is just too damn big."

He nodded and gestured toward the cigarettes. "Hey, give me one of those, would you?" Bill always supported Helen, even when what she was doing was killing her. He lit up and ruminated. "What about this? What about people who have insurance, but never use it? Those fuckers never get sick, right?" Bill knew he wasn't the best original idea man around, but he'd been blessed with a healthy dose of common sense and a skill at refining existing concepts.

Helen beamed at him. "I wish you'd watch that language of yours, but that's good. You're so darn smart...no wonder I married you."

"Well, it sure wasn't for my looks."

She laughed, then became serious. "New York debacle aside, you know in this last little bit, I'm going to throw caution to the wind."

Helen was always meticulous in her research and her hunts. She would never order an attack unless absolutely sure, sometimes even taking up to a year to make the final call. But as the recent botched plan indicated, time was a luxury she could no longer afford.

Her last-ditch approach was going to cost extra lives, and Bill knew it. But that was the way it would have to be. He said, "You're not going to let the religious nutjobs go wild, are you?"

"Lord, no! The collateral damage would be unbelievable."

The Network, almost by definition, had a high percentage of the very religious who thought they were doing God's work by killing vampires. They were a trying lot to manage at times, but their value couldn't be denied. The Harrisons were still able to control these religious zealots, but it was taking more and more effort to keep them reined in.

Bill said, "Sorry I asked. What, then?"

She scratched her head. "I don't know, but I'm going to try to get a big group of them all at once, I think. Maybe this health insurance angle will help."

"I'll put the computer geeks on it once the sun comes up."

"You know your eldest is our head computer geek. Would it kill you to say 'computer expert'?"

"Oh pish-posh, Helen. Molly calls herself a geek all the time."

She couldn't argue with that. After a moment she said, "One more thing. If I'm able to put something big together, I'm going this time."

Bill knew she'd always wanted to go into the field, but never had. As the heart and soul of the Network, she was considered too valuable and had always been dissuaded. It wasn't a prideful thing, just the truth. But the tumor growing in her lung had altered the equation.

"I figured," Bill said. "Me and the girls will be going with you."

The Harrisons' three adult daughters had all been on vampire hunts, but never together. The risk of losing her entire family was too great. For a moment, Helen looked as if she would argue, but she remained silent, probably knowing it would do no good.

Bill said, "You know that if they catch you and figure out who you are, they're going to kill you, maybe worse."

"I thought of that. If they turn me, I'll kill myself."

Bill took a drag of his cigarette and watched the smoke rise, as if hypnotized by it. "Nope. That's not what I meant. I mean, they'll use you somehow to take down the whole Network."

Helen's death, in and of itself, would certainly hurt the operation—but with Bill and his girls left in charge, things would eventually smooth out. He thought it far more risky if the vampires captured her. And where that risk might come from, he wasn't sure.

She smiled. "What? I said you were smart, so now you're showing off?"

"Just trying to do my part."

"Well, now that you've done the heavy lifting, I'll come up with something to make sure that doesn't happen."

"Like what?" Bill asked.

She shook her head, stood, and pulled him to his feet.

"What's all this?" he asked. But he already knew.

"I think it's time for a bedroom break."

He laughed. "You are one lively old gal."

They left the office and walked hand-in-hand to the bedroom they'd shared for over four decades.

CHAPTER 4

After my solo breakfast of coffee and then some more coffee, I packed for my trip to the Vineyard. The house down there was well supplied, and I didn't need to take much. I managed to hit the road by 2:30 p.m., and on a chilly weekday in April, it was clear sailing all the way.

I got a parking space right at the dock. If this had been high season, I would have had to park in an out lot, pretty much as far away from the ferry as upstate New York. I could've looked forward to a bumpy, sweaty bus ride spent squeezed between a fat, smelly woman and a crying baby with a diaper full of high-test shit. I would have counted it a good ride if same said infant didn't blow baby chow all over me.

I hopped on the ferry, which looked like a cross between a flat-bottomed tug and a prehistoric whale. These boats had holds that could accommodate about a million cars, and when one of them was retired, an infrequent event at best, the new replacement looked like it had come directly from the 1940s. But that was all right with me. I liked the 1940s.

I got myself a cold beer and went up to the open-air top deck, where I always liked to ride. It was quite chilly, but temperature extremes never bother vampires that much. We feel cold, pain, or any other sensation, but as we age and learn to control our responses to various stimuli, we find that they don't have to affect us very much at all.

As I stood leaning on the bow rail, nursing my beer, the ship's foghorn blew its ear-shattering blast. We kicked off from the dock, chugging along. The seagulls took flight as our air escorts, pacing the boat in hopes of tossed snacks. The sea air was salty and fine, and I sat back and lifted my face to that rare, wonderful feeling—April sunshine.

I was well past the need to avoid light at this point, but in the first twenty-five to fifty years of vampire life, we are very sensitive to the sun. We don't immediately burst into flames, explode, or anything like that when exposed to daylight, but the sun can definitely kill a new vamp. Third- and even fourth-degree burns can occur within seconds. Much longer than that, and it's bonfire time, a horrible death. If we get out of the sun fast enough, we'll heal—but given this sensitivity, all vampires initially have to be nocturnal. Even after our sun-fearing days are over, we tend to maintain a night schedule. It's much easier to hunt for blood under the cover of darkness.

When the sun rises, we don't instantly drop into a stone-cold sleep or go into a coma. Like humans, we are varied in our sleep patterns. I'm a bit of an insomniac, and sometimes I really enjoy an afternoon nap. And although we have more energy reserves to call on, and can go much longer without sleep, we like our rest and need it, just as humans do.

Our sun sensitivity is from an almost complete lack of effective melanin during that initial period, and it makes us paler than average. Around the twenty-five year mark, effective melanin production kicks back in. Then we become less sun sensitive, on the order of an albino. Shortly after that, we are still sensitive to sunlight, but no more than your average ginger. Eventually, we have no sensitivity at all. I got some pretty shitty burns early on, but I learned fast. Now I enjoy luxuriating at the beach for days on end.

We seem to retain some level of sun sensitivity in our eyes, though. Vampires wear shades more often than the average human, even at nighttime, but probably no more than the ultra-chic types. Now I grant you, this may all be due to the fact that we like looking ultra-chic, too, and as our vision is better than any human's, we can wear sunglasses in the dark and see quite well. So, night sunglass-wearing *is* a mark of being a vampire—or of being an ultra-chic-wannabe dork, unfortunately.

The breeze in my face was crisp and refreshing, and the beer tasted just right. The channel crossing was brief and smooth as usual, and I stood with the cold wind tousling my hair, reddening my cheeks, and watering my eyes. I was content watching the island grow bigger as we approached, and not a single thought crossed my mind. Given the current circumstances, it was a nice break.

Before I realized it, we were docking. The ship's horn blew again, signaling our arrival and making sure the few of us on deck were completely deaf. I picked up my bag, headed for the gangplank, and strolled off the ferry onto the pier. The few cars on the boat were mostly driven out of the hold already, and I slowly made my way along the pedestrian walkway to the street.

I walked through Ocean Park, which served as the town green of Oak Bluffs. It was a well-maintained, open, grassy park with a man-made pond and a gazebo as its centerpiece, rimmed by brightly painted Victorian-style beach houses. During summer days and evenings, it was chock full of sun-worshipping, dog-owning, Frisbee-throwing skateboarders—the way a town green should be. During the night, however, it got its share of post-last call, boisterously loud drunks, which, I suppose, was a necessary evil.

Ocean Park was deserted. The wind was picking up, and clouds were rolling in. On days like this, the gazebo always struck me as a bit creepy. It reminded me of the gazebo in the Stephen King novel *The Dead Zone*. A serial killer in the book used it as his base of operations in King's famously fictitious, bad-vibe town of Derry, Maine. The thought of that story, along with the wind, gave me a shiver. Yes, even vampires get the creeps. As you might imagine, unnerving us takes quite a bit more than it does for humans—but King is the master of creepy. Vampires generally avoid his novels for fear of nightmares.

I continued deeper into the island, walking along street after street of quaint cottages. Residents really got to know their neighbors here on the Vineyard, since past building codes must have required that houses be built no farther than two feet apart, with walls no more than a quarter-inch thick.

I arrived at my place, a modest two-story, three-bedroom house with a nice wraparound porch. It was on a small rise, and even though it was several blocks back from the beach, the master bedroom had a small balcony with an ocean view. The house was well away from the hubbub of the ferry, the beach, and Circuit Avenue, the main drag of the town. But it was only a ten-minute walk from them all. I like isolation, solitude, and privacy as much as the next person, but only if I can get away from it quickly whenever I need to.

Oak Bluffs was definitely touristy, but I liked it because it was convenient and had a lot going on, especially for a small beach town. There were some truly beautiful and isolated areas on the west end of the island, but if you weren't a talented landscape painter, the number-one activity there was watching sand blow onto your back porch.

I took a tour of the house, turning on various gadgets, power sources, water valves, and the like. Everything seemed to be in working order. I thought I'd settle in and maybe read for a bit—but I started to feel distracted, then fidgety. I thought it might be the divorce beginning to weigh on my mind again, but it wasn't. Initially I didn't recognize what was happening, because it had been so long.

I wanted to hunt.

Not the sanitized version of what I'd done for the last twenty years, but really hunt—bringing my victim down, draining him or her dry, and reveling in it. Since my sham human marriage and human life were coming to an end, the scales of my pretense were falling off fast, and my vampire self wanted to burst through.

I had thought I was over this sort of thing. I didn't need that much blood anymore and didn't have to kill—but here it was, the honest urge to do just that. If this crap kept up, I was going to have to see a vampire psychiatrist, and ours are even more fucked up than the human variety.

I was trying to maintain control, but my breathing was getting rapid. I broke into a light sweat, and my hands trembled. I've never had any experience with drugs, but I'm guessing I felt about the same as a junkie in dire need of a fix. What I needed, though, wasn't as easy as slamming a syringe full of heroin. What I needed was to suck several units of warm, pulsing red blood from a torn-open carotid artery while a hapless victim fought uselessly for his or her life.

This was bad, very bad—especially here, on a small, off-season island where I was well known. I mean, it wasn't like I could go on a rampage and leave the place strewn with corpses and not attract attention. But that didn't matter to me at that moment. I wanted to run from the house, ripping throats apart and drinking gallons of blood. I needed to do something, and fast.

CHAPTER 5

In my current state, I wasn't thinking clearly, so the best I could come up with was to get a few drinks in me. There wasn't a drop of booze in the house, so I raced out the door and up Circuit Avenue to the Ritz Cafe. As the name suggests, the Ritz was a dark little dump of a bar that I happened to love.

In retrospect, going there was plumb dumb, as there would be people there—and I should've been trying to avoid people at all costs. But in my defense, I wasn't in my right mind, and even my right mind isn't all that great to start with. I opened the door and looked upon ten or so late-afternoon imbibers. *Ten? Come on! Ten in this little dive on a cold weekday in April? What a bunch of fucking drunks!*

I stared at them the way a jungle cat stares at a gazelle before the kill. My light perspiration turned into a heavy sweat, my rapid breathing got erratic, and my hand tremors turned to full-fledged shakes. It was over. They were all fucking dead. I wouldn't be able to stop myself.

The door swung closed behind me with a slam, and I jumped like I'd been goosed, looking back over my shoulder. When I turned again, everyone was staring at me. I felt a modicum of control trying to come back—but it wasn't enough, and it was way too late.

Jimmy, one of the burly, bearded bartenders that the Ritz seemed to mass-produce, shouted, "Hey, Doc, how the hell are you?"

His addressing me somehow broke the spell. I'm not sure why, but I think it was because I'd known Jimmy for years and liked him a lot. Maybe that was what won the day. The patrons returned to their beers while I stood there like a mute, sweaty dope.

He walked down the bar, looking concerned. "Doc, you okay?"

I closed my eyes for a moment. When I opened them, Jimmy had miraculously ceased to look like food to me. I took a deep breath and lied, "I'm good, Jimmy. You?"

"You don't *look* good. Come on, sit down, and I'll get you something."

"Sounds like a plan," I said with relief. Maybe, just maybe, the Ritz would stay out of the papers tomorrow as the site of a bloody massacre.

"Usual?"

I nodded, and he poured me a shot of tequila, which I gulped down. A quick refill suffered a similar fate. After my fourth, I started to feel better, or at least my hands stopped shaking.

Jimmy leaned in toward me. "You sure you're okay, Doc?"

I managed a smile. "Work's getting to me, that's all. You know how it is."

He straightened up and extended his arms to the grimy shithole that he worked in. With a gap-toothed grin, he said, "Look around you, Doc. I know *exactly* how it is."

I laughed a little. As he turned to take care of some other customers, I said, "Jimmy, leave the bottle."

He nodded and set it down, then moved on down the bar. I kept at the tequila and worked up a nice buzz that helped to quell my blood lust, which must have been psychological. At my age, I required only a pint or so every third day. Granted, by the third day, I didn't feel the greatest, but it was doable. Damn, I felt so screwed up.

I kept knocking back tequila, and my mind drifted into neutral. I wasn't passed out on the floor from the booze, because vampires have an enhanced physiology. Our cells operate at a higher level of efficiency, and pretty much any ingested chemicals or drugs are digested, broken down, and detoxified, rendering them harmless.

This is generally a good thing, as we can't be poisoned, except by garlic. Toxic chemicals have no effect. Anesthesia...nope. Infectious agents? Uh-uh. Our resistance to all infection is due to our overdeveloped immune system, but a lot of pathogens are simply broken down by local digestive effects before they can even generate an immune response.

On the other side of the coin, we can never get high on drugs. The same goes for alcohol. Our alcohol dehydrogenase enzyme, which does the lion's share of breaking down booze, is too fucking good. Most liquor, although it still tastes delicious, doesn't give us the slightest buzz. Tequila, though, is one class of alcohol that gives us a pretty good high, and despite a lot of research, the specifics as to why are elusive. At the moment, I didn't care about the specifics. I just needed to tie one on.

The other booze that gets us really fucked up, even more than tequila, is absinthe. Because of it, I'm afraid the cliché is true: vampires hang out in absinthe bars. If I tried to order absinthe at the Ritz, though, Jimmy would have thrown me out.

Thankfully, the constant flow of tequila seemed to wash away my urge to kill every human in sight. The TV over the bar had the Celtics on, and the good guys were winning. I settled into various conversations with some of the other patrons, getting into the flow of the place and feeling more like myself. Toward last call, I felt the need for blood again, but it seemed like my normal urge this time, not psychotic the way it had felt before. This, I could handle.

"I think I'll skip last call, my friend," I said to Jimmy. I paid my tab, adding a substantial tip for Jimmy's service, his company, and the fact that he had inadvertently stopped me from killing everybody in sight.

He picked up the cash. "Thank you, Mr. Rockefeller. You know, Doc, I got to tell you, I've never seen anyone handle his booze so good, especially a little shit like you."

I smiled at his "compliment." Jimmy may have looked big, nasty, and foreboding, but there wasn't a mean bone in his body. And for the record, I'm nearly five foot eight-ish, almost.

"Thank you so much for those kind words," I replied. "Now I'm so fucking glad I gave you that huge tip!"

Jimmy's laughter followed me out into the chilly, drizzly night. It was time to get some blood, but I'd need to be careful, just like I'd been for the last few decades when I was playing human. I'd use my telepathy.

~~~

I strolled down the pier, which was deserted, quiet, and pitch dark. The drizzle had created a mist that was only a step away from fog—perfect conditions for what I needed to do.

Then I heard the familiar rattle of empty beer cans coming from one of the docked fishing boats. I easily located the source of the noise, as vampire night vision isn't just good, it's pretty much infrared.

The man was huge, slovenly, and reeked of fish and beer. He stumbled about, smashed, muttering to himself, probably looking for one full can among all the empties. I was shocked that he hadn't been at the Ritz. He would have fit right in. It was a perfect, easy mark.

Given the size of the boat, I surmised he was likely both captain and crew. I didn't hear any telltale noise from below deck to contradict my theory. With any luck, I wouldn't have to deal with surprise witnesses.

"Ahoy, captain," I called out in the darkness. "Can I help you?"

He started, shocked, and nearly fell over. Before he could reply, our eyes locked, and his face went slack. Suddenly, he became steady on his feet. This was my lucky night—a susceptible on my first shot. For an old vamp, I'm middle of the road for telepathy, having an effect on over three-quarters of the humans I encounter.

Vampire telepathy isn't a direct form of communication with humans. It's diffuse and nonspecific, and it can't be used to have a complex dialogue with an intended victim. We use it to muddle the prey's mind, taking the fight out of them and making it easy for us to drink their blood. If I were going to drain this dude to death, the telepathy would make it a relatively nice way to go. With telepathy, we can push out single thoughts or feelings. Mine that night, as per usual, was *Relax*. The old skipper did what he was told.

I climbed aboard and advanced on him. I moved his beard to the side, but he was so fucking tall, I couldn't reach high enough to bite. I lowered him to the deck, which was a smart move, as it made what I was doing much harder to see should any late-night passersby show up on the dock. But it was still pretty embarrassing. Humans have really learned to grow in the last two millennia. Back in 30 B.C., if my legion had had a basketball team, I could have been the starting center. Well, at least power forward.

I bit into his neck, and the first pulse of blood hit the roof of my mouth like a fountain. It was absolutely delicious and I felt instantly energized. I sucked hard on the wound, drawing more and more blood into my mouth, greedily gulping it down. The captain had had a pretty good snoot full of cheap beer, and I could taste the alcohol in his blood. You can't order Pabst and blood at the local bar, but it makes a damn good mix, if you ask me.

To further confuse, disarm, or maybe comfort our victims, vampires secrete a sedative/amnestic from our salivary glands, kind of like Valium, when we bite. This happens as a reflex, but as we mature, we can learn to control it, volitionally giving a bigger dose if the donor is large, or holding the sedative back altogether.

Why would we hold it back? Well, some victims may be assholes, and it might not be quite good enough just to kill them. Now, killing them in abject terror, leaving them aware of exactly what is happening, might better fit the bill. I know this sounds horrifying, but I'm one of the nicer vampires you'd run into—imagine what the meaner ones would do. This drunken giant got an extra-large dose.

In the first thirty seconds, I'd taken about a half unit of blood from him. That's my usual rate; I'm a fairly fast drinker. He was so big, I thought I'd take a unit and a half. He could easily spare it.

To us, blood is a total body experience, much more than a drink. The taste is exquisite, all satisfying, and immediately stimulating. The closest I can come to describing it is when I was a legionary, all those centuries ago. Imagine a long, hot, sweaty ten-mile march in full gear, and then happening upon a crystal-clear stream. Imagine how wonderful that pure, clean, ice-cold water would taste. Multiply that a hundredfold, and you still wouldn't be close.

I drank and drank, lost in the captain's blood. Suddenly, I realized that I'd taken too much. I stopped, but it was too late.

I had killed him.

What a fuck-up. This wasn't as bad as wiping out everyone at the Ritz, but it was bad. Even worse, it was sloppy. I intended for him to be a donor, not a victim. When he woke, he'd likely remember nothing, muddled by my telepathy and sedative, not to mention the beer. If he did remember anything, it would be through a haze that he'd probably put off to a dream or a drunken delusion. But now, the captain would never wake again. I had to dispose of the body in the proper way, to make sure he didn't turn into a vampire—and I wasn't prepared.

I needed to think fast. I couldn't just leave him, as accidental turnings were frowned upon these days. A good candidate had to be properly vetted, with all the appropriate paperwork and recommendations submitted in a timely manner. Since the captain here was already dead, that course of action was clearly off the table.

Decapitation was a surefire way of preventing a turning and was my preferred method. I could use his boat and dump him in the ocean. *No . . . no good.* Starting the engine would attract attention, not to mention the fact that I couldn't pilot a boat if my life depended on it. *Damn it.* I had to straighten this out fast.

That was when I smelled the gasoline.

There was a small gas can on the deck. It would be an attention-getter, no doubt—but given all the empties on board, along with my victim's likely reputation as a heavy drinker, it would pass muster, or at least I hoped it would. And fire was as good as decapitation as a vampire prophylactic.

My victim stared blankly into the night sky as I doused him liberally with gasoline, along with the deck of his boat. I lit a match, and for a moment, I thought about staying with the captain and burning right along with him. The last hundred years had been a downward spiral for me. Maybe I'd lived too long; it happened to my kind. I wasn't enjoying life the way I used to. Maybe it was time for me to go. My aunts were much older than I was, but at least they had each other. What did I have? Not much.

I stood, introspecting, with the match burning dangerously close to my fingers. I shook it out in time and joined my dead friend on the deck, staring up at the sky. In my day, in Rome, suicide was accepted as an honorable way to die to avoid disgrace or as a matter of duty. This would be neither. This would be the act of a coward. No, I'd get through the divorce and move away from Boston and on to another life. I'd see what happened from there. If I chose to end things at that point, so be it. I lit another match, tossed it into the boat, and said, "Sorry, Captain."

The captain, along with his boat, went up like a torch.

CHAPTER 6

The next morning found me standing in front of the bathroom mirror, examining myself. It was a ritual I'd developed as of late, and even though I knew it was a bad sign, indicating a worsening of my century long depression, I couldn't seem to stop. Many who knew me thought this extra time spent in the bathroom was due to vanity, and that was true to a degree, but it was mostly my ritual.

I'd slept almost ten hours, unheard of for a near-insomniac like me. I'm not sure if it was a true sleep, or some kind of shocked coma caused from my fuck-up with the captain. There had probably been fire truck sirens blaring through the night, but I didn't hear a single one. I woke up happy that the cops hadn't come knocking at my door ... yet.

I continued to stare at my reflection. It was the reflection of Julian Brownell, but I wasn't really him. Nor was I any of the dozens of other aliases I'd assumed over the years. No matter what, I was still Roman at my core. I was still Titus Acilius and always would be.

I was a Roman soldier when I was turned all those centuries ago, and now I was examining the scars I'd accumulated during my years in the legion. I thought looking at them somehow made me feel human again—but by this time I had no idea how that felt.

As a vampire, I could never gain another physical scar, although the psychological varieties seemed quite abundant. Humans who hunted vampires thought that we'd become heartless, soulless killers. Even many humans who were vampire-friendly shared this opinion. It couldn't be further from the truth.

Sometimes I wished it were accurate, though. It would make things a hell of a lot easier. When turned, contrary to popular notion, vampires remain the same people that they were as humans. They don't become evil, killing automatons. The physiologic urge to drink blood is surely motivating, but that doesn't remove the mental stress of having to kill. Because of this, many vampires take their own lives in their early years.

I loved my life. Sure, I'd had my ups and downs through the centuries, but I'd always dealt fairly well with the blood-drinking and the killing. At one point, I'd even believed that I might be beyond the psychological pressures of being a vampire. But these last hundred years had shot that theory all to hell.

Lately, my physical scars had somehow come to represent everything I'd lost as a human, and looking at them comforted me. Considering all my years as a soldier, I'd been pretty lucky in the face department. There was a thin scar on my right cheek that I had gotten in Spain when I was a baby soldier of only seventeen. At the time, I thought myself mortally wounded, but it hadn't bled that much. Remembering how I'd carried on about the tiny wound made me smile.

Toward the end of my career, my right earlobe had been shot off by an arrow in Egypt. I didn't even notice it until after the battle. Now, only the keenest observers noticed it.

My body definitely told a more vivid tale. A puncture wound through my left flank—a thrown pike in Gaul. A large chunk of flesh missing from my right thigh—a sword slash in Germany. My left pinky finger gone, left behind on some dusty plain in Greece. I turned about with a handheld mirror to examine the prizewinner, my back. There was a long, wide hack right down the middle of it from a battle axe.

That wound, which I'd received in Gaul, was the only one that ever took me from the field of battle. Before I passed out, I managed to turn and impale my attacker through the throat. I almost died from that injury, and most of my comrades thought for sure I would. I fooled them all, but it took me over a month to recover.

With my exam completed, I came to the same conclusion I always did. I looked to be every one of my well-worn forty-five human years. Certainly improved and enhanced by my vampire physiology, but still forty-five, and just the same as I'd been for over two thousand years.

My mind wandered back through the centuries to the night I was turned.

~~~

The child-animal crouched, staring at me from a dirty, dark alleyway. I'd told him to go find his mother, and in response, he howled terrifyingly, standing my neck hairs on end. But I'd seen many a battle, and neck hair or no, I was calm and ready. I didn't want to harm the youngster, especially a sick one like this, but it wasn't like I hadn't killed children before. At times, my legion had put entire villages to the sword—men, women, and children.

The "child" moved inhumanly fast, leaping at me from over ten feet. I thought it had no chance of reaching me from that distance—but of course, it did.

My sword draw may not have been as fast as it was when I was twenty-five, but it was still fast. What I'd lost in youthful reflex, I'd more than made up with experience and precision, or so I thought. My gladius was out in a split second, my draw smooth and oily as always. I made for an overhand strike that would cleave this tiny assailant in two.

As quick as I was, the young boy was faster. He leapt through my guard, backhanding my sword arm and throwing off the arc of the blow. My arm went numb and felt as if it had been hit by a battering ram. Even so, my blade whistled past the child's head, just missing it. Then it clattered harmlessly to the ground.

The boy attached himself to me. I was staggered by the force of the impact but somehow kept my feet. From a distance, I imagine, this looked like a quaint domestic scene with a good father carrying home a child who was too tired to walk. Small arms wrapped around my shoulders, legs around my waist, and a tiny face snuggling into my neck for warmth. Except the face wasn't snuggling—it was burrowing.

My neck was bitten and torn open, spilling blood down my tunic. I roared more from shock than pain, but it hurt like hell. I tried to pry the monster loose, but it was like trying to move stone. I beat it on its head and torso to no avail. I was weakening.

I heard a slurping noise, and the shocking realization hit. This thing was drinking my blood. In that era, there was only one explanation for this—the child was a demon. The thought hit me like a pan of cold water tossed into my face. I bellowed and doubled my efforts, raging, clawing at it, ramming it into walls—but it did no good. I was flagging, my vision was doubling, and I dropped to my knees.

The child-vampire pulled back then, grinning and gloating, with blood—my blood—dripping from its lips. It's never smart to gloat at a Roman soldier, even a dying one. Once again, I became enraged. I wouldn't allow myself to perish on my knees like this, and somehow I found a final speck of energy.

I lurched to my feet. As I was trained to do in a desperate situation, I slid my thumbs into the vampire's eye sockets. I heard and felt satisfying pops as I crushed its eyeballs. The thing screamed, and I let out a weak laugh as it reattached itself to my neck. The last clear memory I had as a human was fighting to the end. By the next evening, I, Titus Acilius, had transformed into a vampire.

~~~

When I came out of my reverie, I thought, not for the first time, that my ritual and these jaunts down memory lane probably weren't the best thing for my already fragile mind. If I didn't find a way to deal with my little psychiatric problem soon, I'd probably go insane.

I made myself some coffee and sat on the master balcony to look at the ocean and think. Turning that boat into a pile of ashes last night was slipshod work, especially for a vampire of my experience. It told me something I'd already known for a long time: I was losing it. I mean, shit happens even to the best of us, but everything had been in my favor. It had been a dark, deserted, foggy night, with no witnesses and a drunken victim. And I had fucked it all up by letting my mind wander as I drained him without realizing it. "Amateurish" would be a kind description.

I'd been in a funk for a long time, and my grand solution had been to lessen my blood intake, moderate my killing, and utterly deny who I was while pretending to be human. That was obviously working just peachy, with me coming inches away from slaughtering ten people at the Ritz. Yeah, that plan was working out fine.

One positive thing I had rediscovered last night was how good a normal blood intake made me feel. And it wasn't just psychological. That morning, I felt as if I could lift the house off the foundation—totally energized, the way I was supposed to feel. How could I have forgotten that?

To top it all off, I'd gotten myself into a sham marriage with a human who had no idea who or what I was. I'd lied to Lisa every day for the past fifteen years. As a vampire, I had the right to drink her blood, kill her even, but I didn't have the right to lie to her. Even if it was a sham, she was still my wife, and if she could be happier with an old, scraggly-ass, toupee-wearing, womanizing fuck, then good luck to her.

I was a vampire—a blood-drinker and a killer, by definition. Denying what I was wasn't helping me. Neither was pretending to be human, or getting myself overly involved with humans. There were no answers for me in that world. I didn't know what the answers were, but I needed to figure them out fast, or I was going to end up crazy or dead. The first step was to head back home and take care of matters at hand. As for the second step, I didn't have a clue.

CHAPTER 7

Bill Harrison was finishing his night rounds at the farm. With all the staff he and Helen had these days, it really wasn't necessary to do this anymore. It'd been quite necessary, however, when they were first starting out and their vampire hunting was little more than a mom-and-pop business. He'd continued it ever since the beginning, as old habits died especially hard for Bloody Bill.

He was about to enter the front door when he noticed that the guard posted at the corner of the house was seated, leaning back in a chair. Bill wasn't fond of night security sitting on duty, but he'd never expressly forbidden it, either. Even though it was dark where the guard was, Bill's night vision was quite good. He could tell the man was asleep.

Bill glided down the porch noiselessly, despite all the loose and creaky boards. He stood over the guard for several seconds, watching him snooze with his chin to his chest. It was Andy Simmons. He was new to the Network, but he had shown a great deal of promise up until now. Bill liked the kid, but that didn't stop his anger from reaching the boiling point. He savagely kicked the chair, sending it and Simmons crashing to the ground.

The other house guard popped up around the corner, his

gun leveled and ready for action. Bill nodded his approval and waved the man away as Simmons stumbled his way back to his feet. He stammered out, "Bill, I—"

"Shut your fucking yap," Bill hissed as he leaned down close to Simmons, backing him to the wall. "How do you think I feel about you sleeping on the job, Andy? Right at my house, no less. What do you think I would have done to you if one of those blood-sucking bastards got by and hurt my wife or daughter?" Even in the dark, Bill could see Simmons turn pale and break into a sweat.

"I'm so sorry, Bill... Mr. Harrison, I was praying and I've been so tired... I must've nodded off. No excuse, I know. I screwed up."

Bill liked the fact that the kid had owned up, but was disheartened to think that Gary Jarvis had his hooks into someone else. Jarvis billed himself a reverend, but Bill suspected the title was bullshit and of the self-proclaimed variety. Jarvis was, however, the center and unofficial leader of the Network's religious wing. Bill considered him smart and dangerous, and believed he had intentions of taking over, although Jarvis would never admit it, of course.

"Oh, I get it. Let me guess. That peacock Jarvis had you up all night at one of his wacky marathon prayer sessions."

Simmons replied, "Reverend Jarvis is a holy man, Bill. You shouldn't—"

His commentary was cut short by the cannon-sized pistol that magically appeared from nowhere and was now pressed against his forehead. Bill was astounding in handling weapons of all kinds, and by the way Simmons responded, he knew that the kid hadn't even known the gun existed until it was already against his skull. Bill knew Simmons was a bit green, but not this green. He'd even considered taking him out on their next mission. He'd have to rethink that.

"No, Andy, *you* shouldn't. I say that phony is a preening, self-aggrandizing flim-flam man. Are you going to disagree with me?"

Simmons' eyes were as big as saucers as he shook his head back and forth. Bill kept the gun pressed against Simmons' forehead, which was now sweating profusely.

"Good. Fortunately for Jarvis, he happens to be damn good at killing vampires, and that's why I still tolerate him. I'm sorry you fell in with him though. You seem like a good kid." Bill turned away from Simmons, still holding the gun to his head. He looked out over his farm and mused, "You know, Andy, I must be getting old. Way back when I was a young buck, if I had found someone snoozing like you, I would've blown his brains out on the spot. Or, if I was in a foul mood, maybe I'd slice his throat." He turned back to Simmons, who looked ready to pass out. "Now you haven't been around here so long, Andy, and you might think that's bullshit. But ask around, if you want. You'll find out that it ain't. You believe me, don't you?"

Simmons nodded, and Bill removed the gun. A huge exhalation burst out of the young man; he'd been holding his breath and hadn't even realized it. He started to sink to the ground, but Bill's iron-hard grasp caught him by his upper arm, propping him up.

"None of that. You keep your feet. Breathe steady now."

Simmons did as Bill instructed.

When it looked like he would stay upright, Bill released him. "I know you think I'm a prick for what I did. But what happened to you was sweet compared to what a vampire would've done to you if you were caught napping."

Simmons gulped. "Yes, Mr. Harrison."

"I'm just plain Bill around here, Andy," Bill replied. "I

know you were itching to go out in the field, and you've got potential, but after tonight, we'd better bump you back a mission or two, okay?"

Simmons looked disappointed. "I understand. It makes sense. Sorry for screwing up."

Bill nodded and went in his front door. Because Simmons had been asleep, Bill took his Mossberg 500 shotgun out of the gun rack and took an extra turn around the house to make sure that all was well. The Mossberg was a no-frills weapon, but extremely effective, just like its owner. On more than one occasion, Bloody Bill had been described as being a "maestro" in its use. When he was satisfied that the house was secure, he re-racked the gun and headed toward his bedroom.

Before he got there, however, he noticed the light at the bottom of his eldest daughter's office door. At a young age, Molly Harrison had enthusiastically leapt into the family business and never married. It seemed she didn't have the time for such doings. Bill always regretted that. She lived on the farm with him and Helen and headed up their informatics and computer section.

Bill paused at the door for a moment, knocked lightly, and went in. As he expected, she was clicking away at her computer, staring at the screen. She'd gotten about a fifty-fifty mix from her parents in height and appearance, and fared quite well in the intelligence department, possessing both Helen's quick wit and intellect and Bill's reasoning capability and common sense.

He said, "You're up awfully late, aren't you, little girl?"

Although Molly was in her mid-thirties, Bill knew she loved him fiercely and didn't mind his little pet name. She continued to work her magic with the keyboard and replied, "This health insurance angle is really something, Dad. It could be big."

"Really? How are you making out getting into the insurance companies' databases?"

She looked up at him and smiled. "Piece of cake. By the way, great idea coming up with this."

Bill replied, "Oh, I didn't do much. Your mother had the idea."

"It really pisses me off when you do that, Dad. It was your idea, and you know it. And it isn't like Mom is some kind of credit hound. I wish you'd stop being so damn self-effacing."

He was going to respond, but she pressed on.

"And don't say 'I don't know what self-effacing means.' Save that good-ol'-boy routine for someone who might buy it."

He smiled down at her for two reasons. First, that was exactly what he was going to say, and second, she'd done her usual first-rate impersonation of him. Bill didn't love her any more than his other two daughters; he couldn't. But because she was his first-born, she'd always be special to him. He loved her differently, that's all.

"Okay, Molly, you got me," he said. "When do you think you might have something we could go on?"

Her expression grew serious. "I got something *now*."

This surprised him. None of their search parameters had ever been effective in so short a time. Finding a vampire was painstaking work that took months, or even longer. He pulled up a chair next to her.

"You know that one in Louisiana, the one Mom has been tracking?" she said. "I lined up her search protocols, what she already had, and overlaid the new one. *Bang*. It spit him out just like that."

Bill leaned into the screen, studying it for a moment.

"Holy mackerel, Molly. You got him nailed."

"Yeah, I think so. With what we have here, we could move on this one anytime."

"That's great. You know, I feel like I'm getting a bit rusty. I think I'm going to go on this one. You want to come with your old man?" As dangerous as it was, he'd always loved going on a hunt with one of his daughters. He felt it was their family tradition.

She smiled. "Wouldn't miss it."

"With this new program, we're going to be able to flush out way more of these bastards than before," Bill said. "Cripes, I'm going to have to start recruiting again."

"Whoa... slow down, Dad. This only happened so easily because I piggybacked onto what Mom had already done. For this to work on its own, it's going to take a lot of effort. There'll be plenty of bugs to work out."

"How long?"

"I don't know yet... but soon."

Bill smiled. "Molly, now I know why you're my favorite. But don't tell the others, they'd be upset."

She shook her head. "Dad, you think maybe it's time to drop that tired old joke? You've been telling all three of us the same thing since we were little kids."

He laughed. "Well, it is old, but definitely not tired. And it's one hundred percent true. The three of you are my favorite."

She hugged him. "I'm going to keep going on this. Mom is going to want to see it first thing. Why don't you get to bed?"

He thought that was an understatement. In the old days, Helen would have been royally pissed if they hadn't woken her with this kind of news. She'd want in on it from the very start. But she was sick now, and things were different.

"Naw, I'm wide-awake now, might as well start right in," Bill said. "Why don't you send me what you got? I'm going to start working on a mission plan. We can add that to the stuff for your mom to look at in the morning."

CHAPTER 8

I got back from the Vineyard and settled into the Boston Harbor Hotel. On the way, I'd gotten a referral to a divorce lawyer and actually spoke to him for a half hour—or two hundred dollars. In my opinion, when dealing with attorneys, it's best to set your timepiece to dollars and cents rather than hours and minutes. Anyway, I laid things out, and he seemed competent and confident, so we set an appointment for the next week.

I texted Lisa and asked if I could come over and collect my things. Texting is such a sterile form of communication, but it was perfect for dealing with her in this situation. I added an apology for losing my temper when we last spoke, along with an assurance that I wasn't going to make a big stink. Shockingly, I think I actually meant it.

I pulled up to my house, which I now had to consider my *former* abode. The concept struck me as odd. Lisa told me she would be gone while I was getting my stuff. I was relieved, as I really wasn't in the mood for another confrontation with her. I let myself in and went up to the master bedroom. The bed was made, and the room was in its usual tidy state. There were no rumpled sheets or used condoms or spare toupees lying about, giving evidence that Leland had been there. I let out a sigh of relief and went about my business.

I stuffed three suitcases full of my clothes in preparation for the acute phase of my impending bachelorhood. I loaded a duffel with my personal effects, which were remarkably few, considering our fifteen years together. Finally, I crammed my briefcase full of my paperwork.

After I downloaded the contents of my desktop into my laptop, I wiped its hard drive, essentially turning it into an oversized paperweight. I know I'm a bit paranoid, but I believe that paranoia in moderation can be very good for your health, especially when it comes to vampires. I threw the suitcases into my car and headed to the garage.

There was a small steel ring, mostly obscured by poor lighting and shadows, sunken into the concrete floor under my workbench. It was at an odd angle, but I managed to hook it with two fingers. Using all my strength, I lifted the ring and the attached rectangular slab of cement. It was a small crypt door that only the most observant human eye would detect. No human could possibly lift it without the aid of a winch.

No, this wasn't a hidden crypt which held my coffin and a bunch of other Goth-type horseshit. Vampires don't sleep in coffins, unless it's a gag or some kind of sexual fetish. Dracula actually did sleep in a coffin, though. I wondered if he found it more comfortable, but when I asked him if that was the case, he said, "No, it's uncomfortable as hell. I do it for the effect." I still have no idea what he meant.

This was a small vault that I'd constructed when Lisa was away on a conference. It was only large enough for one oversized valise, which I fished out. Inside was an emergency stash of bonds, cash, hard currency, and multiple IDs and passports. It also contained an AK-47, a Remington 870 Express Pump shotgun, and a Glock 26. Even with our physical enhancements, in this modern era, I, along with most other vampires, believed we needed extra protection. Especially when considering how technologically advanced hunters had become. There were still quite a few traditionalists, however, that would not use modern weapons of any kind. They considered me, along with the rest of their gun-toting brethren to be . . . well, pussies.

I had multiple stashes of this kind all over the world, and bank accounts in many different countries, Switzerland and the Caymans being my favorites. Even though I had ready access to funds from these banks, I'd always been a firm believer in the "emergency suitcase" in case of the unexpected need to cut and run.

I replaced the concrete slab and headed back into the house. I took a final walk-through, making sure I didn't miss anything important. Then I took a leak in the downstairs bathroom and left the seat up for good measure; that would show her. The car was loaded, and in little over an hour I was backing out of the driveway, setting a new land-speed record for moving out of your house in an "Oh, by the way, honey, I'm a vampire," pre-divorce frenzy.

I headed back to my hotel suite and took in the beautiful view of the harbor while working on my laptop and half paying attention to the Red Sox getting walloped on the oversized flat-screen TV that hung on the wall.

After a while, I called one of my partners in the ER, Liam Giordano, the schedule guy. He was a half-Scottish, half-Italian total nutcase who had frenetic but focused energy, in an ADD kind of way.

He picked up after the first ring, which was a little slow for him. "Hey, Jules, what's up?"

"Nothing good. I'm having a pretty major problem at home. I'm wondering if you can get my shifts covered for the next week or ten days." I could hear papers shuffling, as I'm sure he was looking at the schedule as we spoke.

He mumbled, more to himself than me, "Only one night and no weekends in the next ten days . . . It shouldn't be a problem."

I remained silent.

"You want to tell me what's going on?" he asked. "You don't have to if you don't feel like it."

Actually, I *did* feel like it. "Lisa dumped me for someone else. She's divorcing me."

There was a slight pause. "You're shitting me."

"I wish I were, but no."

"Have you guys been having problems? How long has this been going on?"

I shook my head. "No, that's the thing. She totally blindsided me two nights ago. I figure her mind's pretty much made up, since she told me she's going to marry the guy she's running around with after we're divorced."

Liam let out that cross between a whistle and a *whew*. "Whoa, mama. You want me to kill her for you?"

"No, I'm going to reserve that pleasure for myself," I answered, not entirely sure if I was joking or not.

"Well, you'll definitely be high up on the suspect list, so if you need an alibi, I'm your man."

I wouldn't just be high up. I'd be Number One. But Leland would be pretty damn high on that list, too, since he was such an asshole with plenty of shady deals in his past—and bucketfuls of enemies. Funny thing was I knew Liam's alibi offer was legit.

I said, "Now that's something I might take you up on."

"But seriously, Jules, what can I do?"

That's what a real friend says. He puts it out there directly, because a real friend feels for you and wants to help. No "if there's anything I can do" shit here.

"Nothing I can think of right now, except getting me off the schedule."

"Consider it done. You know what? I always hated the cunt."

Typical Liam. "Now suppose tomorrow I tell you we're getting back together? How are you going to explain your 'cunt' comment?"

Without missing a beat, he replied, "I'd say since you were so distraught at obviously losing the love of your life, I wanted to vilify her so you wouldn't feel so bad that she dumped you—as any true friend would do."

Typical Liam . . . again. I laughed. "You seem to have your bases covered."

"I always do."

"I'll stay in touch. It'll be a busy week, meetings with Lisa, lawyers, and apartment hunting. Fun, fun."

"I say this with all sincerity. Right now, it sucks to be you."

He was right. "Very funny, but I have to agree. Thanks again for taking me off the schedule, and if you don't mind, keep this hush-hush. It's not exactly public knowledge yet."

"You got it. But the rumor mill grinds fast in the ER. One more thing, I'll kill them both if you want and give you my group rate."

I laughed. "I'll keep it in mind. Good night, Liam."

My next call was to Lisa. Ugh. She wasn't anywhere near as quick on the draw as Liam, but she eventually picked up, right when I was thinking I'd be lucky enough to leave a message.

"Hello, Julian," she said coldly.

She never called me that. "How are you, Lisa?"

"I'm great, you?" she replied with a happy voice.

Bitch, I thought. "I'm good. I was wondering if I could come over sometime, and we could hammer out some broad strokes. I wouldn't hold you to it, of course, but if we could come to a general understanding, it might save us a lot of money before the lawyers start picking over our bones. You know, stuff like—"

She cut me off. "Fine. I'm kind of in the middle of something right now. How about tomorrow at seven?"

More likely, she was in the middle of some*one*. "Fine by me," I said in my best curt tone. "Good night."

But didn't she just go and out-curt me by hanging up without a response? Damn it! She'd been frosty toward me, and was probably fucking that old buzzard Leland while on the phone with me, having a great laugh at my expense. This was what came of having human emotions. I really needed to have the damn things surgically removed.

It was now about eleven o'clock and I was wide awake, so I decided to take a walk around Rowes Wharf, where the hotel was situated. The area had been revamped in the late eighties and had restaurants, a marina, and water taxis, but this late on a weeknight in Boston, it was essentially deserted.

I was on a slow stroll and had stopped for a smoke when a slender young man approached me. He looked like he was about fourteen, pale, pimply, and a junkie, no doubt. He brandished what appeared to be a rubber knife without much enthusiasm and didn't seem like the greatest of threats.

"Give me your wallet," he said in a high, squeaky tone.

His voice didn't do much to dissuade me from my opinion. "Fuck off, sonny," I replied, as I was in no mood for his antics. I turned to look at the ocean and continue my smoke.

And didn't the little prick jam his weenie knife right into my back!

It's not that I cared about the wound. I was already healing when he pulled the blade out. But I was wearing a cool black leather jacket, and this asshole had probably wrecked it. *I'm having one hell of a week here*, I thought.

I spun around and said, "You little fuck. I should take that knife and stick it up your ass."

His eyes flew open. I'm sure he couldn't understand why I was still standing, and I figured he would cut and run. After all, I'd already astutely judged him as not much of a threat. Suddenly, he plunged his knife into my chest, definitely wrecking the jacket.

Well, so much for my appraisal of him, I thought. The jacket was bad enough, but this poor judgment showed how much of my vampire instinct I'd lost. I would have never made this kind of mistake back in the days before I was pretending to be human.

"You've got to be shitting me," I said as I plucked the knife from his hand and tossed it into the ocean. I grabbed him by the wrist, feeling a bone or two break. His scream brought a smile to my face.

He was whimpering. I pulled him close until we were nose to nose. In the old days, this kid would have been dead meat, but I was still under the influence of my human pretense. Right at the get-go, I knew I wasn't going to kill him. How could I ever have thought that I was a danger to Lisa, when I couldn't even muster the balls to kill this pimply junkie? What a wimp I'd become. Well, if I wasn't going to kill him, at least I could have some fun.

I said, "You think you're some kind of scary badass? There are a lot worse things than you that go bump in the night, and I'm one of them. Now I ought to make you pay for my jacket, but looking at you, I doubt you even have a pot to piss in. How about killing you? Nah, that'd be way too easy. Oh, I know, how about something worse, you little fuckwad?"

I pulled him closer still, bit him in the neck, and started drinking. Heroin was his poison; I could taste it in his blood. It was a superficial bite, but I didn't use telepathy, and I held back the sedative. With nothing to dull the pain, a neck bite would hurt like a bitch. He was terrorized, letting out a loud, wailing scream over and over again, even more high-pitched than his speaking voice. He struggled to get away, but no soap there, as he couldn't even come close to moving in my grip. After about a half unit, I released him. He stumbled back and fell to the ground.

My would-be mugger had his hand to his neck wound, but I was gentle with the bite so he wouldn't bleed out. He was shocked pale; his eyes couldn't get much wider. He scuttled on the ground backward to move away. I stood there smiling down at him.

"You freak!" he shouted. "You fucking freak. You bit me!"

I took one step forward, and he leapt to his feet and ran down the pier.

He yelled over his shoulder, "I'm going to the cops. I'm going to report you, asshole!"

"Good luck with that story. And, kid, get yourself a job," I called out after him. "You're a shitty mugger!" I guess this was my version of *Scared Straight!*. I doubted it would work, but what the hell.

CHAPTER 9

For my meeting with Lisa, I was determined to maintain as much of my civility and dignity as possible. I'd even stopped to pick up a bottle of wine. On my arrival, I began to let myself in. But then I realized that just walking through the front door, even though it was technically still my house, was probably not legit divorce protocol. I rang the bell instead.

Lisa was in a mid-length dark skirt, heels, and a white blouse. It was her usual work motif, and she looked great. It was funny that only in the last few days, after she'd told me I was yesterday's news, that I thought about how good she looked. I couldn't say when I'd last thought about it, and I definitely couldn't recall the last time I'd complimented her on her looks. How fucking sad.

I held up the wine bottle. "You mind if I open this? It's one of your favorites. I mean, it's not a celebration, it's just . . . I really don't know why I brought it, but I wouldn't mind a drink."

She hesitated for a moment and said, "Sure, go ahead."

I got out two glasses and opened the wine. "So I thought if we met and worked out some issues before the lawyers got too involved, we might save ourselves some time and money. Hopefully, we can do that?"

"Hopefully. What do you have in mind?"

My lips spoke by themselves, my brain lagging far behind. "How about one last pity fuck?" Sadly, I think I meant it.

She took it well, though. "*Now* you're interested? Seriously, Jules, what do you want to talk about?"

I took my foot out of my mouth and sat across from her at the kitchen island. The kitchen always seemed to be the center of our more serious discussions through the years. Sipping on my wine, I shifted into business mode. "Well, I think our assets are easy to tease through. We only have two joint investment accounts, but other than that, our finances are separate. Possessions seem pretty simple to me. You have your family stuff. I have my antiques. We have the house here, and the one at the Vineyard. Now when it comes to alimony—"

She interrupted. "I don't want your money, Jules."

I was shocked. "You don't want alimony?"

She shook her head.

"Your lawyer isn't going to like that," I said. "You'd be due some."

"I know you make more than I do, but I'm doing okay. I think it would be cleaner this way. I told you that once I marry Donald—"

It was my turn to interrupt. "Let's not go in that direction right now." I wasn't ready to include my personal version of "The Donald" into this talk.

She nodded. "It's just that once I remarry, the alimony obligation ends, anyway. Why complicate things?"

She was right. Even in the communist state of Massachusetts, that was the way it usually went. "Okay, it makes sense, I guess. But I still think your lawyer will object, so I won't hold you to it. It's probably the wine talking, anyway."

She hadn't tasted her wine yet, but she smiled.

Now that we were getting divorced, I was really good at making Lisa smile. *Just great.*

She said, "So if alimony is off the table, now what?"

"I think it can be pretty simple. We keep our individual accounts and cars. Instead of selling off the houses, I'd like to keep the Vineyard house, and you can have this one."

"That's pretty generous. This one's worth a lot more, and your lawyer might not like that."

"That's okay, I love the Vineyard, and this is more your town than mine. You're invested in it with your business, and I'll likely move on."

"You'll leave the area?" she asked. "Your job?"

"Yeah, I think so. With us breaking up, there's not much to keep me here. You were born and bred here, but I've always felt it was a bit cold and stiff for my taste."

We paused for a moment, and Lisa looked off through the kitchen window. She seemed sad, and it made me uncomfortable.

"We've got two investment accounts together," I continued. "They're doing okay, and they're within a few thousand of each other. We'll each sign off on one of them."

She nodded, still looking melancholy. "Maybe we can keep the furnishings in each house to make it simple. I'd like my family stuff, and you want your antiques and artifacts. They're like family heirlooms to you, aren't they?"

All my family was dust centuries ago. "Yes, they are."

"We can make up a list of things that we each would want from both places. It shouldn't take very long, but I don't feel up to it now. You?"

I shook my head. "No. It's kind of sad, isn't it? All of

these years together, and we can divide everything up so neatly in about two minutes. It doesn't say much for us being a cohesive unit, does it? Maybe we weren't meant to be together."

"Well, I didn't mind taking the time to figure it out," she said.

"Me neither. The last fifteen years were pretty good, for the most part, right?"

She agreed. "They were."

I was starting to get emotional, so I wanted to finish up before I blubbered or did something embarrassing. I cleared my throat and said, "So why don't we let our lawyers know what we came up with? They can start writing something up, and hopefully we can work through this as cleanly as possible."

"I'll drink to that—" she said, but she pulled up short on the comment before it had fully left her mouth.

"Sounds good to me." I raised my glass and drained it. Lisa raised her glass, but didn't drink. It was one of her favorite wines. Was she having second thoughts about the deal and didn't want to drink to it? *Well, that would be silly. All she has to do is say something.*

I took a good look at her and saw it—the shame written all over her face. It struck me hard, like a brick dropping on my head from a skyscraper. At that moment, I knew with absolute certainty why she was doing this. *What an idiot I am. Second thoughts about the deal, my ass. This just keeps getting better and better.*

"Pregnant!" I blurted out. "You're fucking pregnant!"

It sounded alien, talking about my wife like that when I wasn't the one who impregnated her. I felt totally removed, like an outside observer watching a movie from a third-person point of view—maybe even fourth or fifth.

How the hell had I ended up here? *Happily married,* I thought. *Good job, nice house—but no, not for you, Jules. For you, it reads more like "divorced and thrown over for a slimy old fuck."* Miserable, and who cares about the fucking job? The house, I just gave that up. Oh, and by the way, my not-quite ex-wife is already knocked up by that same-said slimy old fuck! Whoever was writing the script of my life had a shitty sense of humor. The part about me being a vampire and lying to her all these years didn't enter the equation right then, but what the hell. She was pregnant with another man's baby!

Her shame did a quick disappearing act, and it was replaced by a self-satisfied, smug look. I wanted to slap it off her face, or worse. I took a step forward. That pimply junkie may have lucked out. He meant nothing to me. But this . . . this was personal. Right then, I realized, wife or not, I was a threat to Lisa. I managed to keep my rage under control, barely, but I had to know why. I said in a low, surprisingly calm voice, "We've talked about kids a lot. You said you never wanted any. You said you never minded that I couldn't be a father. How could you do this? Why?"

Lisa didn't do the guilt thing well. Historically, even if she were 100 percent wrong, she'd never apologize, and if she did, it always came out sounding about as sincere as a three-dollar bill.

Her eyes blazed with defiance. She answered vehemently, "I'll tell you why—because I wanted to! It felt good to be with a real man. It felt vital, alive, and dangerous, instead of safe and dead, the way it was with you. And why shouldn't I have a kid? Because I ended up with somebody who's impotent and doesn't pay attention to me anymore? So what? Time was running out for me. It was over between us, and I changed my mind. I wanted a child, and I wanted Donald's. It's as simple as that."

I was still livid, but also totally depleted, like every speck of adrenaline in my body had gone on a coffee break. And for the record, I'm *sterile*, not impotent. That's a big difference in my book—although with Viagra and the like, maybe not so much anymore.

I'll never understand human nature. I don't recall it so well any longer. I didn't even know what to say. "You hate me, you really hate me. I never hated you, maybe even not now. Why?"

"You did worse than hate me," she answered, her voice rising. "You *ignored* me! At least I've made the effort to feel *something* for you, even if it is hate. What did you do besides blow me off, night after night?"

After flinching from her outburst, I looked at her squarely. "No matter what I did, you had no right to do this to me. You owed me that, at least."

"Fuck you, Jules," she shot back. "I owe you nothing. I owe myself as quick a divorce as possible so I can be with a man who loves me and pays attention to me. You probably want to renege on our deal now, but it's still good by me. It makes sense, and I want this to go as fast as possible. Even if you wanted this house, instead of that dump at the Vineyard, I'd give it to you, just to move things along. Now please leave, and try to stay out of my life."

Try to stay out of her life? After what she had said, I wanted to *end* her life. I don't know if I honestly could have hurt her then, but it was a definite maybe. Her being pregnant was the X factor, though. She might have escaped being harmed tonight—but that didn't mean everyone would.

"I'll leave the wine," I said. "You may as well drink up. Considering the father, the kid's going to be a retard, anyway."

I'd barely closed the door behind me when the wine bottle smashed against it. And I thought I was the one with the temper.

CHAPTER 10

I drove to the center of town and parked once again at the commuter rail to stew. It was fast becoming my favorite parking lot. But I didn't do much stewing, and I don't think a single thought crossed my mind. My brain and body felt pretty much disconnected. I got out of my car and started walking. My mind may not have been totally in on the master plan, but my legs sure knew what they were doing.

About fifteen minutes later, I was on my soon-to-be old street, approaching my not-my-house-anymore house. I pulled up half a block down and across the street and dropped back into a small wooded section between two lots.

I leaned against a tree, still as death and barely breathing. My unblinking eyes were laser-locked onto our house. I was on autopilot, disconnected and ice-cold. It was the 180-degree polar opposite of the nearly psychotic killing frenzy I'd almost let myself fall into at the Vineyard. This was the way I used to feel when I was a real vampire with some nastiness to attend to—coolly detached. It felt so comfortable, so familiar, just like coming home. At that moment, I can honestly say I wasn't sure what I was going to do, but I was sure it was nothing good.

Of course, Leland's car was already in the driveway. But him being there didn't piss me off. I'd expected it, and it nudged me even deeper into that cold, disconnected place; so all the better.

The sidewalks rolled up early on weeknights in Needham, but a few dog-walkers and their charges went by. They didn't see me, as I was only a shadow in the night. One of the four-legged strollers may have gotten a whiff and stopped for a moment, head cocked and looking in my direction. The mutt quickly broke into a trot, dragging its owner along. *Good choice, Fido.*

I waited an hour, maybe two, but I'm not sure. When I got this way, I could be treacherously patient—and patience is generally not one of my virtues. Then The Donald emerged from the front door with Lisa seeing him out. They kissed long and hard. It almost made me gag.

She was decked out in some kind of black lingerie thing. *Slut.* There were no lights on, but with my vampire vision, unfortunately, I could see their antics just fine. He got into his car, and I started walking at a slow pace. *No need to hurry,* I thought. I knew exactly where he was going.

The China Star, one of the several Chinese restaurants in town, had a nice bar with big-screen TVs. It stayed open late, which was a rare bird in a quiet suburb. Way back when, Lisa told me that Leland held court there three or four nights a week. I planned to wait at his car, which was parked behind the restaurant. No, The Donald couldn't park in front or on the street like the common folk. He had to park in back, at some dumpy garage that had a shady reputation. The owner was a friend of his and provided the private space. Leland didn't know it yet, but it was a bad night for privacy.

Curiosity, or maybe audacity, got the better of me, and I decided to go in. I knew Lisa would have warned him about the cuckolded hubby with the big, bad temper. But I knew the cocky son of a bitch wouldn't listen. He was The Donald, after all. He'd been a boxer in his youth and was reputed to carry a gun. He should have listened to his new chickie, as none of that was going to help.

One might ask, "But, Jules, won't he recognize you? You must have met him, and after all, he is fucking your wife."

And a good question that would be, except for the fact that Leland is that self-important kind of guy we've all met at any number of suburban house parties. Even though he should remember you because there's some minor connection, like working with and fucking your wife, he doesn't. He can't be bothered to make the effort. When you shake his hand, he'll mumble some platitude, but his eyes won't even register you as being alive, let alone at the party. Then he'll quickly be off to the next more important person. If you bump into him later in the night, it'll be like meeting a total stranger. Yep, we all know that guy.

Even so, going in was still a risk. He might have had a fraction of a memory of me, and that could have be enough to get his scent up. But you know what? If I were going to act like a vampire for the first time in decades and do something foul like make this bastard vanish from the face of the earth, I was definitely going to have some fun with it. Shit, maybe I'd even buy him a drink. It wasn't the best plan I'd ever had, but what the hell.

I sat at a table in a dark corner and ordered a beer. Beer is a good thirst quencher, but no buzz for us vampires. I wasn't looking for a buzz, just something to pass the time. Leland was at one corner of the bar, with what appeared to be a group of male cronies and a lone woman. I think her name was Pierce, and I believe she had the reputation of being the town slut. She and Leland were far too cozy, especially since The Donster was an engaged man with a slightly preggers fiancée. There was quite a bit of whispering between old Donny-boy and Pierce, and a lot of overly loud laughter from the cronies.

I melted into my seat, doing my best to remain unnoticed. Several drinks later, Leland made a big show of picking up the tab, the asshole. He gave his lady friend way too long of a kiss goodnight, and she gave his shanky ass a squeeze in return. Then he started the ritualistic farewell of glad-handing and hugging his cronies. He had no idea how much of a farewell it was. I quietly left.

It was fairly dark out back, with only one overhead light casting a meek yellow glow. It didn't illuminate much and only succeeded in creating shadows. But I wouldn't need much light for what I had in mind.

I waited in the darkness, near the front bumper of Donald's ostentatious old-school Cadillac. It wasn't long before I heard him coming. For a moment, I thought he was talking to someone, probably Slutty Slutterton from the bar. *Damn it!* I'd have to do a quick fade and come up with a Plan B. But as it turned out, Leland was alone and he was humming to himself. Man, was he tone deaf. He auto-popped his car doors.

"Hello, Donald," I said.

My greeting startled him, and he dropped his keys. The overhead light shone directly in his eyes. He squinted into my dark silhouette and said, "Who's that?"

"I think you should know who I am. I certainly know who *you* are." My voice was utterly emotionless, mellifluous, and pleasing. I was way down in my cold, icy place, completely at ease, and even happy, thinking of what I was about to do to him. I stepped out into the light so he could get a good look at me.

He took his good look, and just as I presumed, had no

fucking idea who I was.

"Sorry, buddy, but I don't know you," Leland said. "Whatever this is about, it's late, and it's going to have to wait."

Did I see a little fear in The Donald's eyes? I went on calmly, "Well, you should know who I am, you slimy old cocksucker. After all, you *are* fucking my wife, and you even managed to knock her up."

Ah, there it was. The light of recognition flicked on, instantly killing his China Star buzz. I'll give him credit; his fear vanished quickly, as nobody talked to The Donald this way. Now I thought he'd go into blowhard bravado mode, and I wasn't disappointed.

"Look here . . . Julian, isn't it? I don't want any trouble. But I assure you, I can defend myself. I have a lot of friends in the police department, so—"

I cut him off with my oh-so-pleasing voice. "You should have thought of that *before* you started screwing my wife."

"I told you, I don't want any trouble."

"Donald, old pal, you have no idea what kind of trouble you're in."

I took a slow step forward, and he started reaching under his jacket, no doubt for the gun that he carried. Our eyes met, and his face went slack. His hand swam around a bit, then seemed to forget what it wanted to do, and fell to his side. He was a telepathic susceptible, which was good. I needed to keep this little murder as quiet as possible. By the time I reached him, I was grabbing him by the shoulders more to support him than to assault him. With my left hand, I took him by the hair and bent his head to the right. The toupee/implant thing, or whatever the fuck it was, felt greasy and shifted significantly in the process. *Gross.*

I leaned in close and bit him deeply in the neck. His

blood sprayed into my mouth, and tasted fantastic and energizing. Hating this old fuck didn't take away from that, but then again, nothing ever did. I was going to drain him to hypovolemic shock and death.

The human body has about ten units, or pints of blood. In about five minutes, I would drain about 70 percent of old Donny's supply, and that would do the trick. If people have time to adjust to gradual blood loss, say from a slow bleed or bone marrow failure, they won't die. They'll feel crappy, no doubt, but I've seen patients in the ER come in with two-thirds of their blood gone and still functional. They're tired and pale, but they aren't in imminent danger because their bodies had time to compensate and use other fluids to keep their blood pressure adequate.

Not the case with Donny here. The rate of blood loss that I was inflicting upon him was massive and too rapid—kind of like a traumatic injury to the aorta from a car wreck, or a bullet wound through the heart. And when I was through with him, I was going to relish ripping his ugly fucking head off, toupee and all.

Tick-tock goes the clock, and time was certainly running out on The Donald. It wouldn't be long before I stopped this bastard's clock for good. But even assholes like Leland catch a break sometimes, and he got his from the most unusual of sources: me.

This humanness was becoming quite the pain in the ass. It just didn't want to let go of me. I thought about the fact that people have affairs and fuck who they shouldn't all the time. But most of them don't get their blood drained on account of it. As much as I tried to ignore it, that damned concept wouldn't quit.

As I drank, I mused further that to be fair, I was playing human. He and Lisa didn't know there might be a different set of deadly rules for me, being a vampire and all. But did I have to be fair? Leland was a total asshole who had screwed me over royally and needed to die. But I still couldn't kill him. What the hell was wrong with me?

I stopped drinking. Leland was unconscious, and I lowered him to the ground. I took out a black hankie, one of many that I own for such occasions, and put pressure on the wound in his neck. I bit my finger and dripped some of my blood on his wound, healing it. The infectious agent that causes vampirism is readily killed by an intact human immune system. But when applied externally, it will stay functional long enough to accelerate human tissue healing.

My bite mark had vanished in a few minutes. A vampire bite mark, by the way, is basically circular in nature, like any humans' would be, albeit with accentuated punctures caused by our slightly overdeveloped canines. To deliver the famous movie Dracula two-puncture wound, vampires would have to have ridiculous overbites, and deliver the coup-de-grace via some sort of weird, bobble-head, stapling motion.

I was fairly sure Leland wouldn't clearly recall the attack, since he'd nearly passed out from my telepathy, and I'd given him a healthy dose of my sedative to boot. If he did, with no injury to back his story up, who'd believe him? I located his keys, put them in his pocket, and hefted him into the driver's seat of his car. With any luck, he'd think he nodded off after a few too many.

His breathing and pulse were steadying, and I could tell he'd come around soon. Everything looked in perfect order except for his toupee thing, which was still askew. I couldn't bring myself to adjust it, however, fearing if I touched the greasy motherfucker again, I'd vomit. I quietly shut the car door and started walking.

Right when I thought I'd straightened myself out and would kill somebody that I actually meant to kill, I chicken-shitted. There was only one place to go for the hefty dose of guidance that I needed. This night wasn't going even close to the way I'd planned it.

CHAPTER 11

Harrison and his strike team sidled down a dark alley in Shreveport, Louisiana. They'd scoped out their prey and were more than ready to move in for the kill. He'd taken four from his group with him. For a single vampire, and a young one at that, it would be more than enough. He left the rest as backup at observation posts. Bill was turning to give some final instructions, when one of the squad was lifted off into the darkness, as if he were flying. The man barely had time to start screaming before he was cut off.

The ominous silence was broken by Bill's single-word command. "Drop."

The remaining four dropped into kneeling positions in a rough circle, guns at the ready.

Molly whispered, "I didn't even see him move, Dad. You?"

Bill's eyes kept scanning the darkness for some clue as to where their assailant might come from next. "Nope. Must be a heck of a lot older than we thought. I'd guess five hundred, if he's a day."

They waited nervously for some sign, some target, anything at all to shoot at. Bill felt a whoosh of air, and another one of his team was whisked away.

"Steve!" Molly screamed and took off to follow what she

thought to be the vampire's direction of movement.

Bill yelled after her, "Molly! No!"

She didn't listen.

Once she turned a corner, Bill made his decision. "Martinez. On me."

They took off following Molly, covering each other as best they could. They rounded the corner to see Molly hacking away with her Samurai sword, a weapon she favored for close combat. Bill saw blood fly as her sword hit home. He had no shot, however, as Molly was directly in his line of sight—right between him and the vampire.

"Molly, down!" he shouted.

But it was too late. The vampire struck her with a hard backhand, and she flew across the alley, landing in a heap on the cold pavement. He and Martinez opened up, their fire creating a deafening roar, but they hit nothing but air. The vampire moved lightning-fast and disappeared into the darkness like a wisp of smoke.

"Drop," Bill said again.

The two of them took to a kneeling position, once again back-to-back and waiting.

Bill couldn't believe that Molly had broken protocol. She had never done that sort of thing before. He watched her lying still on the ground, knowing very well she might be dying—or already dead. Every fiber of his being wanted to go to her. But he knew if he broke formation again, they were as good as dead. With huge effort, he pushed all of the feeling he had for his daughter to the back of his mind. He was a hard man.

Al Martinez said, "Hell of a pickle, huh, Bill?"

Even though Martinez was born again and a follower of Jarvis, Bill had always liked him. He kept his religion and his work separate, and was cool under fire. Martinez had never made a slip-up on a hunt, and when Bill went into the field, he usually took Martinez with him. He was rock-steady and could always be counted on.

"Yep," Bill answered. "Looks like this one's old school and wants to kill us with his teeth. At least there's that."

"Good thing, too. If it were even using a popgun, we'd all be dead by now."

Bill sensed, more than felt, that whoosh in the air. He pivoted instantly, and his Mossberg shotgun roared to life. "Damn! I almost got the fucker!"

Over the years, Bill had developed a technique for firearm use that he'd called "reflex shooting." It wasn't just shooting at targets, but shooting without hesitation at any kind of movement, or even changes in movement. It was a skill that had saved many lives through the years, and Bill, despite being nearly sixty-one, was still by far the best in its application.

The deadly silence descended upon them once again. Martinez whispered, "Bill, do you think—"

"Quiet, Al," Bill answered softly. Despite the dire circumstances, Bloody Bill let his mind wander. With his eyes half-lidded, he filtered out his conventional senses as much as he could. If someone had told him he appeared to be meditating, he would have scoffed at the concept, but that was exactly what he was doing. He was reaching out with senses that he wasn't sure he possessed, senses that might very well have been figments of his imagination. Or perhaps they were a ramped-up conglomeration of his conventional senses, accentuated by the state he'd pushed himself into. It didn't matter. Whatever they were, he reached out with them just the same, trying to feel the vampire, to feel where it would attack from next.

Bill sensed that movement in the air again, and much

earlier than before. In that split second, he knew—he absolutely knew. In a blur, Bill spun to the inside and upward. As he fell onto his back, he fired from the hip, almost straight up into the air. The shotgun blast went off next to Martinez's head. He recoiled, but held his position. As if falling magically from the sky, the dead body of the vampire dropped right in front of him.

This time, Martinez jumped to his feet and put a burst of machine gun fire into the vampire's chest. When he saw that the body no longer had a head, he looked mollified that he'd been shooting a corpse. "Shit. Sorry, Bill. You took his head clean off. I didn't notice at first."

"Would've done the same thing. Better to be safe."

Martinez turned to add something, but Bill was already crouching over Molly. "She's alive, Al. Go check on Steve and call in the backup."

Molly had taken a solid blow to the head, but she was coming around and appeared to be okay. A huge bruise was already forming on her forehead that would need to get checked out. But at least she was alive. Due to her quick action, Steve Conti was still alive as well. He'd suffered a deep bite wound to his neck, but Al managed to staunch most of the bleeding, even before their pickup car rolled up.

The fifth member of the team wasn't so lucky. Bill found him back in the alley, his neck shredded. Looking at the wound, Bill thought that the vampire most likely did it with his hands and not his teeth, but even so, he couldn't take the chance of letting him turn. He took a large bowie knife from his coat and decapitated the corpse. Considering the damage the vampire had done to the man's neck, it didn't take much effort.

Bill poked his head in the door of the car. Molly was still dazed, but already looked better.

"You're going to have one hell of a shiner, little girl," he said. "How you feeling?"

It seemed to take her a moment to focus on Bill's face. "I'll be okay. Just a little headache, that's all."

Bill looked past her to where Conti sat. One hand was holding a bloody handkerchief to his neck, the other was holding Molly's hand. Bill said to Molly, "I didn't know you and Steve were an item. If I did, I never would've taken you both on the same mission."

"I didn't know, either. Until that vampire grabbed him."

"Oh, I see. Well then, I suppose there was nothing to be done about it. You rest. I'll see you in a bit." Bill then made his way to the driver. "Get Molly checked out with a CAT scan. Standard story. We can't take Steve in with that bite. Too suspicious. Patch him up as best you can and make sure you start the antibiotics soon. Take the vampire's body and get rid of it, but send another car for Joel's. He's at the very back of the alley. I don't want him riding in the same trunk with that fucking monster."

Bill, Martinez, and the rest of the team searched the vampire's apartment but didn't find anything that might lead to other vamps or human helpers. Bill was incensed. "Goddamn it, I thought we'd find something! This one must be a fucking hermit. All right, Al, listen. You and the rest stake this place out and tap the phone. But only twenty-four hours, max. Anybody who shows up or calls, kill them."

Al asked, "Anyone? What if it's, like, a telemarketer or something like that?"

"*Especially* if it's a telemarketer. You'd be doing the world a favor. Joel was a good man. We lost a bunch more in New York. I really want to run up the tally for good guys on this one."

Martinez nodded. "I get it, high body count. I'm on it.

You sure you don't want one or two alive?"

Bloody Bill responded with a smile, and it wasn't a pretty one. There was murder in it. "That's what I like about you, Al. You're always thinking. Sure, one or two might be just the ticket. Maybe after a nice little conversation with me, they'd see the error of their ways. Maybe they'd even tell us all about their vampire pals, huh? You take over here. I'm going to go check on Molly."

Bill hadn't had any recent "guests" in his torture chamber on the farm. He was already starting to look forward to it.

CHAPTER 12

I made the drive into Boston in no time, parked my car, and walked to the top of Hull Street in the North End. The Old North Church was down the other side of the hill directly in front of me, and Copp's Hill Burying Ground loomed eerily on my left as I approached my aunts' home.

Domenic Salvucci, their chief bodyguard, stepped out of a shadowy doorway, holstering a handgun slightly smaller than a tree trunk. It had an oversized clip that I knew was loaded with hollow-tip dum dums filled with garlic extract. There would be almost zero chance of other vampires attacking my aunts, but like a good boy scout, Dom liked to be prepared. The thought of those garlic bullets gave me a shudder.

All vampires are allergic to garlic in varying degrees. The reactions go from mild with itchy rashes and swollen eyes, to severe and deadly. I'm lucky to be on the milder side. We don't suffer a reaction from skin contact or smell; the allergy can only be triggered by ingestion or direct introduction into the bloodstream.

As a matter of fact, I love the smell of garlic and am totally bummed I can't eat it anymore. Back in ancient Rome, garlic was a big-ticket item in many of our foods. It was also used as a medicinal, and I was a total glutton for the stuff. I mean, why does it have to be garlic? It couldn't have been nutmeg or cloves or some other horrible spice that I hate. Pretty much all of my paisan vampires lament the loss of garlic right along with me.

Historically, garlic was a great vampire deterrent. The smell couldn't be missed, and it was common knowledge that the stuff could kill vampires, although way back when, we didn't understand how. So, quite sensibly, vampires stayed away from it.

As time passed, more and more anecdotes popped up about vampires ignoring garlic, or simply removing it from humans and drinking their blood anyway. Doubt was beginning to be cast on the garlic issue.

I had an interesting experience with garlic myself. In the 1300s, in a small village in Hungary, some idiot poured a whole bucket of garlic cloves on my head. Aside from stinking for two days, I was totally fine. But while I was trying to figure out what the hell had happened, my garlic-pouring assailant dropped down from a window, driving me face-first into the ground.

The village was deserted, as there was a wedding going on at its small church. I was passing through, not looking for trouble for a change, and then *bang*, a garlic shower and *pow*, a body slam from the second floor. My attacker was a big boy—the village blacksmith and a vampire hunter, as well. He was an intelligent one at that, since this was broad daylight, and he obviously didn't believe the commonly accepted lore that vampirism was a nighttime-only club. Because most humans at that time *did* believe it, my guard was down.

I quickly picked myself up, but he was already on his feet, delivering a blacksmith-worthy roundhouse rap to my noggin with some type of huge mallet. Now, this dude swung from the toes, and got every ounce of his 250 pounds behind it. I heard—and felt—my skull crack in an explosion of pain. Once again, I was kissing the ground, dazed and very confused.

Between the garlic and the mallet, I guess he thought he had me, because instead of immediately striking again and probably crushing my skull, I heard him rummaging for something. There was the sound of wood clanking about. My head started to clear, and the pain was improving, as we vampires do heal rapidly. In the minute he took to mess around with whatever he was doing, I was almost 100 percent healed and ready for action. Well, maybe more like 50 percent, maybe even 20 percent—but my 20 percent is still pretty good.

I let him turn me over and saw he was holding a huge wooden stake. When it comes to believing stupid vampire lore, human ignorance is vampire bliss—and his belief that a stake to the heart would kill a vampire made me feel pretty damn blissful. I had to respect the guy. No human had gotten the better of me like this for well over a thousand years, and that was when I was a "baby" vampire. *A garlic shower, a mallet to the head, and now a wooden stake? Enough already!*

As he tried to skewer me, I broke the stake in half with a karate chop and then pulled him off-balance, rolling him over me. He was once again quick to get up, but now I was ready, and his "quick" was far too slow. I was on him. I grabbed his head and gave it a sharp twist. The neck cracked like a dry branch. There was a look of surprise on his face as he stared at me, his head facing 180 degrees the wrong way. The surprised look faded rapidly to dead.

My temper was still up, however, and I wasn't done yet.

A few more twists, and I had his head as a bloody trophy. Being a traditional village smithy, he had a thick black beard, which I used to bowl his cranium up the center aisle of the church just as a wedding ceremony was concluding. That caused a bit of a stir. My temper is not a pretty thing, but at times, it can almost be artistic. In vampire circles, by the way, that story is considered a charming anecdote.

As science progressed, our researchers came to understand the physiology of the garlic allergic reaction. The info was disseminated, and garlic was debunked as being an effective vampire deterrent, but not quite. Human researchers, the ones who believed in vampires, also figured it out—and saw the potential for an effective weapon. When forcibly introduced into the bloodstream, say by a bullet, it causes an allergic reaction that is intense, extremely painful, and lethal for those with a severe allergy.

Bullet wounds hurt like hell, even though they heal rapidly. But with garlic bullet wounds, you have an absolute orgasm of pain, and the garlic significantly delays healing. So once again, garlic has re-emerged as an effective vampire deterrent in the form of garlic-soaked or garlic-infused hollow-point bullets.

Now, as Dom approached, he gave an all-clear hand signal to his two machine-gun-toting colleagues who had come up to the fence of the cemetery. They faded back into the shadows.

"Hello, Doc, how are you?" Dom said.

Dom was quite a specimen. He looked like a refrigerator with a large head stuck on top, and he tipped the scales at close to three hundred pounds of solid muscle, but he moved quietly, with a fluid grace. Because of his size, he might have been mistaken for the big, dumb sort, but that assessment couldn't be further from the truth. He was one of the most perceptive humans I've known and was ferociously loyal to my aunts. He'd been their chief bodyguard for the last fifteen years, and they loved him like a son.

"I'm good, Dom. You?"

"Can't complain. They're expecting you, of course."

"Of course." They always knew when I was coming, and it always irritated me a bit.

"C'mon, I'll take you in."

I stopped. I felt like talking. "Hey, Dom, can I ask you something?"

He turned back to me. "Sure, Doc. Shoot."

"Why do you keep doing this? You don't donate blood, right?"

"Nope," he answered. At first blush, you might think it odd that humans would voluntarily donate blood to vampires. But when compared with other fringe human behaviors, it wasn't so unbelievable. What about the masochistic freaks who allow themselves to be put in leather diapers and masks, then led around on a leash and whipped? How about people who tattoo and pierce every part of their bodies? What about fetishers who worship feet or let people piss on them? Voluntarily letting a vampire take some blood seems almost tame by comparison.

There are advantages to being a donor, too. Most vampires who can organize a donor network are often well off and lavish gifts and money on their donors. And being bitten, once you get used to it, can be intensely stimulating on a sexual level. Finally, just being on the inside, hanging with us, when most people don't think we exist, is a thrill in and of itself.

Some who donate are more pragmatic and are in it for the financial gain or the possibility of being turned. Others are there mainly for the thrill, and personally, I have nothing against them. I like a good thrill as much as the next person. A small minority are religious or uber-altruistic and donate blood for God, for a sense of self-importance, or for some other goofy reason. As they see it, by donating, they're protecting others from being attacked or killed.

Although this last category is generally full of crackpots, there may be some truth to their reasoning, as leaving a trail of dead bodies isn't very helpful in maintaining the anonymity that vampires need to survive. What they fail to grasp is that we're predators and killers by nature. And we'll kill anytime it suits us, unless, of course, you've become a pussy like me.

"And you're not looking to be turned, are you?" I asked Dom.

He looked surprised at the question. "Jeez, no. I'm Catholic."

For Dom, that was evidently enough to explain things. But for me, it opened up a multitude of questions. Given my less-than-flattering view of the church and Dom's position on the subject, I let it go. A discussion down that path more than likely wouldn't end well.

"I see. Then why?"

"It's simple, really. I love them. They took me in, and I figure I owe them."

"They wouldn't see it that way."

He shrugged his huge shoulders. "No, but I do."

Dom was an only child whose mother had died when he was a little kid. His Dad, a mid-level Mafioso, was whacked when Dom was only fifteen. My aunts took him in, finished raising him, and put him through school.

Dom continued: "Besides, I like them. They're superior people."

That pretty much summed it up for him. *They're superior*

people. That was especially nice to hear, since most humans wouldn't consider us people at all. "So are you, Dom. Let's go in."

We entered a tiny "little old lady" loft, which was dark, cramped, and filled with 1960s furniture that wasn't in the best repair. The living/dining area couldn't have been more than eighty square feet and was partitioned off by a ramshackle buffet with a large collection of mismatched plates.

A miniature kitchen was crammed into one corner. It had an oven, of the easy-bake variety, one cabinet, a tiny stovetop, and an even tinier sink. A wrought-iron spiral staircase in one corner of the living room led up to the loft, which had barely enough room for a double bed, a small dresser, and an old tube-style TV.

The best feature of the place was its angled roof that was mostly glass, due to two oversized picture windows. And like any card-carrying old ladies, my aunties had completely covered them with the ugliest dark shades imaginable, so that not even a single photon of light could get through at high noon.

Sitting at a two-person table crammed up against a wall was the older of my two aunts, Mary, reading *The New York Times* and drinking coffee. She looked up and smiled. As usual, her lovely smile warmed my heart.

She had interesting, dark, European features, with a small nose and a strong jaw, but it was her eyes that dominated her face. They were large, almond-shaped, and the darkest brown. They didn't miss the smallest of details.

Her eyes were beautiful on the outside, but as they locked onto mine, I could feel the power in them percolating below their surface, reaching out into the room and into me. That energy was a physical, palpable thing. Even after all these years, and all the love and trust I had for her, she still unnerved me a bit, and she knew it.

Her black hair was pulled back in a neat bun, and she wore a nondescript blue housedress that was all the rage among the old hag set. In addition to being the elder of the two sisters, she was also the tallest, at about four foot ten. Katie, my other aunt, was the petite one, at four foot six.

To me, Mary looked anywhere from sixty to a hundred twenty years old, depending on the day. She'd never tell me at what age she was turned, or exactly when it happened, but it was centuries before I became a vampire. She was always coy when I tried to pin her down on the exact time.

She and her sister must have had their reasons to withhold this information from me, but they were never big on randomly divulging information, anyway. After knowing me for two thousand years, they still wouldn't even tell me their real names. One time I told them that I suspected them to be the oldest vampires in the world, and they both laughed long and hard at that.

"Not even close," was their response.

But I did know that they were turned by the same vampire, at the same time. Katie was younger by two years, which she was quite fond of pointing out to Mary whenever it suited her, and it suited her frequently. They really weren't my aunts, of course—but when I looked at it from another perspective, they were so much more. You see, like Dom, they'd taken me in many years ago, when I was lost and alone and in desperate need of friendship.

I hugged Mary and kissed her on the cheek. When she hugged me back, the force that flowed out of her was astounding. If she wanted to, this tiny old lady could keep hugging me and crush me like a bug. We broke our embrace.

"Jules, let me look at you . . . just as pretty as ever."

"I'm not so sure about pretty, Aunt Mae, but you look great."

She waved a hand at me. "Don't lie to your elders. We haven't seen too much of you lately. Why not?"

Dig Number One. She loved playing aunt to me and pushing my buttons, especially when there was an audience. Dom was at parade rest in a corner, and there was a tiny smile on his face already. She knew damn well why not. I was trying to act like a human, and having two ancient vampire aunties didn't mesh well with the idea.

"Just busy, I guess," I fibbed.

She asked sweetly, "And how's that beautiful wife of yours? Aging well, I hope. What's her name again?"

Dig Number Two. She knew Lisa's name and, of course, never approved of my marriage.

Dom's smile grew a bit bigger.

"Lisa, Aunt Mae. Her name is Lisa."

She replied absently, "Oh right, Lisa."

"Actually, that's what I want to talk to you about," I said.

"I know. Well, actually, Katie told me. You know how she gets those feelings."

I did, indeed. They were both off the charts with vampire telepathy, but Katie was especially so.

She turned to Dom. "Dom, sweetie, it's late. Go home. We'll be fine with Vinnie and Marco in the cemetery."

There was no arguing with my aunties, so Dom bent way, way over and gave her a kiss on the cheek. The disparity in their sizes was comical. He said, "Okay, Mae. Tell Katie I said good night, and I'll see you tomorrow." Dom left us alone.

Mary said, "Katie's out back, watching the news. We'd better hurry, or she's going to say I was monopolizing you."

We walked under the spiral stairs to a shabby, knotty

pine closet in the far corner of the room. A clothes hanger protruded straight out from the top of the closet, and hanging from it, of course, were housedresses. Mary moved the dresses to the side and entered a code on a keypad. On the other side of the door, I heard a bolt sliding open with a muffled *clunk*. Mary pushed the door open and walked through it. Although I was no giant, I had to crouch down to follow her.

I closed the door behind me, which on the not-for-show side, was made of reinforced steel. It auto-locked with a louder *clunk* in here, maybe even a *clank* as I entered one of the oddest and most sumptuous rooms I'd ever seen.

Huge, at about seventy feet long and forty feet wide, the room included a living area, a kitchen, and a dining area. Antique, ornate crown molding rimmed the ceiling. A nearly movie-theater-sized flat screen dominated one wall of the living area, and a modern-looking sectional faced the screen, surrounded by several overstuffed classic-style armchairs that charmingly varied in height. Beyond that, the modern stainless steel kitchen was nicely counterpointed by a simple, rustic oak table. Finally, there was the dining area, lavish and banquet-sized.

Nothing clearly delineated the areas, but the wall and ceiling colors gradually transitioned, one into the other, to give a feeling of separateness. The living area, lush with muted gold walls and a pastel sky-blue ceiling, blended into the kitchen's light green walls and off-white ceiling.

Finally we came to the eye-catching colors of the dining area, with its sponge-painted orange walls and textured deep-red ceiling. The colors changed gradually, and somehow it all worked—dramatically so.

To most, this great room would appear to be one big hodge-podge, but when looked at closely, each area made perfect sense. They even all made sense together, like a single, complicated tapestry that told a rich story. What that story was, I had no idea. But I was sure my aunts did.

More than two dozen paintings and other works of art that varied greatly in age adorned the windowless walls of my aunts' secret lair. The average person wouldn't recognize most of them, but there were some that possessed quite a degree of notoriety, especially a certain Vermeer and two Rembrandts, whose previous home had been the Gardner Museum. Mary had mentioned a few times how much she liked them, and Dom made it happen.

Katie sat on the sectional, watching the news. She had the same black hair, brown skin, and features of her sister, but they were finer. Her eyes were of a similar shape and color as Mary's, and although piercing, they were a bit softer and less intense.

She wore a white silk dress, a stylish black sweater, and a simple pearl necklace. This was definitely an "out back" outfit, because in the loft, she would have been decked out in housedress chic. She was beautiful and tiny, standing at about four and a half feet, and she reminded me of a porcelain doll. But of the two sisters, she was by far the more volatile.

I often wondered why they went through this charade of playing little old ladies to the outside world, while living decadently in their secret flat. The answer was . . . well, there wasn't a good answer, except they'd always been ultra-private and loved their secrets.

Katie's voice was soft and a bit gravelly, but it carried. "Jules, honey, come over and give me a kiss."

I did, but then she held me at arm's length.

"You look good, Jules, but not right. I knew you were coming. I felt a little shiver in my mind, but it didn't feel nice, the way it usually does when you come for a visit. You're in some kind of trouble. Sit down and tell us about it. We'll help."

It was such a pleasant offer. Katie turned off the TV, and the two of them settled on the sectional. I sat on an oversized armchair facing them. I didn't know where to start, so I took a deep breath and started at the beginning. They listened attentively, occasionally punctuating my monologue with a concise question or two.

Somewhere along the way, one of them must have switched to Latin, because I found myself speaking in my original language. It felt so good. It's hard to keep track, but currently I speak about twelve languages, and my aunts speak even more. I've forgotten some, but twelve is about the right number. My ability to speak so many languages isn't due to the fact that vampires are inherently smarter or more insightful than humans. As a matter of fact, I've known some truly dumbass vampires. It's that our bodies, including our brains, function more efficiently than humans'. But our original human intellect is still what we're stuck with at a baseline. All the tools around that intellect, however, work faster, better, and more effectively.

My story ended with a wimpy sigh, which is hard to pull off when speaking Latin. My aunts looked at each other and seemed perplexed, but remained silent. I awaited an answer that never came.

"So, what do you think I should do?" I asked at last.

Again, they looked to each other, then to me.

One Mississippi, two Mississippi... "Oh come on, say something!"

Mary spoke. "We don't get it, Jules. There really isn't a question here."

"Or an issue of any kind," Katie chimed in.

"It seems silly that you're agonizing over this. The answer is obvious, just—"

"Just kill her," Katie interrupted. "And Leland, too, and—"

"That dopey son of his for good measure," Mary added.

My aunts had a way of alternating speech and finishing each other's sentences. Most of the time I found it cute, but tonight, it struck me as annoying.

"But that's what I was going to do," I shot back, "and I stopped myself. That's why I came to you. You know, to get some non-killing advice. Maybe an alternative?"

Katie said, "Now you're being silly, Jules. Do you expect us to give you bad advice? What kind of aunts would we be if we did that?"

"You're not buying your own baloney, are you, Jules?" Mary asked. "Just because you were playing house with a human for a few years doesn't mean you bought into it, right?"

I looked from one to the other and answered, "I'm not sure."

Mary blew out a toneless whistle. "When's the last time you killed a victim? Or anyone, for that matter?"

"Last night . . . so there," I answered.

"On purpose?"

"No." I felt embarrassed.

"And before that?"

"Years."

"That's not healthy, Jules," Katie said. "You can get by physically, of course, but psychologically, it's all wrong. You can't go on like this. We never understood why you went in this direction, why you needed to go human, but it didn't matter. You felt like you had to do it."

"And we went along with it," Mary added, "even though

we thought it was stupid and hated that bitch wife of yours. But we didn't think you'd go this far."

"And take it so seriously—seriously enough to deny your own nature," Katie said. "It's not good for you, Jules. You need to kill her."

"Yes, kill her," Mary agreed. "You'll feel better."

I blurted out, "But she's pregnant!"

Mary shrugged. "So what? There are plenty of other humans in the world."

I wanted to scream. It was this kind of harsh, cold vampire thinking that I'd wanted to get away from in the first place, even if I was just pretending.

"And we all know it can't be your kid . . . right, Jules?" said Katie.

They shared a quiet old lady chuckle at this high humor. The sub-virus infection that causes vampirism, among its many other effects, causes sterility in both males and females.

Mary noted my serious look and said, "Oh come on, Jules . . . you lose your sense of humor?"

"And your balls?" Katie added.

They shared a much louder laugh this time.

Katie was still far too amused at her little joke to speak, so Mary said, "Seriously, Jules, you can't really believe all of that human-constructed religious morality crap, can you? Enough of this! Wake up! It's for them, never for us. You know they're only bald-faced lies to control the masses."

"More than knowing it, you've witnessed it directly," Katie added, having recovered from her laughing fit. "Religions are a bunch of fairytales put together by people who were getting beaten up. So of course their central themes are negative."

In a mocking voice, Mary said, "'Even though there's a

steady stream of piss in your face, don't worry! You'll be rewarded in the next life.' Yeah, right. Look at cultures that were on top of the world, like Rome, Egypt, Greece, Babylon, and dozens of others you don't even know about. Always polytheism, male and female. Gods, fun, sex, mingling. Life was good, and then—"

"Then the downtrodden came along. Monotheism, females treated like shit. 'Don't do this, don't do that, or you'll be punished. But don't worry, you'll be rewarded in the next life.' Newsflash: there *is* no next life."

They were getting up to full steam on their anti-religion locomotive. It was a recurring theme for my aunts—and me, for that matter.

Katie went on, "I have to give credit to you Romans, though, you had it figured out the best. Stolen gods from the Greeks here, adopted ones from the Egyptians there, and I don't think a single one of you really believed in any of them."

"Morals are made up by the humans to keep each other in line," Mary said. "You know this, but you need to accept it again. Stop trying to live like a human, and move on."

"You don't think there's anything to it at all?" I replied. "Anything that's worthwhile?"

"No," they replied in unison.

Katie said, "Look at their history. It's obvious . . . they never learn."

"*Our* history," I replied.

Katie rolled her eyes. "Okay, *our* history. Religion causes way more harm than good. It's a fact. Do I need to go over examples? The Spanish Inquisition, the Crusades, Jihad, the St. Bartholomew's Day Massacre?"

Mary picked up. "Or what about all of those pedophile priests diddling those innocent little boys, and the great

Catholic Church spending millions to bury it?"

"And *we're* the bad guys?" Katie scoffed.

"All their silly holy books, writings, and rules. All it comes down to is one rule: treat each other nicely and with respect. But they're too stupid to get it."

I raised my voice. "What has this got to do with me not wanting to kill my wife?"

Mary replied calmly, "Because all the reasons behind that decision come from those human religious constructs, which are one big house of cards. You don't need to play along."

"And you *want* to kill her," Katie added. "You're only stopping yourself."

I wanted to deny that, but I honestly couldn't. "It's still not enough. I'm supposed to kill them just because religions are a bunch of crap?"

Katie answered, "No, you're supposed to kill them because you want to. You *need* to."

I shook my head.

"Why don't you turn Lisa instead?" Mary asked.

I'd looked into that possibility a few years back. Unbeknownst to her, I had run Lisa through a local vampire profiler. She failed on almost every psychological test. The conclusion was that she was too flighty and unstable, with way too much family. Family nearly always proved a deadly complication for a new turnee. "That's not an option for me . . . or her. I went into this as a human, and that's how I'll finish it."

Katie said, "Oh, so when you profiled her, I suppose that was just for fun?"

I was furious that they knew. "How do you know that? There's supposed to be client/profiler privilege! What the hell? Now you're spying on me?"

Katie raised her voice. "And now you're lying to us! If

you weren't acting so screwy, we wouldn't have to spy. We're trying to watch out for you."

I shook my head. "You two are unbelievable. Jesus Christ."

Katie was up and standing over me in a flash. Well, that wasn't quite true; it's possible to see a flash. I didn't see her move at all. Her fists were balled at her sides, and she was breathing heavily. She looked absolutely deadly.

In a dangerously quiet voice, she said, "I told you, *don't say that*. I'm not going to tell you again."

It wasn't about taking the Lord's name in vain; it was that she'd actually known Jesus personally. To use her words, she thought he was "a good kid." Mary, however, had told me that Katie had loved him like a son.

I put my hands up in surrender mode. "Okay, okay. I'm sorry. Take it easy, Aunt Kay."

She continued to glare at me.

"Kay," Mary said softly. When she didn't respond, Mary said it louder, finally getting her attention. "Come on, sit back down. You're not helping."

Katie reluctantly turned from me with barely contained fury and said to her sister, "He really pisses me off sometimes."

As she walked back to her seat, I felt fortunate to be alive, and maybe more fortunate not to have shit myself.

After an uncomfortable pause, Mary said, "Jules, let's look at your problem in a different way. How about from your origins? You started out as a Roman. The Romans were a lot of things, but one thing they definitely had was a sense of justice."

Katie added coolly, "A bit mean about it, though. Bloody, even."

Mary smiled. "It's there right at the beginning of Rome,

with Romulus and Remus. The she-wolf thing is a bunch of baloney, but I like the story anyway. Remus was smart enough . . . and so handsome."

Katie jumped back in. "My goodness, he was beautiful. But he had no backbone, and no common sense, just like you, Julian. The people wanted the brothers to co-rule, but Romulus knew it would end in disaster."

"So he made the hard choice and killed Remus, his own brother," Mary said. "Sure, it was a bit harsh, but it was the best decision for his people and what ended up being Rome."

"That Romulus was cagey and so mean," Katie said, "and not very good-looking with that wall-eye of his."

"Whew, that thing could look around a corner," Mary agreed.

"It was a tough form of justice, but it carried forward, and they kept order and their empire," Katie continued. "Even their common folk felt they could get their day in court."

"Or at the end of a sword," Mary added. "But they meted out their justice according to their law, and it was simple and swift. It worked a hell of a lot better than what goes on today. What would happen to a town or village that rebelled against Rome?"

I replied, "The rebellion would be crushed, and the town destroyed."

Katie looked at me intently. "And the people; even the women and children?"

I saw what they were getting at. "Executed or sold into slavery, depending on the example that was to be made."

Mary clapped her hands together, like a teacher proud of an apt pupil who'd solved a complex problem. "Of course! A bit extreme maybe, but effective. It worked, didn't it?"

I nodded.

Mary continued, "Maybe even saved lives in the end, discouraging further fighting, like dropping the A-bomb on Japan. That was harsh, but it stopped the war, and probably ended up saving a lot of lives."

Katie smiled. "Definitely. What do think would happen, Jules, if you looked up the home village or town of any suicide bomber—"

"Those bastards," Mary interjected.

"—And bombed it into oblivion? Sounds cruel, but they'd think twice about blowing themselves up, along with a bunch of innocent people. It would save lives in the long run."

Mary touched my arm. "Jules, you haven't just read about it in books; you've lived it. Does this bullshit system of so-called justice work? Or did the old ways work better?"

"The old ways were harsher. More innocents got hurt, but the needs of the many were attended to much better."

"And what about you Romans and your extra-long memories when it comes to avenging yourselves?" Mary continued. "Think of how you pissed all over the Greeks all those years over Troy. Not that you need much of a reason to piss on Greeks."

They both snickered at this. My aunts had assured me that it was absolutely true that Trojan refugees were part of the first peoples of Rome. They'd been there to see them immigrate. And because of it, we Romans did take great pride in kicking the Greeks' asses. But that wasn't the only reason.

The main reason we took their land was that we wanted it. It was ripe for the taking, and that was how we operated. They yakked and yakked, spouting the virtues of their ideal democracy, while we rolled up their country.

"I know the history," I said.

Mary snapped, "No you don't! Or you've forgotten it. You're a Roman, Jules, and you'll always be one. You have a long memory for wrongs, and you're used to swift, harsh justice. It's part of who you are."

Katie said, "People don't ever change much. Oh, they might smooth a few edges or make adjustments to some minor things, but they don't fundamentally change who they are. You're pussyfooting around the issue. You know what you want to do . . . what you *should* do."

"You're going to make yourself sick, going over it again and again, and we don't like to see you hurting, Jules," Mary added.

Katie looked at me. "It's this kind of thing that drives some vampires crazy or even makes them kill themselves — even long-lasters like you."

"You don't think we didn't notice you've been sensitive for the last hundred years or so?"

Katie nodded. "Yeah, about a hundred years."

"If anything happened to you, it would kill us," Mary said. "We worry about you."

"We love you," Katie said.

My ancient vampire aunties, who had killed countless thousands, were actually quite sweet. I felt lucky to have them.

Katie went on. "And you seem to have forgotten one more thing. You're a vampire, Jules, and that makes you a predator and a killer by nature. I know you didn't choose it, and neither did we, but that's the fact of the matter."

Mary shook her finger at me. "And just because you drink those horrible test-tubes at the hospital, which is pretty disgusting, if you ask me, and haven't drained anyone dry lately, doesn't change anything."

"You know, Jules, when Rome was at its peak, it was similar to the vampire world in an important way," Katie said. "It didn't take shit, and we don't, either. Because we don't have to."

I put my head down and thought for a moment. I did want to kill Lisa and Leland. There was no denying it. But I couldn't bring myself to do it. Maybe it was my depression or human values that had gotten to me. Or maybe I was having an off day. I shook my head. "I can't do it. I feel like I need to think more."

"We figured," Mary said. "We don't care about you killing them for their sake. We want you to kill them for your own health. But if you can't, we think you should get out of the area."

Katie touched my arm. "It's not our best advice — killing them would be better. Are you absolutely sure you won't kill them?"

"I'm sure, Aunt Kay."

She sighed and said, "Okay, but don't be alone and brood. We think you should tidy up your loose ends, then travel."

"Yeah, visit some of your old haunts and your old friends," Mary added. "Maybe they'll talk some sense into you and give you some perspective."

Now that idea got my attention. Not just picking up stakes and moving on to the next city that I would call home, but traveling carefree. I had a lot of old friends to reconnect with, and a lot of cities to visit. It would be fun, and maybe exactly what I needed to get back in the groove.

I'd seen some of my kind occasionally when I traveled — the cretins and weirdos Lisa had alluded to — but never got to spend any real time with them. Yeah, this was sounding like just the ticket. I smiled. "I think that sounds like a great idea. I'm going to do it."

Katie replied, "Well, I'm glad you always take our second-rate advice. Where to first? I'm thinking New Orleans or Montreal . . . or maybe Rome?"

I couldn't go wrong with those three cities. Dozens of others also flitted through my mind. But I couldn't decide right then. "I'm not sure."

"When you do decide, do what you need to do to get out of town," Katie said. "We'll take care of the rest."

"Great," I said, and then I stopped short. *Take care of the rest?* "Wait a minute. You've got to promise not to kill Lisa or Donald, or the dopey son, for that matter."

In perfect unison and too quickly, they said, "We promise."

They'd never broken a promise to me before, but the way they answered so fast made me uneasy. "And promise not to have anyone else kill them."

"Why are you insulting us?" said Mary. "You know we don't mince words like that. It's the same thing."

She was right. "I apologize. That was out of line."

Katie said, "Apology accepted. What we meant was, email us the name of your lawyer, and we'll have ours contact him."

They had the very best and most expensive lawyers out of New York—vampires, of course. They were bloodsuckers times two, and the bastards never died. She continued, "Sign over power of attorney so you can maybe stay out of court for your divorce. You really won't kill her?"

"No, Aunt Kay."

She sighed.

Mary continued, "Send us any accounts you want us to sweep up into the Swiss and Cayman banks you use."

They had nearly all of my vital info, and I trusted them

implicitly.

Katie chimed in, "Oh, May, we'll have to get a caretaker for the Vineyard house."

My aunties thought of everything. I stood up, but they remained seated.

"Thanks so much for doing this," I said. "Now that it's in my head, I do want to get out of here ASAP. You guys know I'm not in love with the Boston area, but no matter where I end up, I'll come to visit a lot."

"We know," Mary said. "We think it's best if you hit the road soon. One more thing—when you get back, we probably won't be here."

I sat back down. "What? You've been here over a hundred years. Why?"

"Jules, there's another reason for you to leave town," Mary said. "Somebody got close to us, and we think it was the Genealogist."

"That bitch!" Katie added.

The only thing we vampires reliably knew about the Genealogist was that she was a woman. After that, it was pretty much nothing.

I felt nervous. "Close? How close? When?"

Mary answered, "Very close. A few months ago in our New York townhouse."

"Why didn't you tell me?"

Katie shrugged. "You have your own problems, Jules, and what could you do besides worry? The thing about it is I still don't know how she flushed us. I'm pretty sure it was through the computer connections in New York. Maybe I let the firewall slip, I'm not sure. But when I ran a back trace, I think someone was in the system, although I couldn't be sure. That bitch is very good and very careful. She'd make a great vampire."

"We figure it's a matter of time now before she zeroes in on us here, so close to New York," said Mary. "So, we'll beat her to the punch and leave. And you've been affiliated with us around Boston for years now. They could be getting a bead on you, too."

"Where will you go?" I asked.

Katie looked at her sister. "We're not sure. Maybe back to Italy, maybe Spain."

I said, "Tell me what happened."

Katie looked at me, and her lip trembled a bit. "They almost got my big sister."

"Not with you around, Kay." Mary patted her sister on the hand.

Katie smiled, but it was forced.

I was dumbfounded. To think someone, a human no less, could almost take out one of these two ancients was beyond all reason.

Katie was too upset to talk, so Mary continued. "They hit us at four a.m., right at the time we like to nap. It must have been luck, because I don't know how they could have known that. They were loaded for bear—infrared goggles, automatic weapons, and shotguns, all with garlic ammo. They even had flamethrowers. Can you imagine?"

"Small ones, maybe enough for two or three bursts, but enough to do us in," said Katie, who had regained her composure. "They were clearly designed for vampires. They got through the outer electronic perimeter, but they didn't count on how well-trained Dom, Vinnie, Marco, and poor Paulo were. The bastards killed Paulo. Now his two little boys don't have a father. They'll always have us, but if I ever find that bitch, I'm going to skin her alive."

In this modern era, the saying "skin someone alive" is pure hyperbole, but in this instance, Katie meant it literally.

"The second I heard the firefight start, I was up at the window," said Mary. "It was fast and deadly. You should have seen Dom and the boys, Jules. You would have been so proud. They put down five of the bastards, but Paulo caught one in the head right toward the end. He was dead before he knew it. When it was over, Dom checked them all and made sure the courtyard was secure."

"Checking them all" meant Dom put one more bullet in each of the intruders' heads. Quite an effective checking technique, if you ask me.

Mary continued, "He gave me the 'all-clear' sign, and right then, the door kicked in, and I caught both barrels of garlic-soaked twelve-gauge, right in the chest. This son of a bitch was fast, and I didn't have time to duck. I crashed into the wall on the other side of the room. I never felt so much pain in my life. I couldn't even move."

"They've developed some kind of super-concentrated garlic extract," Katie said, "worse than anything we've seen before. We still don't know how he got by the inner security. We're not sure if this one slipped away and got in, or the others gave up their lives as a distraction to get him through."

That was an ominous concept. I'd always thought my aunts liked to play mafia with bodyguards they didn't need. How wrong I was. Katie nodded, as if she read my thoughts.

"You think vampires were involved?" I asked.

Mary said, "We've got our share of vampire enemies, but no. We're sure. We'd definitely know."

"What about one of your guards?"

"No, Jules," Katie answered. "You Guineas know how to hold your water and keep a secret. Now the Irish, they make squealing an art form. You can't trust them. Your wife's Irish, isn't she?"

Dig number . . . I'd lost count. "Hardy har har," I said.

Mary went on. "Well, now this big lug, he was bigger than Dom even, stands over me and takes this flame-track nozzle off a backpack and sparks it up. Right then, I heard one more shot in the courtyard—"

I interrupted, "Were you scared, Aunt Mae?"

"Maybe a bit, I'm not sure. But I remember thinking I'd had a good life, albeit far too long, and that I'd miss Kay. Right then, she appeared out of nowhere, like a miracle."

"Where'd she come from?"

"Katie was on an old-school hunt. You know how much she loves the Red Sox."

I nodded, remembering her New York-specific hunting pattern.

Katie said, "I always like to kill a few Yankees fans when I visit. It's the least I could do for our boys. It's funny how the cops never can figure out that the only thing the victims have in common is that they're all wearing Yankees caps."

The sisters shared another old lady laugh.

When the snickering stopped, Katie continued, "I'd just finished with my third Yankees-loving bastard when I felt something, kind of like when I know you're coming, Jules. But this time, it was that Mary was in trouble, and she's never in trouble. I started on a dead run, and then I heard the first shots. I flew through the courtyard. Dom sensed me running by and fired at me, the darling."

I said to Mary, "That was the shot you heard?"

Mary nodded.

"I don't know how I knew," Katie said, "but I knew I didn't have time for the stairs. The window was definitely out of my jumping range, three stories up. But I guess it was adrenaline, because somehow, I made it."

"Did she ever," Mary chimed in. "She flew through the

window and kicked the lug in the head, just like Jackie Chan."

"I wish I could have seen it myself, because I really love Jackie Chan," Katie said.

Mary laughed. "Anyway, the lug goes down hard, the flame track torches the bed, not me, and Katie's on him—and what she did to him."

"Considering he was going to kill you, I think I was pretty restrained."

"You ripped his balls off and stuffed them down his throat," Mary said.

Kate waved dismissively. "I was easy on him. I only wish he had six or seven more balls to rip off."

Mary grinned. "Then she tore his throat open and drained him dry. For a minute, I thought she was going to turn him, but she snapped his head off like a twig. My baby sister." She was positively beaming.

"I was going to turn him so I could torture him for a few hundred more years for what he almost did to you, sis," Katie said. "*Then* I'd kill the nutless bastard. But I thought we already had enough of a mess to clean up without complicating things."

"Fortunately, we didn't have to deal with the cops. We got everything cleaned up and got rid of the bodies," Mary said. "They had nothing on them that we could trace. We sold the townhouse through a sham company."

"I'm sure going to miss killing Yankees fans," Katie said.

Mary chuckled. "We sent the garlic extract for analysis. It's three hundred times more concentrated than anything we'd seen before. It took me nearly three hours to heal completely."

"You, three hours?" I asked, shocked. For someone as old and as powerful as Mary, three hours to heal was nearly an eternity.

Vampires heal rapidly due to our highly improved physiology. It's a nice side benefit of the infectious agent that causes vampirism, a sub-virus which we call human-to-vampire sub-virus, or HVSV. It's a fastidious organism, transmitted classically by a bite, but can be contracted by blood exposure, or rarely, sexually. The normal human immune system wipes it out one hundred percent of the time, unless the victim's immune system isn't hitting on all pistons—as with AIDS, or in a cancer patient being treated with chemotherapy, or under special circumstances that put a normal immune system under maximum stress, like death.

When HVSV survives in a body, it multiplies rapidly and intercalates itself directly into the genome of the host, causing significant genetic change. The net result is optimization of bodily function on a cellular level. Each and every cell of a vampire is running at near peak efficiency, and this efficiency improves, rather than declines with age. In my opinion, a major design flaw in humans is that their cells and bodies deteriorate with age. It's quite the terrible turn of events and doesn't seem fair. In my mind, it proves that a "divine creator" doesn't exist. Or maybe it proves that there is indeed a God, but that he or she happens to be a mean-spirited bastard.

The HVSV infection turns the host's cells almost completely away from growth and toward a purely maintenance-oriented function. So basically, when you become a vampire, you have exactly what you had as a human, but now, vampire physiology via HVSV enhances it and keeps it running at a near-optimum level.

Without having to deal with the vastly complex function of cellular reproduction, there's no chance of a catastrophic genetic mishap, as when cancer develops in humans. For the same reason, we don't accumulate minor genetic mistakes, so there's no chance of cellular senescence, either.

That's why we don't age. We have the exact same cells, in the same orientation as on the day we were turned, and now they're maintained by the greatly improved vampire biology. They never grow, divide, or age. They stay exactly the same. We go along maintaining ourselves for, well, maybe forever.

The HVSV also makes our bodies adept at repairing injury, but only as far as replacing exactly what was there to start with. And because of our improved immune system, we don't suffer medical illness of any kind.

The biggest change, of course, is our need for blood, and it has to be human blood. No synthetic or animal blood can replace it. Why do we need it? We don't know for certain. But our scientists think some component in human blood is an irreplaceable co-enzyme for a vital process, like energy conversion, for instance.

One thing we do know for sure about blood is that without it, we die. After several days going without, we start to degenerate, reaching a cachectic concentration-camp look within a few weeks, and shortly after that, it's over. Not the best way to go. Not that getting shotgunned and torched by a flamethrower would be much better.

Mary answered me. "Yes, it took three hours to heal. And that super-garlic . . . I've never felt pain like that."

"You're lucky he didn't aim high. At that range, a shotgun blast would have taken your head clean off."

Out of the corner of my eye, I saw Katie wince at my comment. That sort of wound would certainly do a vampire in, and not because of injury to the cerebral cortex. It would be from injury to the brainstem, which controls basic functions like breathing, heartbeat, and blood pressure. If that's knocked out long enough, before it can heal, it'll kill us. We quickly heal standard bullet wounds to the head, just like everywhere else on our bodies. But they're no fun at all and leave behind quite the shitty headache.

In LA in the 1950s, I was a private detective for a while. It was an interesting job, gave me an endless supply of blood donors, and LA was wild fun. I'd sent my secretary home for the evening and was sitting in my office doing some paperwork when I heard some footsteps. I didn't think much of them, as I was expecting a new client. Evidently, though, a hunter had scoped me.

Four guys burst into the office and opened up on me with 45s. I took about a dozen painful close-range wounds, but the one I caught in the head was excruciating. I went down hard behind my desk.

Through the horrible ringing in my ears, I could hear them popping fresh clips into their guns. They were going to come around the desk and unload on me, blowing what was left of my head to mush. I willed myself to move and fished out the Thompson I had stashed in my bottom desk drawer. I'd always kept the machine gun there, not for hunters per se, but for any asshole in general. Back then, LA was that crazy.

I popped up and, through my blood-obscured vision, started shooting, plowing all four of them down. The roar of the Thompson was deafening, and it wreaked havoc on my assailants, the walls, the windows, and anything else in its path. I was screaming the whole time I was shooting, but only realized it when my ammo was spent and I could hear myself over the impotent clicks of my weapon.

When it was done, I came around the desk to find one of them still barely sucking air.

Between last gasps, he managed to squawk out,

"Cheater . . . fucking vampire cheater . . . using a gun."

Can you believe it? He crashes my office with three other guys who empty their clips into me, and *I'm* the cheater? I was about to put a bullet in his head, but he had the good sense to croak.

A good old decapitation will work just as well as a brainstem hit, as it removes the brainstem, along with everything else, from the neck up. There's an urban legend that Dracula was decapitated by an overly pious monk, and sometime later, if the story is to be believed, his head was somehow grafted back on, and he miraculously survived. I've never heard of another vampire surviving such an injury, so I think it's baloney—but if it were true, it would go a long way in explaining why Dracula was so stupid.

Katie said, "These hunters knew their stuff. No stakes or other bullshit with them."

Mary smirked. "I would have let him put a stake in my heart just for the fun of it. Then I would've taken it out and stuffed it up his ass."

We all shared a laugh at that image. We heal heart wounds, too. There's no black magic in wooden stakes that'll kill us.

"May, remember that knucklehead who shot me with those homemade silver bullets?" Katie asked. "He was so surprised when I didn't die or explode or something."

Mary said, "The only silver you're allergic to is the silver-plated kind in cheap jewelry. It gives you a rash."

"You know, he still looked surprised even after I swatted his head off his shoulders."

We burst out laughing, and things were once again feeling normal. When the laughter petered out, I became somber, reviewing in my mind what had nearly happened to Mary.

"On second thought, my trip can wait," I said. "I'm staying right here to help Dom protect you until you leave."

"Nonsense," said Katie. "You'll go on your trip. Grouping up like that will put us in more danger."

"Kay's right. You might end up leading them to us, or we to you."

"I'm always right," Katie sassed. "You go on your trip, and take care of yourself. Dom's already stepped security way up, and we're going to get on the move soon, anyway. She'll have to start from scratch to trace us again."

"You ought to lose the Julian Brownell identity," Mary advised. "You've always been associated with us. She could have a line on you already."

"Maybe they'll hit your house and kill that wife of yours by mistake," Katie said.

I rolled my eyes. "Will you please stop, Katie?"

She shrugged. "You have to admit, it would solve a lot of problems."

"One more thing. You know a vampire from Shreveport named Kolinsky?" Mary asked.

"Yeah. Sort of nutty, a bit of a loner, right? I met him a few times. He's not so bad. Why?"

"Gone missing," Kate said. "Him and a bunch of his people. We figure he's been hit. You might want to stay clear of the area for a while."

"You're kidding me. Two hits, this close in time? The Genealogist has never done that before. Why would she change now?"

"No idea, but you need to be more careful than usual," said Mary. "There's something going on here."

I couldn't believe this was happening. It made my worries about my divorce shenanigans seem downright silly.

As they stood, Mary said, "You ought to get going, Jules."

"Okay, I'll go. But I'm not just going to sit back after what happened to you."

Katie said, "We know, and we know we can't stop you."

Mary stared me down. "But be careful, and don't expose yourself for us. If anything ever happened to you, we'd never forgive ourselves. Now come give us a hug."

I bent down, taking Katie in my left arm and Mary in my right. I kissed them each on the cheek. "I'll be careful, I promise."

Mary said, "Ever since we found you, all those years ago, we've loved you. We'll always love you, Titus."

"That's right . . . always," Katie chimed in. "And coming from us, that means a lot."

"I love you, too," I said, although I don't know if the term "love" quite covered what I felt for them.

I waved goodbye and exited into the "old lady loft." I started down the hill to my car and saw Dom leaning against a building, having a smoke. It was after 3:00 a.m., but I never expected him to have gone home, after what happened in New York. I pulled up next to him and struck up a Cuban.

"They tell you?" he asked.

"Yep."

"I feel like shit about it, you know? Right under my nose."

"You shouldn't. You've always done a great job, and those fuckers were well prepared."

"Well, I learned my lesson and tightened things down a lot."

After a few silent puffs, I said, "They're going to have to leave. You going with them?"

He looked at me, shocked. "Of course I'm going. You

think I'd leave them?"

"No, I don't think you would."

He took a long drag from his cigarette. "You're going to get involved in this, right?"

"Oh yeah," I said.

"Will you keep me in the loop if you turn anything up?"

"I will, and the same for you, okay?"

He'd put out his cigarette and was rummaging for another, but he was all out. "You got it, Doc."

"Thanks, Dom, but I think it'll be plain 'Jules' from now on. I got to run." I started down the hill and flipped him the rest of my deck of Cubans.

He caught them. "What's this? These are way too rich for my blood."

"Try them, anyway."

"Thanks, Julian."

Dom was a quick study. As I turned the corner, I could see he'd already struck up a cigar. By the time I'd gotten to the bottom of the hill, I knew where I'd be going. It had to be New Orleans. I had a lot of friends there, and Shreveport was a little too close for comfort. If something happened down there, maybe I could help, or maybe I'd turn up a lead on how the Genealogist had found my aunts. It was a shot in the dark, but it gave me some direction on where the hell I was going to go.

I got into my car for the short ride back to my hotel. I needed to have a difficult conversation with Liam Giordano. Considering ER docs don't own a practice per se, and the ER business was pretty much "cash in and cash out," what I was going to do was possible, but unseemly.

Even at three in the morning, he answered before the first ring quit. "Jules, you've got to stop calling me at these odd hours. People will start to talk."

"Hey, Liam, listen. I've got to cut right to the chase. I'm going to quit the group and move away from Boston. I need you to cash me out of the business."

After a slight pause, he said, "You're pulling my chain. I'm not buying, buddy."

"I wish I were, but it's true. This thing with Lisa has me pretty screwed up, and I've always hated this area, so I'm going."

There was a longer pause this time. "You're not kidding. Are you sure you've thought this through? Why let her force you to do this so soon? You've got a lot invested in this practice, Jules."

"You know me. Snap decisions are an art form. But seriously, my mind is made up."

He did know me, and well. When I made a decision, I didn't backpedal.

He said, "Okay, I'll organize a little dinner or something."

"No, I'm going to be traveling for a while, and I'm leaving tomorrow. You know I hate those kinds of things, anyway."

"Man, you're going to disappoint a lot of people by leaving like that, me included."

"I'm sorry, pal, but I have to do it this way. It's time for me to go."

I thought I heard a little catch in his voice. "Okay, okay. I'll cash you out and send the money to your account. I'll email you resignation forms from the corporation and the hospital. Anything else?"

"No, I think that will do it."

"So this is it, huh? Not the way I envisioned it."

"Me neither. Will you give my apologies to the rest of the group?"

"Of course." He paused and then added, "We had a real good run, didn't we, Jules?"

I smiled. "We sure did . . . BFF?"

"Fuck you," Liam answered, sounding more like himself.

"I'm planning on circling back here at some point. I'll come in to see you when I do."

"I'm not counting on it, but I hope you do."

"Bye, Liam."

"Goodbye, Jules." He hung up.

Sometimes being a vampire blew. A lifetime of goodbyes can really get to you.

CHAPTER 13

My flight from Boston to New Orleans was right on time. I got a taxi around noon, and as per usual, the New Orleans cabbie had more than a passing acquaintance with the gas pedal. Before I knew it, we pulled up to the Hotel Monteleone. I wanted to be right in the middle of things, and the Monteleone fit that bill, being located in the French Quarter on Rue Royale, only one block south of Bourbon Street.

It was a family-owned-and-operated hotel, one that had passed through the years from father to son to grandson. It was rare for its breed, in that it had not gone downhill through the generations. In fact, it had flourished. I've observed that generational success in business usually doesn't happen. The founder of a successful business is almost by definition a sharp person, but then he or she has to pass it on to a child, whom random odds theory dictates to be less sharp. By the time things dilute down to a grandson or a granddaughter, you've likely got a full-fledged fuck-up on your hands.

In general, most family businesses are down the shitter in two generations max, but the Monteleones had beaten the odds. I think the smartest was the founder, Antonio, but his son Frank, and Frank's son, Bill, were no slouches by any means.

The hotel had originally been known as the Commercial Hotel, back when Antonio bought it in 1886. He, his son, and his grandson expanded and renovated it through the years, making the Monteleone the grand old place that it was today. I'd been staying there ever since Antonio took it over. Before that, it was a poorly run dump known mainly for its syphilitic whores.

I met Antonio when he first emigrated from Sicily in 1879. I'd already been in New Orleans for about ninety years at the time. He was an excellent businessman, but he was never ruthless. He told crummy jokes and always seemed to be in a good mood. He was sharp, but friendly and charming at the same time. I missed him.

When Antonio told me about his plan to buy the Commercial, I put up some cash to help out. I'm a very silent partner in the Monteleone to this day.

When I stepped into the lobby, I got the same feeling that I always did when I was there. I felt like I'd stepped back in time, and that was fine by me. The marble floors shone brightly in the mellow light from golden chandeliers. The extra-high ceiling was decoratively painted and broken into rectangles by thick, ornate crown molding. It was a lobby from an era gone by.

The general manager greeted me in French. I may have been a silent partner everywhere else in the world, but here at the hotel itself, the staff always seemed to know me somehow. "Monsieur Beauparlant, did you have a pleasant trip?"

In New Orleans, Montreal, and some other places, I was known as Christian Beauparlant. Instead of having a wife in every port, vampires usually have a name in every city.

Names are much easier to handle than wives, and they help maintain our much-needed anonymity.

"Yes, Patrice, I did. And how are you?"

"Quite well, sir. It's good to see you again. I've taken the liberty of having your usual suite made ready."

After I checked in and began to walk away from the front desk, he asked, "Will you be needing a reservation for dinner tonight, sir?"

It was a tempting offer. New Orleans has so many fine restaurants, but I wanted to prowl and not be a slave to any appointment. I replied, "A Wednesday night in April? I'll take my chances, but thanks, anyway."

Patrice shot me a prissy, proper look that only top-level managers and concierges at the best hotels could deliver with aplomb. The look said, *Silly man. It is always proper to have a reservation in a civilized society*. But his voice said, "A pleasure having you back, sir."

I smiled, shook his hand, and slipped him a neatly folded hundred-dollar bill. I always tipped extraordinarily at the Monteleone, since I was never charged a dime when I stayed there.

The elevator ferried me to my suite on the seventeenth floor, the top floor of the hotel. *Lavish* would be an understatement in its description, with its rich red-and-gold colors and French provincial furniture. It boasted a large parlor for entertaining, two bedrooms, an office, and a spectacular view of the Mississippi.

Plane travel always makes me feel a bit off, grimy even, so I decided to make a refreshing dip in the outdoor rooftop pool my first order of business. As I suspected, the pool was deserted. Being around 1:00 p.m., it was late for the morning swimmers, and a bit early for the returning tourists to take their late afternoon dip in the sun.

The poolside bar provided me with a tall, cold margarita, and after a few delicious sips, I waded into the shallow end and dove forward. The water washed over me, and I felt instantly purified. I began my swimming motion and immediately sank right to the bottom like a stone.

Vampires' cells are loaded with mitochondria, the microscopic energy factories of the cell, and because of it, we're denser than humans. By appearance, most would expect me to weigh about 160 pounds, but in reality, I'm 225. So it's scales that vampires avoid, not mirrors. This increased density makes us notoriously poor swimmers, and the few vampires who've made the decades-long effort to learn to swim are usually insufferable about it.

The coolness of the water and the warmth of the sun were in a delicious balance as I calmly walked underwater to the deep end. Our improved physiology continually repairs what to humans would be waterlogged, drowned lungs. As a matter of fact, vampires trying to commit suicide by drowning usually stop the attempt due to boredom.

My breathing was slow and controlled. I'd been underwater many times and had gotten somewhat used to the feeling of liquid moving in and out of my lungs. It takes a while, but once you get over the feeling of suffocation, staying underwater is very relaxing. I leaned against the side of the pool, watching the sparkling sunbeams penetrate the water's depth.

I must have lost track of time, because when I glanced upward, I realized there was a head peering down at me from the edge of the pool. *Shit! Another amateur mistake.*

I obviously couldn't swim out, so I climbed up the ladder. Excuses started flying through my mind. *"I'm trying to break the world record for holding my breath."* Idiotic. *"I'm in the middle of deep-sea diver training."* Stupid.

As my head broke the surface, I turned away from my observer, and as subtly as I could, belched out about a gallon of pool water. I turned and looked directly into a pair of oversized, stunning light-blue eyes belonging to a little girl. I instinctively looked for her parents, who'd be an additional worry if they were also aware of my underwater sojourn.

The parents were at the bar with what appeared to be the girl's older sister, ordering food and drinks. By their demeanor, I was certain they'd not noticed me. Vampire telepathy was not an option. It doesn't work on young kids. Maybe at around eleven or twelve, you'll get some traction, but my little eyewitness was younger. I'd have to talk my way out of this.

She was about seven years old, skinny, with long, white-blonde hair, wisps of barely visible eyebrows, and long eyelashes. Her face was pleasing, with a wide forehead, high cheeks, and full lips. Then, recognition traveled forward two millennia and struck my heart like a lightning bolt.

This little girl in 2012 was the exact image of my daughter the last time I'd seen her. My little girl, who'd been dust for centuries. My eyes welled with tears, my throat tightened, and I took in a hitching gasp of air. Her eyes opened even wider, which seemed impossible, since they were already as big as saucers.

"Are you all right, mister?" she asked in English with a slight southern drawl. It was definitely not Latin, the language my daughter would have spoken. That broke the spell a bit.

I cleared my throat. "I'm fine, sweetie. Just fine."

"You were under there an awful long time."

"I was, wasn't I? Why didn't you go for help?"

She piped up with that oh-so-cute drawl, "Well I was gonna, but then I watched you for a little while, and you didn't look like you needed any help. You stayed there and looked around like you were standing on the corner in front of my daddy's restaurant. You looked okay."

"And you were right, of course, because here I am."

"Can you breathe underwater like a fish or something?"

I didn't lie. "No, I can't. Do I look like a fish?"

"I guess not. So how do you do it?"

"It's one of those things, honey," I said.

She was about to ask something else, when her father called out, "Laura, *Lauradarlin*, come on over. I got you something for lunch."

"Bye-bye," she said, and skipped away. It was a truly beautiful sight. The name Laura is Roman in origin. My little girl's name was Acilia.

Acilia . . . it sounds inane, doesn't it? Well, the name was defined by the culture of the time, and she made it beautiful. Only males got two names in Rome, sometimes three, if your family rated—but girls got only one name. That name was generally a derivation of what would be called the last name.

In my case, the family name was Acilius, so she got the feminine version, Acilia. Even if there were two daughters, they'd often get the same name, further differentiated by "the Elder" and "the Younger." When the three-girl mark was hit, parents had to get creative—and if you know any Roman history, you know name creativity wasn't one of our strong suits. Anyway, we never had to worry about another child coming along. My wife, Aelia, had a difficult time with the delivery and had a massive hemorrhage that nearly killed her. She was never able to conceive again.

My daughter was by far the strongest love of my human life. You might ask about my wife, but marriage in Rome back then wasn't anywhere near the same as it is today. It was more of a business relationship arranged by two families. Not to say feelings of love couldn't and didn't develop between husband and wife, but in my case, there wasn't time. You see, we were only together for about nine years, and I was away on campaign for much of it.

Smart and beautiful, Aelia loved to laugh and was easy to get along with. I think even a hard-ass Roman soldier like me would have swooned eventually. I wish I'd had the chance to find out.

Acilia walked and talked early, and was quick-witted. Once mobile, she attached herself to me. She became my shadow when I was at home, and I adored her.

I was away when it happened, on some damn campaign in some damn country—and for the life of me, I can't remember where. I came home to find my house deserted and my wife and child nowhere to be found. I lived with other families in what you might call a very crowded middle-class housing area, or maybe a slum, it's hard to compare to the present times. There were three wooden buildings, three stories each, facing into a common courtyard. It wasn't great, but two years earlier, I'd saved up enough to buy my "unit," so I didn't have to pay rent anymore.

I quickly looked through the house, dread already welling up in me. As I made my way back to the front door, standing there were my favorite neighbors, Quintus Licus and his wife, Gaia. They were both about sixty—fairly ancient for ancient Rome—and had raised children, and now grandchildren, in their small dwelling. They'd become like adoptive parents to me, as my own parents were years dead. I took one look at them and knew.

"How?" I asked.

"Plague," Licus answered simply.

Fucking plague, whatever that meant. Back then, it could

have been anything, since Rome was always filthy with one illness or another. Today's modern conveniences and medical technology are frankly amazing. In my time, life was fast and cheap, and death was always right around the corner.

I nodded. Silent tears ran down Gaia's face, but not mine. I was a good Roman soldier, and tears would be improper.

"When?" I asked.

Gaia looked at me with pity. "Over a year now, Titus."

Over a year. Over a year, and I didn't even know my wife and child were dead. I felt weak, but managed to say, "Can you take me to them?"

Licus and Gaia led me to a small green space outside of the residential area that was commonly used for funerals. As we slowly walked along, Licus told me that he'd sent word, but it obviously hadn't reached me. He assured me that he'd arranged the proper services and had made the proper sacrifices to the gods in my absence.

When we arrived, I could see trees and grass, but not much else. We burned our dead, and since it had been a year, there was nothing to see. Licus had been careful to keep a mental note of the funeral pyre's location. I stood there dumbly, looking at nothing. My mind went blank. There was nothing for me to do, and the nothingness made it worse. There wasn't a marker, a stone, or even a piece of wood—nothing. The world had been wiped clean of my wife and my darling little girl without missing a beat. It didn't seem right.

Then I started thinking about the timing. Over a year ago—it would have been around the time of Acilia's eighth birthday. I asked Licus if he knew the day they died, but he didn't. Prior to Caesar reforming the Roman calendar, our dates were all over the place. Licus knew the month, but not the exact day.

I started thinking I would never know if my little girl had been seven or eight when she died. It was a useless thought. What difference did it make? She was dead. But she was my little angel, and I wanted to know how old she was when this fucking plague took her.

I felt so inadequate, a failure as a father, and so lost . . . so alone. Good Roman soldier or not, I couldn't control the grief. I fell to my knees, shouting out loud at the gods. What a great waste of breath that was. Then the tears came, followed by great sobs. The pain was too much.

Acilia was already ashes under my feet, and I'd never see her again. I fell to my side and lay there, crying like a baby for quite a while. It must have been a long time, because when I finally opened my eyes, it was almost dark. I wiped my face and got to my feet, not expecting to see anyone.

But Licus was standing where I had left him, waiting for me in the fading light. He'd sent Gaia home. As improper as it was for him to witness this display, it would have been worse for a woman to see it.

One of the best traits Romans from my era shared was their sense of duty and loyalty. The one exception was politicians, as some things never change. Licus, a true Roman, waited and did his duty by me at my time of need.

I composed myself and said, "Thank you for waiting, Licus. I'm all right now."

"Good. Then let's go back," he replied. "Gaia will fix you something to eat. You'll feel better."

We walked back with his comforting hand on my shoulder the entire way.

I stayed for about a month with Licus and his family, recovering from my loss. They kept gently reminding me that they could be my family now and that I should stay.

Licus had two granddaughters to marry off, and no doubt I would be a target for one of them. Unfortunately, they both looked like mules, although they were nice kids. I'm sure they both got married and spawned passels of mule-faced children. But I had no interest in such matters. I'd decided that I would never have a family again. What had happened was far too painful to even remotely consider setting myself up for a repeat performance. The only blood I had left was my older brother, Lucius, but he lived in Greece, and I hadn't heard from him in years. We hated each other, and for all I knew, he was already dead.

No, it would be a career in the legion for me. Back when my family was intact, the plan had been the standard sixteen-year hitch, receiving a payout of farmland, hopefully in Italy proper, and then, living out the rest of our lives as farmers. That was all shot to hell with my wife and daughter gone. The legion was all I had left.

It may have been more dangerous than the next job, but life was cheap in my time. We were used to hardship and expected it. Nowadays, people are so protected that only a serious illness, extreme old age, or a strange accident are typically fatal. We weren't protected at all. Anything, even the common cold, could be lethal.

I said my farewells to Licus and his brood. Before I left, I gave him my dwelling. It was already bought and paid for, and I would never return there. He had way too many people living in his place, so it made perfect sense. Loyalty should always be rewarded — misplaced loyalty, maybe more so.

Now I continued my climb out of the pool and made my way back to the bar. I finished my drink and ordered another. As I waited for it to arrive, I toweled off and watched little Laura with her family. She was clearly her father's favorite; the mom seemed to favor the older girl. It was a quick conclusion to make, but I'd bet on it. Sometimes you can tell these sorts of things at a glance.

Parents always have their favorites. My father, who was a sweetheart of a man even though he was a Roman soldier, had always favored my brother. He did his best to hide it, but kids always know. It still bothers me, even after two thousand years.

My drink came, and I took one final glance over my shoulder. I was rewarded by a perfect little smile. I smiled back, thinking I'd never see little Miss Laura again. I was wrong.

CHAPTER 14

After an extra-long primping session for my big splash back into vampire society, I settled on a very vampire-chic outfit: dark jeans, black tee, and a black sports jacket. I was definitely a bit overdressed, but what the hell.

I slipped out into a beautifully sultry night and turned onto Bourbon Street and its eternal 24/7-carnival atmosphere. The whole damn street was seedy, wonderful, outrageous, and alive—and it's been that way for decades. Peppered all along it were eateries, jazz clubs, bars, and strip joints. I loved it.

On the average night, there was enough vomit on the streets to make wakeboarding the preferred method of transportation. And if you couldn't get laid down here without having to pay for it, you probably needed to have your genitals surgically removed.

As I passed one of the many bars open to the warm evening breezes, a barmaid of dubious morals—and of long legs, blonde hair, and ample, pushed-up breasts—offered me a shooter. I wanted to get right into the spirit of things, so of course, I accepted. A shooter in New Orleans is the same as a shooter everywhere else: fluorescent green or purple or red and extra-fruity, with a tiny splash of nondescript alcohol, in a plastic test-tube. It usually costs about three bucks, and after a two-buck tip, it's quite the deal for the barmaid and the establishment.

In New Orleans, it's not the drink you're buying, however—it's the delivery. The "deliverer" sometimes puts the blunt end of the test-tube in her mouth and bends you over for a shooter soul kiss, you drinking from the action end of the tube. Sometimes it's hooked into your fly, and used as a penis surrogate for pretend oral sex. My shooter gal chose well for her delivery technique. She nestled the tube between her breasts and pulled my head down to suck the tube dry. I had no objections.

I have to admit that being so close to her, her scent, and all of the raucous sexual excitement of this place, I really wanted to fuck her while drinking her blood. I was totally unclear as to which would be the primary endeavor. I thanked her, gave her a twenty, and told her to keep the change. She gave me a very sexy smile and told me to come back anytime. I told her that I might do just that, but I'm not sure how much she would have enjoyed my return, since my teeth would have been sunk into her neck.

I continued on through the humid night. The crowd noise was wild, and jazz and rock wafted onto the street from the various bars. The smell of booze and sweat and sex was in the air. I recognized several vampires on the street and nodded hello to them as I passed. I didn't know any of them personally, but I could tell what they were easily enough. Vampires can learn to disguise their smoothly gliding gaits to varying degrees, attempting to make them look more human. But we never seem to be able to hide the hungry, predatory look in our eyes. It's unmistakable.

I was getting close to Fritzel's European Jazz Pub, a regular haunt of mine since it opened in the late 1960s. It's cramped and crowded with plain wooden benches for seats, many of which are so close to the tiny stage that you can reach out and touch the musicians. I love the music and the atmosphere there, but that wasn't why I was going.

An old friend of mine, Jean-Luc Leclerc, owned Fritzel's and he also happened to be the vampire mayor of New Orleans. Vampires don't have organized political structure. But when a city has a high vampire population, like New Orleans, a mayor is chosen by popular acclaim to adjudicate disputes, supervise our businesses, and keep our less delicate activities subtle enough not to attract undue human attention. A mayor can hold the position for life, or until he or she steps down—or in extreme cases, until forcibly removed.

In modern times, once a city hits about the fifty-vampire mark, some loose organization usually develops. At a hundred, a mayor is needed, with attendant administrative help. Given that New Orleans is not that big of a city, it has a fairly large vampire population at two hundred. I know that number doesn't sound like all that much, but it is when you consider the sum total of carnage we inflict on a daily basis. Keeping this sort of bloodshed hidden is no easy trick and requires strong leadership, cooperation, and common sense.

In many ways, our society is a collaborative commune of murderers, and we're quite proud of it. Rogue behavior is bad for everyone, and simply not tolerated. Other larger cities may have higher populations, but even though New Orleans has the highest population density of vampires for a major metropolitan area, it always remains under the radar. Some of this has to do with New Orleans' sleazy side. Its many human-perpetrated unsolved murders and disappearances, do wonders to camouflage the many killings that the vampire population racks up. But most of it is on account of Jean-Luc's superb management skills.

A vampire mayor is usually someone who's been in a city for a long time and is a long-lived vampire. Just as in the human world we tend to equate age and experience with intelligence. My friend had been in New Orleans for the last three centuries and was relatively old, at about a thousand, but he was still a baby to me. San Francisco also has a mayor, as do New York, Paris, Rome, and many other cities. Boston, of course, doesn't. What self-respecting vampire would want to live there, except perhaps a dope like me, playing human with a wife and a nine-to-five job?

Jean-Luc's woman, Simone Desmarais, played hostess at Fritzel's. She stood outside the door, her usual station. She'd been the hostess here for fifty years and hadn't changed one bit—yet no human ever seemed to notice. When she saw me approach, a large, toothy grin grew on her lovely face, and she planted a long, cool kiss on my lips. It was the kind of kiss where my tonsils became acquainted with her tongue. She finished with a playful, blood-drawing bite on my lower lip, which put a charge directly into my groin, something she'd been doing for years.

I held her at arm's length and drank her in. She was stunning—tall and slim with light brown hair, grey eyes, and high cheekbones. Her thousand-watt smile was surrounded by the fullest of lips. When Leclerc turned her 250 years ago, she was thirty. Jean-Luc was lucky in that Simone, his human paramour at that time, agreed to it. Mine wouldn't. But the little French bastard was far more charming than I was.

"Simone, darling, a picture of beauty, as always," I said.

"Christian, my love, how I have missed you. Jean-Luc was away on business, but once he heard you were here, he canceled everything. He should be back in town any minute now."

"I can't wait to see him."

She threw her arms around me and whispered, "We've missed you. We've all missed you. You really are more important to our kind than you give yourself credit for."

Her perfume was distracting, and her natural scent, even more so. "You're way too sweet," I said. "I've missed you, too."

She stepped back with her hands on her hips. "I'm hoping you're done with whatever you were doing in Boston, and you're going to kill that no-good human cunt whom you foolishly married." She somehow made the word "human" sound dirtier than "cunt."

"I have no specific plans at this point, but that's exactly what my aunties told me to do."

"You ought to listen. If you want, I'll kill her for you."

"Thanks for the offer, but I'll take care of it."

She whispered in my ear again, "If you ever feel like going human again, call me. You'll quickly forget all about any human woman."

Being this close to her, with her warmth, the press of her body, and her breath in my ear, was intoxicating. I managed to croak out, "I know I would."

We'd always had an intense physical attraction and had enjoyed numerous sexual liaisons through the years. She was beautiful, skilled, insatiable, and extremely energetic. If sex could kill, I'd want her to be the one to do me in.

Vampires are sexual creatures, and our sexual mores are quite a bit different than humans'. Basically, we don't have any. We can be "exclusive-ish" for extended periods of time, and jealousies can develop, but because we're so long-lived, there's no point to it. We're not going to shack up with the same person for, say, more than two hundred years, anyway. And there are plenty of other vampire and human fish in the sea. So long-term monogamous relationships don't make much sense for us, because our "long-term" is too damn long. I tried it the human way and barely lasted fifteen years.

Vampires pretty much mix and match with only general boundaries. Our way is relaxed, exciting, and an enjoyable and necessary distraction we truly need to help us last for the long haul. Our system is clearly better than humans', but I have to admit, our enhanced physiology, infertility, and lack of sexually transmitted diseases certainly gives us an advantage in this arena.

It was amazing how being in this rowdy town for only a few hours made me start to feel like a vampire again. I'd begun to realize how much of my true nature I'd suppressed for the last twenty years. What the hell was I thinking? I started to have a natural, honest urge to hunt, and the thought of drinking chemically treated leftover blood from a test tube made me want to gag.

Simone and I were starting to attract attention, especially since her shtick as hostess was "the ice princess." She barely spoke to the patrons and pretty much gestured them to their seats. Her behavior was out of character in their eyes.

She also observed the attention and said, "Why don't we go in? I'll clear a bar seat for us."

"Good idea," I replied.

Two seats at the tiny bar miraculously appeared, and waiting at mine was a tequila—hers, champagne. We clinked glasses and downed our drinks. Two more instantly materialized.

We caught up, with fine New Orleans jazz as our background. Things in the Big Easy were going well for Simone, or Kate, as she was known to those not in the know.

We chatted as the drinks flowed and the music washed over us. Simone kept time to the music by playing footsie up and down my leg, and I didn't mind. I felt alive again. She was so distracting, I almost forgot what I wanted to ask her. "Oh, by the way, any news on Shreveport?"

"Nothing. Clean as a whistle, and Kolinsky hasn't shown anywhere. He's always been a bit crazy, so pulling out without telling anyone might be something he'd do—but ten of his VAs have gone missing, too. He must have been hit."

"VA" was the current PC term for "vampire associate." These were the vampire-friendly humans who lived in our world, performing various tasks and jobs for us. I told her about Mary's brush with death, and her eyes widened. "That's unbelievable. And two attempts so close together in time? That's never happened before. What's going on?"

"I don't know, but Shreveport being so near, I thought I might help Jean-Luc come up with something."

She shook her head. "He's already had dozens of vampires and VAs looking into it. Nothing. Just the same as always with that genealogy bitch."

It was interesting that the complete lack of evidence was the only evidence that it had been the Genealogist. Other hunters weren't that good. "Well, in that case, I guess I'm on vacation."

She smiled and checked her watch. "You ought to get going. Jean-Luc will be at the Absinthe House anytime now. I wouldn't want you to miss him."

The Old Absinthe House was pretty much a tourist destination on Bourbon Street. But the Absinthe House Simone referred to was the vampire bar for the New Orleans locals.

I took her face in my hands and kissed her. When I was done, her eyes remained deliciously closed for a beat or two.

"I wouldn't want to miss *you*, either," I whispered.

CHAPTER 15

Lisa sat on the couch in the living room of what was now for all intents and purposes, her house, and hers alone. She liked the ring of that—but felt sad about it, too. Julian hadn't been a bad husband, but he hadn't paid enough attention to the relationship or to her. She was sipping a decaf coffee, finishing up some work on her laptop, and half paying attention to the news on TV, when Donald breezed in.

He got himself a beer, kissed the top of her head, and sat down next to her. Mute, he stared off in the distance.

She looked at him for a moment, amused. "Hello," she finally said to break the silence.

He didn't respond.

Just like him, she thought. *Probably sifting through a dozen deals.* Louder, she said, "Ahoy, Donald. Are you there?"

He blinked, surprised. "Oh, sorry, babe. I got something on my mind."

"I noticed. Want to talk about it?"

He looked at her intently. "I do. Look, you know me. The only way I can be is direct, and so I'll just come out and say it. It's about you and your husband."

He had her full attention now. She knew how controlling Donald could be, and she had clearly told him that she wanted him to stay out of her divorce. It was between her and Julian, and she wanted to handle it without any meddling. "We discussed this, Donald," she said angrily. "You said you'd stay out of it. How am I supposed to—"

He cut her off. "I know what I said, and I knew you were going to be pissed, but I don't care. I smelled a rat, and what am I supposed to do, ignore it? You're my woman now. That's my child you're carrying, and I'm going to protect both of you. That's the way it is, and the sooner you get used to it, the better."

She was fuming now. "I can't believe you said that! I can't believe you'd do this!"

"Look, hear me out. That deal your husband offered you was too easy and too fast, especially with you having the affair and already being pregnant. He could leverage that. It has to be shady somehow."

She wasn't going to let this stand. It would be a bad precedent for their marriage, especially with someone as headstrong as Donald. She said coldly, "Well, you ought to know about shady deals."

He seemed to take this as a compliment and smiled. "Right you are. I pushed them on plenty of dupes, and I can smell one a mile away."

She raised her voice. "I told you to stay out of this. I can't believe—"

He interrupted again. "Two minutes, that's all. If you're still pissed, you can yell at me all you want."

She paused and bit down the venom she was about to spew. "Go ahead."

He pulled out a sheet of paper. "I've got a list here of about six million dollars in assets that your Julian owns. He made a fair effort to hide them, so you weren't going to see any of it in the divorce."

Stunned, Lisa sat up fast and reached for the paper. "Give me that."

Donald held it away from her. "Hold your horses. I want to tell you the odd part."

She really wanted to get her hands on that paper, but waited to hear him out.

He looked at her. "Some of the purchases were made almost a hundred years ago. His name's on them, sometimes with another fellow he must be in cahoots with, but the dates don't make sense. Sometimes the social security number's right, sometimes it's a different one. It's a jumble. I've matched his signatures from the P and S when you bought this house. I'm no expert, but I'll be damned if they don't look the same. And you know what? Some of the documents are from as far back as 1928."

She was dumbfounded. Finally, after a moment she said, "What the fuck?"

Donald cackled. "Yeah, that's what I said."

"What do you make of it?"

"I don't know. But one thing I do know is your innocent little doctor isn't so innocent after all. Maybe you're not the only bad guy in this breakup. And if something doesn't make sense, like this, money's usually the explanation. I'd wager he's pulling some sleight of hand here and pocketing a whole lot of cash."

Lisa extended her hand and asked, "May I see that now?"

"Of course, honey," he answered with a smug smile on his lips.

She wanted to slap it off him. Lisa studied the paper closely and said, "It doesn't make any sense. Have you done anything about this?"

"No, not a thing. Besides me, only you and my

investigator know. I thought I'd let you take a look at it first. If you want to move on it, we'll go ahead. If not, we'll let it drop."

Knowing Donald, she thought he'd move on it no matter what she said, but she'd deal with that later. For now, she reread the list of Julian's hidden assets while Donald smiled on, sipping his beer. She felt as if she'd been struck in the head—perhaps by the same imaginary mallet she'd used on her husband a few nights before.

CHAPTER 16

As I meandered toward the Absinthe House, I ruminated over the fact that in the last millennium or so, I'd gravitated toward vampires of French extraction. I think it's because the French have had it figured out culturally for centuries. They're cool, have it going on—and more than that, the smug bastards know it.

When I first encountered the French in Gaul with Caesar, they were savages, as beastly as any of the Germanic tribes, and I was quite content to hack them to shreds. But with Romanization, they were smart enough to see the good in culture and civilization. They adapted to it and eventually did it better than any other society. I guess I've become an ancient Roman Francophile vampire, if that makes any sense.

The Germans, also savages at the time, were saved from us by the fact that their crummy weather made their country undesirable. The Brits were in this same bad weather category, and were even more isolated from Rome, being on an island. They're tough bastards, though, and became empire builders like us. But they really seemed to miss the culture train. Their food sucks, and they're so fucking boring. You've never been truly bored until you've been cornered at a party by an upper-crust British vampire. They don't need to kill their victims by drinking their blood; they can bore them to death.

As I walked down Bourbon, I noticed several more vampires. One young man, maybe twenty when he was turned, flew across the street. He fist-pounded me, gave me a huge hug, and introduced himself as Jake. He addressed me as "Yo, dude" and went on for several minutes about how cool I was, and what an honor it was to meet me. He hoped we could have a sit-down sometime, hunt together, or do several other things that I doubted very much we'd ever do. I fairly tore myself away as he shouted after me that he'd see me around. I saluted him with a wave and walked on, smiling. Jake may have been a little over the top, but he seemed like a nice kid.

Vampires, being small in number, are a fairly close-knit group. Being a tad over two thousand put me in some rarified air, and unfortunately, made me a bit of a celebrity. At this point in history, getting to be my age should be no great trick, with all of our scientific knowledge, social connections, and even support groups available. Can you imagine—vampire support groups? Whatever the source, though, knowledge is the key to survival, and because of it, I expected most vampires of this era to last for the long haul.

When I was turned, however, it was ancient times and tough to get by as a vampire. In the first place, nobody, not even us, knew what the heck was going on in terms of vampirism. We had little or no support unless it came by sheer luck, as in my case. And right along with humans, we believed the bullshit lore and superstitions that were dreamed up. Humans were essentially our only source of information, and the rest was hit or miss, or on-the-job training.

Back in the early 800s, I was cornered by a mob, literally with my back to a wall in some little pissant village in southern Italy. At its head was this half-assed priest, and he pulled out a crucifix and thrust it toward me. I actually averted my eyes and groaned in pain. Then I realized the cross wasn't hurting me at all. But I still needed to keep my wits about me, as there were about fifty of them. Just by sheer weight of numbers, they could kill me, but the cross was definitely not doing anything.

I straightened up, all confident, and put on my best scary vampire face, showing off my canines. The crowd took a collective step back. I was about to take the opportunity to bolt, but old half-assed stepped forward, reached under his filthy, ragged cloak—which reeked of urine, by the way—and took out a crude bottle. He heaved its contents into my face. *Oh no! Holy water!* I swear I could feel my face burning off, and somehow I half-leapt and half-scuttled up and over the wall, like some kind of crazed monkey. I broke into a full vampire sprint, both hands rubbing feverishly at my face, which I was sure was melted and ruined. I think I ran about ten miles before I stopped and realized I wasn't injured at all.

It's a funny story, and I still laugh about it today. But I was stunned and actually thought I was mortally wounded. If my flight reflex hadn't kicked in, I might have curled up in a ball, and that mob would have had their way with me. I survived through harsh, superstitious times because of my wits, strength, and a number of other reasons—but maybe the most important was luck. Not to mention the patronage of two very old sisters.

The Absinthe House is underground in a basement, which is no small trick, since New Orleans is below sea level. It's in the Quarter proper, and all the robust activity in the area effectively masks vampires' comings and goings. Its secret entrance is heavily guarded, and if any stray humans happen to find their way in, they'll never come out.

The place is big, and it's open at all times. Although it's dominated by a large single room, there are a fair number of side parlors for private meetings and sexual encounters. Many of my kind, however, are not shy about letting it fly right in the main room. I guess I'm among these exhibitionist vamps—not because I'm any wilder than the next person, but because I was raised Roman. You never completely outgrow that initial human life. It sticks with you like old luggage. I mean, once you've been through a Roman orgy or two, most anything seems tame. The orgies were quite a hoot in general, although I attended a few boring ones. Let me tell you, there's no bigger letdown than a boring orgy.

One of my old friends, John Dodd, a physician by training, was turned in Victorian England, and will always be somewhat prudish because of it. When we discuss sexual behavior, he's always fond of saying, "Christian, no matter what the circumstances, if a man puts himself into a situation where there are other erect penises within grasping distance, then that man is a homosexual by definition."

I always counter, "John, I have been in that situation many a time, and I can assure you that I am not homosexual. The key is for women to be readily at hand, and none of the erect penii can be pointing in my direction."

Being the prude that he was, Dodd harbored a prejudice against prostitutes. When he was turned, he went after them preferentially, although he did make a notable exception for an ex-fiancée who had jilted him. It wasn't that he was angry about being a vampire—he was a voluntary. Nor was he ignorant of our ways, since he had been well instructed by the vamp who had turned him. It was that he had this new power and wanted to exercise it. Hence, the legend of Jack the Ripper was born.

This sort of behavior isn't unusual in voluntaries; in fact, it's thought to be psychologically stabilizing. New turnees have that immortal, testosterone-loaded, teenage-type energy running through them and need an outlet. It's like going through super-puberty with no parents around to rein you in. Simply put, Dodd felt like fucking around, and our fucking around can get bloody. His antics proved quite entertaining, with all the wild rumors, speculation, and panic in town. Although, I grant you, it probably wasn't so entertaining for the whores Dodd butchered.

The Absinthe House's décor was of dark wood and dim lighting. A huge, oblong double bar bisected the room, with a ceiling-height mirror facing out on either side. The liquor shelves were stocked with a vast variety of absinthe and tequila, and the wine list was staggering. There were cozy leather booths all around and several tall bar tables, but a lot of room left for dancing. The waitstaff and bartenders, both vampires and human VAs, were sharp, well dressed, and way too good-looking.

When I entered, heads turned, and warm greetings followed from friends and strangers alike. This prodigal son had returned. Vampires have a great sense of community, and I was beginning to feel like a jerk for walking away from it for all those years.

A trio of vamps was playing mellow jazz on the left side of the bar, or Left Bank. They had a cool vibe going, and I settled in to listen while I indulged in a few cocktails. After a short time, there was a tap on my shoulder. I turned to see my dear friend Jean-Luc.

He beamed at me. "*Mon ami*! It is so good to see you!"

We embraced and exchanged kisses on each cheek.

Despite his small size at only five foot three, I could feel the power flowing from him. When he got to be my age, I was sure he'd be far more formidable than I was.

He looked fit and sharp, with dark blue dress pants and a button-down white shirt. His penetrating brown eyes were framed by a neatly trimmed beard and shoulder-length black hair tied back in a loose ponytail. The left side of the beard and the rest of his face were marred by a vertical scar that split his eyebrow and extended down to his lower cheek. The scar had come from a scimitar almost a thousand years ago, when he was a human knight on a crusade. Lucky for him, his helmet had protected him from losing his eye, and he often bemoaned this pre-vampire disfigurement. But I thought it gave his face character, and secretly, I believed he thought the same.

I envied his impeccable facial hair, since it's hard to come by for a vampire. If a mistake is made while trimming, the hair takes decades to grow back. Our HVSV-enhanced physiology is about maintenance, not growth. In the case of hair cells, even though they're not growing themselves, they still retain their original function of producing hair, but at an extremely controlled rate. So basically, it takes about two years for a vampire to get a five o'clock shadow. Growing a full beard takes fifty years. Neat freaks have their hair trimmed once a decade, but most get by with a haircut every twenty years or so.

My last go-round with facial hair ended in the 1920s. I had a full moustache and a big soul patch, and the only vampire who thought it didn't look stupid was me. I attempted to trim it one morning while distracted by a lady friend. After four or five passes of the side-to-side fuck-up, I ended up with a crooked Hitler look. No way to grow that puppy back in less than half a century, so off it came, and

I've been clean-shaven ever since. So a vampire buzz cut doesn't result in miraculous regrowth while we slumber coma-like in a coffin. It results in one bald motherfucker of a vampire, and for quite a long time.

On the other side of the bar, Jean-Luc's private table awaited us. I'd never met him before New Orleans in the 1700s, but I wish I had, as he'd lived a fascinating life. We were similar in many ways, both being soldier types. Although we'd had a rocky start, we'd been good friends ever since.

The mood on this side of the bar was decidedly more upbeat, with a mixed vampire and human band rocking out a loud fusion jazz, and the dance floor was already packed. As we made our way through the crowd, we ran into Jake, whom I'd met on the street earlier.

After he gave me the same "Yo, dude" greeting, he turned to Jean-Luc and said, "Hi, Jean-Luc. How are you?"

Jean-Luc did not stop. "Fine, Jake," he responded flatly.

Jake trailed us, nervously talking about this and that. His monologue was like white noise and not totally unpleasant, but clearly annoying to Jean-Luc. We reached our table, and Jake, showing some intelligence, didn't try to sit at such a big-ticket spot.

"Gotta run, dudes," Jake said. "Nice seeing you again, Mr. Beauparlant."

As he turned into the crowd, I shouted after him, "Jake, call me Christian."

He gave me a nice smile, waved, and was gone.

I turned to Jean-Luc. "Who decided to turn him?"

"It was a mistake. He was left for dead, but my guess is he is far too stupid to die."

"I see. He *is* a bit annoying. Maybe he just needs some guidance."

"Good luck with that, my friend. I have tried, as have many others, but to no avail. He's more like a pet now, and not the smartest one at that."

I was about to respond when our waitress approached. She was human, with dark hair, dark eyes, and ridiculously long legs, despite her petite frame. She had the kind of ideal breasts that only nature can create and youth can maintain—without the aid of a plastic surgeon, that is.

She said, "The usual for you, Jean-Luc? And what can I get for you, Monsieur Beauparlant?"

I read her nametag and replied, "I'll have what he's having, Miranda. I'm Christian...you can drop the 'Monsieur.'"

She smiled and headed to the bar.

"I wish people would stop with that 'Mister' shit," I said. "It makes me feel as old as I am."

"It's a sign of respect. We haven't had a real *ancient* here for a long time," Jean-Luc replied.

I said, "Here's the way I show respect. Fuck you, you little French bastard."

He laughed, and our drinks arrived—tequila and absinthe over crushed ice with a twist of lime. Miranda went out of her way to call me "Christian" as she set the drinks down. She was so damn cute. We ordered a light meal, and I watched Miranda miraculously sashay away without falling off her stiletto heels.

Jean-Luc noticed my gaze. "Now that you've emerged from your human stupor, you appear to be as lecherous as ever, eh?"

With great effort, I tore my eyes from Miranda's behind and said, "It's been a while, but it's all coming back to me. By the way, how did the buying trip go?"

Jean-Luc's out-of-town business wasn't hosting a

vampire conclave or plotting to take over the world. He was purchasing wine. We'd been in the wine import business together for over two hundred years. It was something we both greatly enjoyed, and it was quite profitable, especially with the awakening of the American palate in the past forty years. Americans really know how to consume when they get a taste for something.

Jean-Luc, given his heritage, was the prototypical French wine snob. Oh, he'd occasionally lean toward some Italian varieties, but having to accept the quality of American wine was distasteful to him.

He told me he'd had good success with mainly French wines, of course. I mentioned to him that I was considering a California trip before the year's end, and I would be sure to make some purchases while I was there. He sniffed and dismissively waved a limp-wristed backhand at me, but he didn't say no. In the end, though it was painful, even he had to acknowledge the excellence of the California wines and the amount of money they put in our pockets.

He shifted gears. "So what about this business with your *wiiiiive?*"

Translation: *wife*. He said it with as much disdain as a snotty Frenchman could muster, and that's a lot.

"No big deal... we're getting divorced. I've got some lawyers on it. It shouldn't take too long."

He delivered the perfect snotty, disbelieving Frenchman look, with a head tilt, one eye partially closed, and pursed lips. "*Divorzzzzzed?* Wouldn't it be better if she just disappeared?"

Jean-Luc maintained a heavy French accent for reasons beyond me, but I suspect mainly as an affectation. He spoke multiple languages, and all perfectly. And besides, the French accent of his time had been much different than the one he currently sported. I'd asked him why he did it dozens of times through the years, and had never gotten a straight answer. I guess he had his reasons.

I replied, "Look, I've started this thing, and I'll finish it. I'll have to work through it, that's all."

"That's fair. But if it is because you were married to her and feel sentimental, I would be more than happy to kill her for you."

Jesus, this was getting ridiculous. The offers to kill Lisa kept piling up. I cut him off. "No, I don't want you to kill her. I said I'd take care of it!"

He turned away in a pretend pout. "I'm just trying to help."

I'd raised my voice, and Jean-Luc was a stickler for good manners. I am, too, but one cannot hold themselves up to the French, especially the stuck-up ones, in this regard. I put my hand on his arm and turned him back to face me. "I didn't mean to shout. I apologize. I've had a lot of offers to kill her, but I'm putting you at the top of the list."

He beamed at this, took me by the shoulders, and delivered kisses to both my cheeks. "I will wait for you to give me the word, and I will take care of it personally."

Now we were back on par. The conversation was interesting and danced aimlessly from topic to topic. Miranda kept the drinks and the food flowing. Our light meal turned into a feast, as the food at the Absinthe House was excellent.

Vampires are renowned overeaters. Blood isn't bad as a source of nutrition, but that's not why we imbibe it, and it definitely lacks in some of the daily-recommended vampire vitamins. Just like humans, we're biological creatures that require energy to maintain ourselves. In fact, due to our ramped-up physiology, we have higher energy requirements and end up eating a lot more than humans on average. These same energy requirements make it difficult, but not impossible, to become significantly overweight. If this weren't the case, long ago I would have ended up on the reality series *Really Fat Fucking Vampires*.

We were having such a good time that I didn't want to break the mood, but I said, "You must be concerned about Shreveport. It's almost next door."

"Yes, very. I'm sure Kolinsky is dead. And not a trace, not a clue—the same as always with her."

"Any connections that could lead here?"

"None that I'm aware of, but who knows? I've ordered everyone to update their computer security, and I've put more surveillance on duty, but New Orleans is a big city."

"Well, I'm at your disposal if I can help in any way. And so you know, there was a recent attempt on my aunts, as well. They're fine, but something may be afoot here. The Genealogist might be changing the rules of the game."

"*Incroyable*! That's particularly unnerving, since we've never understood her game at all."

We lapsed into a morose silence as we listened to the music, but after a time, our pleasant banter reasserted itself.

Toward the end of our meal, three female vampires came in and managed to corral a bar table off to our left. In a word, they were outstanding—dressed to party and to show off their perfect bodies. I'm sure they had been hot as humans, but HVSV had taken that hotness and turned up the temperature by about four thousand degrees. Their appearance didn't move my thoughts of the Genealogist a million miles away—but at least a few hundred thousand.

They were baby vampires, all between five and ten years on this side, I'd guess, and maybe twenty-five or so when they were turned. Everything about them screamed "new," and they reveled in what they were, loudly laughing and being overly made-up—none of which detracted from their sex appeal in the least. What should have been the subtlest of gestures ended up unintentionally garish and excessive. It's the way all new vampires are until we master the self-control needed to blend into the world at large. If a vampire is turned by choice and is happy about it, this is the way he or she acts. All of us can act like that when we let down our guard with our own kind.

The three of them were drinking absinthe like fish and chain smoking, even though they could go up like torches and take half of the club with them. Vampires' hundredfold increase in mitochondria, in addition to causing our "weight problem," also, in effect, makes us energy warehouses. Something that's quite necessary to maintain our more demanding bodily functions. The down side is all that additional power lying around makes us much more flammable and forces us to take particular care when dealing with fire. In fact, most victims of spontaneous combustion that you might read about in the tabloids while waiting in the supermarket checkout line are vampires who've erred around fire. We never have gas stoves in our houses. It's always safe electric ranges for us.

Despite this, these three wild women were carelessly lighting cigarettes, one after another. And with the amount of product in their hair, their potential flammability was probably quadrupled. Sure, I enjoy my Cubans, but I don't crazily gesticulate with a lit smoke in my hand.

These women were a pleasure to watch, but it's hard for me to describe the feelings they evoked in human terms, since I've been a vampire so long. But perhaps it's the same for humans when they sit in the park on a beautiful sunny day and see a four- or five-year-old child playing with reckless abandon. I think that may be it, a sort of a wistful, content observation, but minus the push-up bras and fuck-me pumps. It's the way I should've had the chance to act. Instead, I scuttled about for nearly fifty years, not really knowing what I was or what I was doing until my aunts found me.

The girls appeared to be of average height, but it was hard to tell for sure, considering the towering heels they wore. Despite those heels, they moved like lynxes. Two were brunettes, one with dark brown hair, one with red highlights, and the third was a blonde. The blonde was the tallest and curviest of the lot. Red Highlights was a bit trimmer and athletic-looking, and Dark Brown was willowy and smoldering. None of them had that cachectic model look, and I heartily approved. I've always fancied some meat with my potatoes.

Their shoes were stylish, expensive, and black—reminiscent of what might be called Roman sandals, but with lofty heels. Their dresses hung mid-thigh, tight and loose at the same time, showing a lot of cleavage, a lot of leg, and a lot of everything else.

I wasn't the only one mesmerized. These three attracted buckets of attention. The music kicked up a notch to a deeply primitive, base-dominated beat, and the dance floor almost instantly was overflowing.

Jean-Luc interrupted my reverie. "Why don't you put your tongue back in your mouth, and I'll tell you about them."

I turned to him over the din of the music. "I'd rather you didn't. I'll find out in time, but for now I'll enjoy the mystery."

"Suit yourself," he said.

I turned back to leer again and looked right into the

lovely face of the blonde.

"Hi, Jean-Luc," she said to my friend.

He smiled and nodded.

"You're Beauparlant, right?"

"You have me, and 'Christian' will do," I replied.

She looked me up and down in a not-so-subtle way. The tip of her tongue came out and touched her upper lip, which I deeply enjoyed. Pretending to be human and married in Boston . . . what had I been thinking? At that moment, it was difficult to recall.

When Blondie was done with her once-over, her ice-blue eyes locked on mine. "Hi, I'm Maddie. You look damn good for a two-thousand-year-old."

An old standard line popped into my head. "Well you know, I exercise daily, get plenty of sleep, and try to watch who I eat."

She laughed. It was loud and lovely. "Funny, too. I like that. Roman, right? I just love history."

"Then I am your man."

She looked over her shoulder at her two friends. "I'd better do what I came to do before my girlfriends get jealous."

"We couldn't have that."

"We were wondering if you would like to dance with us."

Being asked to dance . . . so wonderful, so quaint, so from a bygone era. "I'd love to."

She smiled. "With all of us . . . together."

I smiled and stood. "Better still. I'm at your service."

She said, "Not yet, but I expect later tonight you might be."

Oh, I like this girl. I took her hand, and she led me toward her friends. I looked back to Jean-Luc and gave him a wave goodbye. He shook his head, smiled, and waved back. I was introduced to Becca of the red highlights. Her lovely face sported dazzling green eyes, a perfect aquiline nose, and very full lips. Jen of the dark brown hair was next. Her eyes, like her hair, were the darkest brown, framed by arresting, high-arching eyebrows. Her neck was elegant and slender.

I kissed their hands in turn, saving Maddie for last. We pushed out to the floor. The beat was strong, and the dance floor was wild. We waded in and joined the mass of vampires, along with some brave humans, moving to the beat.

It was out of control. There was barely room to breathe, let alone dance—but somehow we managed both. My three partners circled me like predators. Sometimes one darted in for close dancing, sometimes two, but it was best when it was all three. We'd leap in the air together, embracing before we came back down. I spun them, dipped them, devoured them. The music went on and on.

Suddenly, Maddie pulled me in for the longest of long kisses. Just when I felt she'd taken my breath away, she broke the kiss. Before I could recover, Becca latched onto me, deep and soulful, and oh, those lips. I thought I could take no more, but I did when it was Jen's turn—and with pleasure. She held me to her by a handful of my hair. The way her tongue worked around my mouth was dizzying.

Despite my lack of oxygen, at that moment, I wished I had two more mouths and about eight more hands. We were spinning around and around, and so was Jen's tongue. Then the music stopped, and the room broke out in applause. Evidently, we'd made quite a scene, and a circle of onlookers had formed around us to watch our antics. I was embarrassed, but made a slight bow for the audience, which I held as I walked off the floor. I wasn't looking for a curtain call. The reason for my hunched-over posture was that dancing with these three beauties had given me a raging erection.

Their hair was now disheveled, their clothing was askew, and they had some deliciously indelicate signs of perspiration on their dresses. Vampires don't sweat much by human standards, but we'd really worked it on the dance floor and had earned our perspiration. They looked wild, tousled, and even sexier.

I bought a round of drinks—more like four, as these girls could sure knock them back—and made to take my leave of them. They protested.

"Ladies, the night is far from over," I said. "As a matter of fact, I've decided to have a little party tonight in my suite at the Monteleone. I would be devastated if you didn't come."

Jen asked, "What time?"

"Three," I replied.

They all smiled.

Becca said, "Oh, we'll be there, all right."

I bade them farewell and returned to Jean-Luc.

He greeted me by saying, "The man-whore strikes again. Did you lose your erection yet?"

"Not quite, but you're just jealous. Hey, could you do me a favor? I'm throwing a party tonight in my suite. Will you make some invitations for me?"

"Of course, and I'll supply the—"

I cut him off. "It's my party. I'll take care of it."

He was disappointed, but he didn't protest. As he walked me to the door, we ran into Jake once more.

I said, "Jake, I'm having a little party tonight at the Monteleone. Are you free?"

The kid nearly fell over and managed to stammer out,

"Are you kidding, Mr. Beauparlant?"

"No, I'm not, and it's Christian."

"Thanks so much, dude... I mean, Christian. I'll be there."

"Great, and by the way, we were never properly introduced. I don't know your surname."

He looked at the floor and mumbled, "I'd rather not say."

From behind me, Jean-Luc cheerfully said, "Lipschitz!"

My mouth moved by itself. "You've got to be fucking me."

With his head still down, he mumbled again, "No, but I wish I were."

Jean-Luc tittered from behind me, but Jake's head snapped up. He looked pale and horrified at his faux pas. If I were another kind of ancient, one who took his age and status more seriously, this could have been interpreted as an insult punishable by death.

Jake would have no way of knowing that I wasn't that type. When I burst out laughing, his expression went from terror to relief in one second flat.

"I'm so sorry dude ... Mr. Beau ... I mean, Christian. I didn't mean to—"

I quieted him with a wave of my hand, finishing my laugh. "That was rich. You're a card, Jake. I'll see you in a few hours. We are going to have to do something about that name. Deal?"

"Deal. But I'm kind of fond of Jake," he said with a smile and then faded back into the crowd.

Another joke by Master Jake, and this time, I think he meant it.

Jean-Luc looked at me disapprovingly. "Now why on earth did you do that?"

"An act of pure vampire kindness. Besides, he's not so

bad."

"He is a twitchy buffoon who fails at everything he tries to do."

"Maybe he hasn't found the right thing to do yet. And from what you've told me, you weren't the smoothest when you were first turned."

"Maybe so, but I was not an imbecile, either," Jean-Luc shot back. "He's going on twenty years now. Nothing has changed, even though many have tried to help him."

"Well, Monsieur Leclerc, I'll pick up the torch and give it a whirl."

That brought a questioning look from him. "May I ask why?"

"Don't know. I feel bad for him. He's lost and alone, even though there are plenty of vampires around. I was out there alone, really alone, for the first fifty years. It sucks."

Jean-Luc snorted. "I think you're getting soft."

"Probably. Weak moment and all that, but what the hell."

CHAPTER 17

Bloody Bill waited patiently outside the holding cell. He could hear some gentle crying and soft conversation, but not much more. He was deep beneath the farm in the Bunker, a complex of over a dozen subterranean rooms that served as the operations center of their entire Network. Helen had come up with the concept for it, and Bill had overseen the construction back in the late '80s. It was where they did most of their computer investigations and research. It also could serve as a last-ditch safe haven, should the need ever arise. Now, however, it served one of its other purposes: as a prison cell for a "guest" of the Harrisons.

The door opened briefly, and for a moment, the sound of whimpering was much louder.

"Any luck, Reverend?" Bill asked.

"No, Bill," Gary Jarvis answered. "I fear her soul is lost forever."

Bill smirked. "I couldn't care less about her soul, Gary. We both know anyone who goes into that room always leaves the same way. It's information I want. She's got nothing? I know New Orleans is teeming with vampires. Shreveport is practically the next town over, for cripes' sake. She doesn't know anything?"

"I'm afraid not. Seems her master hardly ever left town. Didn't allow his humans to travel, either. I believe her."

During Bill's interrogations, he'd often used Jarvis as an aide. He didn't like the man much, but even he had to admit that the reverend had talents. One of them was playing "the good cop" following Bill's harsher techniques. But in reality, when it came to himself and Jarvis, the routine was more like "bad cop, very bad cop."

To Bill, Jarvis seemed as slick as goose shit, but people under extreme duress never noticed. He'd trot out his religious hoopla and promise to save their souls. That, along with his inherent smoothness, often got the detainees to give up significant information.

"Yep, I think you're right," Bill said. "She doesn't know anything."

Bill went to enter the cell.

"Bill, how's Helen doing?" Jarvis asked.

That caught Bill's attention, but he replied nonchalantly, "She's fine. Why do you ask?"

The nonchalant charade continued. "Oh, no reason. It's just that I haven't seen too much of her lately. The last time I did, she looked a bit under the weather, that's all."

Shit, Bill thought. They'd wanted to keep Helen's illness secret until the end. This was Jarvis' subtle way of telling him that he suspected it. He probably expected to be elevated in the command structure once Helen was gone, given his significant influence on God knew how many of their agents. "Helen's fine, Gary. But I'll tell her you were asking after her."

"Would you tell her that I'm praying for her, as well?"

"I will, but if you don't mind now, I'm going to make one more pass at our guest."

"But I thought you said you didn't think she knew

anything. Why not, you know, end it?"

"Just being thorough, that's all. You know how you ministered over that beautiful ceremony for Joel? Think of what I'm doing as my way of honoring his memory, too. Besides, the little bitch deserves it. People get what they deserve, Gary."

This last part he said while staring frostily into Jarvis' eyes. To his credit, the reverend did not flinch and even smiled a bit. Bill knew he got the message. Jarvis was a smart one.

"I'll pray for you, too, Bill," Jarvis replied and then turned on his heel. His sterile-sounding footsteps echoed from the cold, steel floor as he headed for the stairwell.

Bill entered the cell, and the screaming started immediately. He waited patiently until it petered out to a harsh panting. He leaned forward and stripped off the sheet covering the girl. She screamed again. Jarvis always covered them with a sheet when he spoke to them. Bill thought it was a nice touch.

The girl was naked and strapped to a table, conjuring images of Frankenstein's monster. But this was no monster. This was a petite twenty-year-old girl who, if truth be known, reminded Bill of his youngest daughter. But that thought would gain no purchase in Bill's hardened consciousness; he was in business mode. This was an animal and a helper to the vampire who'd killed Joel, and she'd almost done the same for Steve Conti and Bill's Molly. There would be no mercy, and she would suffer greatly.

Her body showed the ravages of Bill's tender mercies. Her face was beaten and swollen, and her arms, legs, and torso had multiple bruises, burns, and lacerations. Her fingertips were caked with blood where the nails had been ripped from them. She was whimpering again.

Bill said, "The reverend informs me you have nothing more to tell us, and that your soul is lost. If that's true, it's too bad, really. If you would tell me something I could use, all this would stop."

Through her whimpering, she started crying, "No," over and over again.

Bill ignored it. "You know, I've come up with something new that I'd like to run by you. But first, maybe I should give you a frame of reference."

He picked up a pair of pliers from a nearby table and approached his victim. She screamed again, and he cuffed her a solid backhand, temporarily silencing her.

"Be quiet. You're giving me a headache." He looked over her ruined fingers and added, "Pretty slim pickings here. Let's change it up some."

He moved to the bottom of the stretcher, grabbed her big toenail with his pliers, and with a quick twist, tore it from her foot. She screeched in agony. By the time she stopped screaming, Bill had already finished tinkering with the next act of his brutal play.

As he approached her, she panted out, "Please, please stop! I don't know anything!"

"That's a shame," he said, "because this next part is going to make that toenail feel like a walk in the park."

He hooked a small clip to each of her nipples. Wires ran from them to a car battery. Her eyes widened, but before she could say anything, he flipped a switch. Bill had thought her quite the screamer before, but the sound that ripped from her throat now made that seem like whispering in comparison. As the electricity surged through her, she bucked and writhed on the stretcher, screeching loud enough to burst her vocal cords.

Bill watched her agonized convulsions, smiling as he did.

It was one of the few genuine smiles in his repertoire.

He cut the electricity, and she flopped back to the stretcher, moaning and soaked with sweat. The smell of her burnt flesh began to fill the room. Bill didn't mind one bit.

"You know, I wasn't kidding," he said. "You really *are* giving me a headache." Bill fished around on the table and finally found what he wanted. "Here they are. My earplugs." He turned to face her again.

"Please, no more," she pleaded. "Please, stop. Please?"

His smile faded, and his eyes turned into merciless flints. "You should have thought of that *before* you started running around with that fucking vampire."

He flipped the switch.

CHAPTER 18

I left the Absinthe House and blended into the night. I needed blood, but that wasn't quite correct. The truth was, I *wanted* blood, and there's a big difference. For the first time in years, I wanted to hunt—not to fulfill a need, but for the pure joy of it. Not going nuts like on the Vineyard, or for revenge like with Leland, but for the act itself. I'd suppressed a lot over the past few decades, and if I was going to come back to my world and get over my fragile psychological state, I needed to do this right.

As I started walking north, I made a frantic call to the Monteleone's night manager. I explained my problem of throwing a 3:00 a.m. party with not one bit of planning. I ordered as much food and liquor as he could get his hands on, and despite my nervousness at the lateness of the hour, the manager assured me all would be well. I hung up, relieved, and focused on the hunt.

When I was on my home turf, I needed to be careful about the possibility of being identified. There would be no such limitations in New Orleans. I still had no idea if I would kill or not. But I didn't fixate on it and resolved to let matters sort themselves out on their own. At times like these, thinking was way overrated.

There was no lack of sketchy areas in the city, but the

sure thing was across N. Rampart, around Louis Armstrong Park. It was a large green space just north of the Quarter, which had become a haven for criminals over the years. As I walked deeper and deeper into the trees, I was feeling a lot less human—and a lot more vampire.

I saw them, sooner than they did me, although I'm sure they thought it was exactly the opposite. There were three of them, a black, a Hispanic, and a Caucasian. I'm all for racial equality in felons. When I stopped, they casually advanced and surrounded me.

Hispanic spoke up. "Hand over the wallet, right now."
I smiled. "What if I don't?"
They pulled their knives in unison.
The black man said, "Then we're going to fuck you!"
My smile grew. "But you guys aren't my type. Besides, I'm really not in the mood."

Caucasian clearly wasn't used to any backtalk from his victims. He appeared shocked by my witty repartee, but then recovered and shouted, "You're fucking dead, asshole!"

He tried to stick me in the chest, but I easily caught his wrist, and with a quick twist, snapped his forearm. He howled and fell to the ground, clutching his newly right-angled limb.

Hispanic waded in low on my right, trying to gut me. I spun too fast for him and struck him in the temple with a backhand karate chop, crushing his skull. He dropped like a stone, dead before he hit the ground. I was going to say that I hit him harder than I meant to, but that's not true. I hit him exactly the way I meant to.

The black fellow managed to get in behind me and jam his knife into the right side of my back. It was a well-placed strike and would have been deadly for a human. For me, it was somewhat painful, but mostly annoying, as I had on one of my favorite sports coats, and this fuck put a hole in it. Between Boston and here, I was losing way too much of my wardrobe. With his left forearm locked around my neck, he twisted the knife back and forth, surely expecting me to slide dying to the ground.

I reached behind me and put my hand over his knife hand, forcing him to pull the knife out despite his grunts and struggles. I slowly turned around, still holding his hand so he couldn't escape. I looked into his now-panicked eyes and crushed his windpipe with one quick blow to the throat. He went down, gasping for air, but that didn't last too long.

I leisurely strolled up to Mr. Caucasian, who was trying his best to crawl away. I grabbed him by the back of the neck and lifted him to his feet as he spat out nonsensical whimpers and groans, with the occasional "no" thrown in for good measure. I spun him to face me, and he screamed, either from the pain in his arm or from the look in my eyes — I don't know which. He was trying to say something, but I ignored it.

"I guess it's time for that fucking," I said.

There'd be no telepathy or sedative for this asshole. I wasn't feeling the love for him right now. As a matter of fact, I wasn't feeling much of anything. I was in that cold, dark vampire place. I thought I'd been there for Leland, but I wasn't even close. I'd either forgotten how it felt, or I was kidding myself. But now, this was the real deal.

I bit into his neck and he screamed, this time meaning it. Not that phony, "my broken arm hurts," or "you scare me" kind of scream, but the "I'm going to die" kind of scream. And he was quite correct.

I drank and drank, he screamed and screamed, and it didn't bother me in the least. It was the way it should be, the way it had to be for a vampire to survive. His blood hit me like a nuclear Red Bull. I felt more alive than I had in years. After a few minutes, he quieted, slipping into shock and going unconscious. I stopped drinking before he was dead, as I was damn sure not going to screw up and turn this jerk into a vampire.

I snapped his neck, twisted his head around three or four times, and ripped it from his body. As I told you, I favor decapitation as a preventative for unexpected turnings. It's completely effective, and I liken it to condom use in humans. Just as the condom prevents unwanted human births, decapitation prevents unwanted vampire "births," albeit in a somewhat more grotesque fashion.

I took his scrofulous head and heaved it deep into the woods. I used one of their shirts to clean my hands and face of the telltale blood. But more importantly, I noted that my black sports jacket was hopelessly ruined.

I looked around at the carnage: three dead gang-bangers, one headless. The cops could have a party figuring out this one, as far as I was concerned. *Fuck them.* I hated cops, anyway. They'd keep it out of the papers, if they could, not wanting bad publicity for the city.

I stood there for a moment, waiting for the guilt to come, but it didn't. I'd acted as my true nature instructed, and I didn't feel one bit bad about it. As a matter of fact, I felt pretty damn good, so maybe I was making some progress. If so, I was hopeful that I could save some cash and avoid having to see a vampire shrink. The idea of having that appointment like every Thursday at 4 p.m. . . . well, for eternity, was daunting.

I admit, this mini-massacre was a bit of an overreaction, and leaving three dead bodies around in a city teeming with vampires wasn't kosher, but since I was a visiting dignitary, it would be okay. For the last twenty years and longer, I'd been repressed or depressed. Now I was coming out of it—at least, I hoped so. I mean, all those self-help gurus on TV always say keeping your feelings locked up inside is very bad. Looking at the three corpses strewn about me, I'd have to say I had most definitely let my feelings out. I think Dr. Phil, and maybe even Oprah herself, would have to approve. I smiled, basking in their presumed support.

I had one more stop to make, with only an hour left before my party. I headed south at a brisk pace toward the Mississippi River.

~~~

Café du Monde, nestled close to the Mississippi and right across from Jackson Square, is one of my favorite cafés. It's a two-trick pony, serving only coffee with chicory and their world-famous beignets. The beignets are simply square pieces of fried dough that are liberally doused with powdered sugar.

You may ask how beignets are different from doughnuts or other types of fried dough, and the answer is, I don't know. But they're heavenly—warm, soft, and delicious—and they melt in your mouth. I've had beignets at other shops in New Orleans, but for some reason, they're not the same. I don't know if it's a secret recipe or the atmosphere, but I do know that every time I eat a beignet somewhere else, I feel like I'm cheating on Café du Monde.

The atmosphere there is pure New Orleans, with high turnover, big crowds, and great people watching. There always seems to be a breeze from the Mississippi, and the powdered sugar gets airborne and lands all over everything and everyone. It's part of the allure of the place.

For vampires, the thing about beignets is that they go particularly well with blood. I know it sounds kind of gross, but it's true. It's the dichotomous flavors—the sharp, crisp, sudden, metallic taste of the blood, and soft, slow, sweet, sleepy taste of the beignets. For humans, it might be like chasing a bite of chocolate chip cookie with a cold beer, or perhaps a fine piece of dark chocolate with champagne.

Going there directly after hunting is a special vampire tradition in New Orleans. I scarfed down two orders of beignets, and as usual, they made the perfect counterpoint to the blood I'd drunk. I took my last bite, savoring it and washing it down with a final sip of coffee. It was ecstasy. I closed my eyes, enjoying the flavors, the moment, the warm breeze, and being back in game. Then I remembered what Du Monde had lulled me into forgetting.

My party! Oh shit!

It was a quarter to three, only fifteen minutes until the party was to begin. I dropped some cash on the table and broke into a vampire-speed run right through Jackson Square, leaping over the fence at the end of it like a high-hurdler. Even with a fair crowd still there, I didn't care who saw me. Around the square at 3:00 a.m., most potential witnesses to my mad dash would be too high or too drunk to be taken seriously.

I buzzed up Pere Antoine Alley, next to St. Louis Cathedral. That alley had always been a great place to hunt through the years. Being right next to the cathedral added just the right touch of religious irony as I brought my victim down.

I turned onto Royal and slowed down. There were too many people around who had a somewhat better chance of having their wits about them than their Jackson Square cohorts. I headed up to my suite in a panic. I hoped I'd still be okay since vampires, like their human counterparts, love to be stylishly late.

Jake sat on the floor outside my door, unstylishly early.

Frazzled as I was, it was great to see anyone who might help. He opened his mouth, but I spoke first. "Good to see you, Jake. I'm running a bit late, and I need a hand."

"You've got it, chief. What can I do?"

Chief, I thought. I liked that. It was a term I used. Maybe I could get to like this kid, fuck-up or not. "First, let's go in and see what room service did."

A lot, as it were. The curtains were open, giving a magnificent night view of the Mississippi and the French Quarter. A bar was set up with the usual poisons, and a cold buffet stood ready to go. The burners for the hot food were there, too. All in all, things appeared okay, especially on such short notice.

"Jake, my boy, I think we're looking good. I'm going to grab a quick shower and change. Get yourself a drink, call the front desk, and have them send up the hot food. Greet anybody who arrives while I'm in the bathroom. Okay?"

He looked like he was about to choke on this little bit of responsibility, but to his credit, he didn't. My status as an ancient can unnerve even the most confident of vampires, so I could only imagine the havoc it was wreaking on Jake. He mustered up as much false poise as he could. "I'll take care of it."

Everyone thought he was an idiot, and maybe he was. But another possibility, maybe not so plausible, was that everyone was wrong. Maybe a little confidence was what he needed.

I stripped down in the bathroom and took another forlorn look at my ruined, pig-stuck jacket. I jumped into a quick shower, which for me, even with paired down primping, was still thirty minutes. I emerged from my bedroom and was disconcerted to find about a dozen people in the room. Jake had done a more than credible job of stand-in host.

There was some nice jazz playing from an iPod, and the hot buffet had appeared. People were eating, and everyone had a drink. I was impressed. I approached Jake, who was at the bar serving drinks to some new arrivals. He saw me coming and handed me an ice-cold glass of champagne.

"I thought you were supposed to be some kind of a fuck-up?" I said.

He shrugged. "I am mostly, but not so much tonight. Maybe you're my good luck charm."

"Maybe so. Thanks for holding the fort."

"Least I could do. I really don't rate this kind of invite."

"You ought to start believing that you do."

Before he could respond, Jean-Luc entered, and I headed toward him. Turning back to Jake, I said, "You're off the clock. Mingle. Have fun."

He saluted me with a raised glass. But when I guided Jean-Luc back to the bar, I was bemused to see Jake still playing sous-host, despite my admonishment. He already had a drink ready for Jean-Luc and another for me.

Then, out of the corner of my eye, I noticed that my three dance partners had arrived. I said absently, "Why don't you guys get something to eat? I've got to do the host thing."

As I walked away, I heard Jean-Luc say, "Host, my ass."

He and Jake were still laughing as I greeted Maddie, Becca, and Jen. "Ladies, I'm so glad you could come."

"We wouldn't miss it, Titus," said Jen.

These girls had done their homework. I hardly gave out my real name to anyone. With a decent amount of legwork or computer savvy, any vamp could track it down—but even so, they'd come up with it pretty damn fast.

"You don't mind, do you?" said Maddie. "It's just that

you seem so much more a Titus than a Christian or a Julian, or even a Texas Jack—although we really liked that one."

I smiled. "I liked it, too. But I seem like more of a Titus because I *am*. I don't mind at all."

My eyes noticed a little spot at the corner of Becca's delectable lower lip. I reached out with my index finger and touched it. *As I thought—blood.* I loved these three; they were a healthy dose of wild energy, mixed with equal parts boldness and recklessness. It was a recipe for disaster, but a thing of beauty at the same time.

I put my fingertip in my mouth, sampling the intense, zingy taste. Even a tiny drop hit me like a shot of caffeine. I closed my eyes, sorting out the flavors, and ruminated, "About twenty-five years old, male...Hispanic and German extraction, I think."

Becca's mouth fell open. "You can't know that!"

The thing was, I could—and I did. A vampire's sense of taste is exquisite, and like everything else with vampires, it gets better with age.

"At twenty-one hundred years old, I have many talents," I quipped, "some of which I hope to demonstrate later."

They smiled together. I was beginning to think that they did everything as a three-woman unit. The mathematical possibilities were staggering.

"We'll hold you to that, Titus," said Jen.

Maddie added, "We'll hold you to a lot of things."

"For now, why don't you grab some drinks and get something to eat," I said. "My self-appointed co-host will take care of you."

They glanced at the bar, where Jake was still mixing and serving. The boy seemed to have recognized an opportunity with me, and for better or worse, was going to run with it. That's a mark of someone who has a chance at being a success—recognizing opportunity and acting on it. I don't mind people who act and fail, but the real fuck-ups in life are the ones who have a huge break sitting right under their noses and are too dense or lazy to notice it.

Jen said, "We always liked Jake. He's a bit goofy, but nice."

Becca raised an eyebrow. "Kind of cute, too."

"Maybe you can teach him a few things, Titus," Maddie said. "Help him out."

"Maybe I will," I said. "Maybe I can teach you three a few things, too."

Again came that trio of perfect smiles. They headed toward the bar. I stood there for a moment, admiring the view, then waded back into the party, greeting and chatting. It was turning out to be a great get-together. It felt so nice to be around my own kind, with no pretenses.

Despite the festivities, I started to feel a bit guilty about the mess I'd left in Louis Armstrong Park. After all, I was a visitor, and this was Jean-Luc's city. My actions, although immensely enjoyable, were somewhat boorish. I approached Jean-Luc. "You have a cleanup crew on tonight, right?"

The sort of chaos I'd left in the wake of my hunt happened on occasion, making cleanup crews necessary—especially in larger cities. There was an on-call team to take care of such things. It was shitty work, but it paid well.

"You know I do. Why?"

Shamefaced, I told him what had happened, giving him the approximate locations of the three corpses and the one head. He didn't respond right away, and I thought I'd be chastised, but instead, he beamed at me like a proud father.

"It's good to have you back, my friend. You and your decapitations . . . It's so old school, but charming all the same. I will take care of it."

He took out his cell, had a brief conversation, and gave me a thumbs-up. I felt instantly better. As for the three I'd dispatched in the park, fuck them. I'd done the world a favor.

The party went on, and before I knew it, dawn was approaching. Some of the younger, sun-sensitive vamps made their apologies and left. The others soon followed suit and left me with a stream of well wishes and thanks. I was genuinely liked here among my own kind. I enjoyed belonging again.

I shut the shades and rolled a food cart into the hall. There, sitting on the floor once again, was Jake. He looked up sheepishly. "I kind of lost track of time. The next thing I knew, the sun was coming up."

"And your big plan was to sit in the hallway until sunset?"

He shrugged. "I didn't want to bug you."

I picked him up by one arm. "C'mon, you're sleeping in my guest room."

He started to protest.

"Jake, please shut up," I said, taking him to his room. "You're welcome to stay as long as you want."

As I approached the master bedroom, I heard a faint sound coming from it. It was subtle, something that only a vampire would pick up, but it was definite. I snapped into high alert mode. Could someone have infiltrated my party? No way. But after what had happened to Mary, Katie, and Kolinsky—maybe way.

I considered my options as I waited, listening, as still as death. There it was again, very soft. This was infuriating; the bastards had come into my suite while I was entertaining. Options flew out the window as I went with the no-plan plan: I'd burst in and kill everyone in the room.

I threw the door open.

Becca, dressed in black lingerie, squeaked and dropped a bottle of champagne. "You scared me, Titus. Shit, you're a quiet one. We thought you were in the parlor."

Maddie and Jen, similarly clad, were sitting on my bed.

"You okay in there?" Jake's voice called out from the other room. Filtered through my lust, it sounded about a thousand miles away.

I responded, "A-Okay."

The night had been wonderful, but this morning looked to be a whole lot better.

CHAPTER 19

I got up and ordered some room service. Jake got up shortly after; I could hear him in the shower. Once the sun had set, the girls joined me in the parlor, and we chatted over our meal.

They'd been good friends in Philadelphia, where they graduated from Penn together. Maddie's double major had been anthropology and history. At some point, she'd become interested in vampire lore, maybe even obsessed with it, and was able to track down some evidence of vampirism in Philly. Although the other two were skeptical, they went along for the ride and discovered that we do, indeed, exist.

They carefully worked their way into the culture, becoming VAs while avoiding becoming vampire food. Although no easy trick, being long in both the brains and looks department surely didn't hurt their chances. They ingratiated themselves with a prominent vampire by the name of Thomas Carson. They proposed being turned as a threesome. Likely thinking with his genitals, he agreed and did the deed. This wasn't a sure thing for the girls, and in fact, the odds were that one of the three wouldn't survive.

The process starts with draining the potential turnee to

death. As the human body croaks, so does its immune system, and then the HVSV runs rampant, doing its stuff. If things work out, reanimation usually occurs within six to twelve hours. For some, it's a bit quicker. For others, it's slower, but if there are no results by the twenty-four-hour mark, it's over. The thing is, the process is totally unpredictable. You can be young and healthy and not make it back, or you can be decrepit and wracked with cancer and come steaming back with flying colors. There's no way to tell.

Needless to say, they all survived and got some basic instructions as to how to live the vampire life. Afterward, they ditched Carson, left Philly, and resettled in New Orleans. Talk about getting taken for a ride. I'm sure old Tommy-boy reasoned he'd have a trio of eternally grateful concubines at his disposal for quite some time. But that's what dick-thinking will do for you. It may have been a tad harsh, but I can't really blame the girls. Turning someone doesn't mean you own them, and besides, Carson is a total tool.

I discovered that they'd been on the ball since being turned, having invested in a small clothing design business. They were getting by money-wise, initially obtaining their capital from thievery of all sorts. Almost all vampires go this route at first, since we have the natural skills to be excellent thieves. After a time, they discovered they needed more stable income. Relying on acts of felony for your funding can get dangerous . . . fast.

Being baby vamps, they required a lot of blood every night. I asked them about their feeding and whether they usually killed their victims or not.

Jen answered for all of them. "We almost always kill. It can be a bitch to cover sometimes, but it's probably easier here than a lot of places."

"That's true," I said. "This is one of the easier places. New York, Las Vegas, Paris, Rome... even your beloved Philadelphia are all pretty good, too."

Maddie spoke up. "Truth is, we like the killing."

I knew how they felt. "Just be careful that they're good and dead. Accidental turnings can be a bitch to deal with."

Throughout history, vampire population has always mirrored human population in size, but our numbers stay lower out of necessity, due to the amount of destruction we cause. As the human population exploded in the twentieth century, ours didn't, and in fact, we had to control it even more carefully, since the age of social security numbers, photo identification, and computers was upon us. It became much more difficult to murder anonymously and get away with it.

By the mid-1950s, the entire vampire race, for the most part, had bought into carefully monitored turnings and a diminished population growth curve. It was the wise course of action, but there were some who advocated an all-out war to establish vampires as a ruling class. We've always had such sub-groups throughout our history. But the truth is, we couldn't manage to take over a single major city during the Dark Ages. How were we supposed to take over the world in modern times?

Becca said with a dreamy smile, "Oh, we're very careful. Not a single accidental turning for us."

They looked at each other and giggled like schoolgirls. I was tempted to inquire after their method, but held off. I'd prefer to see it.

"I hope you're not going to judge us for killing, or give us a big daddy lecture," Becca added.

"Quite the opposite," I said. "I encourage you to kill."

That seemed to catch them by surprise.

"Really?" Jen said.

I nodded. "Sure. As a vampire, to deny that you're a killer is to deny yourself, and that can surely fuck you up. Believe me, I know."

Bold as ever, Maddie asked, "You did it for a long time. You denied who you were. Was it really over a dog, or is that some story?"

"No story. It *was* over a dog. Well, he was the straw that broke the camel's back, anyway."

Maddie said, "Must have been one hell of a dog."

"He was. But the point is, you can't deny yourself or your nature, or you'll screw yourself up like I did for the last twenty, maybe even a hundred years. You should fall into the hunting pattern and killing pattern that's right for you as time goes on. You shouldn't force it, one way or the other, or it'll mess with your heads. That's the way not to last, to be a short-timer . . . and I wouldn't like that."

"I . . . uh, *we* wouldn't like that, either," said Jen.

I told them I'd like to help improve their business. They "reallied" me to death, jumped up and down, squealed, hugged, and kissed me in a decidedly non-sexual, thankful kind of a way. Even so, it was a Herculean act of willpower not to let myself get aroused. Although they probably wouldn't have minded, I thought it would have been unseemly to get a woody at such a moment. In my defense, with all the jumping about, a goodly number of breasts popped out of the Monteleone robes they were wearing.

You may think I was agreeing to all of this because, like Carson, I was being led by my dick, and you wouldn't be totally wrong. But you wouldn't be totally right, either, as I had every intention of mentoring Jake. That wasn't sexually motivated, and could clearly be used as Exhibit A in my defense. As for Exhibit B, these girls were smart, gorgeous, and wonderful additions to our community, and they deserved my guidance. *Extenuating circumstances at best, Mr. Beauparlant,* my inner circuit court judge informed me. *You are guilty as charged of Dick-Thinking in the Second Degree.*

Future business plans aside, it was going to be first-things-first and sticking with basics. I wanted to hunt with them and see if I could give them any pointers on how to satisfy our most primal need. If a vampire couldn't do that well, or at least passably, he or she was totally screwed.

We agreed to meet at 11:00 p.m. in front of St. Louis Cathedral. They got into what little was left of their underwear and dresses. Anyone else wearing those tattered remnants would have looked silly, but they looked sublime. As they were leaving, Jake emerged from the guest room, looking squeaky clean. Considering the time I'd first heard him in the bathroom, I concluded he must have been a fellow long-shower-taker.

I said, "Sit down. I got you some food."

We chatted as he ate. He'd been twenty and a student at Tulane when he was turned in 1992, and it truly was a comedy of errors. I took it from his narrative that he had been a computer-geek loner without many friends. He was in the French Quarter one night and decided to take a walk along the river before heading back to campus. He was just past Canal Street when he was attacked. He recounted, "He came out of nowhere and clubbed me on the head. I was woozy and still half out of it, and he latched onto my neck. I thought, 'This can't be happening.' But I was getting weaker and weaker, and it was getting hard to stay conscious, hard to even breathe."

I nodded, remembering that same feeling.

He went on. "All of a sudden, he stopped and pulled

back. That was the only time I got a good look at him. Small, Hispanic, with mean, laughing eyes and slicked-back hair. He had a cruel mouth and a crueler smile, and my blood was dripping from his little pimp moustache. I don't think I'll ever forget that."

"No, you probably won't."

"Anyway, right then, I knew I was dead. My life didn't flash before my eyes or anything, and all I could think was, 'Not like this, not without at least some fight.' I felt like a dishrag, but that smug look on his face helped me to find some willpower, and I head-butted him right in the nose. I got him pretty good. I think I may have even broken it. His blood flew, and he screamed."

I smiled. Maybe Jake and I had more in common than long showers.

"Before I could do anything else, he grabbed my head and twisted hard. I more heard the snap than felt it. Really, I didn't feel very much at all. There was a quick flash of light, and that's it.

"The next thing I knew, I was floating downriver somewhere, close to shore. Even though it was shallow and I'm a good swimmer, I was having a lot of trouble making it the last few feet in because of the density thing. I must have swallowed about a gallon of the Mississippi."

"That couldn't have been too tasty."

"Saying it tasted like shit would be an insult to shit. Anyway, I touched my neck and moved it all around, making sure I was okay. I realized I actually felt pretty good, maybe better than ever. I decided to go to the cops.

"Already I was in denial, fooling myself, thinking I must have remembered things wrong—you know, the bite, the broken neck. I'd been hit on the head and wasn't recalling things right, that's all. The little spic mugged me and threw me in the river. I didn't even realize it was—"

I finished for him. "The next night."

"Yeah, right. That totally had me screwed up. Imagine trying to make a report at the police station, thinking it was the wrong day. The cops already thought I was just another drunk, full-of-shit kid, and that didn't help."

"You were quite lucky, you know. If you'd turned more quickly, you would have fried in the sun, and we wouldn't be having this lovely conversation."

My comment reminded him of his near-miss. He still looked nervous about it, even though it had happened twenty years ago. "I know, right? Well, anyway, I went back to the dorm and crashed. Luckily, my roommate, who I hated, was out of town. He was Korean and probably even more antisocial than I was. I slept until two o'clock and woke up feeling like crap. Way off, you know? Real thirsty.

"I was lucky my roommate put in blackout shades. He kept a totally weird night schedule, and the room wasn't that sunny to start with, anyway. But when I opened the shades, I felt like I'd been lit on fire. I fell back on the bed, out of the light, thank God, and saw that my arms were blistering and red. I ran to the bathroom to look in the mirror, and my face and upper chest were in the same shape. It hurt like hell.

"I was totally panicked and splashed water on myself, crying and carrying on the whole time. Then I noticed the pain was better. I looked in the mirror again, and my skin now had no blisters and was a dark pink. I watched, and it was like time lapse. Another two minutes, and I'm back to normal. I'm like, 'Whoa, dude!' I took a good look at myself.

"It was like I filled out some, you know? Muscles a bit more defined, and I actually had the semblance of a six-pack, when it used to be a two-pack, at best. I mean, I had been in pretty good shape, but not like this. And then it all hit me. The bite, the sunburn, the healing, the new-and-improved body. I was a vampire! Like, no way!"

I was letting him ramble. I knew the telling of his tale was as therapeutic for him as it had been for me.

"Again, you were lucky," I said. "At least you had enough info to make that leap, as incredible as it was. Remind me to tell you my turning story someday. It's remarkably similar. I was left for dead, too."

He looked shocked. "You, Christian Beauparlant, were supposed to be a meal?"

"Yep. And when I came to, I had no concept of what had happened to me. The information simply wasn't there. I thought I'd caught a disease or an evil spirit from the attack."

Jake nodded. "Yeah. Me, too. I still couldn't totally believe the vampire thing, so I was thinking that the little pimp spic had given me some disease or something. You know what I mean?"

"Yes, I do. I basically stumbled about for nearly fifty years before I was educated. You, at least, had something to go on. You can thank Dracula and Stoker for that."

He looked at me disbelievingly. "Come on. That stuff isn't true. Stoker made most of it up."

"No, some of it *is* true. But go on, I'll tell you about it sometime."

"Okay... so, anyway, I had to do a test. Back to the window, only my hand this time, and *bang*—microwave city. But now I wasn't panicking and calmly watched it. It was truly amazing. My skin had almost blackened, but it healed in less than five minutes."

Five minutes was brief for a new vamp, I thought. Jake might have been more powerful than he knew. "You sure about that? Less than five minutes?"

"Yeah, dude, I timed it. Science minor. Anyway, I spent the rest of the day locked in my room. I drank all the water I had and ate every scrap of food in the place. Having no friends came in handy for once, since nobody visited. I waited for sunset. I was beginning to feel shitty, but if the police wouldn't help me, I was going back to the Quarter and find that little pimp myself.

"And even though I felt crummy, I kind of felt strong at the same time and decided to walk it. I must have got going at a good clip, because the folks I passed gave me some very odd looks. I got to Bourbon Street in record time and started sifting around and wandering through the crowd. Incredibly, I almost walked right into him. He took off, and man, was he fast. I nearly caught him, but he lost me in the crowd."

"Not to jump ahead, but who was he? How old?"

"A guy by the name of Juan Abeyta, Puerto Rican. At the time, he'd been a vampire about one hundred and ten years."

"I don't know him, but not bad. A baby vampire nearly chasing down a centenarian? Go on."

"Now I was starting to feel terrible. I bought a gallon of water and drank every last drop. I got two po' boys and inhaled them. Right after, I felt like I was going to puke, but the po' boys stayed down, barely. I thought, that's it. I'm going to the hospital. As I was approaching the ER entrance, two guys and a girl, all vampires, grabbed me and forced me into a car.

"I ended up in the back room of the Absinthe House, where I met Jean-Luc. He explained what had happened, and gave me some basic pointers for my new life. I still couldn't believe him, you know? So he pulled out a pistol and put three in my chest, knocking me to the floor.

"That convinced me more than anything that it was all true. I *was* a vampire. Then he brought in Abeyta, I think, to try to pawn some of my education off on him. I went nuts when I saw him, but they held me back."

"I would have tried to get at him, too."

He paused for a moment. "I wouldn't hunt at first. They had to force-feed me blood that somebody had collected. But the truth was, it wasn't all that forced. The second it touched my lips, I knew it tasted better than anything I'd ever had.

"There was no way to avoid the blood, unless I was going to kill myself, and I wasn't going to do that. So I learned to hunt, but I'm not very good at it. Jean-Luc helped me set up a fake suicide so nobody would come looking for me. The cops dragged the river for a few days and that was it—the end of Jacob Lipschitz. I've kicked around here, getting passed from vampire to vampire for training, and not doing too well. After about ten years, they gave up on me."

"Why didn't you leave?"

"I really don't have any place else to go."

"Family?"

He sighed. "Yes. You know I didn't want to fake my suicide, on account of them, but there was no other choice. It was the only thing to do."

Jake went on to talk about his family, and my picture of him became clearer. Born in Ann Arbor, Michigan, he was the youngest of three sons. His father, a huge brute of an ex-high school football star, never made the pros as he thought he would. Dear ol' Dad never even made his college team—but he ended up being a success in business. He got himself a young trophy wife, whose main activities were spending money, fucking the pool boy, and taking pills, but not necessarily in that order.

Jake's two older brothers were chips off the old blockhead—big goons and half-assed athletes. Then cerebral Jake came along, with no interest in athletics, but into academics and computers. The dad was appalled, the brothers followed suit, and the mother was too high to give a shit.

There was one silver lining in this fucked-up family—a surprise baby sister born ten years after Jake. Her name was Elise, and they'd adored each other prior to Jake's "suicide." She was twenty-nine, a writer, and living in San Francisco.

The father had the good sense to have a fatal heart attack about five years ago, and that was no great loss to humanity. The two brothers stayed in Michigan and were in the process of running Daddy's business into the ground. The mother still held court in the big house, frying her brain with drugs, and her crotch with various gardeners, tennis pros, and gigolos.

Jake gave not one shit about any of them, except for Elise. He had a recent picture of her that he'd snarfed off Facebook. She was petite and cute with blue eyes, strawberry-blonde hair, and a small, rounded nose sprinkled with some leftover little-girl freckles.

I looked at Jake, who was about five foot ten with a pointed, aquiline nose, dark hair, and eyes. Between his features and the ten-year age difference, it could lead a person to wonder. I'm guessing Mrs. Lipschitz snuck one in under the wire, and I'm willing to bet that thirty years ago, her mailman was a short redhead.

Jake told me he hadn't seen Elise since he was turned, but I knew he was lying. I don't think he contacted her, but I'm sure he'd seen her, probably so he could be close once in a while. I could see it in his eyes, and more than that, given the circumstances, I would've done the same thing.

So Jake, the fuck-up of the family, a loner and friendless, had become one of us by a huge stroke of luck. Surviving a snapped neck is not unheard of, but rare. He'd have been discriminated against initially, as these mistake turnees usually are. But when vampires start showing themselves to be on the ball and useful, that sort of bias tends to fade fast. Sometimes mistake vampires end up being pillars of the community, and the well-planned turnings end in disaster.

So Jake, continued right along being a fuck-up vampire. I understood. Being a goof was a role he was used to, and maybe even comfortable with. Well, I was going to change that, or at least try.

"So what, you don't think you belong here, is that it?" I asked. "You don't deserve to still be alive?"

He mumbled, "Well, that's pretty much the case, isn't it?"

"Oh, boo-fucking-hoo," I answered sarcastically. "I was in the same boat, and I managed to do all right for the last two millennia."

"But you were a soldier. You knew how to survive, and you had skills."

I raised my voice. "I had nothing! The only thing I had was the ability to hold the line and take a chunk out of you with my sword. *You* have skills and knowledge. You're a computer guy, for Christ's sake. And a good one, if I'm to believe you. How do you not exploit that? Vampires love tech guys."

He didn't answer.

I handed him my card. "Look, it's getting late, and I've got some stuff to do. I'm going to be busy for a few days, but we'll hook up after that. Call me, and we'll start your education."

He gave the card a desultory look, stuffed it in his pocket, then got up and quickly headed for the door. "Yeah, right," he muttered.

He thought I was blowing him off, like everyone else. I moved quickly and silently. To him, it probably looked like I'd magically appeared between him and the door. I had him by his lapels, and he was off the ground with his feet dangling and eyes bugged out.

I said calmly, "Now as you've noticed, I'm pretty informal despite my age and standing in the community. But turning your back on me and pouting your way out the door is not going to do. Do we have an understanding?"

He quickly nodded, and I let him down. He smoothed his jacket, keeping his head down.

"Why did you insult me?" I asked. "Why are you putting me in the same category with everyone else who treated you poorly?"

Jake raised his head, and his eyes were glistening with unshed tears. His voice was full of barely contained emotion. "Why are you doing this?"

I answered honestly, "I'm really not sure. Let's just say because I can, and you need it, and you seem like a good kid."

He paused for a moment, wiping his eyes. "Okay."

"One more thing: this is a two-way street, so I'm giving you a homework assignment. Use your computer and come up with something, one thing, to help me."

He groaned like a schoolboy assigned a surprise ten-page essay. Then he brightened. "You mean it?"

"Yeah, I mean it."

"Okay, I'll do it." He shook my hand and left.

I was feeling quite self-satisfied. I'd had a wonderful three-girl fuckathon, and now, a leg up on my Jake reclamation project. I hit the laptop to catch up on the news of my former life. My accounts in the Boston area had all been shut down and transferred properly. Mary and Katie informed me that all was well. They'd closed their house in the North End and were moving to parts unknown. I was sure they already knew where, but as usual, they were being secretive, cryptic, and safe.

It was time to meet the girls.

CHAPTER 20

On his private line, Bill Harrison had just received the call from the field that he was waiting for. The news was good. He collected Molly and headed to Helen's office. Before they entered, they heard her harsh, rasping cough. In the last week, she'd taken a sudden and marked turn for the worse—she had developed an unrelenting cough, and her weight was down. Bill couldn't help but feel that this signaled the beginning of the end for her. He and Molly hesitated until Helen's coughing fit petered out. She hated to be caught in such a way, showing any sign of weakness.

As Bill made his way to his chair behind her desk, he couldn't help his anger at the sight of a newly lit cigarette dangling from her lips. He wanted to slap it out of her mouth, but what good would it do? That horse was long out of the barn for such antics. As he settled into his chair, Molly sat on the corner of her mother's desk. Just as the easy chair was his spot in this office, the corner of the desk was Molly's.

"Well?" Helen asked.

"Great news, hon," said Bill. "Quebec City went as smooth as silk. We got two of them, and six of their human pets. Not even a scratch on any of ours."

Helen beamed, but had to stifle another cough. Bill glanced at Molly and saw the concern on her face. He knew the same emotion was written all over his. Helen got herself under control. "That's great news. The new information seems as good as gold."

Molly said, "The health insurance angle is the real deal. We had these two completely under surveillance before the team even left for Canada. The program is still new, but I've got it paired with a bunch of your search protocols. It looks like we may have a line on a bunch more."

Helen smiled. "Where?"

"Montreal and New Orleans," Molly replied. "We also had one in Boston, but he disappeared. The son of a bitch was pretending to be a doctor. Can you believe it?"

Helen said, "I believe anything when it comes to them. What about the others? How soon?"

Molly shrugged. "I'm not sure . . . but soon."

Bill interjected, "Before we get into that, don't you think we ought to move on Jarvis? He knows you're sick, Helen. He practically told me so. He's going to do something. I don't get why you want to sit back and let it happen."

"You've always been impatient, Bill. I'm not sitting back. Time's not right, that's all. Trust me on this—I know what I'm doing."

Bill scratched at his beard stubble. "Okay, if you say so. What are we going to do if Montreal and New Orleans check out at the same time?"

Helen shrugged. "We'll put two teams in the field, of course."

Bill knew Helen understood that putting even a single team into the field was a huge risk, no matter how good their information was. Putting out two teams pushed that risk up exponentially. Any breech in their protocols might reveal the location of the farm and their center of operations, and bring down the entire Network. Helen must have believed that it wasn't merely the beginning of the end for her. To throw caution to the wind like this, she had to feel that she was further down the road than that. Bill felt his throat tighten with emotion.

Molly said, "But, Mom, the logistics of putting two teams out aside, isn't it too dangerous? We've never done it before."

"First time for everything. And Bill, when you put the teams together, you and Molly don't go. Neither does Shannon or Cathy."

Bill thought, *Two teams going out and not a single Harrison among them.* He was taken aback. "Now hold on a darn minute, Helen. If we—"

Helen said calmly, "I know I'm dying, Bill. But am I still in charge or not?"

Bill winced at the thought of her gone. "You're still in charge."

"Good. Then please do what I say. And Bill, make sure both teams are loaded with Jarvis's men."

CHAPTER 21

I turned down Royal and saw the girls waiting for me in front of the cathedral. I loved punctuality, and my gods, did they look good. Jeans were the uniform of the evening, evidently, and their three pairs couldn't be much tighter. Their hair was pulled back and ready for action, and they wore form-fitting blouses—and my, did those forms fit. I was greeted with kisses. *I could get used to this*, I thought.

I pitched my voice low, too low for humans to hear, and was relieved that they followed suit. They were eager to show me their methods: their hunt, how they kill, and their means of body disposal. I was just as eager to see it. We switched back to our normal speaking voices, the ladies' being several hundred decibels louder than mine, as they led me to a side street. We piled into a '69 Impala that was as big as a tuna boat, with Becca as chauffeur. I slid into the back with Maddie and Jen, who immediately got a little touchy-feely. *Too bad it's a short ride*, I thought. *I haven't gotten laid in the back seat of a car in decades.*

Somewhere east of Elysian and a little south of Route 10, we pulled over in one of the many shitty neighborhoods there. I got out with Maddie and Jen, but hung back.

It didn't take long. It was pitch dark and quiet, with

hardly a light on in any of the houses. It was the kind of neighborhood where people are happy to remain ignorant as to what's happening on the street. A foursome of thugs appeared, and they must have thought it was their lucky night. Two little girls would be easy pickings for robbery, assault, and maybe even rape or murder thrown in for good measure.

Two of the muggers were dropped real fast, incapacitated. The girls were good and very efficient. Jen had her victim in the thrall of her telepathy. She was on him in a flash, draining him dry. Maddie's wasn't so lucky, being telepathy resistant. He went down the old-fashioned way: shocked and trying to scream through the iron-like hand that sealed off his mouth. It was over in minutes.

Jen made a call, and Becca rolled up with her lights off. Maddie told me that if there'd been only one or two victims, they'd take the car to a different area and repeat the process. But as it was, there were plenty of dupes to go around, and they offered the last one to me.

Blood was the most profound gift in our culture. It was the gift of life itself. I didn't need it, but to refuse would have been just as profound an insult. This night with them had gotten me so ramped up, I would have accepted their gift even if I'd drunk down twenty gallons. Before I went to it, though, I watched the other two do their cleanup while Becca drank.

They opened the trunk of the car, which was lined with a plastic wrap. The trunk and dome lights had been disabled. They pulled out two huge contractor disposal bags and wiggled into elbow-length rubber gloves, the kind I imagined nuclear power plant technicians might use. To my surprise and pleasure, they rammed their hands into their victims' chests, crunching through the ribs. They fished around for a while and pulled out the hearts, like adorable, psychotic Aztecs. Man, how I loved these girls. Pretty damn effective for preventing unwanted vampire turnings. *Bing-bang*, bodies and hearts all bagged up and in the trunk.

It was my turn to feed. My guy was coming around, but way too late. I chomped down into his neck, and he let out more of a whimper than a scream. I drained him in record time, and it felt so damn good, but probably not to him. I asked to borrow a glove and took off my jacket. Wrecking another jacket was just not acceptable. I tried the girls' "rip out the heart" technique.

The rib crunching was an interesting sensation, and with my medical training, it was easy to locate the heart. I tore it out and crushed it for good measure. Not bad, but it's tough to teach an old dog new tricks. I liked my method better. I put the corpse in a bag and demonstrated my "twisting off the head" method, which they enjoyed. I said, "Things go a lot easier with a sword, but I left mine back at the hotel."

Now all the stiffs were piled in the trunk like cordwood, and we were off.

I asked, "Where to?"

"We have a lot of dumping areas," Becca replied. "Tonight it's going to be a backwater bayou, but none you'd see on any swamp tour, I'd bet."

The girls had obviously chosen the area well. It was deserted and pitch black. We got into a broken-down eighteen-footer and took a quick boat ride through the inky, dark night. The craft was equipped with pre-tied ropes and cinder blocks, which were quickly attached to the bodies. The bags were slit open a bit so the critters could get in for an easy meal, and *splish-splash*, man overboard. Becca was right. This was no bayou trip a tourist would ever see.

Maddie drove back to the Quarter, while I made out in

the back with Jen and Becca. I could taste their victims' blood on their lips. It was absolutely intoxicating. Maddie cracked a bottle of Cuervo, and we passed it back and forth, capping off one hell of a night.

The car parked, we strolled indirectly toward the Absinthe House. Jen asked for my critique. I didn't have much, as these girls would make seasoned Mafia hit men look like wimps. The car was stolen, and the plates were frequently switched. Cars were frequently switched, too, although they really liked the Impala. I told them not to get sentimental over a car. That could lead to being noticed. The girls ticked off over two-dozen isolated dumping grounds. They also maintained changes of clothing and towels in the car, in case things got messy.

I told them their system was good, but not to get too cocky. No system was perfect, and they should always be willing to change it. "Think of each step of the process," I said, "and how you'd respond if something went wrong."

Maddie nodded. "That's good. Hadn't thought of it like that."

I added, "The biggest potential problems I see are the bags and gloves. You use a lot of them, and they're unusual purchases. That makes them traceable. Vary the purchase locations, and don't use credit cards—only cash."

"Shit, we didn't think of that," said Jen.

"No harm, no foul. Unless one of those bags turns up with a stiff in it."

We arrived at the Absinthe House, and I stopped at the door.

Maddie asked, "You're coming in, aren't you?"

"No, not tonight. I'm going to chill for a bit at the hotel. I need a little alone time."

As much as I wanted to hang with them, I was having a

bit of an after-hunt letdown. A lot had happened in the last few days. Truth was, I was still trying to come to grips with my sojourn into phony human life and my return to the vampire world. But I was feeling a whole lot better, and my humanness seemed to be finally wearing thin.

They moved in for a group hug, and Becca said, "We understand, but don't think you're getting away from us so easily."

I smiled. "I have no such intentions. And remember, we still have your business to discuss."

I got kisses from all three as I wrapped my arms around them.

They said in unison, "We love you, Titus."

Hearing it made me melt. I replied, "I love you, too." And I honestly did.

They walked away from me, tossing little goodbye waves over their shoulders. I waved back, smiling and probably looking like a dolt. I shook my head and strolled up to the doorman. "Those three, put everything they ring up on my tab tonight, okay?"

He responded, "Of course, Mr. Beauparlant."

I'm a perfect gentleman . . . from the waist up.

CHAPTER 22

After a wonderful brunch with Simone, I decided to while away some time reading in Jackson Square. A perfect Mississippi breeze tickled the beautifully warm afternoon. Jazz seemed to flow from everywhere, and the street performers, out in force, went through their paces. I took a moment from my book to watch them. Then I gazed up at the statue of Andrew Jackson and reminisced.

I'd known Jackson personally. In fact, I'd fought with him against the Brits in the Battle of New Orleans. Describing him as crazy would probably be kind. He was definitely a lunatic, but a damn smart and effective one.

During the War of 1812, the predominantly French population rallied to the American cause. It was bad enough that their precious New Orleans had been ceded to these Americans. But to have the British claim it as a spoil of war . . . that would have been intolerable. Even the pirate Jean Lafitte, although bribed by the British, fought with Jackson. Jackson and Lafitte despised each other from afar, but once they met, they realized that they were both cut from the same bravado-soaked cloth and became fast friends.

It was shaping up to be a near-idyllic day, until my

phone rang. In my reverie, I answered it without noticing the incoming number. When I heard Lisa's voice, I winced and asked, "What can I do for you?"

"Sorry to bother you, but I needed to talk."

I was feeling more and more vampire every day, but every time I'd had any contact with Lisa or even thought about her, I felt that insidious humanness at the backdoor of my mind, waiting to come back in and stay a while. I was beginning to hate the feeling. "I'm listening."

"I thought you might be at the ER. I never liked calling you on your cell at work, in case you were with a patient."

How fucking considerate, I thought, but I said nothing.

"They told me you don't work there anymore, that you quit the practice," Lisa said. "Is that true?"

I was annoyed by her discovery. "Not that it's any of your business, but yes."

"Where are you?"

"Again, not your business. Now if this Q and A session is over, I'm really quite busy."

"No, it's not over. You want to tell me about these investments you have all over the world? I mean, six million dollars is a lot to forget about."

I was shocked, but at the same time, relieved. The six million figure meant she hadn't found everything, not even close. I'd bet wherever she got the telltale info, it came from the last century. I'd gotten sloppy during my depression, but I had to know for sure. "What are you talking about? What investments? From where?"

She bit, thank goodness, ticking them off. "Oh let's see, an apartment in Istanbul, a farm in Italy, a bar in Canada, some paintings that are on display in Spain right now. Should I go on?"

She didn't have to. They were all relatively recent

purchases—well, relative when you looked at my 2,100 years of existence. Maybe my carelessness represented a subconscious death wish by having info on the grid that a hunter could find. In my defense, when I'd made the purchases, I wasn't expecting to get married and divorced, then have the legal equivalent of a rectal exam looking into every aspect of my life. If Lisa could get this far, I could only imagine what someone like the Genealogist could do with such a slip-up. But I didn't have to imagine—I knew. She'd kill me.

Suddenly, it struck me that this didn't fit Lisa's behavior. I'd offered her a good deal. She wanted out, and speed seemed to be of the essence. Then it hit me. It wasn't Lisa at all. It was Donald Leland. The realization immediately piqued my simmering anger. But I had to be even more careful. "Oh, that stuff. I did all that years ago. I wasn't trying to hide it from you. I really did sort of forget about it. Look, I can have it assessed and I'll split it with you, if that's what you want."

"No, that's not what I want. What I want is to know how some of that stuff has your name on it as a purchaser in the 1920s. I want to know how you bought something in 1948 with your social security number on the transaction, and your date of birth listed as 1910. Last time I checked, Jules, you were born in 1967."

This was far worse than I thought. "Look, Lisa . . . I admit the deals weren't the most aboveboard. I assumed a previous ownership in a lot of cases, and the records were fudged. I saved a boatload on taxes and fees, and the agent I used made a ton."

It was thin—the best I could do on short notice. But I knew that Lisa was no dope.

"That sounds like bull, Jules. You know what I think? I

think you're some kind of international thief or embezzler or something like that. All that traveling, all those people you happen to meet all the time. It kind of makes sense to me."

If she only knew the half of it. For the second time in the conversation, I went from alarm to relief. Given the facts, it wasn't a bad theory—but far less worrisome than if she'd figured out I was a vampire. "No, that's not it at all. It's just what I told you."

"And who is this Christian Beauparlant? His name turns up on a lot of the documents."

My heart sank again. The ups and downs of this little phone call were becoming dizzying. "He's the agent I used. A real nice guy."

"I don't believe you. Since we're divorcing now, I honestly don't care what you're doing. But do you know what makes me sad? The fact that you were running around being sneaky and lying to me, probably the whole time we were married. This stuff is probably only the tip of the iceberg."

Was that ever an understatement! But where did she get off accusing me of lying and sneaking? Granted, it was true—but she was the one who'd had an affair with Leland and was now carrying his child. Well, if I wasn't going to act like a vampire in the matter of my divorce by killing Lisa, it didn't mean I couldn't act as a typical underhanded human. "Speaking of sneaking and lying, you might want to keep a shorter leash on your fiancé. He's running around with some slut in town."

"Oh come on, Jules. Don't you think that's beneath you? You're jumping on the rumor mill bandwagon to hurt me. Donald stopped seeing other women the minute we were engaged."

I knew I'd gotten to her by the exaggerated evenness of

her tone. If nothing else, this tack might distract her long enough until I could get my six-million-dollar mess cleaned up. I said sweetly, "Oh, am I now? What would you say if I told you I saw your Donald and his paramour myself? I think her name is Janet Pierce, and they were groping each other at the China Star on the very night you informed me that he'd knocked you up. I am presuming, of course, that you two lovebirds were engaged by then. Come to think of it, I think you mentioned that this Pierce woman was an old flame of the Donster."

Her silence was music to my ears, and I went on gleefully. "Let me know if you want to split the six mil. I'd be happy to pay that and more, just to be rid of you. I've so enjoyed this little talk, but I've got to run. Ta-ta."

She started to say something, but I hung up and immediately dialed Jake. I told him the scenario and added fixing this "little" problem of mine to his already assigned homework.

"I can probably handle it, but it will take time," he said. "If you knew who did the research on you, it would speed things up. I could focus my back-trace. Any ideas?"

I knew it was Leland, but he wouldn't have done it himself. He had teams of lawyers, any one of which could have looked into me. It finally dawned on me. This would have been an unofficial, dirty investigation. I remembered that old Donny used a private investigator who was rumored to dig up dirt on his business associates. I shared this with Jake.

"You got a name?"

"No, but you can look it up. I guarantee you there aren't too many private investigators listed in Needham, Massachusetts."

Armed with this information, he seemed confident that

he could take care of things. I hoped that he could; otherwise, Lisa would move way up on the I'm Going to Get Killed by My Vampire Soon-to-Be Ex-Husband List. If that had to be, I'd make sure the Donster would go along for the ride, too.

Human Julian wanted to stew, but vampire Titus was having none of that. I was meeting Jean-Luc for dinner, and before that, I was going to take a nice stroll through the Quarter. If this divorce got too complex, I just had to remember that I was a vampire and could make my problems disappear in the most definitive of ways.

CHAPTER 23

My French Quarter wander was about at its midway point when I saw her, Laura, the little girl from the pool. She was walking with her family about fifty yards in front of me, probably heading back to the hotel. Little Laura lollygagged behind the rest, peeking into shop windows and skipping along, the way girls her age do. She fell a touch more behind, right about that distance when a parent would instinctively look back and say, "Come on, honey, catch up."

Laura's parents never got that chance. Right at the moment of maximum separation from their child, he bolted across the street in a blur, scooped her up with one arm, and was gone like smoke. Before she was carried away, I saw her futilely trying to scream through the hand covering her mouth, her bright-blue eyes shocked wide. At that moment, they met mine, and in them I saw the terror she felt. Even though she was only eight, tops, and couldn't likely crystallize the thought, she knew with absolute certainty that she was screwed. She was going to die.

Maybe, but not if I could get to her first.

A vampire had done the scooping; he was too fast to be human. He bolted full-bore, north through the Quarter. Some vampires have a predilection for kids and the taste of their blood. They claim it's sweeter or more energizing or some other fucking thing. It's our version of pedophilia, and a pretty damn creepy one at that.

I took off after him. The father shouted behind me, but he was way too late. This little race was already a block away. The kidnapper cut through alleys, darted between buildings, jumped fences—everything he could do to elude me. He twisted and turned, but he wasn't losing me. Because of that, he had to know it was a vampire chasing him. I hoped he wouldn't kill her and dump her as he ran. I finally caught up to him in a back alley.

He'd stopped to wait for me, his back to the wall of a deserted building, holding Laura in his left arm. She was unconscious, with a little blood trickling from her forehead; he'd probably given her a rap on the head to stop her from squirming. I was happy that she was still alive, but the idea that he'd hurt her in any way really pissed me off.

The kidnapping vampire was a well-built Asian male, maybe thirty when he was turned. As a vampire, I pegged him at about a hundred years old or so. I approached slowly.

He put his right hand up like a stop sign. "What's this all about?" he said angrily.

"I know this little girl, and I'd consider it a personal favor if you'd let her go."

No vampire has the right to interfere with another's choice of feeding, even if the other vampire is a slimy pedophile. If we did that, we'd have as many wars as humans do. The only exception is a catastrophic choice that could harm all vampires or something of the like, and this clearly wasn't the case. Well, it might not have been a catastrophe for our race, but it was for me.

He said more calmly, "I'd like to help you out, but she's mine. Now if you don't mind—"

I interrupted. "Do you know who I am? Jean-Luc is a very close friend of mine, and I'm sure—"

"Fuck all that and fuck you!" he interrupted. "You've got no right to do this, and you know it. I know who you are—the Great Beauparlant. But that doesn't mean jack to me!"

I was being stupid. I didn't know this girl at all. She just happened to look like my daughter who'd been dead for two millennia. The guy was right. He had no obligation to honor my request and was well within his rights to decline, simple as that.

I ran all of this logic through my head, but it wouldn't wash. Even though it didn't make one bit of sense, I wasn't going to watch a lookalike of my long-lost little girl die right in front of my eyes. And besides, would it have killed this fuck to show a little respect?

"Look, what's the big deal?" I said. "There's plenty more to feed on. Why not—"

His right hand moved to her neck. "*You* look! Fuck off, or I'm going to rip her throat out right now! Either way, she's dead. Now beat it!"

That was it. Having his right hand on her neck made him defenseless on that side. I moved as fast as I could, covering five paces in a blink, and put a straight left directly into his face. Several facial bones satisfyingly shattered, and blood flew from his nose. The impact of the blow drove the back of his head into the brick wall with a loud *bonk*.

He reflexively dropped the girl, and I caught her. He wasn't down, though, so I delivered a half-assed karate kick to his gut, breaking a few ribs in the process. He hit the ground hard. Air whooshed out of his lungs, sounding like broken bellows.

Laura's eyes blinked opened for a few seconds. "Am I at the pool?"

She passed out again before I could answer. I examined her head and found a small laceration on her right scalp. I bit myself and let a little blood drip on the wound; it healed immediately. *What the hell,* I thought. *It'll save her a trip to the ER. Who knows who would have sewn her up—maybe a hack, or worse yet, a medical student.*

I took a look at Mr. Fuck-off. He was breathing slowly and starting to heal. I sat and waited for him to recover, with my Acilia in my lap. About ten minutes later, he started to make some noise. I rolled up my jacket for Laura to use for a pillow and laid her on the ground. I wanted to be ready when he regained consciousness.

He came to slowly, dazed. Considering the damage I'd inflicted, it would take him another few hours to heal completely. When his eyes focused on me, he started back and scuttled away. I stayed seated, watching him and smiling.

He honked out through his shattered nose, "What are you waiting around for, to finish me?"

"Hadn't really thought about that, but now that you mention it . . ."

In an instant, I had him by the neck and banged him hard into the alley wall. The back of his head crashed into it, and his eyes rolled like he was going to pass out again. That wouldn't do at all—but after several face slaps, he was with me again. I squeezed his throat, compromising his airway, and growled, "Listen to me, you dirty little fuck. If I see you even look at this girl again, I'm going to rip your fucking head off. For that matter, stay away from kids in general, you fucking freak. If I hear otherwise, you're dead meat. Understand?"

He was just able to squeak out, "I have the right to feed on anyone—"

I lifted him off the ground, tightening my grip and cutting both him and his airway off. "And I have the right to kill you, asshole. What do you think of that? Now, do we have an understanding?"

His feet thrummed helplessly, and his red, oxygen-deprived face nodded up and down.

"Good," I replied, flinging him across the alley. He crashed into the far wall, then into a bunch of garbage cans. Their discordant metallic clangs were music to my ears. I picked up Laura, who was still out. Luckily, she had missed the entire show. As I walked away, I said over my shoulder, "One more thing: stay clear of me while I'm in town. If I see you again, I'll kill you."

I was three blocks from the Monteleone when I heard a small voice say, "Where am I?"

"Don't worry, honey. You're safe."

Laura was still dazed, but as she got a good look at me, she said, "You're the fish-man from the pool, right?"

"That's me."

Then it hit her and she stiffened, looking over my shoulders and all around. She said, panicked, "Where is he? That man! Is he . . . ?"

I was way out of practice soothing children, but I tried. "Shhh. Shhh. It's okay, Laura. He's gone, and he's not going to hurt you. I took care of that."

She relaxed a little, but stayed on guard. "You sure?"

"Positive. I'm taking you back to the hotel now. Your parents are probably a little worried." *Like maybe to death.*

"That guy who grabbed me was creepy. He looked kind of like Bruce Lee, but a lot meaner."

Interesting. How'd she know Bruce Lee? Her dad was a fan, I'd bet. But she recognized him as Asian, and that might help later. "You don't need to worry about him. He's long gone."

She was quiet for a moment, then looked up at me. "Hey, you called me Laura. How'd you know that?"

She was a perceptive little brat, even after such trauma. I smiled. "I heard your dad call you that at the pool."

"Oh. What's your name, anyway? It can't be 'fish-man.'"

I laughed. "No, it's Christian. But you know what? You can call me Titus. It's kind of a nickname."

"It sounds silly, but okay. Hey, Titus . . . can you put me down now? I feel like walking."

"You sure?"

She nodded. Her eyes were so damn blue, even on this dark street. Down she went, and immediately, she put her hand up. When I took it in mine, a chill ran up my spine. It had been a very long time. We walked, and sometimes she skipped, holding my hand all the way to the Monteleone. It felt like heaven.

The police were already there, and so was Patrice, the general manager. He'd be called in for this kind of crisis. He breathed a sigh of relief when I presented the missing girl. A lot of the sigh was for the girl, since he was a father many times over—but some of it was for the fact that the Monteleone would stay out of the newspapers. He escorted Laura and me upstairs.

Along with Laura's parents and her sister, two New Orleans detectives and two uniforms were stuffed into their room. The sister was sobbing hysterically, and the parents looked about half a step away from the loony bin when we entered. They all went silent for a beat when they saw us.

"Laura!" the girl's mother screamed.

Laura ran directly into her dad's arms, and a family hug ensued for several minutes with a lot of crying and kissing. The police, Patrice, and I waited patiently. When it ended, we made our introductions.

They were the Russos, visiting from Atlanta. The father, Fred, owned a few restaurants back home, a barbecue kind of thing. Expanding to New Orleans had been on his mind.

Next, the cops did what they did best—separate and question. One detective and a uniform took the Russos into the adjoining bedroom, the other two cops stuck with me, as did Patrice. The detective asked if I would answer some questions. He also asked if I needed a lawyer. I told him I had nothing to hide. Out of the gate, I was the main suspect, even though it was absurd. But that's how cops operate. The first suspect is usually the correct suspect in their dull minds. Often that's true, but not always. I mean, a girl goes missing, and some strange guy happens to return her. Senseless or not, I was a suspect, even though I was the one who brought her back. What, did I have a sudden change of heart, or maybe an attack of pedophile/serial killer guilt? Laura could've identified me as her assailant, if that were the case. But it mattered not to New Orleans' finest.

Anyway, the detective asked me all the right questions, and I gave all the right answers. It was easy. I really didn't have to lie. I just left out the vampire part. I saw the guy grab her, I gave chase, and he dropped her and ran. *No, Officer, I didn't get a good look at him, but I think he might have been Asian. Yes, officer, about five foot blah, blah, and about blee, blee pounds, etcetera, etcetera.* It was quite the unshakable story.

The detectives compared notes. Laura had probably described the guy as looking like Bruce Lee, and my Asian comment tied it up, pretty much getting me off the hook. They left with handshakes all around, and I promised to give an official statement the next day.

Patrice excused himself, and I got to meet the rest of the

family, for real this time. The big sister, Lea, was nearly eleven; Laura was eight. Lea had the same features as her little sis, but in a slightly different mix. She was pretty, but not like Laura—although I have to concede a certain bias.

Lea said, "Thanks for saving my sister. I would have missed her something awful."

"You're welcome, Lea. She would have missed you, too. You must be a very good older sister."

"I am . . . and from now on, I'm going to be even better." She excused herself to get ready for bed.

Next came the mom, Julie, who threw her arms around me and covered my cheeks with kisses. She cried and thanked me, over and over again. Fred had to pry her off me, and he apologized for her being so over the top. But given the circumstances, she really wasn't. Her daughter had come back from the dead.

Fred embraced me more like a brother than my own brother ever had. His eyes filled with tears, and he told me that if I ever needed anything and he could help, he would. He then said that he owed me more than his life. I could only imagine how he felt.

We exchanged cards, and I was invited to his restaurants anytime, free of charge. I told him that I loved barbeque, which was a white lie. I also said I would stay in touch—another white lie. If I started communicating with the Russos, all it would do was remind them of what had nearly happened to their little girl.

Fred mentioned they were headed back to Atlanta the next day and had an early flight. I doubted very much that they'd set foot in New Orleans again. The new restaurant would have to land somewhere else.

I turned to Laura for our goodbye. I was distressed at the prospect of never seeing her again, but it would be best for her. What was I supposed to do, play the weird vampire uncle for a stand-in Acilia? I may be fucked up, but not that fucked up. I said, "Well, sweetheart, you've had quite an adventure for one night. I think it's time for bed."

Her big blues looked up at me. "Way past my bedtime. I was so scared until you came for me, Titus. Thank you."

"You're welcome, Laura. I'm glad I could help. But now I think you should get tucked in."

"Yep. I'm real tired." Laura yawned and put her arms up to me.

I looked toward the dad for his permission, and he nodded. I picked her up and hugged her, and she kissed me on the cheek, the same way my girl had done the last time I said goodbye to her. Tears wanted to come, but I wouldn't allow them. She put her head on my shoulder and was starting to fall asleep instantly in that way that only young kids can pull off.

I walked her over to her dad, delivering his precious "Lauradarlin" to his arms. His tears were free-flowing, and he tried to speak—but he couldn't. He squeezed my shoulder with his free hand.

As I turned to leave, I heard Laura whisper sleepily, "Bye-bye, Titus."

I left them alone and intact as a family. It felt good in one way and screwed-up in another. I couldn't help but think of all the people I had killed over the years. All of them likely had some family, and those families likely had frantic meetings about their missing loved ones, like the Russos had tonight. Except there was no happy ending for them. Their family member was dead and never coming back. They would be forever missing, thanks to me.

Tonight, I had saved this little girl from one of my own kind, since I happened to be getting divorced, and because of it, happened to end up in New Orleans. Little Laura happened to stay at the same hotel as me, and because she spied on me in the pool, I noticed how she looked exactly like my daughter from two thousand years ago. Then, two days later, I happened to be walking on the same street as her, and I happened to see her get snatched. Weird and so totally random. I really didn't know what to make of it.

Most of the time, I didn't feel bad about the people I'd killed and all the mayhem I'd caused. I was what I was, and I didn't ask for it. Frankly, I was more confused about Laura looking like my Acilia. I guess this time, I felt like I was able to save her, when I didn't have the chance all those years ago. Well, not Acilia, but a girl who looked like her. Oh, I don't know. But it made me feel good.

CHAPTER 24

I was officially twenty minutes late for my dinner with Jean-Luc. He was persnickety about punctuality, but when I sat at his table at the Absinthe House, he let my tardiness pass. As luck would have it, Miranda was our waitress once again.

I said, "Hello, beautiful. How are you?"

She smiled. "Doing fine, lover."

"Lover . . . I like the sound of that."

Her smile widened. "Just a name . . . for now. From what I hear, I don't think I could come close to keeping up with you."

I hated that she already knew about my sexual gymnastics from the other night. "Don't believe everything you hear."

"Oh really? That's too bad. And to think I was a bit curious." She winked and was gone. I watched her walk away, transfixed.

Jean-Luc said, "Eh-hem. Can you at least control yourself long enough for us to get through dinner?"

"Sorry. I've been a bit crazy since I've come back."

"Yes, I know. What is this about the little girl you rescued? That kind of thing is very awkward."

Vampire news travels fast in New Orleans, and Jean-Luc had eyes and ears everywhere. I told him how the girl was essentially a twin of my daughter and how it had affected me. He favored me with an odd look.

"I understand, Christian. I really do, and I will take care of this. But I would not make a habit of this sort of behavior. It could cause problems."

He was right. This was his town, and he was telling me in a nice way to cut the shit.

I raised my hand in the Boy Scout salute. "I promise to be a good boy."

He laughed. "I understand you've had quite the dalliance with the three little ladies from the other night. I've heard you've taken them under your wing...and under your balls, as well." He tittered at his own comment.

I had no idea what "under your balls" meant. Maybe it was something that didn't translate well from Old French, but I went with it. "Correct on both accounts. I'm trying to help them out a bit. It's a counterpoint to your hands-off approach."

His backhanded limp wrist waved at me in disdain. "Oh, the sensitive Roman killer. Did you ever consider that letting them learn on their own makes them adaptable and self-reliant? That this might lead to longevity? As I recall, neither you nor I had any significant instruction—yet we've lasted and prospered."

There were many more who hadn't. But we'd had this discussion numerous times in the past, to no avail. I decided to cut it short before it went sour. "Nice weather we're having."

Jean-Luc laughed out loud. Changing the subject this way never failed to amuse him. "Titus, I will never understand your fascination with meteorology. Oh, and I understand you have also taken on a new pet, Jake."

"He's a good kid."

"He is, but a word of warning. He's a born screw-up. Be careful. I trusted him once, and it cost me dearly."

I was about to ask him what he meant, but at that moment, Miranda stopped to clear our table. She bent to pick up the glassware, staying there a beat too long and giving me an excellent view of her cleavage. She smiled and then walked away, her hips moving seductively.

I said to Jean-Luc, "So what's her story?"

"Very good VA. Stable, as far as humans go, and she clearly likes our company. She even has a vampire boyfriend who, as a matter of fact, is working the bar tonight. She is a bit torn about whether to leave things alone or become one of us."

"How long has she been torn?"

"Going on five years now."

That was a long time to decide, unless you were going to be a VA lifer, and VA lifers were usually, well, weird. "Five years! Is she weird or something? She doesn't seem it."

"No, not at all."

"Is she a good candidate?"

"Intelligence-wise, *oui*, and quite attractive and charming, too. She has no significant human family situation to deal with. She's had the standard evaluation by our psychiatrist and did very well. As for emotional stability, your guess is as good as mine. She is, after all, a woman— and a human one at that."

"Hmm. I think I'll have a chat with her."

~~~

"What the hell am I doing?" Miranda said to herself as she hustled back to the busy bar. She shouldn't have been taking extra time to flirt with the new vampire in town. Her boyfriend, Nick, was the lead bartender tonight. Even though he was sweet on her, he was a perfectionistic control freak about how his bar was run. He could be quite the prick when things didn't go his way.

She took a glance back over her shoulder and noticed that Jean-Luc was sitting alone. She felt disappointed that Beauparlant was gone, but when she turned back, she was startled to see him standing right in front of her. He looked at her intently. If she'd been susceptible to vampire telepathy, she figured she'd be on the floor by now.

In general, she'd enjoyed him looking at her, but in this instance, she wasn't so sure. He stared into her eyes with a small, unpleasant smile on his lips. Now she was sure . . . she didn't like it. Just as it occurred to her that she might be in trouble, he grabbed her by both shoulders and lifted her off her feet. She'd been around vampires for some time, but had never seen one move nearly as fast, not even Jean-Luc.

She was only able to let out a startled, "Oh!" and then was whisked across the room as if propelled by a NASA rocket. A moment later she found herself dropped on a couch in one of the private rooms that adjoined the bar. The door slammed shut, and Beauparlant was there, leaning with his back against the wall. It was as though he'd materialized out of thin air.

Angered by his manhandling of her, she stood and said, "What's the big idea? If I don't keep moving my drinks, Nick's going to be pissed."

He kept staring at her, mute, with no trace of human emotion. Finally he said frostily, "Don't worry about Nick. I'll take care of him. Worry about me right now. What the fuck are you doing?"

Miranda didn't understand the question. "I'm trying to do my job! What the fuck are *you* doing? And don't think going all vampire is going to scare me. I've been around your kind enough that I'm used to it."

"That's not what I mean, and you know it. You're not stupid, and you haven't been around me. You'd be wise to be afraid."

He leaned toward her, and she couldn't help but take a step back. *He's gone,* she thought. The vampire she thought she knew was gone. Now she was locked in this room with a two-thousand-year-old monster. She could feel the power rippling off him and somehow draining her energy, making her weak. But she'd never been the type to cave. "Okay, I'm scared. Are you happy now?"

"No, not happy, but glad you're sensible," he said, smiling a little. "Now answer my question."

With the smile, a good deal of the monster was gone, but nowhere near all of it. When he spoke, there was at least a speck of feeling. Miranda was relieved, but knew she wasn't even close to safe yet. She understood from experience that although vampires looked human and for the most part acted that way, they were killers who could sometimes go off unpredictably and for reasons known only to them.

Along with not being the type to cave, she'd never been the shy type. "I think you're cute. I was flirting with you. Big deal."

His smile widened, and she thought him a cocky bastard.

"I understand you have a boyfriend, a vampire, no less. What, he's not ringing your chimes?"

Forget cocky bastard, she thought. *He's a total asshole.* "We do just fine."

"How old is he?"

"Not that it's any of your business, but he's thirty-five."

He shook his head. "No, how *oooolllld* is he?"

"Oh, that . . . around sixty-five."

Now Miranda was treated to a smug, purse-lipped smile. "That would explain it," Christian said. "He's a baby, probably a loser before he was turned. I'm guessing self-esteem issues."

Miranda had had enough. She decided she was getting out of this room and away from this ancient psycho vamp. She took a step toward the door. "Look, this is bullshit, and I have work to do."

She didn't see him, but more felt him move, as he took her by the shoulders and popped her back against the wall. Her head struck it with a *thwack*. She saw stars, and for a moment almost passed out. Everything went grey but then slowly came back into focus. When it did, she was looking into Beauparlant's stony, ice-blue eyes and the blank mask of his vampire face.

Feeling sure now that this little meeting wasn't going to end well, she thought herself lost. Defiance would serve no purpose, and neither would self-defense. She could scream for help, but the rooms were soundproofed and she'd be dead before the echo of her shout died. That left begging for her life as a last option, but she'd never do that. She'd known the danger when she'd chosen this life.

She thought herself a good judge of men and vampires, but staring into this killer's blank expression, she felt stupid for being attracted to him. She was certain that she wouldn't leave the room alive, but she would never give him the satisfaction of seeing her blubber or carry on. That thought calmed her. She considered the fact that she had no family, no one to miss her, so it would be all right. But she felt a resolved melancholy at the idea of dying at twenty-seven.

What did I expect from being with vampires? she thought. She smiled, thinking that particular revelation came to her a bit late. But that was her—never decisive, always in between, waiting for options. Well, one thing she wasn't was a coward. She desperately tried to think of some wise, hard-ass, final comment. But this sort of thing was not one of her talents. Given the circumstances, the best she could come up with wasn't very original. "Fuck you."

The vampire replied, "I'm not in the mood . . . yet."

This was too much, and despite her grave situation, she got angry. "You're getting ready to kill me, and you throw me a half-assed James Bond line? What kind of an asshole are you? Look, I *was* attracted to you. Obviously a big mistake, but now I'm bored with this, so why don't you do what you're going to do, and let's get it over with."

The vampire stared on silently, like an old Roman statue.

This caused Miranda to go from angry to livid. "You trifled with me, assaulted me, and now you're just going to stand there? Here, I'll make it easy for you." She stepped forward, brought her knee up, and nailed him squarely in the crotch. She felt a satisfying *squish*.

Beauparlant flinched a little, his eyes opened a bit wider, but for the most part, he remained still as a statue. His eyes narrowed down again and turned an even colder, deeper, icier blue.

Miranda thought, *This is it. He'll bite me or kill me in some good old-fashioned way.*

"That hurt," he said. "But you still haven't answered my question. Let me remind you. What the fuck are you doing?"

She was about to claim ignorance again, but she slowly grasped what he was actually asking. She did understand the question now and admitted, "I really don't know."

He didn't let go of her shoulders, but his hands relaxed some, and his face relaxed too, making him look almost human again. He was still too intense, still very dangerous, but a little less vampire. "Finally, an honest answer."

He was right, and she found it remarkably annoying. "So I like being with your kind. There's plenty of others who do, too. Why me? Why are you doing this to me?"

"You're the one who singled me out, so right now I'm interested in you, not the plenty of others. You've been a VA for five years—that's a long time for someone like you."

"What is that supposed to mean?" she half-heartedly protested.

He scoffed, "Oh, come now, you know. Lifer VAs are either a little wacky, or they're crazy, or they end up being vampire food. You're smart, together, attractive, and even dating a vampire. You've been with us for five years, long enough to see the life. So what's the issue? You don't have family, and you're mostly in our world, anyway. You seem fairly emotionally fit, although, as you demonstrated tonight, a bit prone to hysteria."

"Oh, how witty. Fuck you."

"As I said, I'm not in the mood," he shot back.

She was about to continue along with this witty repartee, when realization hit her. "You fucking jerk! All this scary shit was an act to make me piss my pants and give you a thrill!"

His shoulder grip re-tightened, and *whomp*, the back of her head kissed the wall again, like a post-concussive déjà vu. He didn't use as much force this time, but she once again found herself nose to nose with him.

"Not all of it, you dumb bitch. I could as easily kill you right here as let you walk out of this room. I'm trying to ram through that pretty little head of yours what you're playing with. Oh, sure, you've got a great gig going here. Well-connected in New Orleans, even a D-list vampire boyfriend, and we're very civilized in our little society here, aren't we?"

Miranda huffed.

"But you're cavorting with killers. You humans are fine and dandy, but you're second rate to us, at best. At any time, you could piss one of us off, and you're dead. Maybe you don't even piss anyone off, but a vamp kills you just for giggles. No recourse, no police, no protection—you're fucking dead."

There was no sense in denying it. Even though she hated to cry, her eyes filled with tears. She couldn't stop herself. "At first, it was fun—a mystery, breaking into this world. But now that I'm fully in, I still can't decide. You're right—lifer VAs are always wacky, and I don't want to be one of them. What would happen when I got old and lost my looks? Some shitty nowhere job for the rest of my life? Ending up a crazy old hag, hanging on until the bitter end? And you vampires have a fantastic retirement plan, a quick death. Not the greatest."

Titus released her and sat down, looking weary. "Look, Miranda, I tried for the last several years to be human. I couldn't do it, and do you know why? It's because I'm *not* human. Now you're trying to do the same thing, playing vampire. All I got out of my little foray to the realm of make-believe was heartache, and I nearly drove myself nuts.

"But for you, it could end worse than that. You're too smart to keep going half-assed like this. Decide. Either be turned or not. If not, then get out of this world. Walk away from it before something bad happens to you."

It was perfectly clear to her now that he had been trying to help her all along. She thought his approach sucked, and perhaps he was even going to kill her at one point. But in the end, his intentions were good, without the killing part, that is.

She wiped her eyes. "I've got a good read on the life. I've even gone and watched with Nick when he hunts. I'm just not sure if I can deal with the blood-drinking . . . the killing part. I'm not religious or anything, but committing to that, to murder, for the rest of my life . . . I don't know."

He looked at her and smiled. The monster was long gone, and he was 100 percent sweet, sexy Christian Beauparlant again. "Well, you can't really take drinking blood out for a test drive, but let me assure you, the taste is to die for. Pun intended."

She smiled at his lousy joke. "I believe you, but I've always been such a hedger. And all the killing . . ."

"There are ways around it, but only after the early years. You get used to it, or you die. It's as simple as that. You can get some perspective on blood drinking when you're the donor, though. It's a reversed perspective, but at least it's something. How does it feel when Nick bites you?"

"I've never been bitten. I won't let Nick do it. I told him I'd leave him if he did."

Christian lowered his head, shaking it back and forth. "Pussy," he said under his breath. He moved super-fast again and had her by the shoulders, but gently this time.

At least he didn't whack my head again, she thought. Two concussions in one night were enough. "I thought we were done with the scary part."

"We are, mostly. But it's time for the final part of your education." He opened his mouth and slowly licked his overdeveloped upper canines.

Miranda didn't want this. Or did she?

"No," she said weakly. But she didn't fight as he moved his mouth to her neck. What would be the point?

There was a sharp sting. She winced and moaned, but the pain faded quickly. She felt the sucking on her neck, the drawing. It was intense, sensual, all-encompassing. She was lost, floating . . . and then the visions began. They came in waves. She saw Rome, New Orleans, other places. They were as they are now, as they were hundreds of years ago, seen through his eyes—exactly as he had seen them over the centuries. Egypt, Paris, and the Old West. She thought she must be hallucinating, but at the same time, she knew it was real.

The drawing of her blood, her very life, went on and on. She moved her hand to the back of his head, holding it at her neck. *I want this*, she thought. She started to fade and weaken, feeling herself slipping away. Then there was nothing.

She came around slowly on the couch. When she realized what had happened, she sat up fast, got dizzy, and nearly passed out.

He was there immediately, lowering her back down. "Whoa, take it easy, kid. Just lay low for a few minutes."

She was woozy, but managed to ask, "Am I turned?"

He lit up one of his little cigars, being extra careful around fire, like vampires are. He blew out some smooth-smelling smoke and said, "Naw. Didn't even take a unit. It's the oral sedative . . . it will wear off in a bit."

She had no idea what the oral sedative was, but she was starting to feel better. She touched her neck, and there was no wound.

"You healed the bite with your blood, right?

He smiled. "An old trick, but it works every time."

"I saw things . . . Rome, Egypt I think, the Old West. You, in the West?"

Beauparlant smoked on and shrugged. "Yep, me in the Old West. It was quite fun, actually."

"Those visions I had . . . were they real?"

"They were real, all right. I got a few from you, too. You were raised in Cincinnati, correct?"

Surprised, she said, "Yeah, that's right. But how did that happen? I'm not susceptible to vampire telepathy."

"You don't have to be. With a physical connection, there can be some general thought sharing. Nothing too specific, and it doesn't happen all the time. For instance, I don't know exactly where you lived, but I got a look at your childhood home. And I can't name your pet dog when you were a kid, but I know you had one. It was a poodle, I think."

"She was a poodle and her name was Coco." Miranda thought about her childhood dog, who'd been dead for twelve years. She still missed her. "Does this sort of thing happen between two vampires?"

He gave a sad little smile. "Unfortunately, no. Just vampires and humans."

"When you bit me, it felt good. You made it feel good. Does that happen all the time?"

"Older vamps like me can make it happen. You usually start to get the talent after two, maybe three hundred years. Before that, it's telepathy, and that gets stronger with time, too. What's left after that is our oral sedative, and after that, brute force, which we have in abundance."

"Oral sedative?"

"We secrete it from glands in the mouth when we bite. It gave you that initial swooning feeling."

"But when I'm just starting—"

"When you're just starting, you'll need a lot of blood and you'll have to kill, sometimes brutally, to get it. Some victims will deserve it, some won't, but you'll need innocent right along with the guilty. Look, what I'm saying is, you'll evolve as time goes by. You'll be more skilled and sophisticated in your techniques. You'll be able to choose to kill when you want—but again, it'll take time. At first, you'll be a killing machine. You'll have to get by that period to survive." He stood. "I apologize for the theatrics earlier, but hopefully it did some good. So for now, class dismissed." He turned to the door.

No way, Miranda thought. He was intelligent, urbane, and had her best interests at heart—and she wanted him more than ever. She moved fast, maybe not vampire fast, but fast all the same. "Christian, wait a minute. I want to thank you."

He turned, and she stopped his response with a firm kiss on his lips. They kissed for a long time. He tasted of the cigar and her blood.

After they broke the kiss, he asked, "You sure about this?"

"After everything you put me through, do you think you're getting away that easy?"

Visions came again, exploding, more intense this time. When he'd said this happened with a physical connection, she'd presumed he'd meant with the vampire's bite. She never imagined it would happen when they were connected as a man and woman.

She'd never experienced anything like it. He was everywhere, inside her body, inside her mind. She was elated, and before the end, she lost control and bit his neck, like a vampire would, drawing his blood. The bite affected him profoundly.

Afterward, they made quite a pair lying on the couch— him with his pants around his ankles, but still wearing his shirt and jacket, and her with her blouse undone, no undies, and her skirt hiked up to her chest. He struck up a cigar.

"Hey, give me one of those, would you?" Miranda asked.

He lit one for her and handed it over. They smoked in silence, watching the different patterns of their exhalations as they rose to the ceiling.

"Helluva trick there, that thought-sharing during sex. Thought I was going to die, but a pretty good way to go."

He blew out a smoke ring, absently touching his neck. "Your trick wasn't too shabby, either. Nice neck bite for a human. Shocking in that good, Las Vegas kind of way. You should have no problem with the biting part of being a vampire. Very sexy—it moved me."

She leaned over, smiling, and kissed him. "Yeah, I noticed. I'd love to stay longer, but after all, I am supposed to be working, and I bet I'm in trouble. I'm going to go straighten myself out."

Christian gave her a smug little smirk, an expression she now thought was cute. Her panties materialized in his hand, as if conjured by a magician.

He looked at the panties and back to her. "I was hoping for a souvenir, but . . ."

She snatched them out of his hand. "Very funny." One kiss later, she headed for the bathroom.

Ugh . . . I definitely look like I've been screwed, Miranda said to herself as she looked in the mirror. She got herself together quickly.

Christian was looking his debonair self, pants on and everything. She went straight into his arms and kissed him again. She felt as if she couldn't get enough of his lips.

When she released him, he said, "Putting the sex aside, and that's no easy task, I want you to think about what I said tonight. You need to make a decision soon."

She promised him she would.

"I want you to come and see me," he said. "We can talk, and I can give you more information, hopefully helping you decide one way or the other. And no matter what you decide, you'll always have me for a friend."

Miranda really did like him, especially after he'd stopped

the scare tactics. She thought him so open and willing to share, whereas a lot of other vampires were unwilling—or maybe unable. Perhaps it was his age, or maybe it was just the way he was, but she had to ask. "Since you've been down here, you've been helping out a lot of people—your three girlfriends, Jake, that little girl, and now me. Why are you doing all this?"

He shook his head. "I'm not sure. I've always been that way to a degree, but nowhere near as much as this. Maybe it's because I've locked myself out of my world for so long, and now that I'm back, I'm jumping in with both feet. Might be that I'm a sap, I don't know."

"I don't think anyone would say you were a sap. Whatever the reason, I'm glad you're here."

He smiled, which made him look almost boyish. "Me, too. For what it's worth, you'd make a great vampire."

She beamed and went back to work. The bar was backlogged with tons of drinks and crowded with customers. Nick was working like a madman. He looked up and glared at her, but she didn't care one bit. Christian blew by her and somehow quickly smoothed Nick over. He spent the next hour waiting tables with her, helping clear the logjam at the bar that their tryst had caused.

It was obvious to Miranda that Christian had experience as a waiter. She was starting to wonder if there was anything he couldn't do. He finished his "shift" and bowed to Miranda, kissing her hand. It sent a shiver down her spine.

Christian meandered back to a decidedly unhappy-looking Jean-Luc. Miranda knew she'd have to deal with the fallout from Nick later, but what a night she'd had. She thought of Christian's charming sexuality, his insight, and most importantly, his offer of friendship.

CHAPTER 25

Lisa might have been amused to know that she was stalking Donald in the same way that Julian had, from behind the China Star. She was in no mood for amusement, however, as she waited in her dark car for Donald to arrive. She wanted to ignore Julian's comment, wanted to wall it off like Montresor had walled off the ill-fated Fortunato in "The Cask of Amontillado," but failed miserably.

Despite her best efforts, her suspicion had grown over the last few days. The doubt started as a minor, intermittent annoyance, like a TV commercial jingle that had gotten stuck in her head. But in a short span, it had turned into a constant, full-fledged symphony of misgivings. She may as well have been trying to tune out the *1812 Overture* from a front row seat at Symphony Hall.

She knew Donald's habits and didn't have to wait long. He emerged from the China Star arm-in-arm with Janet Pierce. Lisa gasped when they kissed. Pierce dropped down out of sight, to her knees no doubt, as Donald leaned back against his car. Thankfully, the sordid specifics were blocked from Lisa's line of sight.

She fought back her tears, got out of her car, and approached them, being careful to not see too much. She said, "Donald, if you don't mind taking your dick out of Janet's mouth, we need to talk."

Donald jumped and gave a startled glance to the top of Pierce's head. She popped to her feet, looking every bit as startled as Donald, who was zipping his fly.

He stammered out the well-worn, tired expression, "Now, Lisa, this isn't what it seems."

Lisa actually laughed at that. About two dozen witty responses flew through her head. *What's the use?* she thought. "On second thought, we don't need to talk at all. We're through." She turned and began to storm away.

Donald called after her, "Lisa, don't do this." He wasn't pleading; he was commanding.

About halfway to her car, a powerful cramp nearly doubled her over. She paused and kept going, but by the time she reached her car, she could feel the warm wetness. She looked down. When she saw the blood soaking through her pants, she passed out.

~~~

The following morning, Lisa sat on her hospital bed, waiting to be discharged. It had all happened so fast. She'd miscarried in that dark, grimy parking lot after directly observing Donald's infidelity. The doctor in the ER who'd informed her that she'd lost the child did a lousy job of it. She'd already known, of course—but it still hurt. The doctor's bedside manner didn't just suck; it was nonexistent. She couldn't help but think Jules would have treated a patient more kindly.

A quick trip to the OR was followed by an even quicker D and C, and then to a comfy bed for observation. There was no more significant bleeding, only a bit of spotting at best with that pesky fetus gone. After a repeat stable blood count, she was ready to go.

She was stunned, thinking she couldn't possibly feel any worse, when Donald arrived, disproving that theory.

"What do you want?" she barked.

"Look, Lisa, last night was a mistake. It won't happen again. I don't want it to wreck things. I love you."

That was no apology, only a statement. He didn't sound loving or sorry or repentant or emotional or *anything*, for that matter. It seemed like he was reading off items from a shopping list. She wondered how long it had taken him to think up and rehearse his bland little speech. He hadn't even mentioned their lost child.

What a fool I was, she thought, *trusting someone like him*. She'd arrogantly believed she'd be the one to change him, so she was twice the fool. Her marriage to Julian had ended up being a failure. There would be no altering that, but to have picked this man as his replacement now seemed ludicrous.

Lisa removed the engagement ring that Donald had given her and thought, *Damn, that's two rings in one week*. She held it out to him. "I don't care if you do it again or not. As of last night, it's officially none of my business. I don't ever want to see you again."

When he didn't move to take the ring, she threw it at him, and it fell to the floor. Donald didn't pick it up, nor would she, but now she saw an authentic emotional change in his features. It was indignant fury.

"You dumb little bitch," he said. "I do the dumping here, not you. You'd better come to your senses, get up off your ass, and put that ring back on."

For the first time in the relationship, it seemed Donald had let his true self shine through. Lisa wasn't surprised. Deep down, she'd known it all along.

With a smile she said, "Donald, darling, for a bald-headed, slimy old man, you think way too highly of yourself."

His face reddened, and his fists clenched together. He advanced on her a step.

Lisa's smile widened. "Oh, you're too much. You're going to attack a woman in her hospital room after she just miscarried? Even the great Donald Leland might not be able to weasel his way out of that one."

He stopped, gathering himself. "This isn't over. You have no idea how screwed you are."

"Fuck off, you old buzzard."

His eyes took on a cruel glint. He nodded once and quickly left. Despite all that had happened, Lisa felt better.

CHAPTER 26

I thought I'd be in for some trouble with Mr. Manners—Jean-Luc—and I was right. Leaving him for some personal time with Miranda was fine, but as his guest, waiting tables in his establishment was definitely not.

Vampires always retain what they were in their human lives to some degree. My career as a Roman soldier defined me as having common roots, so helping Miranda wait on tables was something I wouldn't think twice about. Jean-Luc, on the other hand, was born a crusade knight. Accustomed to privilege, and used to being served, he'd always maintained some of the aristocratic attitude that went along with his former high station.

From across the room, I could see his prissy pout long before I sat down. For this battle, I decided on silence as my initial tactic.

He drummed his fingers in counterpoint to my reticence, but finally burst out, "So, did you enjoy embarrassing me, waiting tables like a scullery maid? I'm beginning to think you have lost your mind."

"Look, Jean-Luc, I kind of screwed things up tonight and wanted to help, that's all. Can we leave it at that?"

"No, we can't. Why do you do such things, Titus? Why

not come to me and ask me to get extra help? I only run this town, after all. You always have to be in the spotlight, don't you? I'm quite shocked you've lasted so long with your little masquerade as a human doctor. Oh, but I am sure you were still able to be the star there, too, hmmm?"

Was I that self-centered? Maybe. Does being a vampire make you self-centered out of necessity? Definitely. But I was no more so than any other vampire—or was I?

Jean-Luc was a good and loyal friend, but he could sure get me angry at times.

"I'm sorry if I insulted you," I said. "And maybe I am self-centered, but I just jumped back into our world after twenty pretty screwed-up years, so excuse me if I've ruffled your precious bullshit French feathers. As my supposed friend, I'd think you'd cut me a little slack and be happy for me."

"I am happy for you. As for my bullshit feathers, you did a bit more than ruffle them. First the blood bath in Louis Armstrong Park, then adopting that imbecile, Jake, then saving the little girl. And by the way, do you have to fuck everything that moves? Why don't you start using your brain and give your penis a rest?" The prissy Frenchman was a facade that he would drop only under extreme duress, but he was right. I'd been out of control since I had arrived.

I thought about my history with Jean-Luc. We were now friends, but it didn't start out that way. I came to New Orleans in 1791. Jean-Luc had already been there for thirty years, since the very beginnings of the city, and he was clearly in charge. I immediately fell in love with the place, greatly enjoying the multicultural scene, and I decided to stay. My status as an ancient dictated that I had some input in the running of things. I really didn't care much about such matters, but I'd just been chased out of Montreal by a mayor who I clearly should've been overlord to. Truth be told, I'd chosen that subservient station, but that didn't change the fact that I was still smarting about how it had played out, and I wasn't about to let it happen again.

I didn't try to cut Jean-Luc out, at least not completely. I made him an offer to be co-leaders. He was having none of that. We tried to work it out, but we couldn't, so he ordered me to leave. I politely declined, and he challenged me to a duel, which was all the rage at that time. I accepted.

His weapon of choice would be his crusader's broadsword, a huge blade of nearly three and a half feet. I, being the sentimentalist that I was, had my gladius, which was quite small by comparison. In the case of swords, as in penises, size does matter. He had a distinct advantage in weaponry.

Our training was probably a wash, but being a millennium older tipped the scales greatly in my favor. By force of years, I'd be faster and stronger. But vampire development isn't linear and varies greatly with the individual. Jean-Luc was powerful. This fight would by no means be easy.

We met at night in a dark warehouse along the Mississippi. The entire vampire community, about sixty back then, turned out as witnesses. Simone, a baby vamp of five at the time, was among the spectators and looked as radiant as ever.

For a soldier, remembering the details of a battle can be somewhat elusive. You're immersed in the ebb and flow of the fight, operating more by instinct than thought. I recall Jean-Luc's sword whooshing through the air, making deadly music. It was a devastating weapon, especially when wielded by someone so versed in its use. Even the stonewalls yielded to its force, screeching in protest as huge chunks of rock were torn from them. Being a vampire, Jean-Luc would not get fatigued by the sword's weight and size. I recall wondering how this slight man could have even lifted the weapon when he was human, let alone use it in battle.

I remember stealing glances at Simone, and it cost me. During one of my glimpses, Jean-Luc slashed me across the chest. The wound hurt like hell. I wouldn't make that mistake again.

Jean-Luc was a prick back then, like he was today. Even so, I wasn't out to kill him, although he was definitely trying to kill me. You see, even though he was annoying, I sort of liked him from the start. Like me, he was a soldier, and somehow his ridiculous pomposity fit him.

A few minutes into the battle, I knew I had him. As good as he was, and as powerful, my age was going to be too much for him unless I did something stupid, like ogling his woman and getting my chest sliced open because of it.

I fought a defensive, retreating battle, looking to disable him, killing him only if I had to. I let him back me into a wall. He took a huge swipe, which I barely eluded. His blow raised sparks from the stone, eerily strobe-lighting the onlookers.

He moved to impale me, but I deflected his thrust off-center. He ran me through my right side, and I theatrically screamed louder than I had to, but not by much. It hurt like a bitch. I lowered my guard, grasping at the wound with my free hand.

He did what I thought he'd do, suddenly pulling his sword out and back into a striking position, making to slice off my pretty little head. As he delivered his blow, I stepped inside the arc of his sword, hacking across his right arm with my gladius.

His forearm, still holding his sword, clattered to the floor.

He was looking stupidly at his bleeding stump when *clang*—I struck his head with the hilt of my sword. He was stunned and still on his feet, but defenseless. With a swift forehand movement, my gladius sliced through the air and his neck. I pulled the strike in at the last moment, and although I hacked a deep laceration through the front of his throat, I never touched his spine, leaving his head on his shoulders. I'm a true artist with my gladius.

There was a collective gasp from the audience, but I only really heard Simone's. For a moment, they must have been thinking Jean-Luc's head was about to join his arm on the floor. He was gushing blood, gasping and futilely clutching at his neck with the one hand he had left. Finally, he fell flat on his back.

I was on him in a flash, the tip of my sword under his chin, pointed straight up toward his brain. He was a bloody mess, incapacitated, but cognizant. He looked stoically into my eyes without a flinch, the tough little bastard.

I said in my chirpiest tone, "So what do you say, Jean-Luc? You think we can run this town together?"

His eyes widened in disbelief, and he managed to give me a slight nod of assent. Simone gave me a dirty look as she carried Jean-Luc's forearm past me and placed it against his bleeding stump. He was moving his fingers in no time. A vampire's dismembered body parts graft back on very well when replaced right away. We don't grow missing limbs back, however. We're vampires, after all, not lizards.

His arm and the rest of him healed quickly. After a time, we became friends and had been ever since. But listening to him dress me down for serving a few drinks, I was thinking that I should have killed the son of a bitch back then when I had the chance.

I said, "Go fuck yourself, Jean-Luc. I'm out of here, and

I'm out of your shitty little town." I could be as petty as I believed him to be, maybe more so.

As I stood, he put his hand on my arm to stop me.

"No, wait, I'm sorry. I spoke in haste." He paused. "The truth is, I'm nervous. You've made me nervous coming here after all this time. I need to know what you're going to do. I'm fine, no matter what you decide. I should have asked you right away."

I had no idea what he meant. "No, I'm the one who's sorry. I've been acting like an adolescent ever since I arrived. All I've been doing is fucking up your town and causing trouble. I don't have a clue as to why I got myself so involved with Miranda tonight. I don't even know her. Maybe I'm losing my mind."

"What exactly did you do for Miranda?"

I shrugged sheepishly.

"Oh, I see."

"No, not that," I said. "Well, there was that, but I also gave her a life lesson, and a tough one. I think . . . well, I *hope* I educated her, helped her to make a choice about what she should do. But it's none of my business. I'm still pretty screwed up myself right now. I think I need to be with my own kind. These damn humans, they complicate my life."

Jean-Luc must have realized how unstable I was, because he looked concerned. "Sit," he said. "Sit back down."

I sat, but I hate being the source of anyone's concern. I don't do it well, so I changed the subject. "So what's the problem, my friend? We've known each other a long time. Why am I making you nervous?"

He hesitated. "I know you're traveling and said you had no intention of staying, but I also know how much you love this city. If you choose to stay, I must insist things go back to where they were, with you and me running the city together.

Etiquette and respect would dictate this. It would be just like the old days, eh?"

Now I finally understood. My very first centurion was of the opinion that my mind was made to plod along, but never to run. Times like these seemed to prove him correct. I thought I'd keep my response simple. "Well, fuck all that."

Jean-Luc smiled and seemed to relax a little. "Titus, you always make me laugh. You're quite a card."

"A wild card, Hugh."

Jean-Luc's given name was actually Hugues, but I had a tough time pronouncing that version.

I went on. "Look, I'll say it again. I have no interest in a leadership position. All I want is to get re-acclimated to my people. The city is yours. I can't be any plainer than that."

"Are you sure, because if not—"

I cut him off. "Will you please shut the fuck up?"

For a second, he looked like I'd slapped him. Then he laughed. Now the relief was showing through, loud and clear. Even when we were "co-mayors," he had always been viewed as the junior partner because of my age, and the fact that I'd spared him the night we dueled. I know he resented it, but he dealt with it well. The truth was, he was a far better administrator than I could ever be. He did most of the serious work, while I was more of the PR guy.

When he stopped laughing, he said, "You know I'm not that stupid."

I didn't know what he meant, and I told him so.

"You changed the subject from your problems to mine to distract me," he said. "I'm not that much the fool."

"You know me. I like talking, but not about my problems."

He shook his head. "Doesn't it matter that you're talking to a friend? You are such the stoic Roman."

I was about to protest, but he stopped me. "You don't have to talk, just listen. I'm worried about you, but as I see it, you're mostly okay. You always were a sex fiend, a helper to vampires and even humans sometimes, and of course, a terrific killer. These are all things you are doing here with a little more gusto than usual, shall we say. Your actions make perfect sense since you've been so repressed for so long. It will run its course, and you will get back to the way things were. Otherwise, the police will be on us, or you may fuck yourself to death."

I laughed at that, but I thought he was right. I hoped he was, anyway. One thing I did know for sure was that he was a true friend. I leaned over the table, took his face in my hands, and kissed him on his lips.

His eyes bugged out, then he pulled away and exclaimed, "I take it all back. You're insane!" He looked around the room, mortified, wiping his mouth with a napkin.

A good number of patrons were smiling, or politely laughing, which was wise. Big guffaws at Jean-Luc's expense could be detrimental to one's health. But my kiss was pretty damn funny.

I said, "You're right about the insane part, and I'm so damn glad I didn't kill you all those years ago."

He composed himself. "I'm glad, too, but you couldn't be blamed if you did. I was such a pompous ass back then."

"Back then, huh? Thank goodness you've gotten so modest lately."

He waved his limp wrist at me again and said, "By the way, Christian, for a vampire with your tremendous sexual reputation, you're a terrible kisser."

Now that hurt.

CHAPTER 27

The next few days passed tranquilly. I was beginning to feel at peace, and I hunted every night. Having blood on such a constant basis made me feel energized and alive. I didn't hunt like the pretend-human, half-assed vampire I'd been in Boston. I hunted like the predator I was. And whoever crossed my path went down, simple as that.

I was settling down in my parlor, taking in the view of the Mississippi with a novel and a beer, when Jake arrived, days earlier than expected. He looked serious and exhausted.

My greeting wasn't strictly by the book. "You look like shit."

"Thanks a lot," Jake shot back. "That's because I've been up for three days straight taking care of *your* messes."

That got my attention. I ushered him in, gave him a beer, and sat him down.

He opened his laptop and began. "Leland's private eye was easy enough to find. The guy's name is Garret Dick. And I thought *I* had a bad name."

I laughed. "No arguing on that one."

"Anyway, he's an ex-con, a one-man company and an amateur, at best. But he's dirty, and I'd guess that's why your buddy Leland likes him so much. He's the one who looked into you."

I agreed. "The dirtier the better for that fuck Leland."

"Dick's computer security sucks, and I got in easy," Jake said. "He really cooperated too, because his system in the office is networked to the ones in his home, his laptops, even his hand-held. Anyway, I found your files and fried them. I also cooked twenty other files randomly—you know, to throw off suspicion, but I think they'll figure it was you, anyway."

Jesus, it was hard to believe Jake could do all this. He thankfully spared me most of the technical detail. I wouldn't know what the hell he'd have been talking about, anyway. Despite that, the common sense part of my brain was still working fine. "What's to prevent him from doing another search and finding the stuff all over again?"

He smiled. "Two things. First, I overlaid your transactions with a security system I've come up with. It's better than anything else out there. At least I think so. Second, even if they got through the new system, which they wouldn't, your investments from that list don't exist anymore. I sold them all off. Now they all belong to Jake Lyons Enterprises!" He beamed.

I gagged on my beer and spewed, "What?"

A few days before, I'd given Jake the gift of a new name and new identifications, using Jean-Luc's local connections. I got a good deal, in part due to my status, but mainly because Jean-Luc had squeezed the vamp into giving me a rock-bottom price.

I did it for two reasons. If Jake was going to start going out into the world at large, he couldn't use his old identifications because they were out of date—and, well, because he was dead. The second reason, Lipschitz, needed no further explanation. I never thought this gift horse would bite me in the ass so soon.

Jake looked crestfallen. "Oh crap. I was trying to help. I thought you'd be happy. Here . . . it's all right here on my laptop. You can move everything back to you anytime you want."

He pushed the laptop to me, and I looked over what he'd done, having not the beginning of a clue as to how he had done it. From what I could tell, everything appeared in order. I was shocked. I'd suspected he might have skill, but not like this. "How could you have all this talent and not be a player down here, Jake?"

"I was so nervous, I screwed up at first. I made a few little mistakes and then a real big one with Jean-Luc. After that, it was pretty much over."

"What happened with Jean-Luc?" I asked.

He sighed. "It was a currency move, back and forth between here and Mexico. I did things right, but I was so jumpy working for him. When everything was all set, I hit the *Delete* button instead of *Send*. It was like I was watching someone else's finger push the wrong button. I couldn't stop it."

"You couldn't undo it?"

He shook his head.

"You did everything right? Just hit the wrong button at the end? I would think he'd understand. He's a reasonable guy."

He said, "It cost him."

"How much?"

He sighed again. "A million . . . actually, one point two million."

"Holy shit! No wonder he's pissed at you. Do me a favor. Don't push any wrong buttons when you're dealing with my stuff."

I needed to stew on this. It was a lot to take in. "I've had it with this computer stuff for now, it gives me a headache. Come on, let's hunt. I'll see if I can give you any pointers."

I stood, but he didn't.

He said uneasily, "There's one more thing."

I sat back down, worried.

"Remember how you gave me that homework assignment? You know, to use my computer to find something to help you?"

I nodded, very worried now.

"Well, I didn't count this as part of it. This was kind of extra."

I worked up the courage to speak. "What did you do?"

In one rushed, run-on sentence, he said, "I hacked into all of your bank accounts I could find and locked them down with my security system and then I changed all the passwords you can change them back whenever you want I think I got them all."

I was dumbstruck, mute. I tried to speak but could only manage a few guttural grunts. It was dangerous enough that this goofball kid had done what he did with Lisa's list, but now he had hacked into my accounts, and he thought he got all of them! The same goofball who had made 1.2 million of Jean-Luc's money disappear with a single push of a button. What had I gotten myself into?

I was still speechless but motioned him to spin the laptop to me again. He brought up what he'd done, and I studied it silently for a good twenty minutes. My accounts, except the sham ones, had all been encrypted and firewalled with what I thought was the latest computer shit that I'd purchased from the latest vampire techies. And most of them were under aliases that this kid couldn't have had knowledge of, yet he'd cracked them all in a few days.

To my great relief, everything seemed to be in perfect order, but he could've wiped me out. And if he could do it, then someone else could, too. I looked up at Jake, who was very pale. I asked with surprising calmness, or perhaps shock, "How exactly . . . did you do all that?"

He paused, opened his mouth, closed it, and paused again.

I said, "I withdraw the question. I wouldn't understand it anyway, right?"

He nodded.

"Okay. Let's hunt."

Relief flooded into his face. And I thought I'd had a lot to think about when he'd hidden the six million.

"And by the way, you're hired."

He asked, "Hired for what?"

"I have no idea, but I'll figure it out."

CHAPTER 28

Bill ambled his way down to the computer room in the Bunker. He opened the door, expecting to see Molly, but he was pleasantly surprised to see his other two daughters there, as well.

"Well, ain't this a treat," he said. "It's a rare occasion when I can catch the three of you in the same place at the same time."

His youngest, Shannon, looked up from her computer screen. She nonchalantly flipped her mop of dark hair from her eyes. It was a gesture she'd made use of ever since her hair got long enough when she was just a little girl. Seeing it made Bill smile.

She smiled back. "What's so funny, Daddy?"

"Oh, nothing. Taking a stroll down memory lane, that's all. So what'd you call me down here for?"

Cathy, his "blondie girl," as he often called her, answered, "Big Sis asked us to help out with her latest search. And when Big Sis asks, she must be obeyed."

Molly stuck her tongue out at Cathy and said, "I think we got it, Dad. Nailed it would be more like it. Both targets are multiples and confirmed. Montreal and New Orleans, but with the new search protocols, it went way easier than I even expected. Better than Quebec City, even."

Shannon said, "Molly worked some more bugs out of the system. It's going to get better and better."

Bill asked, "When could you give the green light?"

"Now," Molly said.

Bill was surprised. "Really? Let me have a look at that."

He studied all three of his daughters' screens. After about thirty minutes, he said, "It sure looks rock-solid to me. Better than some stuff that used to take us months."

"Dad, why can't we go on these hunts?" asked Cathy. "It looks like—"

Bill interrupted, "Now, Cathy, I don't want to go through this again. Your mom didn't want it that way. She had her reasons."

Cathy, his most rebellious girl and his most deadly on vampire hunts, said, "Yeah, Mom *always* has her reasons, but—"

"No 'buts,' girl. You ain't going, and that's it."

Cathy pouted. This was something she'd been doing even longer than Shannon had been flipping her hair. "Fine. I'll stay here and be bored out of my mind."

Bill almost cracked a smile over the pout, but held it in check. It would have really pissed Cathy off.

"Should we let Mom know?" Molly asked. "She always likes to get things hot off the presses."

That statement sobered Bill's mood. "It'll hold until the morning. She tucked in early."

His daughters appeared surprised.

"This early?" Shannon asked. "That's not like her at all. Is she doing all right?"

Bill felt his throat tightening, but he choked it down. He would never let his girls see him weak like that. Helen was dying, and there was nothing that could be done about it.

But he could control himself and be strong for his daughters. That, he could do. "No, not really, honey. These last few weeks have been tough. That damn tumor seems to be ripping through her, sucking the life right out of her. Her appetite's going, and she's lost weight. I wish I could do something, but I can't. We'll have to get along the best we can."

There were some glistening eyes, but no tears. These were Bloody Bill's daughters, after all.

Cathy smiled. "Then we're going to make these the two best missions we ever had. For Mom."

~~~

Later that night, after he'd finished his rounds, Bill crept silently into his pitch-dark bedroom. He thought Helen was asleep and began to lie down.

"Finished your rounds, did you?" Helen said.

"Just now."

"How's Molly doing?"

"I think she's got it nailed down pretty tight. Both cities. She's double-checking some stuff. Even got Cathy and Shanny to help her. If it all goes like I think it will, I'll start with the team assignments and training, first thing."

Helen replied, "That is good news. Remember, have some of Jarvis' men on both teams."

He'd expected a tongue-lashing since he hadn't informed her of Molly's progress right away. In the past, she would have. It saddened him. "I won't forget. Are you going to go?"

"I'm getting worse, but I'm not dead yet."

"Now, Helen, that's not what I meant."

"Oh, hush, Bill. I know. But I'm feeling so crappy, I might screw something up. I'd hate to get someone killed on account of my pride."

"That's fine by me. I hated the idea of you going into the field, anyway."

Helen remained silent for a minute, and Bill thought she was stewing up a good retort, but she began crying.

Bill reached for her in the dark and took her into his arms. "Now what's all this, girl? I'm here, Helen. I'm here for you."

When she'd settled down, she whispered, "I'm so damn frustrated and so afraid, Bill."

"You've never been afraid of anything a day in your life. Even the damn vampires don't scare you. Remember that first one? I nearly wet myself, and you were as cool as a cucumber."

"I might have been cool, but wet undies or not, you sure put the bastard six feet under."

Bill smiled at the memory. *Our very first kill together.* "Well, I certainly did. But I couldn't have done it without you."

"That's just it, the frustration of it. All those monsters we took care of, all these years, and hardly anybody knows. All the people we've saved and protected, and they have no idea. Probably wouldn't care if they did."

"*We* know, Helen. That's got to be enough."

She went on as if she hadn't heard him. "And now, to die like this, in a meaningless way, on account of this damn cancer. I'm not afraid to die, Bill, but to suffer a death with no meaning? It scares me so."

"You've done all this good. Been a good wife to me and raised three fine daughters. There's meaning to your life, and a lot of it."

"But when I'm gone, what's going to happen to you and the girls? Who'll take care of you?"

"I'll take care of the girls, Helen."

"But what about you? I'm so afraid for you. I'm afraid I could falter at the end and mess it all up. End up hurting you and the girls—and worse."

Bill had no idea what she meant. "I don't understand."

Again, she continued as if he hadn't spoken. "You can't let that happen, Bill. You can't let me falter. You have to promise."

"You know I'll be there for you. Right to the end."

"No, that's not good enough. You have to promise. Swear it."

She sounded frantic to Bill, and she'd never sounded that way before. "Okay, I promise."

"No matter what, no matter how it seems to you, you have to be strong for me. Follow my lead, do what I say. Swear it!"

"Helen, what am I swearing to? You can't expect me—"

"Swear it on our daughter's lives!" She was outright hysterical.

He didn't answer for a moment. Helen breathed heavily in his arms, waiting for an answer. She'd been secretive with him at times in the past, and he'd tolerated it because it had always been in the best interest of the family and the Network. He'd always obeyed her. She'd never given him a reason not to, but this time, it felt like he was selling his soul.

Nevertheless, he said, "I swear."

This seemed to relax her immediately. She nestled into his chest, her breathing steadied, and she was fast asleep in minutes. Bill stared into the darkness, silent tears running down his cheeks. Sleep didn't find him for some time.

CHAPTER 29

The hunting didn't go so well at first, as Jake was, in a word, inept. I persevered, and by the end of our little training session, I began to feel there was some hope. On our return to my suite, I found Jean-Luc waiting for us, and he didn't look happy. The three of us sat in my parlor.

"We've been hit again," he said.

Those four little words chilled my blood, right along with the blood I'd just appropriated from tonight's victim. "Jesus Christ! Is this going to be an all-out war?"

Jean-Luc replied, "I don't know. And as per usual, there was not a shred of evidence. No clue as to how she is finding us so easily now. Our computer people are once again stymied."

"Well, we'd better figure it out soon, or we'll be extinct. Where? Who?"

"Quebec City. Michelle Berger *et* Andre Marineau."

"Oh, damn," I said weakly. They'd both been my friends.

Jean-Luc added, "I turned Andre all those years ago. He was a good man."

"We can't sit back anymore. We have to do something."

"What do you propose we do? Nothing has changed. There is not one bit of computer or physical evidence as to how she did it. What can we do that we haven't done before?"

Jean-Luc and I stewed silently, and then my eyes turned to Jake. He fidgeted as I stared at him. He obviously had great talent in informatics, as he'd just done wonders for me. But on the other hand, I hardly knew him, and he didn't have the greatest track record for success. It was quite the conundrum. So, as usual, I went with my gut. "Jean-Luc, Jake showed me a computer security system this evening that seems to be top-notch. And he easily broke into all my accounts that I thought were locked down. I think he could help here."

Jean-Luc and Jake oddly replied in unison, "Now wait a minute." They looked at each other in surprise.

I ignored them. "I know you've had a bad experience with Jake, but he worked magic for me. Take him to your geeks and see what happens. What's there to lose?"

Jean-Luc thought for a moment and nodded. He turned to Jake. "Titus is correct. What's there to lose? Let's go."

Jake appeared as if he'd faint, but collected himself and his laptop.

I was about to tell him "don't worry," or "do your best," or some other bullshit, but that would have been a pack of lies. I told him the truth. "Jake, this is for keeps. You did great by me, and you need to do great now. You can't afford to screw up. Lives are at stake."

He tried unsuccessfully to gulp down his Adam's apple and said, "Okay, Titus. I won't fuck up."

~~~

Three hours later, a knock on my door woke me. I'd fallen asleep on the couch. Jake and Jean-Luc had returned, and I could immediately tell by the look on their faces that things had gone well.

Jean-Luc smiled and clapped Jake on the back. "Great promise. Great promise. Our experts think his system could significantly help us. They are expediting testing, but hopefully within the next few days, we'll begin to lock down New Orleans. After that, we can spread it to other parts of the country. The business details will have to be worked out, of course, so that Jake here can be appropriately compensated, but this is a start in defending ourselves."

I took Jake by the shoulders. "Well done. Really well done."

But Jake looked somber, and now, so did Jean-Luc.

"What? What's wrong?" I asked.

Jake answered, "We overlaid my hacking technique—you know, the way I got into your accounts—onto the firewalls of the Shreveport and Quebec City vampires. And then by regression—"

"Enough! In English."

"There's nothing I can back-trace specifically, but we could tell there's all kinds of activity centered here in New Orleans and in Montreal."

"You mean . . . ?"

Jean-Luc nodded. "Jake believes that is where we will be hit next."

My very best friend in the world lived in Montreal. He was a relative youngster, not the most detail-oriented when it came to his own safety, and the mayor of Montreal hated him.

As if reading my mind, Jean-Luc said, "You know I do not approve of your oversized playmate, but I do not want to see him dead, either." The truth was, Jean-Luc hated him.

"Last time the two of you met, you almost killed him," I said.

Jean-Luc scoffed. "I was merely amusing myself, but no

matter. You should go to your friend. We will be fine here. After all, we have master Jake."

Jake blushed.

"Are you sure?" I asked. "Because—"

"I'm sure. I know how you would worry. Go to the imbecile and make sure he is all right. But now, I must get back to work. I need to make sure New Orleans is safe. I'll send the vital information along to Montreal, as well."

Jean-Luc and I embraced.

"You take care of yourself, you little French bastard," I said.

He smiled. "Always so uncouth. And to think you Romans civilized the world. Be careful, Titus." With that, Jean-Luc was gone.

I turned to Jake. "I'm going to get the earliest flight I can. But, Jake, I am so proud of you."

He was about to answer when my phone rang. Considering everything, I thought certain it would be more bad news, but it was Miranda.

She sounded deadly serious. "I need to talk to you in person."

I already knew what it was about, so I didn't ask. "Okay. You know where I am. When can I expect you?"

"I'm almost there now; I wanted to call to make sure you were in."

The phone went dead. I really didn't have time for this. I wanted to get going, but I'd offered her my help and couldn't back out now. Jake made for the door, and I said, "Where do you think you're going?"

"I heard. Miranda's coming, so I thought I'd give you two some privacy."

"Stay put. I may need you."

About five minutes later, Miranda was at the door. The

two suitcases in her hands suggested her situation had become complicated. I took her luggage, and she came in and sat down in the parlor. She'd cleaned up, but it was obvious she'd been crying. Jake hung back, standing near the kitchenette, and I sat across from her.

She looked up at Jake and said, "Hey, Jake. How you been?"

He looked at her impassively, even a little coldly, which was very much unlike him. "Fine."

Oh, great. The two of them had obviously had dealings with each other. This was just what I needed, more fucking complications. I let it go for now. "So I think I can guess why you're here. You've decided?"

She looked directly into my eyes. Hers were outstanding. They were the deepest, darkest brown. They looked barely under control, though, like they might fly out of her skull. "I've decided. I want to be turned. By you."

As much as I wanted to get to Montreal, after the routine I'd pulled on her, I felt I had an obligation to see this through. I said, "You sure you don't need a bit more time? Maybe talk to somebody about it first?"

She shook her head. "I've taken enough time already."

"Okay. You want to have dinner? A last supper, just in case?"

"That's not fucking funny," she answered in an appropriately nasty tone.

My mouth was clearly running ahead of my brains, as usual, but my, the language on her. "Sorry, bad joke. How about a drink?"

"Definitely. What do you have?"

"A beer?" I offered.

She scoffed. "I'm facing death, and you offer me a shitty beer?"

"Sorry, I haven't stocked this place too well," I said weakly. "I've been going out a lot. I think I've got some champagne, but it's not cold."

She answered as if she were trying to explain quantum physics to a retard. "Hard stuff, Christian. I need a real drink."

I brightened. "Okay. That I can do. I've got gallons of tequila."

She wrinkled up her nose. "I hate that crap. Is that all?"

"Pretty much. I think I have some absinthe somewhere."

She rolled her eyes and gave me an "I don't believe this shit" look. "Even worse. I'll take the tequila."

I smiled. "If I were you, hon, I'd start acquiring a taste for both of them."

I got the booze and glasses, and Miranda managed to gag down three shots. On each round, Jake took his drink and retreated back to his standing station.

"First, what's with the suitcases?" I asked, pouring her another drink.

She put it away with a quick flip of the wrist, followed by a slightly smaller gag than the first three drinks had produced. "I told Nick I wanted to be turned, and he freaked. He didn't want me to do it, but he didn't have a good reason, either. He said it was because he was afraid I'd die, but I thought it was because—"

In a flat tone, Jake finished for her. "If you turn, he loses control of you."

She smirked and said sarcastically, "Go figure. Right. You nailed it, Jacob."

"Don't call me that... you know I don't like it." He sounded angry.

"Sorry," she said, but she didn't sound sorry at all. "I told him if I stay human, I'm definitely going to die. It's a matter of when. When he realized that I wasn't going to change my mind, he suddenly decided he wanted to be the one to turn me. First he says, 'Absolutely not,' and then he insists on being the one to do it."

"More control," Jake intoned from the boondocks.

Her head snapped toward him. "Okay, genius. Lay off that control shit!"

"Just my opinion," he replied.

"*Shove* your opinion."

It was time for me to break this up. "You kids need to learn to play nice. What exactly is up with you two?"

Jake answered, "I dated her before Nick convinced her I was a fuck-up. I treated her well, and all he wanted to do was control her. I always told her that."

Jake dating Miranda. I almost couldn't believe it.

The tequila had clearly loosened Miranda's tongue, and she brayed out, "Oh blah, blah, blah, control, control, control. Can you play the flipside of that record, Jacob? Okay, I'll admit it—Nick's a tool. But he was right. You *were* a fuck-up."

"Enough!" I shouted.

They fell quiet.

I continued in a normal tone, "All this bullshit bickering is grating, so please stop. And by the way, she's right, Jake. You *were* a fuck-up, but that's old news. And Miranda, you do seem to like being controlled. But starting tonight, that's all in the past. Both of you need to get over it. Deal?"

I could tell Jake still cared for her, as the emotions he wore on his sleeve clearly showed.

"Fine by me," he said coolly.

Miranda had her arms folded under her breasts and a pout on her lips. Her lips and breasts always looked good, but in their current pushed up/pouty state, they were absolutely fantastic. "Fine," she half-whispered.

"Since you took the suitcases," I said, "I'm presuming you and Nick are no longer an item."

"Damn right. I packed as much as I could, and fast. I thought the fangy fuck was actually going to kill me."

Jake stiffened at the comment, but I laughed out loud. I loved her term "fangy fuck." She poured herself another shot of gag-o-matic. Somehow even her gagging managed to be cute.

"I still have a lot of stuff there," she said. "I figured I could go back and get it later . . . if there is a later."

That statement sobered the mood, but not for Miranda. She was sloshed.

"All right, before we start, a few things," I said. "Success rate is over fifty percent in general, and given my age, that success rate goes up to about seventy-five percent. Once you die, we'll know within twenty-four hours. So if you're ready, let's do this before you pass out from all that booze."

My success rate was actually around sixty-five percent, but padding the number a little wasn't the biggest lie I'd ever told. She was more than a little slurry now, but managed to down one more shot.

"Good idea," she said. "Let's get this show on the road."

Jake moved toward the door.

"Where are you going, numb-nuts?" I asked.

"Don't call him that!" Miranda shouted, nailing me with a verbal bitch-slap.

I guess sleeve emotions cut both ways. I wanted to get out of town, but no, I'd decided to help some youngsters out, and I'd stumbled into a soap opera. *Why don't I ever mind my own fucking business?*

I said politely, "Sorry. Where are you going, Jacob?"

At that, she laughed out loud.

"Very funny," Jake said. "Since you don't need me, and I really don't want to see this, I thought I'd take off."

I knew it might be tough on him, but I didn't fancy waiting alone, especially if it didn't work. "Would you mind sticking around? I could use the company."

He nodded.

I asked Miranda, "You ready?"

Her eyes looked like they wanted to bolt again, but she said, "As ready as I'll ever be." She pushed past me to Jake and hugged him. "I'm sorry I hurt you. I didn't mean to. And truth is, I still care about you."

He was choked up, but managed to say, "I've always cared about you."

She turned to me, exposing her neck. "Now, Christian—before I chicken out."

No time for dawdling. I stepped in and took her with a firm, smooth bite. Her knees unhinged, but she stayed on her feet. The first gush of blood hit the roof of my mouth in a pulsing fountain. I'd definitely clipped the carotid artery. This was going to go fast.

Miranda held on tight and closed her eyes. I could feel her draining away.

She said softly, "I was so afraid, but this isn't so bad. No matter how it turns out, this isn't so bad."

Then I felt her connect to me again, via the visions of my life. And I saw more of hers. Suddenly, the visions stopped. *Miranda* stopped.

After it was over, Jake and I carried her to the master bedroom and laid her on the bed. She was drained of blood, ashen, and Jake didn't look much better. As corpses go, she was a pretty good-looking one.

Jake and I went back to the parlor to begin our vigil.

CHAPTER 30

Donald Leland sat in his office waiting. Finally, Garret Dick arrived.

Garret heaved his substantial bulk into a chair. His usual self-assured smile adorned his rather large, fleshy, and unappealing face. He fidgeted, finally lighting a cigarette, and plopped his feet up on Donald's desk.

Donald disapproved of both actions, but held his peace. Dick was a valuable asset, so he got a very long leash. Donald waited patiently while he remained silent, puffing smoke rings up to the ceiling.

Finally Dick rumbled, "You're not going to like it, Donny."

With a lead like that, Leland didn't like it already. "I'm listening."

"I couldn't find any other dirt on Brownell, or that other guy, Beauparlant."

Donald pounded the desk. "Damn it!"

"You might want to save some desk beating for later, because it gets worse."

Donald sat back and steepled his fingers.

Dick went on. "That stuff I'd already dug up, the six mil . . . gone. Not a trace of it."

Donald leaned forward again and said incredulously, "What?"

"Yep, gonzo. Like it was never there."

Leland couldn't believe it. "How?"

Dick took a big puff and replied, "I have no idea, and I'm pretty fair around a keyboard. I even subbed it out to a guy I know who's a lot more than fair. And do you know what he came up with? Exactly squat."

Donald was fuming. He spewed out, "But we've got the printouts."

Dick shook his head. "With no hard data to back them up, they're not worth the paper they're printed on."

Donald opened his mouth to speak, closed it, and sat back to think. This had been so promising, and now it was a dead end.

Dick said, "What's the difference, anyway? If you ask me, Janet Pierce did you a big favor by sucking your cock in that back alley."

Donald was only half paying attention. "What do you mean?"

Dick laughed. "Well, aside from the fact she can suck a golf ball through a garden hose, your little indiscretion ended up stopping you from marrying that Brownell bitch. I always told you it was a big mistake, and not just because Lisa's so full of shit. It was a bad idea for you in general. You've been down that path more than once. Marriage ain't for guys like you and me."

Donald had to smile, thinking of garden hoses and the fact that he truly liked Garret Dick. He might be a violent felon, a sociopath that most normal people would naturally abhor, but the two of them had an understanding, a relationship even. They'd gotten each other out of multiple problems in the past, and Garret was the only person

Donald could let down his guard with and act completely himself. It felt refreshing.

No one else got to peek behind Donald's mask. If anyone ever did, they'd run away from the monster as fast as their feet would carry them. Anyone who was sane, that is. It took someone like Dick, a nearly inhuman, hardened career criminal, to truly appreciate Donald Leland.

Donald smiled. "Garret, my friend, you're right. You usually are, but I'm not going to drop it."

Dick did not appear surprised. "How come?"

"Two reasons. First, the doctor is not what he appears. He's got something to hide, and he's good at it."

"But with Lisa gone, how's that any of your business?"

"Oh, it isn't. But whatever he's in to, it's lucrative, and maybe it's a business that someone like me, or you, would like to be involved in."

Dick smiled. "Donny, you're always thinking. And the other reason?"

"Because I'm not quite done fucking with Lisa. Did you think she could dump me, for any reason, and get away with it?"

"Let's see, you fired her, ended her career, maybe wrecked her financially, and now what? You want to ruin her life completely?"

"That's why I enjoy you so much, Garret. You truly understand me."

"I like your style, Donny, but we still have nothing to go on. What're we going to do?"

"It's simple, really. I'm going to flush my little Lisa and see where it leads us."

"You think she's in on it?"

Not for the first time, Donald pondered the possibility. "Maybe. But you'll be able to figure that out for us."

"How so?"

Donald started dialing his new cell phone. "Because, my friend, you'll be following her."

~~~

Lisa was sitting at her kitchen table when her cell phone rang. She answered it, not recognizing the number, but when she heard Donald's voice, she nearly hung up. "What do you want, Donald?"

"How are you doing?"

"Let's skip the bull. I don't have the time. If you're calling to ask how I'm doing, I'm hanging up."

"Actually, I'm calling to do you a favor."

Lisa scoffed, "Do me a favor? Right. You fired me and blackballed me, and now you want to do me a favor?"

In his most soothing tone, Donald said, "Now, Lisa, that wasn't personal, it was a matter of business. How could the two of us work together after what happened? As for blackballing, I did no such thing. The job market is tough out there. You ought to know that."

His firing her couldn't be more personal, and she suspected he had, in fact, used every resource at his command—and they were substantial—to keep her from getting another real estate job.

He continued, "I wish things had gone differently between us, but that doesn't mean I don't still care about you, or want to protect you, even. That's why I need to warn you about your husband."

Lisa was certain that Donald not only didn't care about her, but despised her. Notwithstanding, the comment about Julian piqued her curiosity. "What about Julian?"

"Well, all that information I found on him is gone."

"What do you mean, gone?"

"It's gone, my dear, like it was never there. And now the

little we can find on him, or Beauparlant for that matter, is boringly squeaky clean. Now how would a plain old ER doc have that kind of skill? Or maybe more importantly, what's he trying to hide?"

Lisa was stunned. She wondered, *What the hell is Julian up to?* "Maybe it's a mistake."

"It's no mistake. Garret checked it very carefully, and you know how thorough he can be."

She grimaced at the mention of Garret Dick's name. "Ruthless" was a far better term than "thorough" to describe him. "If your pet arm-twister can't dig up any dirt, I don't know what you expect me to do."

"I don't know, either. I'm just passing along the information, and hopefully it will do you some good."

Lisa thought that last statement rang as hollow as could be. Donald had his reasons for sharing this with her. He had reasons for everything he did, but it didn't matter. She needed to think.

"I have to go," Lisa said, abruptly hanging up. She poured herself another cup of coffee and tried to figure out what this could be about. She never believed Julian's excuses, of course, but this made it all the worse. Not only had Julian pulled off some shady deals, but he was expert enough to cover them up when he'd been discovered. He'd always been good with a computer, but not like this—not good enough to evade Donald and his team of bloodhounds.

Lisa reflected on how Julian hadn't returned any of her calls as of late, and she admitted to herself that it hurt a little. She knew she had no right to feel this way, but it didn't change how she felt.

After hemming and hawing for a bit, Lisa left a message, even though she hated leaving messages when information was so important. She told him about the breakup with

Donald, sparing the sordid details—but not for sympathy. In fact, she suspected that Julian would likely delight in the knowledge. But Lisa didn't care—their divorce settlement had to be altered now because she wasn't getting remarried. She had no job and, quite possibly, no future in real estate, thanks to Donald. She needed money and would get her due.

She'd also mentioned in her message that she had lost her child, and that was clearly for sympathy's sake. After the fact, however, she wished she hadn't told Julian. Not that he would gloat over such a serious matter, but on the other hand, how could he be expected to care, given the circumstances?

After multiple attempts at reaching him, she finally received a curt text in response:

> *Sorry. Understand need to change settlement. Be better if we work thru lawyers rather than directly. JB.*

That short text hurt her far more than his not responding at all. Of course Julian wanted nothing to do with her. What was she thinking?

She reflected on her lousy choices in men. First, Donald had screwed her royally and would continue to do so at every opportunity. Then there was Julian. He was a nice enough guy, but in recent years, not at all engaged in the marriage. As she had slipped into boredom, she'd slipped into Donald's bed, and felt badly over it afterward. Julian didn't deserve that, and she considered herself the villain in their story because of it. But now, with what Donald had learned, Julian had obviously been into some nefarious activities, as well. How bad it was, she had no way of knowing.

He'd lied to her, probably through their entire marriage, and she most definitely hadn't deserved that. It didn't excuse what she'd done, but all the same, it assuredly grayed the black-and-white scenario of the cheating wife and the cuckolded husband. She found herself getting angry.

Lisa would settle for nothing less than a substantial portion of Julian's money, both legal and illegal, as far as she was concerned. Money certainly motivated her, but that wasn't what prompted her to act. Though jobless, she had reserve funds and plenty of time to wait for the lawyers to tease through the divorce.

What prompted her to act was her anger. Both Julian and Donald had treated her underhandedly, and she'd had enough. Lisa had never been a pushover, never a person to trifle with, and she wasn't going to start leaning in that direction now. Always active in seeking out what she wanted, she'd never passively waited for anything to come to her.

She began studying Julian's mysterious list of holdings again and said to herself, "I don't know what the hell I'm going to do, but I'm going to do something."

~~~

Donald put away his cell, smiled at Garret Dick, and extended his arms, palms up. The gesture said, *See how easy it was?*

Dick said, "It won't be long, will it?"

"No, I don't suspect so. And Garret, do you know what she called you? She called you my 'pet arm-twister.' I rather like that."

Dick smiled back, but there wasn't a hint of good humor in it. "Yeah, me too. Before this is all over, maybe I'll get to demonstrate some arm-twisting for her."

Donald grinned. "Perhaps you will."

CHAPTER 31

Sunrise came and brought no change to Miranda. It'd only been five hours, so there was still plenty of time left. Shortly after dawn, Jake started pacing. He had on some big, dopey cowboy boots, and he kept *clomp-clomp-clomping* back and forth, all through the suite. It was driving me nuts.

I'd reached my limit and turned to tell him to stop, when I noticed he walked right through a shaft of sunlight coming through the bottom of the window shade. It hit him squarely on the back of the hand, and he didn't even flinch. I knew he was distracted, but even so, he should've felt something. When he made his monotonous *clomping* return trip, the same thing happened, but with the other hand. Again, nothing.

"Let me see your hands," I said.

"Why?"

Without answering, I took Jake's hands and studied them. There were no burns. I took him over to the window. He'd been turned about twenty years ago and was on the early side to lose sun-sensitivity, but Jake was evidently full of surprises. I took his hand and put it into the sun. He yelped, but I held firm. There was no burning.

"Hey!" he yelled. "Stop!"

I smiled. "You yelled out of reflex. I noticed you walking through the sunbeam. When's the last time you checked for sun sensitivity?"

"Maybe two years ago. It didn't seem so bad then."

"Come on," I said.

Jake looked scared, but in the end, he did it. He rolled his sleeves up and put his arms in the sun. *Nothing*. He tried it with his chest, back, and the grand finale, his face. *No burns.*

I said, "Let's go, day-walker."

We sat by the pool in the early morning sunlight. I didn't speak as I remembered what an epiphany, what a joy it had been to be able to go out into the sun again. He sat, smiling serenely, with his face tilted to the sun. He had that expression that people get when they unexpectedly run into a long-lost love. After a while, we went back in.

"You've only got a little sunburn on the face," I said.

He was shocked. "I do?"

"Calm down, it's already fading. You'll be a tad sensitive for a few months, nothing that some sunblock won't take care of. Then it's beach time for you, my friend."

He smiled. "Cool."

Losing his sun sensitivity distracted him from Miranda for a bit. But he must have suddenly remembered, as he bolted to the bedroom. He was back fast, shaking his head. Then, to my chagrin, he started that fucking pacing again.

I stopped him. "Jake, we may have a long way to go, and you're driving me bug-shit, walking up and down like that. You look beat. Why don't you sack out on the couch? I promise I'll come get you if anything changes."

"Okay, I'll lie down. But no way in hell I'm going to sleep."

About five minutes later, hell found a way, and he was snoozing. I must have nodded off, too—but about an hour later, I woke up abruptly. Something in the back of my head said I heard something.

I took one look at Miranda, and I knew. There was the faintest bit of color in her cheeks. No human would have seen it. I waited and waited. Finally, she took a small breath. I felt her wrist for a pulse. She was kicking along at the breakneck rate of one heartbeat every three and a half minutes. It would be soon now, a few hours at most.

I woke Jake up. "Somebody's going to want to see you in a while."

He jackknifed off the couch and flew into the master bedroom. When I caught up, I found him sitting on the bed, holding her hand.

He said, "I didn't see it at first . . . her color. She's coming back."

"It won't be long now."

Her breathing steadied, and her heart accelerated to twenty-five, an average figure for vampires. Her color kept improving. She had been a looker as a human, but the HVSV sure put on the finishing touches. The lips were fuller and a deeper red, her neckline perfect, and her cheekbones somehow seemed higher. Her hair, full to start with, was even more so, and had taken on some red highlights. I couldn't wait to see her eyes. She was outstanding.

Then it came . . . the reawakening. Miranda didn't do it demurely, like Sleeping Beauty waking from her long nap. She took in a deep, hitching breath and bolted upright. Her arms flew out, and her eyes opened wide. My gods, were they gorgeous.

She blurted out, "Shit!"

I admired the eloquence. She appeared as if she didn't know where or even who she was. Jake held her, calming her, and she finally focused, looking at me.

"It worked . . . didn't it?" she said.

I did a small, theatrical bow. "Correct, beautiful."

She looked around the room, as if fascinated by its everyday appearance. "I see so much . . . I feel . . . great."

I was so relieved that she'd made it. "What do you say we get you something to eat?"

With the reawakening, new vamps needed buckets of energy and usually were starving when they first came around, but she only had eyes for Jake. She smiled, and then it turned into something else—something with a bit more intent. She wrapped her arms around him and kissed him hard. When the kiss showed no signs of breaking, I said, "Don't mind me, I'll let myself out."

I left to give them some privacy. I could call room service later. I dawdled about, giving them some time, but when I returned, there was a worrisome banging noise coming from my bedroom. It sounded as if they'd made it through the headboard and were now working their way through the wall.

I yelled, "Enough already! You're going to wreck the place! Give it a rest!"

Suddenly, the silence was deafening. Then I heard whispering and giggling, just like a couple of silly kids on a sleepover.

Oh, this is just great, I thought. I ordered up a feast, and they eventually emerged. Jake managed to get back into his clothes. Miranda was in my bathrobe. Though it ran to the floor on her, she looked utterly charming. She was flushed, and her hair was beautifully tousled.

We sat down to enjoy our lunch, and Miranda tore into it like a starving wild beast. She needed the energy to jumpstart her new vampire physiology. At the end of her smorgasbord, she let out a massive belch and leaned back in her chair, replete.

"Excuse you," I said. "How do you feel?"

She replied dreamily, "Pretty good, but . . ."

I finished for her. "Something's missing, right? We'll wait 'til sunset, and then we'll take care of that."

Her dreamy look was quickly replaced by a serious one.

"Smile, would you?" I said.

She hesitated and gave me a forced smile. Her canines were now a bit overdeveloped and very dangerous. I thought they were cute.

She said, "I'm scared."

"You'd be stupid not to be," I replied.

The sun finally called it quits for the day, and when we were about to leave, Miranda suddenly hugged me. She was shaking like a leaf, the poor kid.

"I love you, Miranda," I said. I really meant it. It wasn't the moony-eyed "let's get married" kind of "I love you," but that didn't make it any less true. It made me feel like I had family again.

She said, "I love you, too, Titus."

Now Jake moved toward us with a dopey smile on his face, his arms open, trying to turn things into a group hug. But that would have been too much touchy-feeliness for an old Roman like me.

I backed away and growled, "None of that. Come on, we've got some business to attend to. Let's get into character."

We went to the Quarter and hunted. I stalled Miranda, having Jake go first, and then me. By the time it was her turn, she was literally bloodthirsty. It would make it easier for her. She would have preferred a criminal, or someone she could have justified murdering, even if she'd been kidding herself. But you can't always count on that.

It ended up being what appeared to be a workaday middle-aged woman. Maybe she'd finished an evening shift and was heading home, but she never made it. Miranda was quick, efficient, and deadly. She cried afterward, but that isn't unusual after a first kill. I hoped Miranda would get used to the killing, and fast. If not, she'd die. No one felt much like celebrating, especially Miranda, so there'd be no beignets tonight.

We headed back to the hotel. Jake and Miranda quickly tucked in. I heard some whispering and some crying, but I fell fast asleep. It had been a long day.

~~~

The next night didn't go so smoothly. In counterpoint to their guilt over killing, fresh turnees often feel invincible with their newfound power. Miranda fell into this trap, got careless, and took six bullets to the chest on account of it. It was a harsh lesson, and getting shot hurts like a bastard. But vampire pain, even if it's severe, doesn't equate with being debilitated. It's a tough disconnect to learn, because as a human, you're conditioned to accept that pain equals incapacity. After she was shot, she fell to the ground because that's was she thought she was supposed to do. In the end, she'd been able to get up off the deck and dispatch her assailant by tearing his throat out. She didn't shed a tear over him, and I didn't think she'd ever be careless around a potential victim again.

When it was over, she was covered in gore and breathing heavily from blood loss and exertion. The sucking sounds from the chest wounds were somewhat unsettling. She looked down at her chest and said, "Gross."

I hugged her like a proud papa, wrecking yet another jacket, but I didn't even care.

Jake said, "Just for the record, Titus, I was really paying

attention to the lesson tonight, so don't feel like you need to take me out and get me shot to pieces or anything. But maybe we ought to get moving. Even New Orleans police respond to gunshots once in a while."

"Good point. Take the head like I showed you, and toss the stiff in the trunk."

As I got behind the wheel of our car, Jake did indeed take care of the body as instructed, but what I didn't notice was that he kept the head. He pitched it into my lap, catching me off guard. I squealed like a schoolgirl and pelvic-bucked the severed head onto the passenger seat.

Jake and Miranda howled with laughter.

I spewed, "Oh, that's fucking funny. So mature."

They laughed even harder at that, making me laugh, as well. After all, it was a good gag.

That night went a long way toward turning Miranda into a real vampire, and maybe even Jake, for that matter. The next day, I left for Montreal, hoping that nothing bad happened up there.

CHAPTER 32

After an uneventful flight, I landed in another of my favorite cities, Montreal. It was founded in 1642, fortified in 1725, and took off after that. I arrived around 1730, and despite the Brits taking it in 1760 when they won the French and Indian War, I managed to stay there for another thirty years or so. It's a modern city that holds onto its Old World French charm. Old Montreal was the whole of the city when I'd first arrived, and I like it best. Go figure.

I checked into the Le Saint-Sulpice Hotel, right in the shadow of Montreal's version of the Notre-Dame Cathedral. After a fairly quick cleanup and change, I took a pleasant walk to McKibbin's Irish Pub. I was hoping to catch my buddy there—and hoping nothing had happened.

Despite my long life, and the multiple famous, infamous, and not-so-famous characters I've known through the years, he was by far the most interesting of the lot. He was an Irish Quebecois, and as he told it, his original name was Colm Callaghan. But I knew that was not completely accurate. Most vampires and humans alike called him simply "the Squid."

I first met him in 1740 when he emigrated from Ireland to Montreal. Surprisingly, there were quite a few Irish in

Montreal at that time, as there still are today. During the French and Indian War, historians report that Irish soldiers were in the French army, and the historians have that right. Squid was one of those Irish soldiers, and so was I, although my ancestry leaned more toward the Roman-Irish extraction.

He arrived in 1740, at twenty years old, with a bit of cash and a lot of energy. He planned to open a tavern and sought me out as an importer. Squid told me that all he ever wanted to be was a tavern owner, a claim that held true for almost three centuries. Beer and whiskey were a given, but he knew he was dealing with the French and wanted a good stream of drinkable wine. I was the man for that.

He opened his tavern, the Owl's Eye in Old Port, and it quickly became popular. Squid was affable and funny; he charged fair prices and hated the British, regaling any who'd listen with various stories of how much they sucked. In Montreal, there was a sizable audience of folks who'd listen. You couldn't help but like the guy, and I was among his steady customers. We became friends. Although I know him extremely well, many things about him are mysterious.

Various hokey stories surrounded the origins of his nickname, none of which were to be believed. He claimed it was a seafaring name at one point, but I knew for a fact that he hated ocean travel and had vomited all the way across the Atlantic when he emigrated. He sometimes claimed that a retarded cousin gave him the name. Other times, he'd say it came from a retarded friend, due to a mispronunciation caused by a speech impediment. The retarded friend's name was supposedly "the Goon."

As to why he had come to Montreal, Squid claimed he'd killed his new bride due to an argument over what to name their pet cat. He preferred Emily. She, the ill-fated Constance. In later years, he told the same story, but said the pet was a goldfish. When I reminded him goldfish were not available as pets in the 1730s, he looked perplexed, since he clearly remembered having one.

The only fairly certain fact is that he had left Ireland to come to New France. Did he kill his wife? Maybe. But I'd wager he killed someone, at least, and was fleeing a bad situation.

I got to McKibbin's right about seven o'clock. It was a standard-fare Irish pub of dark wood, shitty food, and a stupendous assortment of draft beer. An old-style bar ran the length of one wall and dominated the place. Over the years, there'd been so much beer spilt that it saturated the bar top, the tables, and even the floor, giving the place that sharp, stale, and not-completely-unpleasant smell. Any seasoned pub-crawler would recognize it as the mark of a long-lasting, hard-drinking establishment.

As luck would have it, my buddy was tending bar. You really couldn't miss the Squid, since he was six foot five and filled out. You'd never call him thin, but not fat, either—just plain big. Despite his size-based physical menace, he had a friendly face. If you saw him approach you in a dark alley, you'd be scared shitless until you saw his face. Then you'd be relieved—right up to the point he bit into your neck.

As I watched him mixing a drink, he must have sensed something. He turned, looked right at me, and smiled. Putting his hands flat on the bar, he did a smooth side leap over it, his large mop of brown hair flying back from his forehead. Concerning the Squid, the descriptive "smooth" required some qualifiers.

First, he made his hurdle without paying attention to two young patrons at the bar, probably McGill undergrads, who miraculously scattered before he landed on top of them. They were either quite perceptive or not totally smashed yet, as it was still early. One of them shouted, "Jesus, Squid, watch it!"

Second, as a human, the Squid wasn't the most coordinated of specimens, and this translated to his vampire life. The move looked clunky, maybe even uncoordinated, but at the same time, it was done with perfect vampire fluidity and grace. I know that makes no sense, but the Squid somehow maintained a certain elegance about him, even if he was a klutz.

"Chrissy, so damn good to see you!" he said, bear-hugging me.

He had always called me "Chrissy" over the years. Granted, it's not the most endearing of nicknames, but coming from him, it sounded right.

"Damn good to see you, too, Squid. Nice move over the bar—you nearly killed those two kids."

He chuckled and ushered me toward a stool. "Fuck 'em. It's good for them to use their brains once in a while. They don't get much of a chance at McGill." He laughed at his own joke.

I laughed too, as I took a seat at the end of the bar. He settled in behind it and poured us two tall, tasty beers from the microbrewery du jour.

Funny thing about the Squid, even though most vampires switch to tequila or absinthe, he'd always stuck with beer as his preferred drink. Before he was turned back in 1765, I had to explain a lot of things to him, most of which he had me casually breeze over. The one big exception was beer.

I told him about the absinthe high, and he nodded knowingly, although I knew he didn't know what absinthe was. There was no tequila to talk about yet. It didn't penetrate North America until the 1800s. He did, however, make me go over beer repeatedly and in detail.

"So when I drink it, it will taste the same . . . but I won't get drunk?" he had asked.

I replied with exasperation, as, at least in my mind, there were many other more important issues to discuss. "Yes, for the second time."

"And it will take a vast amount to make me feel full? And I won't gain weight or get sick from too much drink?"

I said slowly, as if speaking to a small child, "Yes. That's right. Can we move on now?"

At that point, the Squid had become silent, a rare event for him. His eyes glazed over, and he gazed up at the ceiling as a smile formed on his lips. He had a look on his face that could only be described as . . . love.

Now he said, "I heard the news. Too bad about you and Lisa. I thought she was nice. I liked her."

The Squid pretty much liked everyone, at least initially. That's the way he was. Lisa met him on a trip to Montreal. He was the only vampire that I ever formally introduced her to. He played the perfect, charming host, touring us around town for a few nights. At the end of the trip, Lisa told me she hated him and thought him an overbearing idiot who never shut up. I kept this piece of information to myself. It would've hurt his feelings.

Lisa couldn't have been more wrong. Squid just liked to talk. By his look, you might expect a "Me Tarzan" type of conversation. It could be a shock to the system when, instead, he rapid-fired you with his clipped, staccato verbiage. He was quick-witted, stand-up-comedian funny— but stole most of his humor. Sometimes you don't realize it for a few weeks, and sometimes never. He was an excellent thief.

I gave him a bullet presentation of my break-up.

"That bitch!" he yelled. "She's way off my Christmas card list!" He actually did send Christmas cards.

"Yep... and get this. The guy then goes and dumps her, and she lost the baby."

He looked distressed. "That's too bad about the kid. She's probably better off being dumped, though. The way you describe this jerk, sounds like he would've dumped her sooner rather than later." The Squid was sympathetic to a fault.

"She called and left messages, telling me about what happened," I said. "With her not getting married now, I'm going to have to pay alimony and all that, but I don't mind. I didn't answer when she called. I feel a little bad about it, especially when I heard about the miscarriage. But I'm feeling better. Talking to her drags me down, and I don't want to go there again."

He nodded. "Understandable. But there's no way you're getting dragged down in Montreal. The two of us are going to tear the town apart. Right, buddy?"

"Right you are," I agreed.

The Squid was the one vampire I had kept in touch with consistently all through my married years. He was a great friend and the most "human" vampire I knew. I mean, the guy had a poker group. He'd played with the same stiffs for over twenty-five years. A group of half-soused French and Irish drunks, they'd miraculously failed to notice that Squid hadn't aged. Oh, the wonders of booze.

I wanted to talk a little bit about the Genealogist, to make sure he was being careful, but the minute I brought up New Orleans, he asked, "Did you see Simone when you were down there?"

Squid had quite a thing for her. His attraction was almost to the same degree that she wanted nothing to do with him.

But he always loved a challenge. He was very patient and could wait decades to score.

I said, "You bet I did, and she may come up for a visit." I was lying, of course, but I couldn't resist pulling his chain.

His eyes flew open. "You're shitting me! When? You need to take me out clothes shopping!"

The Squid was not the best of dressers, although tonight, he was far more spiffy than usual. For nearly a decade, he had favored a red-checked shirt that looked like it had come off a table at a cheap Italian restaurant.

"Slow down, big fella," I said. "Not any time soon. I just left there, and Jean-Luc—"

"That fuck," he growled. "What does she see in that little prick, anyway?"

In the early 1900s, we'd visited New Orleans together, and the Squid made the mistake of impersonating Jean-Luc's phony French accent. It was spot-on, eliciting a fair amount of laughter. But Jean-Luc did not like being the butt of a joke and took exception to it. Squid took exception to his taking exception, and they started in. The age difference was too much, and the Squid got the snot beat out of him.

He wouldn't quit, though, and kept coming back for more. In the end, Squid was nearly unconscious on his feet and couldn't even see Jean-Luc, let alone fight him. He wanted to keep going at him, but I knew Jean-Luc would've killed him. I led Squid away, although I'm sure he didn't know who was doing the leading. It took him nearly a day to heal after all of the punishment the petit Frenchman had heaped upon him. Needless to say, they'd not particularly liked each other since.

I replied, "He's an old friend."

"In his case, your taste in friends sucks. Anyway, if Simone does come up, I'm assuming that we'll all go out together? That'll give me a chance to work my magic."

I smiled and threw some gasoline on the fire. "Sure. And by the way, she told me to say hello."

This was also a lie, but I did it all in the name of some potential fun. He tilted his head to one side, his eyes intense and narrowed, giving me the classic "Squid-eye," his way of silently saying "I think you're full of shit." Difficult as it was, I kept a straight face, since one tiny fissure in my facade would give me away. He kept the Squid-eye on me at full bore, trying to break me. The pressure was astounding.

Finally, with Academy Award-worthy flair, mixing innocence, irritation, and confusion in just the right proportions, I said, "What?"

Maddeningly, he still didn't speak, but I noted the eye had slipped a notch or two in intensity. The relief was palpable. After what seemed liked days, he said, "Really?"

I let out a huge mental exhale. The hook was set. He wanted to believe, but great care needed to be taken. I said again, a tad more annoyed, "Really . . . what?"

"Simone said hello?"

The Squid and I did get off on fucking with each other. It's a guy thing that we'd thoroughly enjoyed for going on three centuries. Now, with the right touch of exasperation, like he was being a dope, I said slowly, "Yes. Simone said hello."

He paused for a moment, and then did a growl that sounded like it came from a brain-damaged Tony the Tiger. "I think Simone is finally going to be introduced to the ninth tentacle."

I have consistently reminded him through the years that squids are actually decapods with ten limbs, so he should refer to his dick as "the eleventh tentacle." The octopus is a cephalopod with eight tentacles. Since his nickname is not "the Octopus," I felt it my solemn duty to once again remind him of these facts.

Before I could open my mouth, he raised his hand to stop me, giving his usual retort on the matter. "Shut the fuck up. I know, but everyone thinks it's eight, and 'eleventh tentacle' just doesn't have the same ring to it." He drained his beer with a swallow. "What say we go grab some dinner?"

"I'm in."

He rearranged the staff to fill his bartending slot, as the place was starting to hop. He spot-hired one of the McGill students he'd almost crushed as a novice busboy. I'm not sure the Squid's management style was particularly effective, but it certainly had panache.

During dinner, whenever I tried bringing up the Genealogist, he put me off, calling me an old lady, a worrywart, and a faggot, but not necessarily in that order. After my sixth rebuke, I decided to give up, for a while, anyway. After a wonderful meal, the big boy wanted to go dancing. And talk about a train wreck—his beautifully grotesque dancing was a thing never to be missed.

We found a place close by, and the Squid waded into the crowd. Without a word of introduction, he took some unsuspecting petite thing by the hand and pretty much dragged her onto the dance floor. She didn't know what hit her and had little choice. Fortunately, she was more than a bit drunk. He hit the floor in full stride, with the little gal in tow, while a techno-pop dance mix blared. The dance floor parted before him like the Red Sea, and he revved up.

I figured the Squid must have an internal metronome that he heard but obviously no one else could. The timing of this metronome didn't seem to have anything to do with the beat of the music, or any music in the history of the world, for that matter. His rhythm was so far off, it was actually on.

But if you watched closely, his movements, although seemingly random, did indeed relate to the music, but in an offbeat, syncopated, and for lack of a better description, Squid-like manner. The gestures are like him: large, overdone, and compelling. Throw in vampire physiology for that gliding sleekness, and there you have it—a sort of ongoing, upright seizure that's quickly noticed.

There were a few jeers at first, but then the crowd began to see the "art" in his freeform spasms. The jeering turned to encouragement, and he responded by increasing the pace of his convulsions, twisting and leaping with delicate landings that nobody his size should be able to do.

He started to sweat almost immediately, and that's another thing that's funny about the Squid. Vampires sweat, but with our improved physiology, perspiration doesn't come easily and would take more effort than a minute of dancing. I don't have a good explanation, but as a human, Squid was a sweaty bastard. He could break into a free-flowing sweat while reading a book in a blizzard. Maybe it carried over, or maybe it's because he's more human than most vampires, or maybe he likes to sweat. I don't know.

His dance partner, scared to death at first, now noticed that he—and therefore she—was getting noticed. She liked it and dove into the dance full tilt, doing a goodly amount of that ass-grinding that people her age seem to like to call dancing. The Squid did not mind. The group that the girl was plucked from, obviously the jealous-for-attention types, joined her on the floor and did another thing people nowadays seem to do a lot of—group dancing. They surrounded my buddy, and again, the Squid did not mind.

The extra ladies motivated him more, and he stepped it up another notch. Now he clearly moved in ways no human could move. As drunk as the other patrons were, they were starting to notice, and we vampires make our living by not getting noticed. I began to feel uncomfortable.

Fortunately, the song came to an end, but if the dumbass didn't finish with a back flip—an Olympic-style, Russian-gymnast, one-hundred-percent-official fucking back flip. He landed it perfectly, but in the process, being Mr. Coordination, bumped three other dancers. He didn't even realize he'd touched them, but with his size and momentum, they got flicked off him like bugs, flying out in all directions.

Squid put his hands in the air, eyes closed to the cheers of the crowd. The fucking ham was drinking it in. In the meantime, his three human projectiles bowled over fellow dancers, tables, and chairs.

I quickly moved past him, saying, "You really stuck that landing, Nadia. Smooth fucking move."

He opened his eyes, lowered his hands, and said, "Oh shit."

We checked everyone as fast as we could, but now the club staff was involved. Fortunately, no one was hurt. We paid the bouncers a few hundred for their trouble and any breakage, then bought a round for the place. The Squid's dance mates were fascinated with him and wanted to hang. But when the opportunity arose, we slipped away as quietly as possible.

As we cleared the club, I said, "Almost two hundred fifty years, and you still haven't learned a fucking thing. Isn't it bad enough your size gets you noticed all the time? Do you think doing a gymnast routine in a human bar is such a bright idea?"

"Stop being such an old lady. I was just having some fun."

"What if you got arrested? Thrown in jail for a few days

when you needed some blood? Then what?"

He didn't miss a beat and went right into a James Cagney, old-time gangster dialect. "Those coppers will never take me alive, see. You're the guy that gave it to my brother, see. Now I'm gonna give it to you, see. Top of the world, Ma!"

His impersonation was spot on. Even though I tried not to, I started laughing. "You're a fucking idiot."

"A dancing idiot."

"Emphasis on 'idiot.'"

We walked on randomly, shooting the breeze and doing a lot of laughing. It felt good.

I said, "Hey, all fun aside, I was worried about you, and don't put me off again. Did you get the info from New Orleans? That Genealogist bitch is going wild. You're being careful, right?"

The Squid was notoriously lax when it came to matters of safety—when it came to matters of anything, really, except having a good time. "Yeah, I got it. I'm fine."

"I'm serious. Don't blow this off. There's something going on. Quebec City is practically next door, and it looks like Montreal may be a new target."

"I knew the two that got it in Quebec. Good vamps. I liked them. But I'm not sure there's enough in what I saw to say Montreal is on the hit list. Looked like a bunch of computer geek gibberish to me."

"It's the best we've got on short notice."

"Well, it doesn't matter what I think. Adrienne's pretty much locked down the town, anyway."

"Good. I hauled ass up here to make sure you were okay."

"To make sure I was okay? Who saved your butt at Ticonderoga? What about Algeria?"

"I'll give you Ticonderoga, but Algeria? You talked me into joining the Foreign Legion and nearly got us both killed. And I'm supposed to thank you for that?"

"Details," he replied with disdain.

I couldn't argue about Ticonderoga, though. During the French and Indian War, my unit had been on patrol near Ticonderoga, or Carillon, as the French called it. Squid was my second-in-command, and we'd walked right into an ambush. The first volley dropped me as I took several shots, one catching me right behind the ear. It must have hit near my brainstem, because I was paralyzed. I thought I was dying.

Then the big oaf, still human at this point, mind you, came lumbering up the trail through a hail of gunfire. How the Brits missed someone so big and so slow is beyond me. He heaved me over his shoulder and retraced his suicide run, although at his extra-slow speed—I'd call it a suicide trot, at best. A second hail of bullets left not a scratch on the Squid, but I got hit three more times. Does that seem fair?

Not that we needed it, but what he did for me that day cemented our friendship even further. It also gained him another nickname, *Calmars l'Intrepide*, or Squid the Fearless. It sounded good back then, but nowadays it made me think of a spicy appetizer.

We walked in silence for a while.

I said, "Hey, not to change the subject, but I had a business idea that might fit up here. Don't worry, I won't try to convince you to give up your sacred calling of running a bar, but maybe you could point me in the right direction." I was thinking of Becca, Maddie, and Jen.

"Maybe this time, I'd be interested," he replied.

I stopped. I supplied wine for his bar and was a minor investor in it, but that was it. I'd wanted to have him as a partner in something else, but he'd never had an interest. "Really? Why? It's not like you to be interested."

He smiled. "Two things. The economy sucks, something I'm sure someone with all your money never notices, and maybe, just maybe, I'm getting a bit bored being a barkeep."

"Go figure. You've only been doing it for two hundred seventy years."

We continued on our walk, wandering toward the waterfront with a discreet, purposeful randomness. It was a good area to hunt.

"So tell me more about this new business," he said.

"It's a fashion and clothing design business."

He snorted. "Oh, great. Right up my alley."

"You don't need to be an expert, but you know everyone in town. You must know some folks who could help."

He looked thoughtful. "I may know some people. Who's running it?"

"As a matter of fact, it's being run by three very new—and very hot—vampire lady friends of mine."

"Really?" he said, growling like a tiger again.

"You know, you ought to stop that growl thing, it's embarrassing."

"Never."

We hit the river and turned west. It quickly got less crowded, not deserted, but empty enough for us to do what we needed to do.

Hunting could be tough for the Squid at times. His size got him noticed. If there were an unseen witness to one of his attacks, he'd be identified. It was hard to miss a six-foot-five near-giant, so he had to be extra careful. If I get spotted, the description goes like this: "average height, average build, average this, average that." It's a great advantage to appear average in the blood-drinking business. Vampires operate best when unnoticed, dancing back flips aside.

His size was one of many reasons why I had been advised not to turn him, and he was quite patient in his hunting because of it. He sometimes took hours to scope out the right victim in the right circumstance. Fortunately, his telepathy was good, and that helped a lot. He was better off hunting in pairs, or groups, because if victims saw him with a bunch of other normal-sized people, strolling and chatting, they tended to relax more. The problem was that he was very private about hunting. I think a part of him found it distasteful, but he'd never admit that.

Soon enough, a solitary male came walking toward us. He looked to be about twenty. Squid pulled out a cigarette, an old standby move of his, and said, "Hey buddy, you got a light?"

When the guy looked up at him, Squid pulled his hair back from his forehead, creating an exaggerated widow's peak. He exposed his upper canines and did an over-the-top, old movie vampire impersonation. "Good eeeeevening."

This always killed me, and I started laughing. If the telepathy didn't work, the victim usually called him an asshole, and Squid took him or didn't, depending on how hard he'd cracked himself up. This time, the telepathy worked, and he drained the guy without a struggle.

When he was done, and so was the victim, Squid asked, "You?"

I could have skipped it, but I always liked hunting with friends. "Sure, let's keep looking around here."

We stored the body in an alley, and I started chuckling. "That fucking 'good evening' thing cracks me up every time."

He smiled. "A classic."

It didn't take long. Mine was a middle-aged man who

looked to be a borderline alcoholic. My telepathy didn't work, so it was a bit of a struggle. I didn't have to kill him, but I did, anyway. I didn't want to make Squid feel bad. The guy fought a lot, and that got me in the spirit of things. I drained him dry.

We carried him back to the alley where we'd left the other one. Squid, being a student of mine, was a decapitation fan when it came to making sure that he didn't have any mistake turnings. From under his jacket, he pulled out a machete. It was larger than any gladius I ever used. Squid was so big, he could conceal a bazooka, and when it came to this sort of thing, I envied him his size.

He completed the task quickly and was fastidious when handling decapitations. He didn't get a drop of blood on him, and there was hardly any telltale gore left behind. It was quite the visual contradiction, seeing a huge beast of Squid's stature hacking the heads off a couple of corpses in such a dainty way. A heinous and horrific act by any standards, but the way he was so prissy about it almost made it appear delicate.

I pried up a sewer cover we'd seen in the alley, and in everything went. *Plunk, plunk, splash, splash.* Being this close to the river, who knew where the bodies and heads would end up, but it was highly unlikely they'd ever be discovered. They'd be two more missing persons in the annals of missing persons. A stroke of bad luck for them.

We started strolling again. I smoked my Cubans, him, his Camels.

He ruminated. "That was fun . . . like old times."

"Yep, it was. It's pretty late. You want to crash in my hotel room?"

"Thanks, but I feel like walking."

I nodded. "You'll get on that business stuff?"

"Starting tomorrow. You know you're going to have to see her. Tomorrow night at the latest. Any longer is disrespectful."

He was talking about Adrienne Du Vivier, the vampire mayor of Montreal. She'd been there since 1648, and when I arrived, she was ruling Montreal with an iron fist. Although I was far senior to her in age, she being just over four hundred years old at the time, my desire to lead in Montreal was far outweighed by my desire to sleep with her. She was stunning—petite, with a non-existent waist, raven-black hair, and wild black eyes. It was lust at first sight. Given her controlling personality, trying to assume a leadership role would've killed the relationship, and frankly, I preferred sex to leadership any day. I know it wasn't the most mature of positions to take, but in my defense, I was only 1,750 years old.

Adrienne had a mean streak, even by my standards. She was of high birth, and she never let me forget it. She was also unpredictable. If things didn't go exactly her way, she might laugh it off or scratch out an eye. The relationship wasn't ideal, but it didn't lack excitement and was actually pretty good until the night I nearly killed her.

"You're right," I said. "I'm not some fledgling skulking into town. No matter what our past, I should pay my respects. Tomorrow night, then. You'll come?"

"*D'accord*," he replied, bending down to give me a hug. "Really good to see you, Chrissy."

I thought maybe I shouldn't have asked him to come with me to see Adrienne. She'd pretty much wanted him dead ever since she met him, and that was way back when he was still human.

I asked, "How are you and Adrienne getting on these days?"

"Long story. I'll tell you tomorrow."

"Okay. And by the way, nice job with those heads tonight, Mary."

"Hey, I meant to ask you, that old guy who's fucking your wife . . . I bet he's tall, isn't he?"

Always too quick for me—and far worse, he was right. Leland *was* tall.

I stammered, "You stole that . . . from somewhere." It was the best I could do on the spur of the moment.

He smiled. "Uh-huh, but I do it so well."

CHAPTER 33

From the rear window of the cheap New Orleans hotel room he'd rented, Al Martinez stared intently through infrared binoculars. The room gave him an excellent line of sight to the back entrance of the building that his team was working in. They'd been in there for a fairly long time—not worrisome yet, but it was getting close.

From behind him, the one member of the team he'd kept with him, Andrew Simmons, asked nervously, "Are they out yet, Al?"

"No, not yet," Martinez replied. "Hey, why don't you put on the coffee? I could sure use a cup." He hoped the task would help distract Simmons from his anxiety. Nothing had worked so far, and Martinez, although a patient man, was beginning to get annoyed. Simmons had trained well, performing coolly under pressure in all the simulations. But the minute he'd gotten into the field on his first mission, he had fallen apart.

Martinez thought it was too bad. Simmons was a smart kid, but he'd seen this happen before. It wouldn't be a total loss, though. Simmons would still be valuable to the Network somehow, but not on hunts.

Simmons' inability to perform that night, however, had

been a particular stroke of bad luck. He had advanced training in explosives, which was what Martinez planned to use, even though it went against protocol. It would have been nice to send Simmons with the rest, but he was so wired, he might have gotten the entire team wiped out. There'd be no fiascos for a team led by Al Martinez.

As the coffee finished brewing, Martinez saw movement. It was his men. He counted them silently as they exited—one, two, three, and four—all there. He breathed a sigh of relief. From the way they moved, with a careful, measured quickness, he could tell they were not under attack or duress. By the amount of time they'd been inside, he could safely surmise that all had gone well and the bomb was set. He would find out for sure in a few minutes when they reported in.

As Simmons brought over the coffee, Martinez said, "They're out."

A hesitant smile jittered spasmodically over Simmons' clammy face. His pasty complexion gained a bit of color. "That's great, Al. Will we be going home soon?"

This normally would have been a dumb question, as their procedure dictated that after a hit was made, they'd clean up and leave immediately with no further exposure for the team. But this mission was so far afield from normal procedure that the question wasn't dumb at all.

One of the Harrisons' basic guidelines in this dangerous game prohibited the use of what could be categorized as diffuse weapons. They thought the risk to the innocent was too great. Explosives definitely fell into the category of diffuse weapons. Martinez's only fallback was that another basic Harrison rule encouraged improvising in the field. He would have to make the case that using explosives on this mission was a necessary improvisation.

Martinez respected Helen Harrison and all that she'd accomplished. He maybe even loved her, like a dutiful son loves his mother. He respected and feared "Bloody" Bill Harrison. His nickname was well deserved for his ruthless efficiency in dispatching vampires and his mercilessness in dealing with humans who aided them. Despite this, Martinez, who'd been born again, was answering to a higher authority now: Lord Jesus, as He was represented by Reverend Gary Jarvis.

Jarvis, a longstanding member of the Network, had helped Martinez and many others find the Lord. He didn't openly oppose the Harrisons, but had differing ideas about how the Network should proceed, and he didn't fear bringing his viewpoints up for discussion in any forum. Jarvis, for instance, felt it impractical to continue to go up against enhanced beings so directly. He pointed out that the mortality rate of field agents was astounding. Beyond this, they were extremely difficult to replace, considering the amount of training needed to prepare them.

When the Harrisons pointed out that the death of innocents was not acceptable, Jarvis countered that the Lord had told him that they were in a Holy War and that if innocents were killed, they would soon be rejoicing in heaven. This particular line of reasoning often infuriated "Bloody" Bill.

The Harrisons thought their cut-and-run system was wisest. Since the team was already in the field, Jarvis thought, why not have them stay out, carefully observing and perhaps gathering intelligence? Or maybe even take out an additional vampire or two?

The Harrisons moved with care and caution, using meticulous planning and study prior to any field operations, and despite this, they still lost many agents. Jarvis thought this strategy was a defensive battle doomed to failure, and he favored an all-out war against the vampires. It was what the Lord had told him was necessary.

This difference of opinion had been on a "friendly" level until recently. Jarvis had become more aggressive, and the Harrisons more wary of their leadership position because of it. It created a tension in the group that threatened to become a schism. It made Martinez, along with many other members of the Network, quite nervous. But if push came to shove, as much as he respected the Harrisons, Martinez would support Gary Jarvis, and therefore, his Savior.

Before he left for this mission, Jarvis prayed with him and spoke to him about God's holy and cleansing light. In so many words, he encouraged Martinez to use explosives. Martinez was not a stupid man and knew Jarvis was maintaining deniability. Given his position, Martinez would have done the same. He considered his options and, after praying more, decided that he'd go against protocol and use a bomb. He reasoned that the Lord had called on him to be an agent of change, and that this change was needed if they were to win this war.

If he wavered, he had the option of contacting Jarvis on a "safe" cell phone. Any contact with a team in the field was also against security procedures. But Jarvis gave him the option, not to break protocol, of course, but to pray with him if the need arose. Martinez did not waver, and it was his experience that when it came to cell phones, none were safe.

Martinez said to Simmons, "I'm not sure when we'll leave. Let's see what the boys have to say about things when they're back."

The bit of color Simmons had temporarily gained faded back to a pasty white. He said, "You think infusing the explosive with the garlic extract will do any good?"

Martinez smiled. "It couldn't hurt."

CHAPTER 34

I made my way to McKibbin's the next afternoon, and we met in the Squid's basement office, which was more like a broom closet. The building itself was very nice, so why my idiot friend had chosen a cold, drafty basement phone booth for an office was a mystery to me. The place literally made me itchy. Its interior design could be best described as classic "a grenade just went off in here" style.

A tiny desk was jammed up against one of the walls, all of which were lined with shitty bookcases overstuffed with various out-of-date record books and ledgers. There was barely room for the second bare-bones chair that sat across from his desk.

The one modern touch in the office was the computer he was tinkering with. I shimmied into my seat, using all six inches of space I had to work with. Squid was jotting down various notes on little scraps of paper, which the top of his desk was awash in. He smoked a huge cigar, blowing out cumulus-cloud-sized puffs and driving the visibility down to the level of a Turkish steam bath.

The desk was so tiny compared to him, he actually appeared to be wearing it, right along with the rest of the room. He finally looked up from under the cover of another huge billow of smoke and shuffled all of his scraps together, seemingly at random. "Okay, I think I got it."

"Good, give it to me quick. If you drop that cigar in this shithole, we're going to go up like a bonfire."

Squid focused on me contemptuously and said, "Stop being such a pussy." He started re-sorting the scraps, handing me some and keeping others, while mumbling to himself.

"Can't you email me this stuff?" I said.

"Jesus, you are a faggot! I thought, you know, maybe two people could get together in person, not on the Internet or some other fucking thing, and go over some business. So sorry I don't have a PowerPoint presentation ready. You probably can't wait to get out of here so you can get on Facebook or some other bullshit."

"All right, all right . . . let's do this. Give me one of the stovepipes you're smoking, and can we get any booze down here in this rat trap? And for the record, I'm way too old for Facebook."

Now I was getting in the spirit of old-time business. He punched a button on an intercom straight out of 1965, and in no time, a bartender was down with a bottle of tequila. He pulled out two dirty, and I mean, *dirty* water glasses from his desk drawer and poured.

I batted my eyes at him. "I'm touched you still remember my favorite."

Expressionless, he said, "You done? Can we do this?"

"Okay, Mister Serious. Go ahead."

He'd done a bang-up job, tapping his multiple connections in town. After about an hour, we were winding up. The Squid still could surprise me after all these years. Just when I thought he wasn't into something, or not paying attention, I found that he was. Even when he seemed totally disinterested, he somehow always ended up being capable.

"In this economy, office space is dirt cheap," he said. "But since most stuff happens online, the physical space will operate at a loss, no matter what. But it should be stylish and sexy to draw the human crowd. I've got a couple of places scoped out. It's risky, probably a bust—but if it catches, it'll be a home run."

He's really done his homework, I thought. "And what's your price for being the onsite manager? Fifty percent?"

"I was thinking more like sixty."

"Fuck you. To be discussed later."

"Sounds like a plan. If I'm going to be involved in the fashion end, you'll need to take me shopping for some new duds. You know, kind of gay, the way you dress."

"Fucking funny. Do you think we should loop Adrienne on this tonight? After all, she is the boss up here."

I already dreaded having to meet with her, and now bringing her into a business deal? It was unavoidable, though, as we vampires kept commerce all in the family. Starting a business in her town without her approval, her cooperation, and her cut of the profits was unthinkable. It was within her rights to snafu the entire deal, and since she hated me, and Squid maybe more, that very likely would be the way this played out. Resigned to try, I planned to do some serious ass-kissing in the process.

He took a long drag and blew another cloud of Cubano in my face. "I already did."

If I could have fallen out of my chair, I would have. But there wasn't enough room for me to hit the floor. "You already brought it up?"

He nodded.

Now this was truly amazing. Adrienne, as far as I knew, hadn't passed a word with the Squid for 250 years. Their last conversation had taken place as she was doing her best to rip his head from his shoulders.

"I didn't realize you two were on speaking terms," I said.

He leaned back, contemplating the ceiling tiles, and intoned the infuriatingly noncommittal "Mmmm-hmmm."

For a moment, I thought he was trying to make me drag it out of him, but he actually looked confused.

"How long?" I asked.

He leaned forward, and the desk creaked under his weight. If he crushed it, it would land directly on my knees, and I had no place to run, as we were essentially stuffed into a vertical coffin for two. His dazed reverie cleared a bit. "Thing is, I think we're sort of a couple, but I'm not sure. I'm kind of afraid to ask."

I was flabbergasted. The Squid was the one person in this world that Adrienne hated the most. I was a close second, but that order was debatable on a year-to-year basis. I stammered out, "You and Adrienne, a couple? You've slept with her?"

He said nonchalantly, "Oh sure. A bunch of times."

This was unbelievable. Now I leaned in. Ominously, the desk groaned even louder than before. I rolled my right hand toward myself in a loose, repetitive circle. "C'mon. Wake up and dish. Don't make me beg."

He poured off another two drinks. "I don't know, about two years ago or so, word on the street was that she had started acting weird. Really bitchy."

"That's pretty much standard for her."

"Yeah, right... but no, I mean, way out of control. Dressing vamps down in public, getting physical with them, and messing them up pretty good. She actually banished a couple from Montreal for no reason. Can you imagine, banishing someone in this day and age?"

I couldn't. As far as I knew, nobody had been banished since the 1700s.

He went on. "And that's not all. Her business decisions got sloppy. Her hunting habits got sloppier and just plain nasty. You see that stuff in the papers a few years ago? The shit cops sold as some sort of weird gang warfare?"

I did remember. There were five or six dead, all horribly mutilated. "Her?"

"Her. She was getting shitfaced almost every night, and she isn't the nicest of drunks, if you know what I mean."

Adrienne liked her booze as much as the next vampire, but she almost never let it get the best of her. This was nuts.

"About a year ago, the grumbling started. You know, 'what is she doing,' 'she's bringing too much attention,' 'we might have to act,' 'we may need a new mayor' . . . stuff like that."

In the past, when a mayor or other high-profile vamp hit the wall or lost it, a revolt could begin, and it was always ugly when it went down. This was serious. Adrienne would be a bit over seven hundred years old now (and to think I'd forgotten her birthday for the last 247 years) and maybe she was getting tired of living. It happens. I hadn't exactly been the most stable vampire for the last hundred years, myself.

I asked, "Did anything get off the ground?"

"Close. They came to me to be the leader. Can you imagine? Me doing a Pancho Villa up against her?"

I couldn't. He was way too smart. "You're too tall to play a Mexican."

He smiled. "I know, right? And throw in that I don't fancy her bashing my brains in."

"Again."

"Right . . . *again*. So this is all secondhand for me at this point. I never saw her because I was still doing my best to avoid her. You know, for health reasons."

"You've been damn good at it, lasting here this long."

"Hey, I love this place. In the mid eighteen hundreds, it got easier when things really took off and expanded. But those first fifty years after you left were touch and go. I'd bump into her now and again and beat a quick retreat, but she always gave me that look. You know, that she still wanted to kill me, but at the same time, she didn't want to fuck with you by doing it. I think when you threw her through that wall, that may have convinced her."

"Might have helped. Even so, most people would have left."

"I made up my mind she wasn't going to chase me out. Hell, who did she think she was? I spilled blood fighting for Montreal."

"I don't think falling down and getting a big splinter in your ass counts as spilling blood."

The Squid had made it through the entire French and Indian War without a scratch. Toward the end, a mortar shot landed relatively close, knocking us down. We weren't hurt by the blast, but he ended up having a big splinter in his butt, and had always claimed it was shrapnel.

"You're such an asshole," he said. "It was shrapnel!"

I didn't want to take him off track, as he could talk for hours about his "war wound." I put my hands up in mock surrender. "Okay, you win. It was shrapnel. Now go on, please."

He took a deep breath and shot me a dirty look. "Asshole. Where was I? Oh yeah, I hadn't seen any of her screwed-up behavior firsthand, since I avoided her like the plague, but I was weighing my options. You know, what to do, where to go. I certainly didn't want to stay and be part of a vampire revolt. Even if I stayed out of it, she probably would've killed me and made up some shit about me being involved."

It was a spot-on presumption. I said, "By the way, thanks for telling me about this when it happened."

"Oh, fuck off. You were still playing Joe Human at the time."

I hate when he's right, I thought. I remained silent.

"So I'm having a rough night, thinking about all this crap, and I go to the Bily Kun to tie one on."

Bily Kun was a dark, moody absinthe bar that played host to both vampires and humans. It wasn't the Squid's best move, as Adrienne owned it, and I told him so.

"I know. But she was supposed to be out of town, and I like the place. Evidently, she got back early, went there first thing, and got totally splashed. So I'm walking in and she comes staggering out, takes about five steps, falls down, and rolls into the gutter. Nobody's there but me. She's totally out, but it's still her, so I start walking by. But I couldn't do it, you know? Couldn't leave anybody like that." Squid was chivalrous to a fault.

"Again, not a great move."

"Yeah, I know. But anyway, I went over to her, slowly, mind you, on guard like I was approaching a cobra. I carefully lifted her out of the gutter and started trying to bring her around, saying, 'Adrienne, it's me, Squid. Don't hurt me, I'm trying to help,' and shit like that. I was fully expecting her to come to and swat my head off. Eventually she started to wake up, and her eyes were glassy, but at the same time, so sad. Then her eyes sharpened and she said, 'You!'"

I poured myself a huge knock of tequila, leaned back in my chair the full six inches the tiny office would allow, and let the Squid tell his tale.

~~~

Oh shit, I thought. "Yep, me. Look, you fell down, I was trying to help."

"I don't need your help, Squid," Adrienne said. "Let me go!"

I let her go immediately; it was a reflex.

She dropped like a stone back into the gutter. Adrienne let out a squawk and said, "You big oaf! Help me up!"

I set her on her feet, and she swayed to a strong breeze that wasn't there. I reached out a hand to steady her. "Why don't I take you home?"

She slapped my hand away and broke two of my fingers. It hurt like hell.

"I don't need you to take me home. I need to hunt." She spun on her heel and promptly face-planted on the sidewalk.

She was giggling a bit, but crying, too, I thought. I turned her over, and she fought me some, but not too much.

"I really ought to take you home," I said.

She slurred out, "I need to *hun*." The *T* didn't make the cut.

I said, "Adrienne, right now, you couldn't bring down a quadriplegic."

She brayed out laughter. Man, I'd never heard of her acting like this.

"Oh, you're funny," she said. "*Thas wha* everyone says."

Then she did an amazing thing. She closed her eyes and lifted her arms up, like a little kid. I was kind of shocked, thinking it was a trap, but I picked her up anyway. I carried her to my car and drove her home. She was out cold for the ride, and the doorman let us in. I tucked her into bed as best as I could. I'm not too good with that kind of thing. Then I let myself out.

I went back to McKibbin's and polished off about a

gallon of tequila. The encounter with her had me so distracted, so worried, that I actually forgot to hunt—and then I couldn't fall asleep until the wee hours. I'd just nodded off when the call woke me up. It was her, sounding as cold as ice.

Without a hello, she said, "It seems I'm in your debt."

I actually felt like I was going to faint for a second and managed to stutter out, "No, not at all."

She ignored the comment. "I'd like to speak with you. Come over to my place in an hour. I think you know how to get here." *Click.*

That was it. Not a request, a command. I had to go, no question. I showered, grabbed a coffee, and drove out, thinking this was it. It was a fine day, cloudless and dry. *Not a bad day to die*, I thought.

The doorman buzzed me up, and she opened the door without a word.

Adrienne turned and walked back into her apartment. I followed, tippy-toeing after her. She was wearing some very high-end jeans, black heels, a white top, and her hair was pulled back. She was so petite, so beautiful—but oh-so-deadly. I felt like an ogre just being in the same room with her. I'll never forget how she looked that day. She led me into the living room, where she had a bottle of absinthe cracked and going. She turned quickly to face me, and I nearly stumbled.

"Drink," she said.

I'm not sure if it was a question or an imperative, but even though 9:00 a.m. is a bit early for me, I thought, *What the hell.* She poured a huge drink into a nice glass, and we sat across from each other. Her eyes were black, blazing, and intense, and she took me in. She stared and didn't speak for what seemed like forever, but it was probably more like five seconds. I fought not to fidget and barely won.

Finally she said, "I'm surprised you came."

I shrugged. "You're the mayor, and besides, if I didn't, you'd have found me. I prefer to walk in and face things rather than be hunted down."

"True enough. But you could have run to your old friend to hide behind him."

"Not my style," I said.

"*Calmars L'Intrepide*, eh?"

I shrugged. "Right about now, more like 'Squid the Scared Shitless.'"

I wondered if I'd really seen the flicker of a smile on the corner of her lips. I thought, *No way. Not this cold bitch. My eyes must be tricking me.*

She went silent again, thinking—or maybe deciding.

I drained my drink. Finally, I couldn't take it anymore. "Look, I appreciate you being genial and all, but I'm about as nervous as a one-legged man in an ass-kicking contest. So if you got something you need to do, let's get to it. I know how it's going to turn out, but I'm not going to just lie down. I apologize in advance for any breakage. Nice place, by the way."

I stood, trying to look intimidating, but not feeling that way at all. She looked up at me, bemused. We both knew she could kill me with little effort.

She said, "Sit down."

I did. The bitch knew how to boss.

"You certainly have heard about my, shall we say, *odd* behaviors."

I was glad I wasn't dead yet, but I still didn't like this line of questioning. "Yep, the whole community has."

Her eyes sparkled evilly. "Yes, but the architects of the potential revolt did not go to the whole community for a leader. They went to you."

Now I really didn't like this line of questioning. No sense in denying it. She already knew. "You're right, but I turned them down."

"Why?"

I decided to be as honest as I could. "A lot of reasons. First, I didn't think you deserved it. I mean, you might be acting a bit fucked-up right now, but not enough to do that sort of thing. Revolt against you, I mean."

"What sort of thing would you do?" she asked.

"Talk. That's one of the things I do best. Although, you're not exactly one of the most approachable vampires I've ever met."

No doubt about it, I definitely saw a small smile this time. "Really?" she said. "Go on."

"I don't like the idea of our kind warring with each other. Chrissy really impressed that on me."

She quickly lost her smile. "I see."

I stumbled on. "I don't like being the leader of anything. I'll do it only if I'm forced. I do much better from the second- or third-banana spot."

"Not very fearless, hiding in the back rows."

I actually got testy. "It's nothing like that. It's where I'm most efficient, that's all."

She nodded. "Anything else?"

She already knew this part, but I said it anyway. "Sure. Last time I butted heads with you, I seem to recall it not turning out so hot for me."

The little smile came back again, probably at the memory of beating my brains in, but it sure did make her look cute. "Next question. With all of our history, why did you stop to help me last night? I wouldn't have done it for you, and in all likelihood, it could still end up not being in your best interest."

I shook my head. "I don't know why I did it. I guess it looked like you could use a hand."

She contemplated this for a moment. "By the way, that night when we butted heads, as you say, why did you stop him from killing me? And don't give me the standard 'vampires aren't supposed to kill each other' answer. You and I both know it happens."

I thought about that, but I didn't have a good answer. "I don't know. It seemed like the right thing to do."

"Even though I was clearly going to kill you?"

"Maybe *especially* because you were going to kill me."

She paused. "You realize, of course, that makes no sense at all."

"I do. But I thought it would sound kind of cool, and throw in that I'm scared to death right now, and there you go."

"Last question. Any cheap looks or feels last night?"

Normally, I'd take this as a change to playful banter, but with her, it could be putting my head in the noose. I raised my hand. "Scout's honor, not a one of either variety."

"And why is that?"

Did she sound a bit insulted? I replied with an overcooked Irish brogue, "That's the kind oh ting me priest tells me will set me on the path straight to hell. The devil's work, it is."

She let out a brief, high-pitched laugh. It was lovely. She looked as if she'd been goosed and covered her mouth with her hand. She composed herself and said, "I see." She took a big pause again, making me want to jump aboard the fidget train. Finally, she said, "I want to thank you for helping me when I was indisposed... and for choosing not to butt heads with me."

I was confused through most of this encounter, and after this last statement, even more so. "You're welcome?" I replied lamely.

Her eyes said, *What a dope*, but her mouth said, "Also, I want to apologize for how I've treated you through the years. I thought you were a poor choice to be a vampire. It seems that my judgment was in error."

My mouth went dry. For one of the few times in my entire life, I was speechless. I think I made a few gargling noises and then gestured toward the bottle. She nodded, and I poured myself another stiff morning jolt. I popped it down, coughed, and cleared my throat. "I don't know what to say. I'm sure you had your reasons."

"And my reasons were correct, but you've proved them wrong. I know I've made it hard on you here, but right now, I'm glad you stayed. Again, my apologies."

I was still feeling surreal, but a few one-liners shot through my head. I thought, *Down boy, I'm still walking a thin line here*. When I'd arrived, I was sure I was dead, but now I was thinking it was more than likely I would leave her apartment alive. I didn't want to fuck it all up now. "I'm glad I stayed, too. I love Montreal. Apology accepted."

There was another awkward silence, so I set my glass down. "Well, I'm happy about how things worked out here. I really ought to get going."

She cut me off. Her voice sounded shrill. "I haven't dismissed you yet."

My knees unhinged and I flopped, rather than sat, back down. *Ker-plop*. She'd bossed me again, and it seemed all I could do was obey. I hated that. I was lucky the couch was well made and didn't break—but it sure groaned some.

I was a little pissed. Can you imagine? *I wasn't dismissed*. Talk about your old aristocratic crap. I was about to say something flip, but then I took a good look at her and saw it all. Despite all her money and power and entourage and lovers, something had gone terribly wrong with her. It was clear to me right then that she was lonely, maybe even totally alone and desperate. At that moment, I stopped being so afraid *of* her, and was actually afraid *for* her.

I said, "As you wish. But does this mean you won't kill me?"

She replied absently, "I'm not quite sure."

I thought, *Shit!* I didn't know if she was joking or not.

I guess she was joking, because we ended up sitting and chatting about a lot of inconsequential stuff. She didn't actually speak a whole lot, but that was okay, since I generally talk enough for two people, maybe more.

The booze got put away, and she actually let me make her breakfast. I finally left in the afternoon. She saw me to the door and shook my hand. It was something she wasn't accustomed to doing, as it was stiff and formal, and I'm pretty sure she broke another one of my fingers. We said our goodbyes, and I left, happy to be alive, and very confused.

~~~

The Squid looked at me through another cloud of cigar smoke and went on. "And that's how it started. A few days later, she called and ordered/invited me over again. Same thing—we talked over brunch, light on the booze this time, mimosas only. She cooked omelets, and they were phenomenal. A helluva lot better than the crap I made her."

I was stunned. "She *cooked* for you?"

"Yeah, lots of times now. She's very good."

I had been with her for like forty years, and she'd never even made me a piece of toast.

He said, "Then we started going out for lunches. She started talking more, smiling, and even laughing."

The Adrienne I knew hardly ever laughed, and when she smiled, it meant *watch out*. I asked, "Did she tell you what tipped her over?"

"No, not yet, anyway. The few times I asked, she promised to tell me soon, when she was ready. I let it go at that. Anyway, about four months passed, and the lunches turned into dinners, and I started hanging with her at Bily Kun and V Bar. We even hunted a few times together. She loves the 'good eeeeevening' thing, too. Really cracks her up.

"So I became her escort. Mind you, I hadn't laid a hand on her; maybe a kiss on the cheek when I dropped her off, but that was it. She was clearly not looking for anything else, and the way she is, I wasn't expecting anything. In my book, we were just friends, for whatever damn reason. If something did happen, she was going to have to be the one to make the first move. It's her nature, and frankly, I was still scared of her."

"Good call. Is she happy with that small dick of yours?"

"She tells me it's a lot bigger than yours, and she's ecstatic that I don't have your premature ejaculation problem."

"Oh, now I *know* you're lying."

"Man, you've got a one-track mind," Squid said. "Is sex all you think about?"

"Pretty much."

"Can I go on?"

"I'm waiting."

"So her behavior was getting better, and she actually seemed happy. Her drinking went back to normal, businesses got tightened up, and no more blood baths. The revolt talk went on the fade, and everyone up here took a deep breath. She even un-banished the two vamps she'd sent away. She told me she wanted me to be her business manager and wanted all the business in town to run through me. Can you fucking imagine, Chrissy? Through *me?* I went home that night on cloud nine. I slept like a baby."

"Like a baby whale," I added.

"Nice. So about two weeks later, I was way short on bartenders and had to cover on a Friday night. We had dinner plans, and I called her to apologize. We rescheduled for the next night. So I nearly fell over when she walked into McKibbin's. Can you imagine? Adrienne in a place like McKibbin's?"

I couldn't. Pubs were decidedly not her thing.

Squid smiled. "Well, she wore tight jeans, pumps, and a white silky tee, with some cleavage on display. Her hair was pulled back, and she had on blood-red lipstick. She looked on fire hot. She turned every head in the place.

"I stared at her, dumbfounded, but after a few beats my mouth came back to life, and I said something like, 'Adrienne, I didn't expect to see you here' or some shit like that. She reached up, grabbed the back of my head, pulled me toward her, and planted a long kiss on me. Everybody in the place went, 'Whoaaaa.'"

"Jesus, I bet they did."

"She said she'd always wanted to see me at work, and you know me, always the ham, but with her as my audience, shit, I was Dangerfield. She laughed all night, drank beer, and ate bar food! I'll never forget the sight of Adrienne swilling down nachos. Anyway, she closed the place with me, and we walked the streets holding hands.

"We hunted and took down a couple that also happened to be walking hand-in-hand. Kind of ironic, but fuck 'em, they shouldn't have been out at four in the morning. So I got her to her door and bent to kiss her cheek. She shook her head, took me by the hand, and led me in."

I leaned forward, elbows on the desk, chin in my hands, wearing a big, stupid grin. "Details, details."

"Fuck you, you old pervert," Squid said. "Anyway, we spent the night together, and the only detail you'll get is that it was great. She told me I saved her life. When I asked how, she said that I make her laugh and that I taught her how to love life again. I understand the first part, but the second part? I don't get it."

I did. "So it seems to me that you're a couple. Why aren't you sure?"

"I don't know. We haven't talked about it directly. We see each other every day, but we're not living together. I still have my place, but I'm at hers most of the time. I get the sense that she likes us having our own places. Just in case, you know? And I haven't been with any other women since I started with her."

"What about her?"

He shrugged. "Haven't asked."

"You pussy. Why not?"

"Don't know. Maybe I don't think I deserve someone like her, and if I ask, it'll screw things up. Or maybe she still scares the shit out of me. Probably both."

"So all this growling and shit about Simone is a bunch of crap, eh?"

"No way. My lecherous growls are always legit. I'm just not completely sure if Adrienne and I are exclusive or not, that's all."

"Well, if it's bugging you, ask her. It doesn't exactly sound like she'd take your head off anymore."

He nodded in agreement and glanced at his watch. His eyes widened. "Shit, she's expecting us, and we're late!"

He got up fast, his knees jamming under the desk, nearly toppling it onto me. But I was ready and caught it.

Whenever I'm around the Squid, I'm prepared for the uncoordinated havoc he can wreak.

I said, "Take it easy, Squid the Pussy-Whipped."

CHAPTER 35

Lisa Brownell sat in her living room, firmly planted behind her third glass of wine. She'd racked her brain for the last several hours, trying to come up with some course of action, and had exactly nothing to show for her efforts. It left her smoldering with anger. She thought herself to be a person not to be trifled with, and Donald—and maybe more importantly, Julian—had pushed her too far. Now, aside from her need for cold, hard cash since she'd dumped Donald, she wasn't going to let this bullshit stand. Lisa Brownell wouldn't sit back and wait for the lawyers. Hell, given what she knew, Julian might be able to hide every asset he ever had and then disappear.

Lisa was about to give up for the evening and go to bed, but took one more look at Julian's mysterious list of international holdings. She didn't focus on the specifics, just stared at the printout as a whole. Slowly, one particular item began to crystallize in her mind. After reading it again and again, she said out loud, "How fucking stupid am I?"

It was the bar in Canada—Montreal, to be specific. Julian was listed as part owner of a McKibbin's Irish Pub there. Although she had no evidence, she knew that one of the other owners would be that big lout, Colm Callaghan. She'd met him about a decade ago, back when she and Julian had taken a trip to Canada. He was pleasant enough, but at the same time, she'd thought he was an overbearing windbag. By the time they left Montreal, her ears were ringing, because Callaghan never stopped talking.

Julian loved the guy, however, and spoke to him frequently by telephone. She could always tell when it was Callaghan on the line by the way Jules constantly broke out laughing. She felt certain that Montreal and Callaghan was where Julian would run. Even if he weren't there, she'd hunt down Callaghan and charm—or maybe wring—some information out of him.

She was sure that if Jules was into something nefarious, that enormous dope from Montreal would be in it along with him. Even if it proved not to be the case, it would at least give her something to do.

Lisa mentally kicked herself for not coming up with the connection earlier as she got on her computer to get a flight. It was too late to leave that evening, but she booked one for the next day. Then she called a chain hotel in the center of Montreal and reserved a few nights. She was ready for action.

~~~

So was Garret Dick. He leaned back in his office chair and smiled. He'd tapped Lisa's phones and computers days earlier. He'd be waiting for her in Montreal when she arrived.

CHAPTER 36

We were running late, so we hopped in a cab and headed for the Plateau area to a bar/half-assed restaurant called Elsie's. It was a nice little neighborhood establishment with an interesting and eclectic cast of regulars, from old stiffs to college students to the occasional vampire. Just the idea of Adrienne meeting us in a place like this spoke volumes about how she had changed.

We arrived after a short but uncharacteristically silent ride, considering that Squid was in the vehicle. He'd drummed his fingers on the armrest the entire way and was actually nervous about meeting his girl with me in tow. How cute he was!

"Yo, Pussy-Whipped, pay the fare," I said, as I was never one to pass up easy pickings. I was shocked by his lack of a comeback and thought he must not only be nervous, but on the verge of panic.

Elsie's was small and crowded. I scanned the room and saw Adrienne standing by a table in the back. She looked beautiful, with a deep-purple blouse and her hair casually falling about her shoulders. She was already assessing me, and I must admit that her gaze unnerved me a bit. But then, it always did.

I could read nothing in her eyes, but when she looked at the Squid, her face changed in an instant. Her features softened, her eyes sparkled, and she smiled widely. For a moment, I had trouble recognizing her, because I don't think she'd ever worn that expression in all the years I'd known her. She looked happy. I hadn't seen her in two and a half centuries, but in that instant, my mind flew back to the last time we'd been together. I could feel the crisp bite in the air and the snow crunching beneath my feet. I could recall exactly how her delicate throat felt as I throttled her, and how her neck tissue groaned beneath my grasp as I started to rip her head from her shoulders.

~~~

The final treaties which had ceded New France to Britain were signed in 1763, but a good year and a half before that, the Squid was in serious trouble. What started as a simple limp had turned out to be a virulent form of arthritis. A lot of quacks around town would call it a lot of different horseshit diagnoses, and would try to treat it with even more horseshit remedies. But of course, none of them worked.

It started slowly, but soon it involved multiple joints crippling the man. I can't even describe how much the poor bastard suffered. With no real medical care, no physical therapy, no joint replacements, and not even a fucking aspirin, he was bedbound by 1764. He drank heavily to kill the pain and went downhill rapidly from there.

I was helping care for him and his tavern. Depending on how he felt, I'd lug him down to the bar and sit him in a stool or chair, and he would continue to hold court at the Owl's Eye as best he could. He was the best friend I ever had, and it killed me to see him like that.

I thought about turning him, of course, but he really was

a horrible candidate. We weren't as stringent about such matters as we are today, but we did have some rules and criteria, and Squid fit none of them. He'd never been a good criteria-fitter. And technically speaking, since Adrienne was the leader of the vampires in Montreal, I needed her approval to even attempt to turn someone. She was dead set against it and had hated him since the moment she met him. I came to accept the fact that I was going to have to let my friend go. But that's not what happened.

By early 1765, Squid's ticket was clearly punched, and he was on the express train to the dead. I had gotten my hands on some laudanum, which was a liquid opioid and a powerful painkiller, like morphine. Booze was no longer even close to doing the trick. Even back then, we knew that combining it with alcohol could be deadly, so I was careful with it.

I was running the tavern, but not doing a good job of it. It was so hard to see him that way, and my heart wasn't in it. A lot of nights, I didn't open the tavern at all. Instead I sat with him and chatted, or maybe read to him. He put up a good show, but much of the time, he was soaked with sweat and writhing in pain. He was never more fearless than he'd been over the years of his illness. But the night finally came.

He'd drunk as much whiskey as I'd ever seen him drink, and most of a new pint of laudanum. But he was still quaking with the pain that he once described to me as "deep in the bones and white-hot." His eyes were glassy from drink, but also grimly determined. He held the mostly empty bottle of laudanum up in the air and wagged it back and forth. "You've got a new bottle of this shit, I presume?"

I pulled it out of my pocket. I was choked up, but managed to say, "Right here."

He slugged down the rest of what he had and dropped

the bottle onto the floor. He reached out a gnarled, arthritis-deformed hand to me and said, "Would you mind taking the cork out? My tentacles aren't what they used to be."

I handed him his liquid death. He took a good slug and remained the jokester to the end. "I'd ask you to join me, but I'm drinking alone tonight."

"Look, Squid—"

He cut me off. "Don't say anything sentimental, Chrissy, or I might lose my courage. I've had a good run. We've had a good run, haven't we?"

I whispered, "One big party."

His eyes lit up. "Yes, that's right, isn't it? A big damn party. I can count on you to take care of things after?"

"Of course," I replied.

He wagged that accursed bottle again and smiled. "Now time for you to go. It's last call."

I bent and kissed him on the forehead. "Goodbye, Squid."

Never at a loss for words, he said, "Now I see why Adrienne is so besotted with you. What a kisser!"

I actually laughed.

"Goodbye, Chrissy."

I turned for the door, walked maybe three steps, and stopped. There were a lot of reasons not to try what I wanted to try, but at that moment I didn't care. He was my friend, and I couldn't lose him without at least bringing it up. "There may be another alternative."

He looked at me questioningly. "Unless you're the Lord Jesus Christ himself, and believe me, I know you're not, I don't see it."

"I'm a vampire, and I could try to make you one."

"And what exactly is a vampire?"

There was plenty of folklore during that era, but it was

still over a century before Stoker and Dracula really outed us. I gave him a quick, condensed summary. By the end, he looked quite entertained. "So now I'm supposed to believe you're some kind of a demon? And you can turn me into one by killing me, and I could live forever, as long as I drink blood?"

"Pretty much, yes."

His smiled. "Jesus, Chrissy, I knew you were crazy, but not this crazy. Could it be you're telling me a nice bedtime story before it's lights out for the Squid?"

"It could be, but that's not it. And I know you know I'm serious."

He sighed. "Yes, I do, and I'm worried about you. But there's not much I could do about it now, is there?"

I thought for a moment. "Have you noticed that I haven't aged in the twenty years since we've met?"

"You've aged, not much, grant you ... but you have some gray now that you didn't before, and some wrinkles."

I'd forgotten about that. He was right. Vampires are not shapeshifters, turning into bats or anything like that, but we can alter our appearance slightly to feign aging. It takes practice and a lot of effort. Most of our kind can do it at about the five-hundred-year mark. It's becoming somewhat of a lost art in modern times, since a lot more can be accomplished with cosmetics.

"Fine," I replied. "How's this then?" I relaxed and felt myself revert to my usual pretty-boy self. Even if I didn't feel it, I would have known it had worked by the way Squid's eyes widened in shock.

He stammered out, "That's some kind of a trick, or this damn drug you're giving me!"

I decided on the crash-course option and took out the long knife I always carried hidden in my topcoat. I opened up my shirt to expose my chest.

He said nervously, "Here, here, now what are you up to?"

"Just this," I said and plunged the blade through my chest and out through my back. Blood splattered onto him and the bed, and he gasped. It didn't feel very good, but I think it got my point across.

I calmly sat looking at him. He was in shock—gaping, and probably waiting for me to fall over dead. I didn't. I brought my hand up to stifle a yawn for effect. He slowly reached out and tapped the handle of the knife a few times with his finger. Then with some effort, due to the arthritis, he took the handle in his hand and moved it back and forth.

"Hey, stop that!" I yelled. "It hurts!"

His hand jumped off the knife, and I yanked the blade out. It made a sucking, wet sound, drawing another gasp from him. I cleaned the blade and replaced it. I cleaned the blood off my chest with one of his blankets so he could see clearly and appreciate that the wound had already stopped bleeding. In another minute or so, it had completely disappeared.

He said, "It's *gone*. There's not even a damn scratch."

"Still think it's a trick? Or the laudanum?"

He looked confused. "I'm not sure. That day on the battlefield, that's why you lived even though you were shot to pieces? And you were heavy, way too heavy for someone your size."

It was stupid of me to have never thought of that, and more stupid to never consider that he noticed. "Yes, being heavier is part of it too, but you move lighter. And that day on the battlefield was a close call. If you hadn't come for me, the next barrage may have finished me."

"I still don't believe you, but . . ."

Then the questions came. They were all pretty insightful, except the one about beer.

"So how long would it be before I could go out in the sun again?"

"About twenty-five years."

"Shouldn't be a problem. I hardly get out of bed before three o'clock. And the rheumatism would be gone?"

"That and all other maladies."

He looked at his deformed hands. "I could live with that. Tell me about the blood again."

"You'll need it. Your body will crave it, you'll want it, and it will taste better than anything you've ever tasted. But you're still you. It's not automatic—you still have to come to terms with the act, the killing and drinking blood."

He was thoughtful for a moment and said, "Fuck it. Plenty of British around. And with food, I can eat as much as I want, and it's nearly impossible to get fat?"

"Yes, and sex is the best ever. More intense."

"Well, that would be an improvement. But living, maybe forever . . . I mean, all of this is hard to believe, but somehow that's the hardest part."

"I'm eighteen hundred years old."

"Holy shit! You don't look a day over a thousand."

I laughed. "If we're going to do this, let's get on with it before you talk me to death. Anyway, if it works, we'll have plenty of time to continue this discussion."

"What are my chances?"

"About fifty-fifty, but that's a guess. I don't know how your illness may affect things."

He nodded. "It's a lot better odds than I'm looking at now. I still don't believe you, but how can I pass up on the idea of you biting my neck? It's way too titillating."

"And besides, what have you got to lose?"

"You're damn right about that."

"You ready?"

He took one more belt of whiskey, turned his head to the side, and said, "Dinner is served."

I dove right in.

"Ouch, that hurts!" he yelled. "I can't believe you're doing this. You really are fucking crazy. And by the way, don't spill a drop, that's Grade-A stuff!"

The idiot got me laughing, and I mumbled through his neck and a mouthful of blood, "Will you shut up?"

He didn't, of course, and despite my laughing, I was somehow getting the job done.

But he kept going. "Don't think this means I'm easy . . . If you want some salt with that blood, I'll pop down to the tavern and get it . . . Hey, if you were a barber-surgeon, you'd save on tools . . ."

He was starting to fade. It didn't take long, since he was already at death's door. But he kept talking right to the very end. It was the only way I've ever shut the Squid up for more than a few seconds—by killing him. He looked truly serene in death, amused, with a smile on his face.

He was on the fast side, turning at just over six hours. Before I was sure, I was worried, of course, pacing about, drinking all his good booze. And there wasn't much good booze at the Owl's Eye. Luckily, I knew at about three hours. It was his hands. The swelling was going down and his fingers were straightening themselves out, looking normal again, even better than before he was sick. At four hours, his color came back. At five, he started breathing. An hour later, he opened his eyes, as calm as can be. He looked around the room and sat up in bed, stretching and moving his neck all around.

Squid looked at his hands and said, "Damn." He

leisurely cracked his knuckles, relishing the feeling and the snapping sound. He threw his covers off and got up smoothly, with no hint of the pain-addled movements that had plagued him for the last several years.

He was wearing one of those ridiculous long nightshirts, which only made it to his knees, making it look even more ridiculous. It was stained with sweat and pee. Breaking into a stretch, he rotated his back with some more snaps, crackles, and pops. It must have felt great, because he had a huge grin on his face. Free from his former pain, he bent over and touched his toes, putting his palms flat on the floor, something he could never have done even on his best day as a human. He straightened up, still smiling, and looked at me. "You feel like this? All the time?"

"Pretty much," I replied.

"Thanks for not letting me in on it earlier, asshole."

"Don't be so damn smug. You've got more than a few obstacles to get by yet."

He waved at me dismissively. "I'll be fine."

And you know what he did then? The big oaf started dancing, slowly at first, picking up speed as he went. It was grotesque, as it always was, and always would be, but captivating all the same.

Squid started mouthing a chant. It wasn't singing so much as shouting random monosyllables, timed to the beat of his dance—"hey, hi, ho, ha," repeated over and over again. But it sounded perfectly beautiful to me.

He looked like some gigantic and insane version of Ebenezer Scrooge, discovering that he had not missed Christmas Day. Faster and faster his movements became, with frenzied spinning, jumping, and dashing about the small room. He knocked over the nightstand, a chair, and pretty much everything else in his path.

He's just as coordinated as ever, I thought.

He finally slowed to a stop. His respirations were at a good vampire rate of nearly non-existent, but he looked flushed and alive—and was sweating profusely, of course.

I asked with a smile, "You about done?"

"Yeah, but I'm so thirsty."

"Let's go down to the bar and talk over some drinks. But you may want to change out of the piss-stained look."

He looked down at his crotch. "No argument there."

Squid joined me downstairs, looking pretty sharp for a change. Even his color was good. Although he had some of our initial pallor, it was still far better than it had been when he was ill. He was standing up straight for the first time in months, and his movements, although still Squid-like, had a vampire's natural grace and fluidity. It was a pleasure seeing him like this.

He moved to his usual spot behind the bar, poured us some beer, and we toasted to his being alive.

Squid stopped me in mid-sentence, covering up his left ear and asking me to repeat whatever I'd just said. I did.

He said, "I heard you perfectly, way better than before— even out of my Squid-ear! It's fixed, just like that?"

"Just like that," I replied.

As a child he had suffered a bad cold and infection. He'd had horrible earaches and nearly died. The end result was deafness in his right ear, probably from a punctured eardrum. It was vampire-perfect now.

The Squid-ear might be gone, but I'll still have that damned Squid-eye to contend with, I thought.

"Unbelievable. Next thing you're going to tell me is my dick has gotten bigger."

I smiled.

His eyes grew wide. "You're serious?" He started to

undo his pants to look.

"That's something I really don't need to see," I said. "Stop fooling about. We've got a lot to go over."

"Well, we do have time for this: I want to say thanks. Thanks for not leaving me sick as hell, leaving me to die."

"No thanks needed. You're my friend. Besides, I owed you. That day on the battlefield, you didn't leave me to die, did you?"

"No, I guess I didn't."

"By the way, how the hell did all those Brits miss someone your size?"

Even though it was far in the past, he looked nervous as he remembered it. "I have no idea."

We laughed, drank a lot of beer, and he managed to rustle us up a half-decent meal as we talked. I told him how Adrienne had forbade me from turning him. "She hates your guts, by the way."

He rolled his eyes. "Tell me something I don't know. Exactly how powerful is she?"

"Four hundred years old, and our leader here in Montreal. Pretty powerful."

"Hold on . . . you're way older than that. Didn't you tell me that we get stronger as we age? Why aren't *you* the leader?"

I shrugged. "I've done that sort of thing many times before, and I don't want the responsibility any longer. She was here first, and would have taken it badly if I had tried to move her out. And she'd never fuck me again. I'd rather have her body than the job."

He nodded. "Good point."

"Anyway, let's be crystal clear on this. Stay away from her until I smooth things over."

"Hey, it's me!" Squid said. "I'll be charming."

"That's what I'm afraid of. I'm serious. You need to be careful. She can be deadly without warning."

"I'll be carefully charming, then," Squid replied.

"You're not getting this. She could take your head off with one blow. Stay away from her until I tell you otherwise."

"Come on, Chrissy. She's about three foot six. Am I supposed to believe that she could—"

As he was gas bagging, I walked around the bar and grabbed him by the belt. With one hand, I lifted him over my head. "And I'm about four foot six. You get it?"

I dropped him to his feet. He was a bit shaken. "Yeah, I guess I do. I'll steer clear."

To my surprise, he did stay away from her—but Adrienne didn't stay away from him. Initially, she was incensed that I'd defied her and turned him, but then she seemed to calm down. Unbeknownst to me, she wasn't calm at all, but was lying in wait for an opportunity. That opportunity came that winter when I went on a business trip to Quebec City.

Fortunately, it went well, and I returned to Montreal a night earlier than expected. Although it was quite late, I thought I'd go to the tavern and scare up a drink. As I approached, I heard a hammering sound and thought it an odd time for someone to be doing work. When I realized the sound was coming from the Owl's Eye, I broke into a run.

I burst into the bar and found Adrienne throttling the Squid, pounding his head into the floor. He was a mess, with his left arm shattered and his frontal skull caved in. There was blood everywhere.

If it weren't so horrible a sight, it would almost be silly— a tiny little woman like Adrienne manhandling a giant like Squid. Her hands were wrapped around his neck, with her fingers dug into his flesh. She kept hammering his head into the floor as she strangled him, tightening her grip, surely with the intent of tearing his head off. He was unable to breathe, beaten nearly to death—but he kept fighting.

I came in behind her, and although livid, I felt calm at the same time. I clamped onto her wrists and thought that this was the way it would have to end. Slowly, I pried her bloody fingers from Squid's ruined neck. When they were clear, he took in a huge, whooping breath.

I spun her to face me as she struggled in my grasp. But she may as well have been fighting stone. She actually hissed at me, like those vampire bitches do in old horror movies. I whirled her around and threw her directly through the thick back wall of the bar and into the alley behind. I followed her through the hole she'd made, meaning to finish this once and for all.

"No, Christian," Squid rasped from behind me. "Vampires don't kill each other. You told me."

True enough, but it happens on occasion, and it was going to happen now. She was hurt from her non-door exit from the Owl's Eye, but was up and ready. Like Squid, she was not going to lie down and die. *All the better*, I thought.

I approached fast and knocked her down with a punch to her beautiful face. She got up quickly and lashed out, puncturing my left eye. I didn't even put up a hand to stop her blow. One eye would do me fine. She shot out a well-placed kick to my groin, but I hardly felt it.

I was a calmly enraged, unthinking automaton. She'd tried to kill my best friend, and now she was going to pay with her life. I kept coming, caught her wrist, snapped it, and pummeled her to the ground. I climbed astride her and took her thin, pretty neck in both hands and throttled her. It felt absolutely delicious.

I was going to do to her what she was going to do to Squid. I'd rip her no-good, fucking head off her shoulders and toss it into the St. Lawrence. I smiled at the thought. That was when Squid grabbed me and tried to pull me off.

Through my killing haze, I wondered at how he had managed to even get off the floor, let alone struggle with me, considering how badly Adrienne had hurt him. It didn't matter. I was going to finish what I'd started.

He kept trying to pull me off her and panted, "Christian, don't do this. We shouldn't kill our own kind. Stop, stop!"

Way back in my mind, I thought that was true enough. *But tough shit for this little bitch.*

He let me go. Then I went for the grand finale. I felt the tissue of her cervical spine start to tear, and I grinned. What I didn't realize was that when the Squid let me go, he wasn't *really* letting me go.

He'd backed up about twenty paces to do the only thing he could do to shake me loose of her. He ran at me full tilt and hit me like a modern football player hits a tackling dummy. I felt like I'd been struck by a baby freight train as he knocked me free, landing on top of me. It was Adrienne's turn to take a huge, gasping breath.

Only a little delay, I thought, *that's all*. I easily lifted Squid off me.

He fought hard, grabbing hold of me and yakking in my ear the entire time. "No, wait! Chris, hold on. Don't do this."

I pushed him off and advanced, but he grabbed on again.

"Look, you can still kill her, all right?" he cried. "Look at her. She's not going anywhere. Just talk to me."

I looked at Adrienne. Her neck was stretched at an odd angle, and she was barely breathing. He was right. She wasn't going anywhere anytime soon. I turned toward him and said, "All right, talk."

Speaking out loud somehow broke the spell. I was no longer a thoughtless killer. I was Christian once again, and I think Squid knew it.

"You don't need to do this," Squid said. "It's wrong, and you know it."

"She deserves it. She was going to kill you!"

"Maybe . . . but it doesn't make what you're doing right. She's in the wrong. Everyone will know it. So don't join her. Besides, I'm fine." He gave me a well-practiced, over-the-top idiotic grin that looked even goofier due to his battered face.

I laughed.

"Look, you told me we don't kill our own kind unless absolutely necessary," Squid said, "and that's not the case here anymore."

The adrenaline was starting to fade, and I felt deflated. He may have been right, but I thought he was making a mistake. "You're being a fool. She'll come at you again—she or her cronies."

"Maybe, maybe not. After what you did here tonight, I'm guessing she'll think twice about trying it anytime soon."

I thought about that for a moment. Then I squatted next to Adrienne, and she looked at me in terror. I said, "I'm not going to hurt you anymore. The man you were just trying to kill convinced me not to."

She glanced up at Squid, and her eyes went from terror to rage in an instant. I jerked her head toward me, and she cringed. We were nose-to-nose. My voice dropped a register, but it was sweet and perfectly reasonable. "But if you try it again, the last thing you're ever going to see is your own bowel. Because I will finish what I started tonight and rip that beautiful head of yours from your shoulders and stuff it directly up your pretty little asshole. Am I clear on this?"

She nodded, wide-eyed, and I knew she believed me.

"You do understand that I'm not joking, don't you, dear?"

She nodded again, but it wasn't good enough for me this time. I shook her roughly for effect, and she screamed.

"That's enough, Chris," Squid said.

But it wasn't. "Tell me you understand."

She rasped, "I understand." There was pure dread in her voice.

"Good. And one more thing. I'm going to that shithole you call your home and picking up my belongings now. If I should see you there, even for a moment, I'll kill you."

I dropped her back to the ground and said to Squid, "You think you might be able to scare up a wagon for me at this time of night?"

He replied, "Of course."

Toward 1790, Squid had begun to lose his sun sensitivity. Adrienne had cast a pall on the city for me, and I wanted to move on. I tried to convince him to come along with me, but he wouldn't. Montreal was his home. He would by no means be safe from Adrienne, but with his wits, strength, and now, ability to travel during daylight, at least he would have a fighting chance.

~~~

Adrienne waved to us from her table at Elsie's, and that broke me out of my reverie. We made our way through the crowd.

Squid said, "Adrienne, sorry we're late, we—"

She pulled him down by the front of his shirt, and her lips were on his, a direct hit. It wasn't one of those open-mouth, porno sort of kisses, but it meant serious business and was the kind of kiss that got the job done. Only the drunkest of the drunk didn't scope out this action. Squid looked breathless when she released him.

"You really must stop apologizing for such trivialities," she said. "I can certainly wait for someone as special as you."

Adrienne was serious, and I was floored. She turned those sparkling black eyes on me, and they lost quite a bit of their sparkle.

Taking both of my hands in hers, she said, "Christian, the same as always."

I didn't know how to take that, but I bowed, eighteenth-century style, and kissed her hands. "I'm not sure how this can be possible, but you look even more beautiful than I recall. My friend must agree with you."

She looked up at Squid and gave him a hundred-watt smile. The best I ever got was about five watts. "He certainly does."

Squid said, "You, too, Addie."

Oh, how nice . . . a pet name. My gorge was starting to rise.

She said to Squid, "Would you mind running to the bar and getting us a round? You know, that beer I like."

Squid gave me a quick look of caution and turned for the bar.

She looked at me with a tiny smile, and her eyebrow arched a bit.

I said, "Alone at last."

She smiled more broadly. "It's nice to know that your sense of humor is still trifling."

"Ouch! I guess I'm still recycling the same old jokes. I forgot you've heard them all already."

She laughed. It was genuine, and coming from her, that was foreign to my ears. As we sat down, she said, "Christian, I want to apologize to you because of how poorly I treated you in the past. Our relationship was superficial, and I was using you. I conspired to take away your friend, just because I couldn't understand what friendship meant. I was nasty back then, and still am to a degree, but I'm getting better, thanks to him. I'm so happy you saved him that night. He's saved me. Again, you have my apologies."

I was completely stunned by her speech and didn't know what to say. "Accepted. And I want to apologize, too, for—"

She cut me off. "Don't blurt something out because I did. You don't have to."

"You're right. But one thing I can say right off is I'm sorry for nearly killing you that night."

She nodded.

I asked, "Adrienne, what's this all about? Squid, me, this apology? What's going on?"

She thought a moment. "It's like the Alcoholics Anonymous twelve-step program. Except in my case, it's not for drunks. It's for mean vampire bitches."

I laughed, and she joined me. I never remembered her taking a poke at herself. She *had* changed.

"May I ask how Squid saved you?"

She shook her head. "I haven't even told him. I can't do it yet. Maybe someday. Then he'll tell you, won't he?"

"I expect so."

"I feel so lucky to have him."

I agreed. "Me, too. Squid's a hell of a guy."

Squid interjected, "I'll drink to that!"

He'd sidled up with our drinks as we were immersed in our discussion. We settled into some mildly uncomfortable small talk that soon turned the corner to comfortable. Adrienne said, "Neal told me about your business idea. It sounds like it has potential."

Hold the fucking phone. Neal? Fucking Neal! What the hell is this? I looked at Squid. "Neal?"

He shrugged and didn't answer.

"Oh, Neal told me about your silly little game," Adrienne said. "You two ought to grow up."

Silly little game? Grow up? We'd made a pact, a deal, maybe even an oath. Well, maybe it wasn't an oath, but it was at least a fucking agreement!

We'd never told each other our real names. I guess it was a silly guy thing, but it was *our* thing, you know? We promised not to look each other up and would have to disclose our names directly. We'd never done it, because the one who told first would certainly be screwed by the other.

Now he'd given up his real name to his girlfriend of what, about three minutes, and she'd blurted it out to me. This went against every rule in the Guy Code. He'd broken our treaty. Now it was war, and I was going to enjoy it.

Squid said sheepishly, "You wouldn't want to tell me *your* name, would you?"

I ignored him and spoke to Adrienne: "You know, I think you're right, we really should grow up. What's his surname, by the way?"

Squid fidgeted.

"O'Sullivan," she said.

"I see. You know, before we got here, uh, *Neal*—Neal O'Sullivan, that is—and I were discussing the fact that he has some confusion about your relationship."

She raised her eyebrows. "Really?"

"Now wait just a damn minute," Squid-Neal stammered.

I continued to ignore him. "Yes, indeedy. He tells me he's been faithful to you since you've been together. But he wonders, if I may be a bit indelicate here, if you've been screwing anyone else?"

Squid made an odd grunting noise.

Adrienne played right along. "You may inform him that I have not been screwing anyone else."

I turned to Squid, who had somehow already worked up a sweat. "Neal, Adrienne is not screwing anyone else."

His response was curt. "Asshole!"

He downed his beer as I turned back to her. "That's gratitude for you. And Adrienne, there is one more thing. Neal wonders why the two of you don't live together. Neal would like to, but I think he's afraid to ask. I presume if this is acceptable, it would be your place, because Neal's is such a shithole."

She was grinning now, really enjoying it. "You may tell Neal that he may move in tomorrow."

I turned to Squid once again. "Neal, Adrienne says you may move in with her tomorrow, if it's convenient."

He was sweating even more, and he'd drunk my beer, too. He started, "You no good mother—"

Adrienne quieted him with a touch of his arm. "Don't grow up just yet. I could learn to enjoy this little-boy behavior . . . *Neal*."

We shared a laugh, although Neal's was a bit reserved. I'd busted his nuts big time, but I'd done him a huge favor, in a kind of backhanded or maybe underhanded sort of way. That, though, was in no way going to stop him from exacting some payback. I shuddered as I saw in my mind's eye the gears of his horrible Squid-brain working on a devastating scheme.

Adrienne excused herself.

Squid started right in. "Asshole! If I weren't sure to get my ass kicked, I'd kick your ass! Where do you get off with that exclusive shit and that moving in stuff, anyway? That could've completely fucked me up because of the fucking name thing."

He was cute when he got mad, with a little stutter and everything. But I wasn't going to let him off the hook. "Oh, shut the fuck up. I did you a favor. And let's not forget who broke the pact, *Neal*. We swore a sacred oath, and you gave it up to Adrienne after a five-day relationship? You're lucky that's all I did."

"The name was a game, anyway, you dirty old Roman fuck. You wait, I'll get you back but good."

"That would have worried me before. You know, when you weren't so pussy-whipped."

Before he could respond, Adrienne rejoined us. "Are you boys behaving yourselves?"

Squid was brooding, so I answered, *"Mais oui, mademoiselle."*

She smiled, Squid stewed, and we turned to business. First, we discussed the Genealogist's attacks in some detail. Adrienne was concerned but hadn't been able to turn up a single lead from Quebec City. Despite Jake's discovery, trying to fight the Genealogist was still like going up against an invisible phantom. It wasn't much, but Adrienne had taken Jean-Luc's report to heart and had done her best to safely lock down Montreal against attack.

The conversation drifted to the more pleasant discussion of my fashion business proposal, and I was happy to discover that Adrienne would be very supportive. I couldn't wait to let the girls know and have them up to Montreal.

Afterward, we went out on the town and ended up at the V Bar, the city's vampires-only establishment. It had posh red velvet décor, and was subterranean, like New Orleans' Absinthe House, adjoining Montreal's underground shopping area. As I think of it, a lot of vampire hangouts are underground. I always thought it was for the privacy factor, but perhaps we actually are creepy.

As the night bore on, the degree to which Squid and Adrienne were in love started to wear on me. It didn't make one lick of sense any way you cut it, but there it was in every look, every gesture, and every touch. It was all over them. I envied them, but things like this were built for speed and not made to last. Don't get me wrong—there have been some long-term vampire relationships, but they're just as rare as they are for humans. I knew Adrienne and Squid's relationship was the real deal, but I gave it a century at most, maybe two.

Now I'd gotten myself into a mood. I mean, I was happy for them, but it made me think about all my deficits in the relationship area through the centuries. Lisa was currently at the end of a very long list. It seemed, at least at times, that some women had loved me. But it's as though I'm constructed only to entertain women and be courtly to them. They seemed to sense it and avoided real commitment with me like the plague. I guess it was the way I was put together. Since I hadn't gotten it right with a woman in two millennia, it didn't take a genius to figure out that I would never get it right.

Suddenly, I needed out. I didn't want to see any more of "The Neal and Addie Show" as they frolicked about, all in love. And what the fuck is "frolicking," anyway? I spied a door at the back corner and made for a stage-left exit.

Out of nowhere, Adrienne appeared and blocked my escape. "Leaving so early, Chris?"

"Yes, I'm a bit tired and got a lot of work to catch up on," I lied.

She nodded, knowing I was bullshitting. "I see. You haven't even said goodnight to Squid."

"I'll catch up with him tomorrow. You call him Squid, huh?"

"Of course. It's the stupidest name I've ever heard, but it somehow grows on you."

"It does, doesn't it?"

"And by the way, I only called him 'Neal' to get you two going. It was amusing and resulted in him moving in with me. A win-win."

I laughed. "You were always the smart one. Before I go, I've given it some thought, and I would like to apologize to you."

"You don't have to."

"I know, but I want to. First, I'd like to retract my apology for nearly killing you. You deserved it, and I'm not sorry about that."

Her eyes and mouth flew open in shock, but she still wore a little smile. These days, she always seemed to be smiling, no matter what.

"You did deserve it, and you know it," I continued. "But what I'd really like to apologize about is the way I treated you before that. I took you for granted and used you for prestige and sex. I had you pegged for a bitch, and I never put any effort into our relationship. It's no wonder you wanted to hurt me. It's too bad that Squid got in the middle of it. I'm truly sorry, and I hope we can always be friends."

She was speechless for a moment. "I *was* a bitch, but you couldn't have said this two hundred seventy years ago?"

"Slow learner." I kissed her on the cheek. "You should get back to your man."

I made my way to the surface and started the walk back to my hotel. I'd had a lovely night, but right then, I felt so alone. And right on cue, the Squid strolled around the corner. I guess I wasn't so good at sneaky getaways.

He said, "Not very nice, taking off like that."

"I wanted to get going, sorry."

He looked me over, not quite the Squid-eye, but it could've easily headed in that direction. "I see. By the way, come on, tell me your real name."

I was lonely, he'd magically showed up, and I loved the guy. "What the hell. It's Titus, Titus Acilius."

He smiled. "Thanks. One more thing: Neal O'Sullivan isn't my real name."

I smiled right back. "You're full of shit. First, you wouldn't have the balls to lie to Adrienne, and second, I looked you up years ago."

He fumed and spewed out, "Cheating little Roman prick!"

"Oh, calm down. And for the record, Titus Acilius isn't my real name, either, dopey."

He stopped his phony fuming. "Oh, sure it is. I looked you up, too."

We both smiled.

"Come on," he said. "I'll walk you back to your hotel."

CHAPTER 37

Al Martinez wasn't one to panic, but he was certainly damn nervous. They'd planted their bomb upward of eighteen hours ago, and still nothing. He had a member of his team watching the front door of the booby-trapped building, and he was taking his shift watching the back from the window of their rented room. He was fairly certain that the target was still inside, but vampires were clever and skilled. They might be anywhere. Always cautious, Martinez deployed two of his men to guard the entrances of the hotel.

He was contemplating a plan to go at their targets with a conventional direct assault, or simply cutting, running, and calling it even. With their explosives either discovered or ineffective, the mission could get ugly fast, and he was leaning toward taking off. He looked over his shoulder toward the man who had set the bomb and said, "Charley, are you positive you hooked everything up right?"

Charley Evans jerked his thumb angrily at Simmons. "For the tenth time, I rigged it to the stove exactly the way this pussy here told me to do it."

Martinez was about to reprimand Evans for his comment, but his remark was stopped short somewhere below his vocal cords by an ear-shattering explosion. They all dropped to a cover position.

When he deemed it safe, Martinez took station back at the window with his binoculars. Evans and Simmons crowded in behind him. But he didn't need his binoculars to see the carnage that the bomb had caused. It looked like it had taken out not just the target apartment, but the entire floor, as well. The two stories above slowly collapsed into a fiery, smoking wreck.

"Shit!" Martinez blurted out. "Charley, how much C-4 did you use?"

Evans was red-faced. He rounded on Simmons and shoved him to the floor. "I used what this asshole told me to use!"

Martinez pulled Evans away. Simmons was lying on the floor in the fetal position with his hands over his eyes.

"Stop it, Charley," Martinez said. "That's not going to help. There's nothing we can do about it now. I hope we got them, because if we didn't, we sure took out a lot of innocents for nothing."

Simmons moaned from the floor, "Jesus, Al, what're we going to do?"

If things had gone smoothly, Martinez would've stayed to observe the blast site and maybe get lucky and scope another vampire or two. But that was all out the window now. They were getting out of there, pronto. As the team leader, he'd have to face the music and, more dangerously, the Harrisons. The idea of facing Helen was bad enough, but facing Bloody Bill? The thought chilled his bones. He would pray long and hard before that meeting took place.

"First, Andy, get the fuck up off the floor," Martinez scolded. "Charley, call in the rest of the team. We're out of here."

~~~

The three girls who had done everything together in life ended up dying together, as well. The bomb had been rigged to go off when their stovetop was turned on. The morning it had been set, Becca, Jen, and Maddie had had a particularly raucous night. They'd come home and crashed right to bed. When they awoke, Jen thought she'd cook a light meal before going out for the evening. They were in the kitchen when Jen turned on a burner.

In the end, they knew no pain—only white.

CHAPTER 38

Reverend Gary Jarvis sat in the Harrisons' office, waiting for them to arrive. He was attended by one of their oversized security guards, who silently towered over him. Jarvis knew the man, but the guard ominously did not exchange a single word with him. After what had happened in New Orleans, this was by no means an audience with the Harrisons; it was an inquisition. Jarvis knew that his very life depended upon how he performed this morning.

Despite this, he was serene. He knew—as he always knew—that he was in the hands of God. He calmly watched the first morning light slant through the office windows. The view of the acres and acres of young corn was spectacular as it swayed slightly in the breeze, dancing in the early morning sunshine. Jarvis said a prayer, thanking the Lord for such a sight—a sight that might prove to be one of his last.

After a few minutes, the Harrisons filed in. He'd expected Helen and Bill, but when the oldest daughter, Molly, was there too, Jarvis thought that the meeting might be even more interesting than he'd expected.

Helen sat at her desk, with Molly propping herself on one corner of it. Bloody Bill sat in his big easy chair, scowling away. Jarvis thought he resembled an impatient attack dog, waiting for the command to pounce.

Helen smiled and began. "Reverend Jarvis, thank you for coming on such short notice."

As if I had a choice, Jarvis thought. "You're welcome, Helen. You know I'm at your service whenever you call on me."

"You, no doubt, know about the disaster in New Orleans," she said.

"I do. It was unfortunate. But we're lucky the authorities seem to be chalking it up to terrorism at this point."

Bill said, "Well, Gary, I doubt very much the twenty-seven innocent people who got torched would consider it lucky."

"Bill, this is a holy war," Jarvis said. "Those innocents are in heaven now. They're in the bosom of the Lord."

Bloody Bill casually leaned forward, and a large pistol appeared in his hand, pointing directly at Jarvis's head. Bill said sarcastically, "Suppose I put one in your eyeball and send you along to that same bosom? What do you think of that idea?"

Jarvis closed his eyes for a moment and thanked the Lord for giving him strength. Then he looked calmly at Bill and the canon-size barrel of the .357 Magnum that was pointing right at him. As much as he feared and disagreed with Bloody Bill, he still had to admire him. He hadn't even seen a hint of the movement that had produced the gun. Quite a feat for anyone, let alone a sixty-one-year-old grandfather. But Bloody Bill had always been a unique specimen.

"Do what you must, Bill," Jarvis said. "I'm right with the Lord."

Bill scoffed.

Helen said, "Put that thing away, Bill. You're not

helping." She glared at him for a moment and then went on. "I apologize, Reverend, but Bill's a little upset. We all are. This is why we've always frowned on explosives. A little mistake can cost a lot of lives, and the team leader on the mission was one of yours."

Jarvis spread his hands and smiled. "Al Martinez has found Jesus, and I helped him do it—but every member of the Network is yours, Helen, not mine. We all know that."

Helen smiled right back. "Well, thank you, Reverend, but we also know that you have quite a bit of influence around here with more than a few of our operatives."

Jarvis's smile somehow grew wider. He thought, *If I have my way, it won't be more than a few, it will be all.* When he finally took over as head of the Network, he would take the fight directly to the vampires. The Lord had instructed him to do so, and who was Gary Jarvis to argue with the Lord?

"If you want, when Martinez comes in, I'll speak to him," Jarvis offered.

"Oh, he's already in," Bill said. "He's down in the bunker, being debriefed right now."

Jarvis nearly choked. The usual protocol was to take two days—or in some cases, up to a week—to bring a team in from the field. This was to make sure they weren't being followed and leading vampires back to the heart of the Network in Iowa. Jarvis had planned to pray with Martinez, and of course go over his story with him. He sputtered, "Well, perhaps I could see him now. Maybe I could . . . could—"

Bill cut him off. "Jeez, Gary, you look a little pale. Let me put your mind at ease. Martinez hasn't given you up about the explosives, and I doubt he will. He's a good man."

Jarvis mustered up some fake indignation. "I take offense at that suggestion, Bill. In no way did I direct Martinez to—"

Bill cut him off again. "Oh, I know damn well you didn't direct anything. You're too smart for that. But I'd bet dollars to donuts you sure as hell suggested it in one of your prayer sessions."

"I did no such thing!"

"Doesn't matter now, does it? By the way, did you know the Simmons kid was on the mission, too? He's a wizard with explosives. He's the one who infused the garlic extract into the bomb. But he kind of cracked up in the field. He's as nervous as all get out. What do suppose he might say about your involvement if I put a little pressure on him? Huh, Gary?"

Jarvis felt what little color was left in his face drain away. They had him. This was it. He desperately tried to think of a way out of this predicament.

Helen said, "Could we cut the baloney, Reverend?"

Jarvis didn't know if this was meant to elicit his final confession, or if there actually was hope of a reprieve. He remained silent, unsure of his best move.

"Maybe you did tell Martinez to do it, and maybe we could prove it," Helen said. "But we all know you sure as heck hinted at it, and don't bother denying that. What would you say if I wasn't so dead set against these kinds of tactics anymore? What would you say if I wanted to step things up, sooner rather than later?"

Jarvis was surprised, but not shocked. He'd acquired some sketchy information that Helen Harrison was ill—terminal, in fact. But he couldn't confirm it until now. She'd operated the same way for decades, and only her impending mortality could explain this sort of change. The possibilities were endless.

If she came around to his way of thinking, there wouldn't be a civil war in the group after she was gone. She'd give Bill and their daughters their marching orders, and they'd obey. It would save Jarvis having to kill them, and they were all valuable assets. Perhaps he could even help Helen find the Lord again before she passed. He would like that.

Jarvis said, "You know, I'd welcome that, Helen. Is that why you put two teams in the field at once this time?"

She nodded.

"Where do we go from here?" he asked.

She smiled. "First, I want you to contact your boy on the other team. If they're planning to use explosives again, I want you to make absolutely sure it's a controlled blast. We can't have any repeats of New Orleans."

"It's against the rules to contact a team in the field," Jarvis said. "Even if I wanted to, you know that—"

Molly spoke for the first time. "Cut the bullshit, Gary."

"Now see here, young lady—" Jarvis said.

Molly interrupted him. "At last count, you're three years older than me, so let's drop the 'young lady' crap. I'm into your secure cells and computer connections. I know for a fact you've contacted teams in the field before. You want me to get the recordings and the printouts?"

If Jarvis had been able to, he would have strangled Molly Harrison right then. "Those contacts were for prayer only!"

Helen said, "That doesn't matter now. Make contact, and make sure they're careful with any explosives. After they're back, we'll have a meeting and go over how things will be moving forward. Is that acceptable to you, Reverend?"

"Very much so. I'll handle that issue with the other team immediately." He got up to leave. "The Lord be with you."

"You'd better hope the Lord's with you, Gary," Bill said. "If that Montreal team screws up, you're going to be seeing him a lot sooner than you expected."

Jarvis gave Bill a sour look and left.

~~~

Helen turned to Bill and said, "Did you need to do that right at the end?"

"It was a little joke."

"Not very funny."

"I thought it was," said Molly.

"Oh you hush, girl," Helen spat. "You're dad doesn't need any more encouragement when it comes to the reverend. You shouldn't have gone off script so much, Bill. You could've ruined my whole plan."

Bill did particularly enjoy ruffling the reverend's feathers, but he'd acted with purpose. "I needed to shake him up a bit. It gets his tongue wagging."

"Well, it might have worked, but it was risky," Helen said. She turned to Molly. "Did you get that list done?"

Molly slid in next to her mom and printed up a list off her computer. She appeared conflicted, hesitating, holding onto the printout. Helen reached out and said, "Well, come on, girl. Hand it over."

Molly did so reluctantly. "It's not like it's a lock. Jarvis' people don't exactly come out of the woodwork and volunteer that they're mindless followers of the good reverend. But it's the best guess I could make, all things considered."

Helen whistled. "This many? There's over one hundred twenty on this list."

Bill added, "Yep, and there's another ten we don't have quite enough on. You sure it wouldn't be easier to have me put a bullet in the reverend's head?"

"Maybe easier, but he'd be a martyr, and it would destroy everything. If my plan works, it'll flush them and cut them all out like a cancer, once and for all."

Bill wished the same could be done for his wife. "I sure

hope you know what you're doing, Helen."

"Me, too."

Molly asked, "What if your plan doesn't work, Mom?"

Helen looked surprised at the question. "Well, then we'll have to take care of that list ourselves," she said matter-of-factly.

Molly looked horrified at the prospect of killing one hundred twenty of their own. Bill simply nodded, knowing it was the right thing to do.

Helen said, "And Molly, the ten we're not sure about . . . add them to the list, too."

CHAPTER 39

Lisa arrived in Montreal on a mid-morning flight. She'd been unable to find Callaghan's address by any means and couldn't remember where his apartment was from their brief meeting all those years ago. She checked into her hotel and took the only course of action open to her—she went to McKibbin's.

Although it wasn't quite noon, the pub was open and manned by a bartender who Lisa thought may have been sixteen years old, at best. He told her the Squid was not at the bar. Lisa cringed at the mention of Callaghan's inane nickname. Each time Julian brought it up to her, she had the same response: "It's stupid."

The baby bartender wouldn't give up Callaghan's address right away. Lisa then implied that she'd had a tryst with the Squid the night before. She winced internally, even though it was only an imaginary affair. She said that he'd left his wallet at her place, and she wanted to return it to him.

The baby bartender suddenly took on the countenance of a lecherous old man and winked at her. Lisa nearly vomited in her mouth. He offered to hold the wallet at the bar until the Squid showed up. But Lisa protested that she couldn't possibly do that, as she felt it was her obligation to return it, safe and sound. He finally relented and gave up the address. As she was leaving, he told her that he got off work at six and asked her to come back for a drink. She turned about, gave him a solid slap in the face, and left the bar.

Disgusted, she caught a cab and headed to the Squid's apartment.

CHAPTER 40

My cell rang right about noon. I thought it would be Squid, but it was Jean-Luc.

"Christian, we've been hit again," he said in a dreadful voice.

Thoughts of potential victims—my friends—raced through my head. "Who?"

There was a pause and then he said, "The girls. Becca, Jen, and Maddie."

I felt like the breath had been sucked out of me. "All three?" I asked dumbly.

"*Oui* . . . all."

I sat down, dumbfounded. I couldn't get it through my head that those beautiful, lively girls were dead. "How?"

"You probably saw it on the news. The bomb last night."

"That was them? They said it was a terrorist attack."

Jean-Luc replied, "I thought it was, too. It wasn't until this morning I was told the girls had gone missing and that it was their building in which the bomb had gone off. Even so, explosives are not the usual calling card of the Genealogist. It wasn't until an hour ago that I was sure. I sent someone, a vampire, over to try to find out anything that they could. And do you know what happened?"

"No."

"She nearly died when she got close to the building. It was an allergic reaction. They'd—"

"Put their super-garlic in the bomb?"

"It would appear so."

"Jesus. Are they really going to start an all-out war?"

"Perhaps, or maybe it's a lunatic fringe group at work. In any case, I wanted to warn you directly. I've put the information on our blogs, locked down New Orleans even tighter, and advised other mayors to do the same."

Stunned, I remained silent.

Jean-Luc went on. "And for what it is worth, I'm very sorry about the girls. I know they were special to you."

"They were . . . they were special in general. I'm going to miss them. Jean-Luc, could you keep an extra close eye on Jake and Miranda for me? I think he's okay now, but he's still a little—"

"Goofy. Consider it done. And be careful, my friend."

"You, too."

I wanted to sit and mourn for Becca, Jen, and Maddie, my beautiful girls. But I couldn't, at least not yet. This attack was unbelievable and gave me a Grade-A case of the jitters. I dialed Squid, and when he didn't answer, the jitters turned to dread.

I dialed Adrienne next, and there was no connection. No ring, no message, no nothing. My dread turned to panic, and I bolted out of my room, bounding down the stairs. Despite all the witnesses to my midday vampire sprint, I ran as fast as I'd ever run. But it was still too late.

CHAPTER 41

Lisa arrived at Callaghan's apartment just as multiple fire engines and ambulances went blaring by. She entered the old-fashioned building, walked up three flights, and knocked on the door. She thought she heard someone inside, but there was no answer. She thought maybe Julian was hiding in there and was about to knock again when the door opened.

The man who opened it wasn't the huge Callaghan by a good foot and more than a hundred pounds. He said, "Can I help you?"

Lisa said, "Oh, I'm sorry. I was looking for Colm Callaghan. Does he live here?"

On the mention of Callaghan's name, Lisa noted recognition flash in the eyes of the slight young man. "Yes, he does, but he's not here right now. May I tell him who came calling for him?"

"Lisa Brownell. I need to speak to him. Do you know when he'll be back?"

"Brownell? You're not related to Julian Brownell, are you?"

Lisa was surprised. She wondered what was going on. "Why yes, but how did you know—"

The handgun now pointed at her stopped her comment cold. A voice from inside the room said, "What'd you do that for, Wally? We don't have time for this. We're pulling out. Now you're going to have to kill her."

Lisa gasped.

Wally smiled. "I'm improvising, like we've been taught. I'm not going to waste a potential source of information like Lisa here. I'm thinking Bloody Bill might want to chat with this gal a bit."

Lisa thought, *Bloody Bill? Jesus, what have I gotten myself into?*

Wally rapped her on the head with his pistol, and everything went dark.

CHAPTER 42

Adrienne couldn't be happier. She'd had a wonderful night dancing until dawn. She was so content, and Squid was especially pleased about how things had worked out between Christian and her. He was a happy man by nature, but she'd never seen him so delighted. After the V Bar had officially closed, she and Squid stayed for hours, chatting with friends.

Afterward, they'd both felt totally energized—and starving. They took in a long, leisurely brunch, and by the time they returned to Adrienne's apartment, it was afternoon. As they walked down the hall, they passed a man. Squid didn't seem to take note of him. But Adrienne did, for two reasons. She'd never seen him in the building before, and he looked very nervous.

~~~

He had good reason to be. That morning, Reverend Jarvis had called and told him he needed to adjust the amount of explosives in their homemade bomb. He'd answered, "But Gary, it's already planted, and she could be back any minute. It would be pretty dangerous to go back in now."

"Get the fuck back in there and fix it," Jarvis had replied. "That's an order, and you'd better not screw up. I only want that apartment torched—no one else's. If you fuck this up, there's going to be hell to pay. Do you understand?"

Although he was shocked to hear the reverend swear, he told him he did indeed understand. He'd never heard Jarvis ever say a four-letter word, let alone two. He went back in and made the adjustment to the explosives on the fly, hoping he'd done it right. He'd barely made it out of the apartment when the two vampire targets went right by him in the hallway. He'd nearly rubbed shoulders with them, and the bitch had eyeballed him like she knew. He thought for sure he was a dead man, but the two monsters kept walking. The second he cleared the building, he was going to remotely detonate the bomb.

~~~

Squid flopped on the living room couch and silenced his phone in his usual pre-nap ritual as Adrienne walked toward the kitchen to get a drink of water. She stopped when she noticed the coat closet door slightly ajar. A stickler for details, she said, "Have you been in the closet near the door?"

"Naw, I never go in there."

Squid noticed the expression on her face as she entered the living room and he rose. "Addie, what is it?"

She was about to answer when she heard a soft *tha-whump* come from the closet. She had no way of knowing it was the sound of a detonator going off, igniting the main explosive—but she did know that noise shouldn't have been coming from her closet. The stranger in the hall and the open closet door had already made her edgy. Now with this odd sound, she knew they were in peril.

She moved as rapidly as she could just as the blast ignited, running headlong into Squid and propelling him toward a window. Even if he had the time to ask why, he didn't need to—he had a crystal-clear view of the fireball expanding toward them as Adrienne drove him backward.

They hurtled through the window, with the deafening explosion and white-hot flames in close pursuit. Adrienne screamed in pain as the blast hit her back. They fell five stories, but Squid executed a perfect back flip, far better than any he'd ever done on a dance floor, protecting Adrienne and taking the brunt of their landing. As they crashed to the ground in the alley behind the apartment, he tossed her horizontally as hard as he could, changing the direction of her momentum and lessening her impact.

The Squid screamed in agony and when Adrienne finally rolled and skidded to a stop, she tried to get up and go to him—but couldn't. The pain in her back suddenly intensified so much that she almost passed out. As she fell down again, her back burst into flames, and she shrieked in shock and anguish. She rolled, trying to beat the flames out, but despite all her efforts, the blaze increased.

Between rolls, Adrienne could see Squid limping toward her, until he noticed his right leg was also on fire. He stopped, feverishly beating at the flames.

Adrienne screamed and screamed. Several hundred years ago, she'd been burned by fire. The pain had been terrible, but this felt a thousandfold worse. Despite her best efforts to extinguish herself, it was a losing battle, and she knew it. She stopped rolling and willed herself to silence despite the agony. She wouldn't let Squid's last memory of her be screeching death throes. The thought helped her find some serenity, and the pain seemed to lessen.

She turned to where she thought the Squid would be. She wanted one last look at her love, but he wasn't there. She thought, *Oh no... he's already burned.* The smell of Adrienne's sizzling flesh filled the air as the flames grew stronger, and then a suffocating darkness crashed down around her.

CHAPTER 43

A few hours later, Donald Leland answered his cell phone. "Hello, Garret."

Dick, not much for pleasantries said, "I lost her, Donny."

Donald was surprised, but not angry. "Really? My little Lisa must have some hidden talents to lose you. How'd it happen?"

"I trailed her to an apartment building, and she never came out. I figure she went out the service entrance."

"Whose apartment?"

"That's the funny part. She'd just been at a bar named McKibbin's. Ring any bells?"

It sounded somewhat familiar, but Donald wasn't sure. "Maybe."

"Exactly how I felt. Anyway, I thought I'd seen it recently, and then it hit me. It was on the list of the good doctor's mystery assets."

"Damn. One big coincidence, isn't it?"

"Definitely. I went back to the bar, and there was this kid working, running the whole place. I squeezed him, and he gave up who Lisa went to see. It was a guy named Colm Callaghan, the main owner of the bar."

"More and more interesting. I hope you didn't squeeze

the kid too hard."

Garret laughed. "No, it didn't take much. Anyway, I went back to Callaghan's apartment. There was no answer at the door, so I let myself in and tossed the place. Didn't find anything interesting."

"Do you think Lisa spotted you?"

"No way. But I'm figuring this Callaghan did, or maybe he just assumed she was being followed."

Donald smiled. "My, my, my. What could dear Lisa be up to?"

"She might have gotten herself into some trouble, and that's why she's gonzo."

Donald thought about that for a moment, but it didn't wash with him. It was all too fast, too coincidental. "Maybe, but I doubt it. She's in on it, somehow."

"In on what?"

"That's the question, my friend. That is the question. But whatever it is, we're going to find out."

"What do you want me to do?"

"Hang there for a few days. Her hotel, McKibbin's, Callaghan's apartment . . . maybe you'll get lucky."

"That's spreading myself pretty thin. Besides, I think she and this Callaghan are long gone."

"You're probably right," Donald said, "but give it a try, anyway. If nothing turns up, I've got some work waiting for you right in good old Needham. Lisa's got a lot of family around here. I don't think she'd disappear on them. She'll eventually come back—and when she does, we'll be waiting."

CHAPTER 44

I got to Adrienne's before the first fire trucks and ambulances arrived. The fifth floor, Adrienne's floor, was a smoking wreck. I tried Squid's number again, but it had now joined his girlfriend's in ill-omened silence. I tried to get up there, but when I hit the third floor, I started wheezing, unable to get a full breath. It was garlic again—a garlic-infused bomb.

I beat a hasty retreat back down the stairs, and in a few minutes, my breathing started to normalize. But my mind was empty, a void. My best friend was dead. I sat on the curb with my head down and broke into huge, hitching sobs. A fireman gave me some oxygen and tried to console me, but I shooed him away.

The din increased as more and more rescue vehicles and sirens and police and gawkers kept coming. I sat and cried. There was a noise that my mind was too boggled to identify. It came again, and now it annoyed me. It stopped and started again, and I realized it was coming from me. I fished my phone from my pocket and looked at it stupidly, unable to remember what to do with it. The shock of what had happened had wrapped my brain in thought-proof insulation.

The phone rang again, and I nearly fumbled it into the gutter. I keyed the *Send* button, but didn't speak. After a moment, a hoarse, gravelly voice said, "Chrissy, is that you?"

I sort of recognized the voice, but it sounded different. Finally some of my brain insulation started to fall away. I thought, *Nobody calls me Chrissy... nobody but Squid.* "Squid?" I mumbled into the phone.

There was no reply. I wasn't sure if I had imagined him speaking to me or not. I felt my heart lurch and said louder, "Squid?"

Still the infuriating silence.

I increased my volume, shouting into the phone over and over again, "Squid? Squid! Answer, damn it! Squid!"

I heard a loud cough, and then he said, "Jesus, take it easy, Chrissy. When you didn't answer, I thought it might've been someone else. With your phone, you know?"

Fresh tears sprouted from my eyes, but now I was grinning. "I thought you were dead! Christ, I was sure of it. What happened? Are you okay? What's wrong with your voice?"

He said, "Yes... no... I'm okay, mostly. It was a bomb. They put garlic in it. Can you believe it, fucking garlic? It's not enough they want to kill us; they want to make us suffer, too. You need to get over here right away. Adrienne's hurt bad. She needs a doctor."

"What do you mean, 'she needs a doctor'? She'll heal."

"I'll explain when I see you. Get over here. Tell me where you are, and I'll send a car. And make sure you're not followed."

Twenty minutes later, I was at a safe house in the Plateau area. Squid looked okay, but he was moving stiffly and winced in pain when I hugged him. I said, "Sorry. What happened?"

"It was a bomb in Adrienne's place. She knew somehow and body-blocked me out the window right when it went off. When we landed, my leg was on fire, but she was worse—her whole back was burning. I put myself out and did the only thing I could think of to put her out. I fell on her. I got lucky and smothered the flames, instead of the both of us going up."

I thought, *Squid the Fearless*. Then I saw his hands. They were still bright red and covered with blisters. "Has this healed at all yet?"

He looked at his hands. "I'm not sure, maybe a little. But it still hurts like a bastard."

"Where else?"

"I can wait. Adrienne needs your help."

"Show me where else."

He opened his shirt, and I gasped. His chest, going down to his abdomen and likely beyond, was burnt black. It was a third-degree burn, maybe even a fourth. He said, "Don't ask me if this is any better. I can't tell. It doesn't hurt as much as my hands, though."

I went into doctor mode. "It's a more serious burn. It takes out the nerve endings. That's why it doesn't hurt as much. When it heals, it'll hurt plenty."

He looked uncharacteristically serious. "*If* it heals."

"Take me to Adrienne."

He took me into the next room, where the wreck of Adrienne lay face down on a bed. Although she was unconscious, she was moaning in pain. Her entire back was burned far worse than the Squid's chest, and yellow drainage was oozing through some makeshift bandages he'd fashioned. The burn was so bad, I could see parts of her ribs where the flesh was completely seared away. The room reeked of a barbecue gone bad. My gorge tried to rise, but I wouldn't let it.

Despite her ruined body, somehow the worst part for me was her frazzled hair. It had been so long and luxurious and now was burnt up to a pageboy length. Its smell mixed horribly with the odor of burnt flesh and filled the air with a suffocating stench. Luckily, her hair hadn't burned off completely, but it would be a long while before it grew back to its usual length—if she survived.

While I examined her, Squid spoke quietly from behind me. "After I put her out, I threw her in the car and came here. We were gagging and coughing all the way, the fucking garlic. We're lucky neither one of us is all that allergic. I stripped both of us down and put her in the shower. I had to, you know, to rinse the garlic off, and Jesus, how she screamed. I've never heard anyone scream like that. I thought she was going to break her vocal cords. But I had to do it. What other choice did I have?"

He made a choking sound, and I caught him wiping tears from his eyes.

He said, "You're a real doctor, right? I mean, you went through the training and everything—you didn't just fake it. You can help her, right?" He sounded desperate. He *was* desperate.

"I don't know. This must be caused by the combination of the fire and the garlic somehow, but I have no idea how that would work. The only thing I can do is treat her like a human burn victim and hope that's enough."

"Okay . . . at least that's something."

"Can you get your hands on some medical supplies?"

"Give me a list of what you need."

CHAPTER 45

The next two days were horrible for Adrienne as she hung in the balance between life and death. But in many ways, they were worse for Lisa Brownell.

When she regained consciousness, she found herself in the trunk of a car, bound and gagged. She tried to scream and fight her way loose, but she could do neither. Hours later, she was shocked into the light of day when the trunk was thrown open.

She blinked, wide-eyed, as she was roughly taken from the car and led into a barn, where a metal door stood open in the floor. She was led down several flights of stairs and locked in a cell. She screamed after her captors but was ignored. Lisa couldn't begin to fathom what had happened to her or why—but she knew it was somehow related to Julian. She sat on her cot and waited, and as it turned out, she didn't have long to wait.

A gangly middle-aged man entered her cell, locked it behind him, and smiled down at her. He looked like a kind older man, almost like an oasis of sanity in this surreal nightmare she'd been thrust into. He said in a friendly tone, "Hi, I'm Bill. Quite a quandary we've got ourselves into, isn't it, Lisa?"

"What the fuck is this about?" she screeched. "You've got to help me! I didn't do anything! Why am—"

He shushed her. "Now hold your horses, missy. I think we can straighten things out, if you answer a few questions."

"You've kidnapped me, and now I'm supposed to answer your questions? Who the hell are you people? I want a lawyer."

He chuckled. "The legal system is kind of on hiatus down here. If you want to get out anytime soon, I'd suggest you play ball."

She was about to say something nasty, but kept her peace. She was stunned, but she wasn't stupid. She knew she was in serious trouble and needed to hear this old gent out to get an idea of what it was about. "I'm listening."

Bill was all smiles. "That's better. Okay, let's start. You've been married to Julian Brownell for the last fifteen years, right?"

"That's right, but we're getting divorced."

He said sympathetically, "Oh, that's too bad."

Lisa noted there was not one bit of sympathy in his eyes. "Look, if he's in some kind of trouble—"

Bill cut her off, sounding nowhere near as kind as he first did. "I'm asking the questions here, girl."

She bit off another nasty reply.

"Good. You're a smart one, aren't you? Smarter than most I've had here, I'd reckon. Anyway, you were in Montreal looking up a Colm Callaghan. What was that all about?"

Lisa thought the best way out of this was to be truthful. "Julian's got a business with Callaghan. He's got a bunch of things like that he's hidden from me. I thought he was trying to cheat me out of some money for the divorce, so I figured I'd look into it."

"Uh-huh. Isn't that the kind of thing you leave to the lawyers?"

She didn't have a good answer for that. "I thought Julian was screwing me over, and I wanted to get to the bottom of it myself, that's all. I admit it wasn't the smartest thing I've ever done."

Bill smiled. Lisa thought his smile was genuine, but not at all in a good way.

"Oh, I agree with you there," he said. "Say, you running around with that husband of yours and then going to see Callaghan hasn't got anything to do with the fact that they're vampires, does it?"

Lisa thought she couldn't have heard him correctly. "Excuse me?"

In that moment, Bill Harrison was gone. Lisa was now dealing with Bloody Bill. His eyes got flinty hard, but he said in the same friendly drawl, "You know . . . vampires? Bloodsucking murderers? It's hard to believe you lived with one for fifteen years and didn't know it. I mean, he'd have to be awfully good at keeping secrets, or you'd have to be pretty dumb."

Lisa's mouth fell open in disbelief. She thought up to now the current course of events had been as surreal as it got—and now, things were taking a turn for completely fucking nuts.

The old man patiently waited until she found her voice. He wore a bemused smile and it infuriated her.

"Are you crazy?" she exclaimed. "Vampires? *Hello*, they don't exist. Fairytales, made-up, make believe, whatever. This is fucking ridiculous. You're a bunch of bunker-living wackos that are all off your rockers, is that it? So we must be in the Midwest, right? Like this shit could happen anywhere else. You mean you kidnapped me because you think, what,

I'm some kind of a vampire helper? How do you know I'm not a vampire loony-tunes? Maybe I'll bite your scraggly old chicken neck right now!"

Bill was still smiling. "You all deny it, at least at first," he said genially. "But I can be pretty darn persuasive in getting you to see the error in that. I've got to admit, though, your little speech there was pretty funny. As for you being a vampire, we know you're not. You don't move the right way, and you went down too easy with the knock to your noggin. Your teeth ain't right, either. But to be sure, we put a cut on your arm, and it didn't heal up the way they do. No, you're human all right. Just working for the wrong side, that's all."

She looked at her arm, and there was a fresh cut there. That was the final item that pushed her over the edge. Lisa stood. He was an old man, and she had training in Kung Fu—a brown belt, in fact. This might be her best chance with no burly guards around. She said, "Look, I've had enough of this. I don't want to hurt you, but you're going to let me out of here."

Bloody Bill looked amused. He chuckled, and his eyes fairly twinkled with malicious glee. "Oh really? I'd sit back down if I were you, little girl."

Lisa snapped out a kick, aiming at his groin. It was crisp, on target, and she was sure it would land. But instead, she crashed face first to the floor, her arm painfully twisted behind her and Bill's large foot planted on the back of her neck. She had no idea how it had happened. Bloody Bill exchanged his foot for his knee, ratcheting up the pressure, and twisted her arm to the breaking point. She gasped as he leaned his face close.

She could feel his breath tickling her ear as he said, "Before this is even close to being over, you're going to wish we had done this the easy way, you vampire-loving bitch!"

CHAPTER 46

Jake Lyons awoke from a dead sleep in the early morning. He'd just tucked into bed with Miranda a little over an hour before. He could immediately tell he wasn't going to get back to sleep anytime soon, so he eased himself out of bed, careful not to disturb his girl.

A dream had woken him. Jake dreamed often, but always had a difficult time remembering the dreams. He could usually bring back the general theme, but not the specifics. He'd always been frustrated by this and envied people who could recall their dreams in vivid detail. In this case, the theme of his dream was crystal clear: *garlic*.

Garlic, understandably, wasn't an unusual subject for vampire nightmares, especially considering the events of the last few days. But this hadn't been a nightmare at all. He went to the kitchen to get a drink, feeling the way a person often does in this situation—that what he couldn't remember in the dream was somehow important.

He sat at his kitchen table, drinking his water and ruffling his own hair, something he did when he was trying to jog his memory. He said to himself, "Come on, Jake. Think."

He exhaled, closed his eyes, and sat back in a perfect repose for meditation. He remained that way for almost five minutes when the first specks of realization seeped into his mind. He waited longer. The seep became a trickle and then a steady stream. When his thoughts hit flood tide, his eyes flew open. "Garlic! Fucking garlic!"

He raced to the bedroom and shouted, "Miranda, wake up. I think I got it. It was so simple—it's garlic!"

Jake's shouts shocked Miranda out of sleep. She sat up, bleary-eyed. "Jake, what are you talking about? What is it?"

He smiled. "Miranda, honey, that's how we'll find her—the garlic. I've got to get to my computer."

CHAPTER 47

Two days isn't a very long time for a vampire, but it felt like an eternity as Squid and I waited for Adrienne to wake up. Watching her suffering and writhing in agony was bad enough. Watching Squid's response to it was nearly as bad. He was a mess.

The two of us never left her side. I did my best, treating her as I would a human burn victim, which large amounts of IV fluids, various burn ointments, and frequent dressing changes. But in the end, it was up to her to heal herself, if she lived long enough to do it.

I was encouraged when, in about a day, Squid's chest and hand burns started to heal, albeit much slower than usual. Around the same time, Adrienne began waking sporadically from her coma, mumbling a few words before she lapsed back into unconsciousness.

By mid-morning of the second day, I noted that her breathing had lost some of its rasping harshness. When I changed her dressing, the wounds still looked heinous, but I could no longer see her ribs. I was dead tired, so I blinked and looked again to make sure I was right.

I woke Squid, who'd fallen asleep in a bedside chair. "Come on, take a look."

He looked at her back and cringed. "What are you showing me that for?"

"No more ribs."

He appeared puzzled, but then looked again. It finally dawned on him. "Yeah, I could see them before, but the burn still looks like shit. You think—"

"I think she's going to be okay."

He hugged me, and when he was through wiping a fresh set of tears from his face, he said, "Thanks so much. I owe you big time."

"My pleasure. You don't owe me a thing. Anyway, I am . . . *was* an ER doctor. This is right up my alley."

He was about to answer when my phone rang.

It was Jake.

Right on top of my hello, he said in a rush, "Titus, I got it, I got her . . . it was garlic. I'm so fucking stupid. I don't know how I didn't see it before. Anyway, I was focused on finding her through her computer trail, but she's too good for that, and stupid me keeps plugging away at a dead end, anyway. Then, with the bombings, I was concentrating on how she scoped us out—you know, it seemed more important. But garlic, it kept bugging me, in the back of my mind mostly. Last night, I woke up and I had it. It's so fucking simple—garlic."

When he finally took a breath, I was able to speak. "Jake, I have no idea what you mean. Now slow down and tell me what this is all about."

I could hear him take a steadying breath. He said, "I've got her. I've got the Genealogist."

A cold, deadly calm fell over me. "The Genealogist? Are you sure?"

Squid turned to me, looking very focused and uncharacteristically deadly.

I put my phone on speaker and said, "Tell me."

"It was so simple. The garlic was the key. According to our guys, her new super-concentrated stuff is still a natural product, not synthetic. So it takes garlic to make it."

My mind evidently was still plodding along at a slow pace. I had no idea how that mattered. "We know they make it from garlic. I don't see how it helps."

"It's not that the stuff is made from garlic—it's the amount. To make a super-concentrated extract from the natural substance would require a huge amount of it, no matter how you look at it. Maybe they make it by distilling it down over and over again, I don't know, but they'd need a lot of it."

The light started to eke into the shadows of my mind. I was beginning to see.

Jake went on. "Anyway, I figured the amount required would be way out of line, you know, like food distributor amounts, or supermarket chains, like that."

"It makes sense to me. How long would it take for you to run a trace?"

There was a slight pause. "I already did. I've been working on it all morning. It wasn't so hard. It was just like I thought. For places ordering big amounts, there were distributors, supermarkets, and the like . . . and one small corn farm in the middle of Iowa. Now what do you suppose a corn farmer would want with all that garlic?"

I glanced at Squid again. His look had gone from deadly to absolutely savage. I'd never seen that look on him before. It was frightening.

I asked, "Anything else?"

"Yep. A William and Helen Harrison own the farm. I tried to backdoor their computer system, nothing too serious, nothing that would set off any alarms, and you know what? They've got more security on their shit than the fucking Pentagon."

"Who else knows about this?"

"Only you and Miranda."

I took the phone off speaker. "Put her on."

"Hi, Titus," Miranda said on the other end.

"We're going to move on this, Miranda, and I'm going to need Jake. You can't come."

"But—"

I interrupted, raising my voice. "There are no 'buts' here. You're not a day-walker, and therefore you're a liability. This is too important to fuck around with. You have to promise me—no funny business."

There was a pause, and I hoped she was seeing the logic of what I'd said. "Okay, you're right. But you have to promise me something, too. Promise me you'll watch out for Jake."

I answered honestly, "I promise to try my best. That's going to have to be good enough."

"Okay, Titus. I guess it'll have to do. Good luck. Here's Jake."

"Jake, call Jean-Luc. Tell him to meet you and go over all this with him in person. Don't give out any info over the phone no matter what, and don't talk to anyone else about this. We can't be sure who's being watched at this point. Tell him to get a team together. Five, six people max. Heavy arms, short-range communications, and body armor. I'll do the same here. Tell him I'll be in contact later today."

"Got it. Anything else?"

"Yes. I need you especially, loaded with every piece of techno crap you can imagine. Shit, take stuff you can't imagine, I don't know what, but be ready on that end. And one more thing. You know how to use a gun?"

"No."

"Learn. You've got twenty-four hours."

I hung up and looked at Squid. "Same for you. Me, you, maybe three or four others . . . you pick them."

He nodded. "Body armor? You sure? Seems like overkill."

"After all this? Yeah, I'm sure. Any little thing might help. They're too good, and we need to be careful. I'm going to bring in one more group for backup."

He was about to say something when Adrienne croaked out from her bed, "I'm coming with you."

She started to lift herself off the bed. Her dressings fell off, and I could see the muscles in her back working with the effort. There was no skin over them yet. I eased her back down, and she glared at me like she used to in the old days, making me feel a little nostalgic.

Squid moved in and sat on the edge of the bed, tipping it precipitously. He took her hand and said, "Addie, you can barely move yet. You know you can't go. Besides, even if you were healthy, I wouldn't want you going, anyway."

Her eyes immediately softened, and now they were filled with fear. "And how do you think I feel about *you* going?"

He smiled at her. "Come on, it's me. In all the baloney I've been involved with, the worst I ever got was a splinter in my ass."

A-ha! I thought. *Not shrapnel, a splinter!*

Adrienne smiled and looked like she wanted to laugh, but it would take too much effort in her sorry state. "A splinter in the ass is acceptable. Anything more, and you'll have to deal with me."

He bent down and kissed her. "You've got it, kiddo. I'd better get on the phone."

He left the room, his staccato verbiage trailing behind

him. I thought Adrienne had lapsed back into unconsciousness, so I turned to go.

"Christian, promise me you'll protect him," she said.

I paused. "He means the world to me. I promise."

She smiled and closed her eyes.

I left the room, thinking, *Oh, sure! Protect Squid. Protect Jake. How about someone protecting* me *for a fucking change?*

When Squid finished his call, I gave him my watered-down version of the Squid-eye.

"What?" he said. "Oh, fuck you. Before you say it, it *was* shrapnel. I only said 'splinter' to make Adrienne feel better."

"Oh, right, I forgot . . . shrapnel."

CHAPTER 48

Bloody Bill entered Lisa Brownell's "accommodations" in the Bunker. Her screams were muffled and choked off by the soaked towel covering her face. She was strapped naked to the examining table, her limbs straining against the leather straps that firmly held her as she was slowly suffocated. Andy Simmons continued to pour water down onto the covered face of his helpless victim. Bill thought Andy might not be such great shakes in the field, or as a night watchman, for that matter, but he sure was taking to "interrogation." He smiled serenely and actually whistled as he waterboarded Brownell.

Bill said, "Andy, hold up a minute. I'm going to take over for a while."

Simmons looked disappointed. "You sure? I'm happy to keep going."

Bill had to raise his voice to be heard over Lisa's waterlogged, tortured breathing. "Yeah, I'm sure. You've been at it for twelve hours straight. Go home and take tomorrow off."

"But, Bill, I don't need a day off. I want to help."

"You *are* helping. But I need you fresh. Take the day off."

As Simmons headed out of the room, Bill clapped him on

the shoulder and said, "You're doing some fine work here."

Simmons beamed at the compliment and closed the door behind him. Bloody Bill removed the towel from Lisa's face, and she panted out ragged, whistling breaths, spewing water from her mouth and nostrils.

When her breathing slowed some, he said, "You know, Lisa, you're by far the most interesting person I've had down here. I got to say, that husband of yours was an ass, and that bastard Donald? What a jerk."

He paused and looked at her for a moment. Her eyes were vacant. She had defensively withdrawn into herself in response to forty-eight sleepless hours of near-constant torture. He'd seen that before, but he knew she hadn't snapped yet. She was playing possum. When she didn't respond, he went on. "But all that stuff you admitted to about vampires is a crock. I've got some experience with this sort of thing, and I'm darn sure you're making it all up. Now I wonder if you really didn't know about your husband, but that's silly, isn't it? I think you've been conditioned somehow. Conditioned to resist. Anyway, I told my wife, Helen, about you, and she wants to meet you. You'd have no way of knowing it, but Helen's never met one of my guests before. It's quite an honor. So, we're going to get you cleaned up and take you upstairs in a bit."

Bill started to walk to the door, but paused and turned back. He did a fairly good job of making it look as if he'd done it spontaneously. "But you know what? First, I want to make sure all our cards are on the table."

Lisa's respirations increased exponentially as he returned to the table with his pliers in hand. He looked her up and down. "Let's see, you're down about six fingernails and four toenails. I'm getting kind of bored with that. You?"

Lisa began mouthing out a strangled, whispering sound.

"Oh, that's too bad," Bill said, "because I am. You know, our last guest didn't like me running electricity through her nipples. But you seemed to do okay with it, somehow. I guess I'll have to get more creative."

As Bill turned to set up his electrical apparatus, Lisa found her voice and shouted, "No! Please, no! I've told you everything!"

Bill ignored her and turned back holding two alligator-clip electrodes. "I'll apologize in advance. Getting this circuit right is going to take a little doing. It might sting a little."

As Bill advanced the electrodes toward her pelvis, she let out an ear-shattering shriek. But that was nothing compared to what she did when he turned on the electricity.

CHAPTER 49

I was once again examining my battle scars, but this time in the stark fluorescent light of a cheap motel bathroom in Iowa. For the first time in a long time, I actually felt good about it. I looked at them, not as a part of my lost human self, but as a part of me—Titus Acilius.

Over the last weeks, in New Orleans and then in Montreal, with the help of my own kind, I'd begun to find myself again. I was far from right, but I was better. I still didn't understand what had happened to me over the last century, and maybe I never would, but I felt better. Being the practical Roman that I was, that was all I needed. Perhaps I was a tad simplistic, but I thought deep reflection was way overrated.

My feet felt like they were on the right path again, and maybe they'd been set there by a sense of family. Not family as humans would define it, but family nonetheless—my vampire family. Squid, Jean-Luc, my aunts, Miranda, Jake, and maybe even Adrienne. Perhaps they were the key to my survival.

Now I had to fight for that survival—maybe for the survival of my entire kind. This battle was that important. That was fine by me. These bastards had attacked my aunts, killed my friends in New Orleans, and nearly repeated the trick in Montreal. Now it seemed they were trying to wipe us all out. That would not stand while I was drawing breath.

I picked up my gladius, hefted it, and spun it in my hand. It felt as it always did—just right. I didn't care if I lived or died this night. It was of no matter. I would do my duty.

I took one more look at myself in the mirror and smiled. I felt as I always did before a battle—poised, ready, and happy. After all, I am Roman.

~~~

I walked out of the bathroom, pondering our game plan for the attack.

"Jesus Christ, what did you do, fall asleep in there?" Squid called out from the tiny bed he was currently crushing.

"Very funny."

As he stood, the many beer cans he'd drained while I showered tinkled and rattled around the bed.

He eyeballed my gladius. "What exactly do you have in mind for that pig-sticker of yours?"

"Oh, I don't know. I'll come up with something. You ready?"

"I was born ready."

So far, things had gone quite smoothly. We'd met on the outskirts of Des Moines. Our team had five members, as did Jean Luc's, which included Jake and Simone. I wished she hadn't come, but I knew once Simone's mind was made up, there was no stopping her. I also wished Jake hadn't had to come. I liked the kid, and this assault would be dangerous. But we needed him.

Late entries were Dom Salvucci and his "associates" Vinnie and Marco. Some of the vampires thought it foolish to involve humans in our team, but I knew how Dom and his crew performed. Besides, the Harrisons might not expect human attackers, and that surprise could give us an edge. Though I'd be damned if I could figure out what that edge might be. With Dom's group, it brought our total to thirteen. It's a good thing I wasn't superstitious.

We performed a brief recon for the layout of the farm and to get some idea of their security. Jake did some passive monitoring to gain whatever information he could and to figure how to best shut down the farm's systems. But he did nothing that would raise any computer flags. We knew how smart our enemy was.

The farm had a main house, a silo, and a barn—and that barn had way too much activity around it. There were anywhere from eight to twelve guards on the place at any one time, and they had advanced electronic security. Although Jake ended up gaining little information from their computer system, he was sure he could shut down their security and power.

The plan was pretty basic. We'd set up a perimeter, Jake on the only small hill on the farm as our observer/coordinator. He'd have one hour to do an active hack into their systems in an attempt to get some hard intelligence. If his intrusion was discovered before the hour was up, he'd signal, and we'd move in.

Our part was simple. Kill everybody on the farm, except the Harrisons. We'd need at least one of them alive, hopefully more, so they could be used as leverage against each other. Then we'd do anything and everything we needed to get information out of them that would crash their entire operation. Once we got it, Ma and Pa Harrison would be dead meat.

We would start the operation at 2:00 a.m. If everything

went as planned, we'd be done by dawn. It was time to go.

I said, "You stick close to me tonight, Squid. And no foolishness."

"*Moi?* Hey, it's me. Not even an ass splinter, Chrissy."

CHAPTER 50

Lisa Brownell stared at the floor, not really seeing it. She had only a vague and incomplete understanding of what her situation was at this point. In her current state, she couldn't recollect her own name, let alone any pertinent details of her life. Her thought process had been crushed down to a basic level and her mind had switched off in self-defense. If she had been able to think, she would have considered herself lucky. She would have been grateful that she wasn't in horrible pain and that she was away from "the nasty old man," as she now thought of Bloody Bill. It was the same feeling a dog might have when its master stopped whipping it.

~~~

Helen Harrison sat at her desk across from Lisa Brownell. Considering what Bill had told her, she thought it might be interesting to interview their captive directly. But unfortunately, Bill had already done his usual thorough job. In a word, Lisa Brownell was a wreck. Helen thought it would be nearly impossible to get Lisa to focus on a question or two, let alone engage in any kind of meaningful discussion.

Helen was about to try to ask Lisa a question when all

the lights winked off. After a moment, the generator kicked in, and lower-level emergency lights slowly revved up to their less-than-ideal intensity. Lisa cringed in her chair and put her head in her hands, sobbing.

Helen tried her cell phone. No signal. She thumbed an old-style hardwired intercom that connected her to the Bunker. "They're here, Bill," she said. "This is much earlier than I would've guessed."

Bill's distorted voice came back over the squawk box. "They're ingenious bastards, but with all our extra activity, we knew they'd find us. But you're right. Earlier than I would have guessed."

"We ready?"

"As we'll ever be. But . . ."

"But what?"

There was a pause. "The girls are here."

"All three?"

"Yep. All of them."

"Damn!" Helen muttered. "Well, that can't be helped now. Do your best by them. At least tell me that Jarvis is still here."

She heard the smile in Bill's voice. "Oh, he's here, all right."

She let out a sigh of relief. "Good, at least there's that. Now you make sure to wait for my signal, okay?"

"I'll wait. And Helen . . . I love you."

She smiled. "I love you too, Bill. Kiss the girls for me." She thumbed off the intercom and pulled a semi-automatic pistol from her desk drawer. She looked at Lisa, who cowered and sobbed in her chair. "Well, girl, looks like you've got yourself a front-row seat for tonight's show."

CHAPTER 51

To give myself some credit, the first part of the operation went swimmingly. Jake got his full hour of computer hacking, and then we quietly took out the guards. They fell like ninepins. The silo was deserted. Once the barn was secured, we converged on the house. We searched it until we found the old lady sitting at a desk in her office, a gun at the ready. There was another woman in a chair with her back toward me, probably one of the Harrison daughters, I surmised.

As we had planned, Squid drew Helen's fire, and I moved in and disarmed her, while he covered the daughter. The move went off just as we had planned, but with one slight complication.

"Holy shit," said Squid from behind me. "Lisa?"

A barely audible voice said, "Julian?"

I turned and looked at my wife, who was sitting in the office of my greatest enemy. I thought, *What the fuck? Did she give me up? Was she the reason the hunters were finding us?*

Then I took a good look at her. She was drawn, with a dirty, tear-streaked face. It was a hell of a contest as to what was wilder looking, her hair or her eyes. I'd put it at about a dead heat. Her fingers were covered with dried blood. What the hell had gone on here?

I took a step toward her, and she recoiled in her chair. I hesitated, and she looked up at me again and burst into huge, hitching sobs. I moved toward her and took her in my arms. She latched onto me fiercely, trembling as she continued to cry.

From behind me, Helen Harrison said, "My, my. What a touching family reunion."

I turned to see her eyes dancing and a smug smile on her face. But she didn't wear it for long.

With one hand, Squid lifted her out of the chair by her neck. Her smugness evaporated, replaced by red-faced choking, but she kicked at the Squid for all she was worth.

"I'd shut the fuck up if I were you, granny," he hissed, and nonchalantly tossed her back into her chair.

As she caught her breath, I settled Lisa down. I managed to detach her from me, and I turned to Helen Harrison. "What's she doing here?"

She shrugged. "We picked her up in Montreal when she was looking for you. She said she didn't know you were a vampire. We didn't believe her, of course, but couldn't get anything useful out of her. You must have trained your little pet well, Dr. Brownell."

I shouted, "She doesn't know, you dumb bitch!"

I could have killed the old lady. I was done with Lisa, but Jesus, I didn't want this for her. I wanted things to end in the routine, extraordinarily painful, human-divorce type way. I'd never wanted her in my world, but there was no going back for Lisa now. They should've just killed her. They pretty much already had.

"The language on you, Doctor," Helen said. "Now why would we presume she *wouldn't* know? It doesn't make any sense. Why would you keep up the pretense for all those years?"

I calmed myself. We didn't have time for this. "Fair questions, but not on the agenda for tonight. Now let's get down to it, Helen."

"Oh, we'll get down to it, all right," she said as she smiled at me, thumbing the button on an intercom a few times.

Squid raised his gun to her head.

"No!" I shouted. "Don't, Squid!"

She said calmly, "You might as well let him pull the trigger. It doesn't matter."

Jake's voice came over my headphones. "Titus, I've got movement, and a lot of it, coming out of the barn."

Then the gunfire started.

CHAPTER 52

Jake watched from his vantage point up on the hill and shouted warnings into his mike, but short of that, there was nothing he could do. They came out of the barn, a strike force of at least fifty, and opened up with machine guns, shotguns, and flamethrowers. They quickly overran the vampires who had still been near the barn. There had to have been a hidden room in it, something the team had missed.

The battle was fast and deadly. Some members of his group were already dead, but from where Jake was, he couldn't tell who they were. He was about to contact Titus again when he saw a group of four break away from the main force and head directly for him. *Shit! How'd they know where I am?* Then he said to himself, "Duh. It's an ambush."

He picked up his laptop and his rifle. He'd have to leave the rest of his equipment behind. This was life or death, and the way things looked, death was the safer bet. He retreated to a small copse of trees. It would provide some cover, but not much. As he settled in, he wished he could somehow use his laptop to shoot. He was so good with it, and frankly, he sucked with a gun.

In his defense, he'd only had a day to practice, and most

of that day was taken up on getting the tech side of the assault ready. As he sighted on his first attacker, he vowed that if he got out of this, he would learn to shoot. But before he could pull the trigger, someone pressed a firm hand over his mouth.

CHAPTER 53

We killed quite a few of our attackers, but not nearly enough, and they in turn killed many in our group. Those who remained were forced to retreat back into the house. Only Dom and I were untouched. Jean-Luc had some minor wounds that were healing, but Squid's ass-splinter luck had run dry, as he and Simone were shot to pieces. They sat on the floor, propped against a wall, breathing heavily.

The rest were dead.

Simone had been machine-gunned down and was about to be torched when Squid made another of his suicide runs and scooped her up. The guy really was fucking fearless—or maybe stupid. He caught several garlic-laced rounds for his effort and barely avoided a flame burst, just making it back into the house. If we got out of this, Jean-Luc might have a very different opinion of him, or at least, I don't think he'd try to beat Squid to death anytime soon. But us getting off this farm was a pretty big fucking "if."

Helen Harrison had that same damn smug smile pursing her lips once again. Her coal-black eyes sparkled. Lisa was on the floor in the fetal position, with her eyes closed and hands over her ears. Jean-Luc, Dom, and I stood guard at the windows. We were surrounded.

Outside, a tall, gangly old man walked out into the open, carrying a white flag. I thought it was cute, but had to suppress the urge to put a bullet in his head. From the photos I'd studied, I recognized him as Bill Harrison.

"Far enough, Harrison," I yelled out the window.

"I just want to talk."

"Do it from there."

"Look, you're not getting out of that house, plain and simple. Give up, and we'll make it quick and painless for you. Otherwise we're going to torch the place."

I laughed. "Great terms, Bill. Sounds like 'death or death' to me."

He shrugged in response.

"You know we've got your wife in here, so how about this? You let us go, and we'll let her go."

He shook his head. "I'd like to do that, I really would, but Helen and I already planned for this. That ain't happening. She's ready no matter how this goes. Decide."

"I need to discuss it."

He nodded.

I turned back into the room, and Jean-Luc said, "I prefer not to be burned, but I won't give up. So as I see it, we only have one tactical choice. Stall for as long as we can, then attack. Perhaps one or two of us will get through."

Jean-Luc and everyone else in the room knew that last statement was bullshit. But it didn't change the fact that his plan was all we had.

I glanced down at Lisa, feeling badly once again that she'd been sucked into this. Then, I stared at Helen. "The only good news here, Helen, is that I get to rip your fucking head off. I'm going to toss it out to old Bill right before we go out. You know I've done that sort of thing before. I kind of get a kick out of it, and it can be quite distracting. I figure it might take Bill off his game a touch."

Her smile never faltered. "Do what you have to do. I've got lung cancer. I'm dead in a few months, anyway. The way things have been going lately, you'd be doing me a favor. As for Bill, he's ready for anything. He's going to put you all down."

Squid coughed up some blood and gurgled out, "Jesus, Chrissy. I thought *we* were supposed to be the bad guys."

Helen laughed. "You're a funny one, Mr. Callaghan. We can't exactly be sweet dealing with the likes of you, can we? And this will be by far the biggest single killing of your kind we've ever made. I count thirteen vermin exterminated."

Dom spoke up. "It's ten. I'm human, and my two friends were, too."

She turned those black, black eyes on Dom. The phony facade faded. She looked as much a monster as any vampire I'd known. "You betrayed your own kind!" she spat. "You're worse than they are. Worse than cockroaches. You'd better hope Bill doesn't take you alive."

Dom looked as if he might shoot her right then.

Squid said, "Jesus, lady. Can you lighten up?"

The room was silent for a beat, and then Jean-Luc tittered, and we all laughed as Harrison glowered at Dom. Leave it to Squid to crack the room up even in dire circumstances. He'd done it again and again over the two and a half centuries I had known him.

It was time. Simone was as good as she was going to be, and that wasn't very good. Squid wasn't much better. But Bill Harrison was too smart to give us much time, and I didn't fancy going up in one big fucking marshmallow roast. I said to the room, "Ready?"

I got silent nods from everyone, except Squid. He said, "I'm ready, and thanks for coming up with this brilliant fucking plan, Chrissy."

Jean-Luc was helping Simone up and laughed again. "He's right, Titus. Not your best."

Squid was struggling to his feet and now, Jean-Luc helped him up as well.

"Thanks, Frenchie," Squid said. "I owe you one."

Jean-Luc looked at Simone, and back to Squid. "No, it is I who owe *you*. But I fear I will never be able to repay you."

I turned to Helen Harrison. "Well, Helen, I think that bell is tolling for you. It's going to be an absolute pleasure ridding the world of the famous Genealogist. It *is* you, isn't it, and not your husband? You're more the type."

Her black eyes fixed unwaveringly on mine. It was unsettling. "Of course it's me, Dr. Brownell. Do what you need to do. But know this—you'll still lose in the end."

"Maybe, but you won't be around to see it."

As I reached for her neck, the yard erupted into a cacophony of gunfire and screams. I peeked out the window, wary of another ambush. The scene that greeted me would have been ridiculous if it wasn't so horrifying. Our attackers were being efficiently destroyed in a gruesome bloodbath—their heads knocked from their shoulders, faces caved in, limbs ripped from their bodies.

The ridiculous part was that all this devastation was being meted out by two little old ladies. My aunts flew about the yard, dodging gunfire and flame bursts, picking off Harrison's strike team one by one. The finishing touch on this surreal exhibition was that as they danced about the black-clad, body-armored, gun-toting assailants, they themselves were weaponless and wore nothing but brightly flowered housedresses. I laughed at the sight.

Then a thought struck me, and my good humor quickly fled. I turned to Dom, seriously pissed that he would withhold this from me.

He put his hands up defensively. "Jeez, Julian, I swear I didn't know. You think I'd want them in this kind of danger? They must've followed me."

I believed him. I didn't have time to do otherwise, since Mary and Katie needed help. As fast as they were, Harrison's troops were not panicking and had settled into back-to-back defensive positions while laying down significant fire. Simone and Squid were still too badly hurt to be of use outside. "Simone, you watch Helen here. If she moves, shoot her."

Simone smiled, as beautiful as ever, even though her face was covered in blood. "With pleasure."

I told Squid to cover us from the house. He was still nearly immobile due to his wounds. For once, he didn't argue. He knew he'd be a liability out there.

Jean-Luc had already drawn his broad sword and said, "Old school?"

I drew my gladius. "I wouldn't have it any other way."

Dom, Jean-Luc, and I burst out into the fray.

CHAPTER 54

Bloody Bill Harrison had certainly killed his share of vampires and was used to how fast they could move. But he'd never seen anything like this. His attackers were like wisps of smoke—there for barely a blink and then gone. Only the death screams of another one of his team alerted him to the attackers' location. Those of his group who were still alive kneeled back-to-back, laying down heavy fire in a last-ditch effort, fighting now for their very survival. Bill wished he could have gotten to his daughters, to stand with them, but he couldn't make it. His only solace was in knowing how well they'd been trained. He was with Jarvis and Martinez. All religious shenanigans aside, he could have done a lot worse. They were both cool under pressure.

Bill's strike team was holding its own for the moment, but he knew it wouldn't last—the vampires holed up in the house would join the battle any time now. He couldn't see his new assailants. Bill didn't even know for sure how many there were, but he thought there were two—and he needed to take them out to have any chance of survival.

Like he'd done in Shreveport and countless times before, he let go of his conventional senses as much as he could and tried to "feel" the vampires. A pattern was there; he just needed to recognize it. In the middle of a firefight, once again, Bloody Bill meditated.

~~~

We charged out into the yard as Squid laid down heavy fire from the house. Dom took cover on the porch and opened up with his machine gun. Jean-Luc and I waded into them, hacking away with our swords. We were both hit several times with those bitchy garlic bullets, but in our ramped-up state, they didn't come close to stopping us. I think it was the archaic barbarity of being attacked with swords that finally broke the vampire killers into a panic. They tried to flee, and the slaughter began.

As he moved off the porch, Dom was shot. He hit the ground, clutching his thigh. I turned to help, but Katie had already slowed and swerved toward him. From the corner of my eye, I saw Harrison pivot with blinding speed and fire his shotgun. Katie's head, from the jaw up, was gone in an instant. She fell to the ground, dead.

I couldn't hear Mary's scream; my own was ringing in my ears. Stunned, I couldn't move—but Mary could. She went right at Harrison, but as if expecting her, the old buzzard switched to a flamethrower and laid down a long burst. She veered off at the last second. Otherwise, she'd have been incinerated. My self-preservation response kicked in, and I got on the move again and back into the fight. It didn't last much longer, and in the end, only Harrison and his two companions remained. They simply laid down their weapons, now useless and spent of every bit of ammunition, and quietly awaited their fate. Considering the expression on Mary's face, I expected Harrison's death to be particularly nasty.

~~~

We marched our three captives into the house. On the

way, I allowed Harrison to check on a seriously wounded woman whom I presumed to be one of his daughters. She had a huge, sucking chest wound and wouldn't last long, but she still might serve as a bargaining chip. He carried her into the house.

To my surprise, Mary didn't kill Bill Harrison immediately. Her voice was devoid of all emotion as she said to me, "I suppose you need him, for a while, anyway."

I still couldn't believe Katie was dead. But her headless body lying in the front yard rammed that reality home. "For a bit... then he's yours."

When we got in the house, Harrison put his surviving daughter on the floor.

Helen stood and said, "Shannon? Cathy?"

All Bill Harrison could do was shake his head.

No wonder, I thought. If they were the two girls who'd been close to the wounded one, they had died horribly.

Helen Harrison sat back down and burst into tears. "You murdering monsters," she said. "You killed my girls."

Mary walked up to the desk, intently studying the Genealogist for a moment. "So you're the one who's been killing us? You don't look like so much to me."

Helen Harrison continued to cry, and Mary walked toward the door.

"Aunt Mae, where you going?" I asked.

"To be with Katie."

Her statement didn't sink in at first, but then I raced into the yard after her. She turned to me, and I could see it in her eyes. It was over for her.

I said, "Please, Aunt Mae... don't."

Her smile was beautiful, like always. She patted me on the cheek. "It's okay, Titus. I've lived long enough, and I don't want to live without Katie."

"Please, don't. What will I do without you, both of you? Don't do this."

I felt a hand on my arm. It was Dom's.

He said, "Come on, Jules. Let her go."

I snapped and shoved him to the ground harder than I meant to. "I thought you loved them!" I shouted. "Katie's gone, and now you want to let Mary kill herself?"

Dom struggled to his feet, his leg wound freely bleeding again. "You're damn right, I love them! I love them enough to know they're no good without each other. You know it, too. Let her go."

Mary said, "Dom's right, honey. Dom, come here and give me a hug."

He obeyed her, as he'd always done. He actually got down on his knees and hugged her with his head against her chest, letting out huge sobs. After a time, she whispered in his ear, and he quieted.

He finally let her go and turned to me. "Your turn, Titus."

I went to her with tears flowing.

She whispered, "When this is over, go to our lawyers. We've left some things, quite a few things, for you. You know, Titus, next to my sister, I loved you the most. You've been like a son to me." She lowered her voice even more. "We were Sumerian when we were turned, a little over six thousand years ago. Katie's real name is Ninbanda. Mine's Enanatuma. Thought you'd like to know. Now go in there and take care of those bastards. And remember, we'll always love you."

I said, "I'll always love you, too."

She walked away and picked up a stray flamethrower. She knelt over her sister, gently patted her on the back, and struck up a flame. They ignited and burned brightly. Mary didn't make a sound. Dom and I watched until the flames went out.

The sisters were together once again.

CHAPTER 55

I returned to the house, crushed by the loss of my aunts and not particularly in the best of moods. But there were other matters at hand. I eyeballed the two non-Harrison captives and said, "Now let's get down to business."

I grabbed one of them and smoothly decapitated him with my gladius. Blood flew everywhere, and Lisa screamed and screamed. I hefted his head, as if trying to choose a fresh cantaloupe at the supermarket, and heaved it out a window. Lisa's screams finally stopped; she'd passed out.

I'm pretty sure I had everyone's attention when I said to Helen Harrison, "You're going to give me a list of all of your agents and the search parameters that you used to find us."

She actually looked amused. "I'll do no such thing."

"Oh, really? Well, your daughter's next, and then Bill." I took a step toward the wounded Harrison girl.

"I know how they're finding us," said a voice from behind me.

I turned around to see Jake. I was so happy, I bear-hugged him.

"Jesus, kid, I thought you were dead!"

"Yeah, me too. I would've been if it weren't for your aunts." He looked around the room. "Where are they?"

I could only shake my head.

"Oh no," Jake said, distraught. He turned to Helen Harrison.

I've never seen him look so angry, so vampire-like. Old Helen brought out the best in us, I guess.

I asked, "Jake, what've you got?"

Still glaring at the Genealogist, he replied, "They've got a lot of minor crap, but the biggie is people with health insurance who don't use it. That's been the real killer lately."

Bill Harrison said, "Shit."

"What about a list of agents?" I asked.

"Couldn't find it. It may not exist at all."

Helen said, "Your boy's right about that. It doesn't exist."

I turned to her. "Well, Helen, without that list, the need to keep you alive just dropped precipitously, unless you'd be willing to contact your group. There must be a way to do that, some encrypted shit or something that even Jake here couldn't trace."

The Genealogist smiled. "Maybe there is. But why would I?"

The conversation was interrupted when Dom, nearly passed out from blood loss, let himself down to the floor.

"Jean-Luc, will you help him?" I asked.

Jean-Luc cut his arm open and let his blood drip onto Dom's wound. It stopped bleeding immediately and healed in a short time. Helen, Bill, and the other captive watched, fascinated.

"You'd instruct your group to disband," I told Helen. "Say it's too dangerous or that you're retiring, or that God told you to. I don't care what reason you use."

"What would I get in return?" she asked.

I thought about it. As dangerous as Bill was, he'd be the only thing she'd bargain for. "I'd let Bill go. Twenty-four-hour grace period."

She snorted. "He'd only need ten minutes to lose you."

"Helen, no!" Bill begged.

She shot a look at him. "Quiet, Bill. Remember, you promised me. You said you'd obey me at the end, no matter what. You swore it. Would you break that oath?"

The old man bowed his head for a moment. Then he looked into her eyes and said, "You know I wouldn't."

Helen turned to me. "But that's not good enough. My daughter, too. And you have to heal her, just like you did with the big man."

"No," Bill protested. "You don't know what that'll do to her."

"Hush, Bill. It worked fine on their pet human. What other chance does Molly have? At least one of my girls is going to walk away from this, goddamn it!" She paused and turned to me. "Well, Dr. Brownell, what do you say?"

I looked at the daughter. She was deathly pale, and her breathing was erratic. She had minutes left, maybe. "No guarantees with your daughter. She may be too far gone. But if you disband your group, it's a deal."

Lisa screamed from her spot on the floor, "No! Don't let him go! Kill him, Jules! Don't let that fucking monster go!"

Bill smiled kindly at Lisa as she shouted, but on second glance, there was nothing at all kind in that smile.

Helen said, "Deal."

Jean-Luc once again spilled some of his own blood, this time into the chest wound of Molly Harrison. After a few minutes, her breathing normalized, and the sucking sound coming from her chest stopped. She was still badly hurt, but now it looked like she would live.

I said to Bill, "Time to go, Pops."

He stepped forward and kissed his wife goodbye, saying,

"I love you, Helen. Be strong—don't give them any satisfaction."

"Remember that night when I told you I wasn't afraid of them?" she murmured. "Well, I lied to you. One of the few times I ever have. Truth is, I've always been afraid of them, deathly afraid. But tonight, I'm not anymore. Getting a close look at them like this is what did it. There's nothing about them to be afraid of at all. Oh, they've got their advantages, all right, but they're as fallible as we are, maybe more so.

"I was so worried about the cancer getting me, about dying a meaningless death. It's better this way, honey. We won, and you and Molly get to walk away. The two of you go to ground for a while. But then you take it to 'em, Bill. Take it to them hard. I believe in you, and I love you so much."

The other prisoner spoke up. "Bill, Helen, what about me? You can't leave me here after what they did to Al."

Helen answered, "Now, Reverend Jarvis, you wouldn't leave me alone in my hour of need, would you? I may want to say a prayer before the end, and there's nobody I'd rather say it with than you."

Helen and the man she'd called "Jarvis" stared at each other for a long moment. A lot passed silently between them. I didn't know what it might have been, but I didn't care.

She said, "You go now, Bill. I'll wait long enough for you to get away before I do anything. Go and take care of Molly for me. You're all she's got now."

He nodded. His flinty eyes glistened as he kissed his wife for the final time. He turned and looked at each of us slowly, marking us.

Squid didn't appreciate it when his turn came. "You'd better stop eyeballing me, old man. Get out of here while you still can."

Bloody Bill said, "I'll be seeing you around, big guy."

Squid answered, "For your sake, you'd better hope not."

Harrison nodded and scooped his unconscious daughter off the floor. He turned once more to his wife and said, "Love you, doll."

She smiled, and he vanished into the night.

Jean-Luc said, "You realize that she is going to screw us. You let a very dangerous man go for no reason."

I nodded. "Yep. But I couldn't resist seeing it play out. It's so much more interesting than just killing them, don't you think?"

Jean-Luc scoffed at my response. I was bullshitting for the audience and took a huge risk that likely wouldn't pay off. But even so, I hoped the Genealogist would slip up, and we'd get something worthwhile in the end.

After thirty minutes passed, I said, "Bill's had plenty of time now, and as you can see, we're not chasing him. Time to pay up, Helen. Jake, get her computer running again. If she tries anything funny, rip her arm off."

With Jake hovering over her, she sent the email to disband her group.

"She did it," Jake said. "It went through. It looks okay . . . wait, wait a minute. The message is bouncing back. Undeliverable."

Squid said, "Frenchie was right, Chrissy. She screwed us. Want me to get after the old coot?"

"No, he's long gone," I said. "Helen, want to tell me what went on here? Before I kill you, that is."

She said, "I kept my part of the bargain. I sent out the email like I said I would. Problem is, I'd already disbanded the group. Well, technically, I didn't disband it. I took a lesson from our Muslim friends and broke it into cells. Small groups, operating independently, absolutely isolated, with no contact with other units. They don't even know where or who the others are." She smirked. "You see, Dr. Brownell, we knew you'd be coming, not quite this fast, but we knew. The cells might not have the power of the old Network, but it'll be almost impossible for you to find them all. Even if you do manage to pick off one or two, there's plenty more to go around. And they'll still be in the business of exterminating you."

I never really expected to clear the deck of the Genealogist in one fell swoop, but this was bad news, and pretty fucking smart of the old bitch. We'd be dealing with terrorist-like strikes for years to come.

She went on. "Even though I technically didn't break the bargain, I don't want you to go away feeling cheated. If you'd like, I'll give you a partial list of our operatives."

I said sarcastically, "Oh, that's really big of you, Helen. Sure, hand it over, would you?"

She took a folded piece of paper from her blouse and walked it over to me.

I looked at it. There were well over a hundred names on it. "All right, you had your joke. What is this?"

"It's what I said it is—a partial list. They all happen to be religious wackos, like him," she said as she pointed to Jarvis.

His eyes bugged out. "Helen! For the love of God!"

She ignored him. "With me gone, there will be nobody to keep them in check, and they'll go crazy doing the will of the Lord. They'll take out a lot of you, for sure, but the collateral damage to innocent people . . . well, I couldn't abide that."

"Like New Orleans," I said.

"Like New Orleans," she agreed.

This was shocking. On the one hand, I couldn't believe she'd give up her own people like this, but on the other hand, it made sense, albeit in a sick way. "Just like that. Now we're supposed to exterminate your problem for you?"

"Oh, come now, Dr. Brownell, they're your problem, too. It isn't like you and your kind need much of a reason to kill. You do it on a daily basis. Here, let me show you."

She turned, smoothly drew a hidden snub revolver from her blouse, and fired twice—directly into Jarvis's chest. Stunned at first, I recovered and took her gun away. Jarvis was knocked back by the impact, but kept his feet. He looked down at the blossom of red growing rapidly on his shirt.

Helen said, "That's for planning to kill my husband and daughters, you bastard. Tell the Lord I said hello."

Jarvis took two shambling steps and fell dead to the floor.

Squid said, "Jesus, this old bag makes us look like pansies."

Helen Harrison looked up at me serenely. "I'm ready now, Dr. Brownell."

I took a deep breath and reached for her throat, but my hands stopped, floated in midair for a moment, and returned to my sides. I lowered my head and closed my eyes. This place was an insane asylum, and everything that had happened in it was dirty and tainted, even by vampire standards. This wasn't a farm, it was a fucking crypt, and I'd had more than my share of killing for one night. I wanted nothing more to do with this place, and nothing more to do with the Harrisons. I didn't even want to touch this woman, for fear she'd somehow infect me, poison me with the evil Machiavellian machinations that ran through her twisted mind.

Dom said quietly, "No worries, Jules. I got this."

I didn't even flinch when Dom's huge gun roared beside me. When I opened my eyes, Helen Harrison lay dead on the floor, a neat bullet wound through her forehead. She looked peaceful in death, maybe even victorious. If you could ignore her brains splattered all over the walls, that is.

"I really need to get the fuck out of here," I said. "Jean-Luc, can you handle the cleanup?"

"*Oui*, I'll contact the locals. If we can't bury it completely, we can certainly make it look like a cult gone bad."

Simone said, "Not a big stretch there, by any means. We should implicate the old man. The authorities might help us find him."

I handed her the list. "Good idea. Will you take this for now? I don't want anything to do with it."

She nodded.

I started for the door, but I noticed two things: nobody else moved, and there was a deafening silence. I turned and saw what I'd forgotten . . . Lisa.

She was still cringing in a corner on the floor. Everyone in the room looked at her with death in their eyes. In that horrible room, covered with blood and gore and smelling like a shooting gallery, my little group did indeed look like what humans think we are—monsters.

Lisa noticed the attention and didn't like it one damn bit. She looked around at them, looking for a shred of human emotion, a shred of mercy—hell, a shred of anything. Squid couldn't stand it and turned away.

She finally focused on me. "Jules, I want to go home. Please take me home."

It broke my heart to hear it. There wasn't much I could do for her now.

When I didn't respond, she continued, quickly climbing the scale to hysterical. "Okay, Chrissy, take me home. No? What about 'Titus, will you take me home?' Or Julian, or whoever you are . . . take me the fuck home!"

After she finished shrieking, I replied, "All right, Lisa, I'll take you home."

Jean-Luc stepped in front of me. "Titus, you can't do that. She knows too much. It's too dangerous for you . . . for us. She'll talk eventually, and even if she doesn't, Harrison or one of his cells will find her. And then what?"

I knew he was right. "I can't. I can't just kill her after all of this."

"Turn her, then. It's the only other choice."

Lisa screeched, "Turn me? Into one of you? No! Stay away from me! All of you stay away from me!"

I shook my head. "No, she's all wrong for it . . . and never like this. She'd go insane."

He nodded and said softly, "If you can't, I will do it for you, my friend."

This was the second time he'd offered to kill Lisa for me. The first time I had taken it as a joke, but this time, it was deadly serious. I wanted to take him up on his offer, I really did, but this was my mess. It would have to fall to me.

"No. I'll take care of things, I promise—but not here. I'm going to take her home." I paused, waiting for a challenge that didn't come.

"Are you sure, Titus?" asked Jean-Luc.

"No, not at all. But I'll take care of it. You have my word."

CHAPTER 56

We crashed for the day in our motel just off Route 30, and then Squid flew us back to Massachusetts in his private jet. He'd first learned to fly in the 1920s and was an excellent pilot. Jake came along for the ride, maybe for moral support, but maybe because Jean-Luc asked him to keep an eye on me. Still in shock, Lisa slept the entire flight.

Squid let us off at Logan, and Jake promptly stole a car from one of the outdoor lots. Before I knew it, we were back at my old house in Needham. It had only been a matter of weeks since Lisa had told me we were getting divorced, but it felt like centuries. The place looked and felt foreign to me, like something half-remembered upon waking from a dream. A fleeting memory there for a moment, quickly fading to nothing and never to return.

Lisa did not look well. Her pocketbook was long gone, and so were her keys. Dumbfounded, she faced the locked front door with no idea what to do next. I got the spare house key from under the doormat and opened the door. She stumbled over the threshold and shuffled to the kitchen, our place of great discussions.

Jake said, "I need to hunt. With all of the excitement, it slipped my mind. Do you want me to wait, until . . . you know?"

I smiled at the boy. Just a little while ago, he had been leaning on me. "No, you go ahead. It's best if I'm alone for this."

"I'll be back in a while," he said as he left.

Lisa and I sat at the kitchen table in silence. At first, her drifty eyes looked at me, disinterested, but soon she sharpened up, as if tapping a secret source of power from being back home. "So here we are again, the happy couple," she said with some of her old sass.

I tried to smile but couldn't. "A hell of a thing, isn't it?"

"It's all true, isn't it, Jules? Is that what I should call you, 'Jules'?"

"Yes, that's what you should call me."

"I mean, that dirty fucking old man screwed me up pretty bad. I'm not sure I'll ever get over it, but I wasn't drugged, right? All that stuff actually happened. You and your friends are vampires."

I said lamely, "Afraid so."

"Why, Jules? Why'd you do it? Why marry me? Why the pretense all these years?"

I paused, thinking for a moment. "First, because I loved you, or at least, I thought I did. No knock on you, but I don't know if I even have a clue what your kind of love is anymore. Also, I wanted to try to remember what it was like to be human again. Pretending to be human was the best I could come up with."

"Did it work?"

I shook my head. "No, not really."

She laughed. "And I thought Donald was fucked up."

As if she'd conjured an evil spirit by saying his name, Donald Leland magically appeared in our kitchen, along with an overweight, mean-looking sidekick.

"I hope you don't mind me letting myself in," Leland said cheerily. "I saw your light on and had to stop by to say hello. Dr. Brownell, this is my associate, Garret Dick. I don't believe you've met before."

Dick tipped an imaginary hat in my direction, but his eyes were all for Lisa. I didn't like it at all.

Lisa said, "Donald, I don't know what you want, but I'm tired. Why don't you and your little playmate—"

Her sudden silence caused me to look at our guests and right down the barrel of the rather large gun that Dick was holding on us.

"Now that's better," said Leland. "This is how things are going to unfold. You, good Doctor, and you, Lisa, are going to tell me all about those little international purchases you've made over the years, and exactly how you made them disappear so effectively. If I like your answers, you may well live to take on Garret and me as grateful partners."

I said, "You've got to be shitting me."

Leland's face went from cheery to crazy mean in a blink. He would have fit right in with the group of nuts we'd left behind in Iowa.

"I assure you, I'm not," he said. "Do you think I've only buried people in business deals, Dr. Brownell? Because if you do, I could show you some burial grounds right at our own town dump that would certainly shock you."

Lisa said matter-of-factly, "No, Donald, I doubt he'd be shocked at all."

I let out a brief laugh. Then it began to dawn on me, the reason Lisa had been caught up in all this.

I turned to her and asked, "Is *that* why you were following me? For money? Not because I was a ... not because of that other stuff?"

"Uh-huh, but it wasn't just the money. I'd been fucked

over by this dickhead, and then I found out you were lying to me, too. It was too much for me to take."

Due to her traumatized state of mind, we hadn't talked about how she'd ended up at the Harrisons', but I'd presumed it had something to do with me being a vampire. Now I understood. It had begun with this silly little human divorce and ended as one very nasty coincidence for Lisa. Boy, did that suck for her.

Red-faced, Leland said, "You watch who you call dickhead, you no-good bitch. You two had better start talking, because I'm getting tired of—"

I interrupted, "No, Leland, I'm getting tired of *you* and your fat boyfriend here. Now fuck off, if you know what's good for you."

"Boyfriend, huh?" Dick growled. "Why, you little prick. First I'm going to fuck that bitch of yours every which way but loose. Then, I'm going to kill her, and you're gonna watch the entire show!"

"Even if you could find your cock under all that fat, I doubt you could get it up."

Dick's face drained of color. He looked at Leland, who nodded once. Then he shot me four times in the chest.

I let myself fall back against the wall, saying, "Ouch . . . ooch . . . eech . . . yikes!"

Lisa giggled.

I started to slide down the wall, and Dick advanced on me. When he was close enough, I grabbed his wrist and snapped it, while helping myself back up. He screamed and his gun fell to the floor, but I really wasn't interested in this henchman, just Leland.

I reached for Dick's neck, but I have to give the fat shit credit. He moved fast and blocked me with his good arm, which I also broke for good measure. I reached for him again, this time snapping his neck. His huge body crashed to the floor, shaking the foundation. His feet drummed for a few beats and went still.

Lisa giggled again. Her mental stability was long gone, but even so, she got off a pretty good one, saying, "I'm not sure, Donny, but I think Julian's mad at you."

I laughed and moved toward him. He'd gotten over his shock well enough to pull his gun.

"Oh, come now," I said.

"What the fuck are you?" he screamed as he fired, putting three more holes in me.

I'd had quite enough of being shot, and slapped his gun away.

Terrified, Leland looked to Lisa and stammered, "Lisa, for God's sake, help me."

"Yeah . . . right," she said.

"I guess it's down to you and me, Donster," I said. "You know what? I've had your blood before, and it kind of left a bad taste in my mouth." I lunged forward and bit into his neck.

He shrieked as I ripped a big, bloody chunk of flesh out of him and spat it on the floor. His carotid artery sprayed blood everywhere. The old buzzard staggered about a lot longer than I expected before dropping dead, joining Dick on the kitchen floor.

Once again, Lisa and I sat in silence.

She finally said, "You're supposed to kill me, aren't you?"

"Yes, I have to. I know you don't understand but—"

"No, I actually do. I get it. I'm one big liability for all of your vampire doings. That little Frenchman was right. That old fuck Harrison, or somebody else, will find me. And let me tell you, with what he'd do to me, I'd crack in a second.

I'd give up you and all your friends to make him stop."

"Lisa, I—"

"Jules, if you don't do it, I'll go crazy, anyway."

I was desperate. "Lisa, become one of us. I could do it."

She raised her voice. "No! No, Jules. I wouldn't want to live like that. I couldn't."

I looked at her. What could I say?

She broke the silence. "Do me a favor? Use a gun. Not that other way, please?"

I nodded and picked up one of the discarded guns and pointed it at her. My Lisa did not flinch while the moment played out for an eternity.

~~~

After it was over, Jake returned. He looked at the three dead bodies on the floor and asked, "What is it with you?"

EPILOGUE

Once I crossed from New Hampshire into Vermont, I called Squid. He answered sleepily, "What, did you forget to tell me how much you love me?"

I heard some mumbling, and he continued, "Adrienne says hello."

"Say hello right back. And I do love you, but I need some help getting over the border . . . and with some body disposal."

His voice lost its sleepiness instantly. "Okay. How far out are you?"

"About two hours."

"Good. Plenty of time. Pull off at Swanton. There's a convenience store right at the exit. I'll be waiting for you."

"You don't have to get up. Just send somebody."

"Hey, what are friends for?" Squid said and hung up.

~~~

I met him as planned. Ten minutes later, we were driving through the woods on an old logging road.

He said, "I had somebody at customs tonight, but I didn't want to take any chances. You never know who might see you, or if your car gets picked up on video. They've got cameras all over the place. So, what happened?"

I gave him a condensed version of what went on in Needham. "So at the end, we left things as they were, and Jake and I torched the place. Jake got into some of Leland's accounts and made it look like Dick had stolen quite a bit of money from him. Not a big stretch, as Dick is ... was ... a convicted felon. So Leland figures it out, dead bodies, burnt house, stolen money, and Garret Dick goes missing, thanks to this car's big trunk and your help. Pretty neat, huh?"

"No, not really," Squid said with disdain. "Sloppy as hell. Fortunately for Julian Brownell, though, if he chooses not to vanish from the face of the earth. He never left Montreal in the last week—I'll have a dozen witnesses to back it up."

"Are you kidding? The Brownell identity is already gone. And I'd advise you and Adrienne to lose your currents, too."

We cleared the woods and got onto an access road.

"Dick, huh?" Squid piped. "What a name. You'd think he would've changed it."

"Yep, should've been a no-brainer."

At that moment, a soft, muffled noise came from the trunk.

Squid looked at me. "I shouldn't have to ask you this, but are you *sure* Dick is dead?"

"Yeah, I'm sure. Dick is dead," I said.

We heard an even louder sound.

"I give up. If Dick is dead, then where's the noise coming from?"

"Lisa, if I had to guess."

"I see. Wait, I thought you killed her."

"Well, I did, stupid."

"Oh, oh ... I see. So I'm to presume she's one of us now?"

There was a muffled grunt and then some banging on the

trunk. I heard Lisa's voice: "Julian! Julian, where am I? Julian, please let me out of here."

"Why doesn't she force the trunk open?" Squid asked.

"She probably doesn't realize she's a vampire yet."

Squid's mouth dropped open, nearly spilling his cigarette into his lap. Somehow, though, it defied gravity, clinging miraculously to his lower lip. "Let me get this straight. You turned her, but she didn't know about it? She thought you were killing her?"

I blurted out, "Well, yes . . . no. I guess. She wanted me to use a gun on her, you know, instead of biting her. But I felt shooting her was . . . well, uncivilized."

"Have to agree with you there. Gunning her down would've been kind of heartless."

"Yeah, that's right, it would've been heartless. So I bit her. I know the end kind of sucked for her, especially after everything she'd been through. But it was over in a few minutes, and I was more comfortable killing her like that. I mean, I *am* a vampire. And the way I saw it, being the one doing the killing, I'd have to live with what I'd done for a lot longer than she did. If she didn't come back, that is."

Squid drove on in silence for a bit. He finally said, "I can sort of get the biting-versus-shooting thing. It makes sense in a warped sort of way. But at the last minute, you drained her dead, and then did nothing to prevent her from turning? Even though she's a horrible candidate, and it was completely against her will?"

"Yep. That's pretty much it. She absolutely forbade me from turning her. Thought she'd be better off dead than going nuts or being one of us, or maybe both. Pretty stupid of me, huh?" I chortled like a moron.

"And everyone says *I'm* an idiot? Boy, Jean-Luc is right. You *are* the sensitive Roman killer."

Lisa's pounding grew louder and she shouted, "I can hear you up there! Let me out of here! Wait. I'm in a trunk? A fucking trunk *again?* Get me the fuck out of here!"

Squid asked, "What does she mean by that?"

"I have no idea. What, now you and Jean-Luc are best buddies?"

"Maybe so. You'd already left that fucking corn farm when Simone gave me a huge hug and kiss on the cheek and thanked me for saving her. She stepped away, and right behind her was Jean-Luc. I couldn't see him there at first because the little fucker is so short. Anyway, he reached up for me, and I thought, here we go again, he's gonna beat the shit out of me. And do you know what he did? He pulled me down, kissed me on both cheeks, and then he planted one right on my lips! Now I say I'm from Montreal, I get the cheek-kissing, but what's up with the lips? And do you know what he said? He said he learned it from you. Now what the hell does that mean?"

I laughed. "Never mind. Just drive."

We crossed the border undetected and were now on a two-lane road. Lisa shrieked, "There's a dead body in here! Julian, or whatever your fucking name is, get me the fuck out of here!"

"My, the language on her," said Squid. "But fun is fun. I'm letting her out of there."

As he started to pull over, I said, "By the way, did I ever tell you what Lisa really thought of you?"

Squid stayed in the right lane, slowing down, but didn't stop. "You said she liked me."

"That was a lie. I didn't want to hurt your feelings. Let me get this right. Now, I'm paraphrasing a bit, but she said that you were an 'overbearing oaf, and that if she ever had to hear one of your monotonous, pointless stories again, she'd rip her own ears off.'"

"No shit?"

"No shit," I answered.

He accelerated back into the left lane. "I guess she can stay in the trunk a while longer, then."

Lisa's muffled voice floated into the car again. "Colm, is that you? It is you! Squid, let me out of here!"

Squid said, "Oh, *now* she calls me Squid. By the way, with Lisa in the trunk, isn't your alibi one body short?"

"Not really. When Jake went out to hunt, he just so happened to bring down a woman right around Lisa's size. He went and fetched the body, and *bang, bang*—a couple of well-placed face shots, and no more dental record matches. I figure after sorting out the barbecue, all they'll have is a bunch of burnt-up flesh. They'll think it's Lisa, all right."

Squid shook his head. "And I thought it was sloppy before."

Lisa screeched, "Julian, you let me the fuck out of this trunk! I'm still your wife, goddamn it! You let me out of here!"

Squid laughed. "She's got you on that one, Chrissy. Technically, you're still married. I think you might've even set a legal precedent. You may have to go through the first vampire divorce in the history of the world."

I said dryly, "Oh, you're so witty. Very fucking funny, Squid."

"No, I'm serious. I think you're screwed here."

"I don't know how I put up with you all these years."

"It's because you love me so much," Squid said. "Hey, it's a little late tonight, but what do you say tomorrow night you, me, Adrienne, and Lisa all go out on a double date? It'll be a hoot." Squid grinned like a big dope.

"Keep it up, asshole."

He laughed. "We're getting close to the body dump. I can't wait to see what happens when you open that trunk."

I had to laugh myself, thinking about how it might go. "It's going to be interesting, no doubt about it."

Squid looked at me and said, "You know, Chrissy, turning Lisa may be the stupidest thing you've ever done. Maybe even stupider than turning me."

I thought about that for a moment. "Not stupider, but pretty damn close."

Right then, Lisa screamed, "Let me the fuck out of here!"

Squid and I looked at each other. We burst out laughing.

END

A HISTORY IN BLOOD

Chris DeFazio

ABOUT THE AUTHOR

Chris DeFazio, is a practicing ER doctor and physician assistant educator who lives in the Boston suburbs with his family.

A History in Blood is the first in a series of novels revolving around the colorful life of Titus Acilius, the Roman legionary turned modern-day vampire.

Made in the USA
Charleston, SC
26 February 2014